Going All the Way

DAN WAKEFIELD

Going All the Way

INDIANA UNIVERSITY PRESS
BLOOMINGTON & INDIANAPOLIS

Grateful acknowledgment is given for permission to quote lyrics
from the following song:

"A Home on the Range" collected, adapted, and arranged by John
A. Lomax and Alan Lomax TRO (appearing on page 278).
Copyright © 1938 (renewed 1966) by Ludlow Music, Inc., New
York, NY. Used by permission.

The paper used in this publication meets the minimum require-
ments of American National Standard for Information Sciences—
Permanence of Paper for Printed Library Materials, ANSI Z39.48-
1984.

Manufactured in the United States of America

Library of Congress Cataloging-in-Publication Data

Wakefield, Dan
Going all the way / Dan Wakefield.
    p.   cm.
ISBN 0-253-21090-9 (pbk. : alk. paper)
I. Title.
PS3573.A413G6   1997
813'.54—dc20   96-35010

    2   3   4   5   6   02   01   00   99   98   97

FOR ALL
THE HORSES
OF THE
STERN MOON

THIS EDITION
IS ALSO DEDICATED
TO THE MEMORY OF
SAM LAWRENCE,
WHOSE ENTHUSIASM
AND PUBLISHING GENIUS
MADE THIS BOOK A SUCCESS
(AND WHO WOULD HAVE
LOVED THE MOVIE).

"The story of my boyhood... is important only because it could happen in any American family. It did, and will again."

EARL EISENHOWER, BROTHER OF
PRESIDENT DWIGHT D. EISENHOWER,
APRIL 4, 1954

"Farther along we'll know more about it
Farther along we'll understand why...."

AN AMERICAN GOSPEL SONG

FOREWORD

Kurt Vonnegut Jr.

Dan Wakefield is a friend of mine. We both went to Shortridge
High School in Indianapolis—where the students put out a *daily*
paper, by the way. His publisher is my publisher. He has boomed
my books. So I would praise his first novel, even if it were putrid.
But I wouldn't give my Word of Honor that it was good.

Word of Honor: Mr. Wakefield has been a careful and deep
author of nonfiction for years—*Island in the City, Revolt in the
South, The Addict.* . . . *The Atlantic Monthly* gave him an issue all his
own for *Supernation at Peace and War.* Word of Honor: he is also an
important novelist now.

Going All the Way is about what hell it is to be oversexed in
Indianapolis, and why so many oversexed people run away from
there. It is also about the narrowness and dimness of many lives
out that way. And I guarantee you this: Wakefield himself, having
written this book, can never go home again. From now on, he will
have to watch the 500-mile Speedway race on television.

This is a richer book than *Portnoy's Complaint,* with wider concerns and more intricate characters, but the sexual problems are
much the same. Wakefield shows us two horny young Hoosiers,
and it is easy to imagine their meeting Alexander Portnoy in a
Howard Johnson's—midway between Indianapolis and New
York. If they were candid with one another, they would admit
that they were rotten lovers, and they might suppose mournfully
that rotten lovers were not welcomed by women *anywhere.*

Going All the Way is a period piece, incidentally—set in ancient times, at the close of the Korean War. And every book is a period piece now—since years or even weeks in America no longer resemble each other at all.

This book is full of belly laughs, but I am suspicious of belly laughs as entirely happy experiences. The only way to get a belly laugh, I've found, is to undermine a surface joke with more unhappiness than most mortals can bear.

After a series of low-comedy sexual failures, for instance, one of Wakefield's heroes cuts his wrists lightly with a razor blade, ". . . so that rivulets of blood began to fiow together, forming a thick little puddle." This isn't funny, and the scene becomes less funny as it goes on: "He started smearing the blood over his face and over the front of his torn shirt, like an Indian painting himself to prepare for a ceremony—a battle, a blessing, a death."

So much for sexual comedy. Nobody dies in the book, but a lot of people would like to, or at least wouldn't mind.

Wakefield's reportage of life in Middle America, as one might expect, is gruesomely accurate and enchanting. His sex-addled fools drive their parents' automobiles through a vast pinball machine whose bumpers and kickers are strip joints and taverns and gas stations and golf driving ranges and hamburger stands. They seek whorehouses, which, it turns out, have been closed for years.

They return home periodically to their smug and vapid parents, grumpily declining to say where they've been. Their stomachs, already churning with hamburgers and beer, twist even more grotesquely when their parents want to know when they are going to settle down to nice jobs and nice wives and nice houses in Indianapolis.

Finally—there is a tremendous automobile crash.

And, finally again, this wildly sexy novel isn't a sex novel. It is really about a society so drab that sex seems to the young to be the only adventure with any magic in it. When sex turns out to be merely sex, the young flee to more of the same elsewhere—and they play dangerous games with, among other things, automobiles and razor blades.

How old are Wakefield's protagonists? About the same age Ernest Hemingway was when he returned to Middle America as a quiet, wounded, authentic hero of World War I.

PREFACE TO THE
INDIANA EDITION

My friend and fellow Hoosier Kurt Vonnegut is right about most things, but I am happy to say he was wrong in predicting I'd never be able to return to Indianapolis after writing this novel ("he will have to watch the 500-mile Speedway race on television"). For a while, though, it seemed his assessment was all too accurate. When the book came out, there were angry feelings back home in Indiana that *Going All the Way* had gone too far. Some people (mostly ones I barely knew) thought I'd exposed their most intimate secrets, while others felt I had cast aspersions on their community and its values, the place of my own birth and upbringing. At first I wished I'd followed an early anticipation of this kind of misunderstanding and set the book in Cleveland.

But in fact I could never have set the book in some other city—not because everything in my novel could not have happened in any American city in the midwest in the nineteen-fifties—but because no other place evoked such feelings in me, called forth the kind of emotion and love set off by the very names of the streets I grew up on *(Winthrop, Guilford, Carrolton)*, my old neighborhood *(Broad Ripple)*, or the drive-ins of my high-school days *(The Ron-D-Vu, The Tepee)*, or bars *(The Red Key, The Melody Inn)*, or the few bodies of water in that landlocked home we proudly learned in grade school was "the largest city in the world not on a navigable waterway" *(Fall Creek, White River, The Canal)* or the lakes beyond with the Indian names where we partied and swam and water-skied *(Wawasea, Maxincuckee)*.

Happily, time does heal, and healers seem to materialize out of the blue to help the process. Librarians are the angels of writers (the ones at the Broad Ripple branch library nourished my love of reading from age six), which was proved again by Ophelia Gorgiev Roop, who as director of adult services for The Indianapolis–Marion County Public Library invited me to give a talk there in 1985, assuring me *Going All the Way* was no longer a source of controversy, but a favorite reading-group selection. Drawn by the warm invitation, I agreed to make my first public appearance in Indianapolis since the book was published in 1970; the library announced my talk as "A Prodigal Son Returns."

For their newsletter's announcement I wrote: "I see myself on this return like the aging warrior, wrinkled and weathered, with feathers turning to gray, raising a hand in blessing and saying 'I come in peace.'" That's how I was received, and my old gang from high school assembled for a party that was one of the happiest events of my life. I've returned often since to give talks and workshops and visit with friends.

There seemed a lovely symmetry in the fact that while *Going All the Way* kept me away from Indianapolis when it first was published in 1970, it brought me back for the longest time I'd spent there since college when the movie script I wrote of the novel was filmed there twenty-six years later. Film rights to the novel had been optioned before, but a movie wasn't made until two young men of talent and commitment appeared in my life in the fall of 1994 and told me this was their favorite book and they wanted it to be their first feature film.

Director Mark Pellington and producer Tom Gorai wanted me to write the script, keep the story in the nineteen-fifties, and film it in Indianapolis. They invited me to be on the set and offer my advice. This is a rare privilege for any writer, and the opposite of my former novel-into-movie experience, when the person who bought the rights to *Starting Over* refused even to speak to me about it on the telephone, and the movie bore almost no relation to the book.

The movie of *Going All the Way* is as true to the "novel" as it's possible for movies of books to be. That in itself will cause controversy in some quarters (it already has), since the novel expresses the anger and confusion of a young man rebelling against the religion he grew up with, and the expression of that is portrayed in the movie. I would no more "censor" it from the movie than I would go back and excise it from the novel. Its re-publication in this edition will no doubt raise questions and criticism from those who feel my writing in the realm of spirituality during the past decade—beginning with my article "Returning to Church" in the *New York Times Magazine* in December of 1985 that led to the book *Returning: A Spiritual Journey*—is somehow in opposition to the novels that were written previously.

"Do you now renounce your earlier work?"

A young woman in the audience of a talk I gave at St. Bartholomew's Episcopal Church in New York City in 1994 asked me that when I was there on a book tour for publication of *Expect a Miracle: The Remarkable Things That Happen to Ordinary People.* I said I did not at all renounce my earlier work, citing the view of novelist Ron Hansen, author of *Mariette in Ecstasy,* who said in an interview that a book was "religious" not because it was "about religion" but because it told the truth. I know that one person's "truth" is the next person's lie, but I mean "the truth" in the sense of it being the expression of the deepest feelings of a human being as he or she knows it; the kind of truth Willa Cather meant when she said "Don't try to write the kind of short story that this or that magazine wants—write the truth, and let them take it or leave it." No writing is worthwhile, Cather told an interviewer, if it doesn't "cut pretty deep . . . the main thing was always to be honest."

Going All the Way cuts pretty deep in the literal way, when Sonny Burns takes a razor to his wrist in a time of desperate frustration and despair. That was the truth of that character in that circumstance, just as his anger at the itinerant evangelist Luke Matthews was true, and his anger, in fact, at God. To "renounce" such scenes would be for me to "renounce" the truth as I see it as a writer of the people, time, and place I am trying to portray.

A writer I know and respect who read my screenplay of *Going All the Way* wrote to question my inclusion of the Luke Matthews scene, now that I am a person of declared religious faith. I answered him in a letter that "It would never occur to me to betray my own truth of that era of life by some kind of 'religious revisionism' imposed retroactively with the outlook that came thirty years later."

By the same token, I would feel it a travesty to try to go back and revise the young men's blighted views of women and women's anatomies to adhere to the political correctness of a more enlightened era. I hope both male and female readers will understand, as most have over the years, that the blatantly sexist attitudes of the time, expressed in the thoughts, language, and behavior of the characters, were as destructive and de-humanizing to the men as to the women; that I no more advocate such attitudes than I advocate people cutting their wrists or cursing God; that in trying to tell the truth of the dark forces of life I hope to expose rather than encourage them, as all serious writers have done throughout history.

When people have asked me what this book is about I have said "it's about friendship." It's also about seeking, questioning, risking, rising from despair and defeat, beginning again, finding the joy and love of being alive, in the moment, as Sonny Burns does in the end, when he is able to experience and appreciate the taste of pumpkin pie, the smell of coffee, the scene and color of autumn leaves, the flow of life that is moving within him, moving him on, again, to begin.

October 1996

PART ONE

1

When the two soldiers boarded the train at St. Louis they caught one another's eyes for a moment in a mutually questioning gaze that broke off teasingly short of recognition, like a dream not quite recalled. The short, boyish-looking soldier moved away into the crowd, his apple cheeks burning brighter, as if they had just been shined, and he climbed in a coach farther down. Something about the face of that other soldier he had seen hinted of the past, and that was precisely what the young man wished to avoid on this of all days, which he felt marked the start of a whole new part of his life—the "real part," he hoped. Settling into a seat by a window, he closed his eyes and breathed in deeply as the train jolted forward, nosing into the future, unlimited.

As soon as the conductor took his ticket he started for the club car, hoping for something that would cool as well as calm him. The air-conditioning system was on the blink, and it was one of those muggy, midwestern days in May when everything seems to stick to you. Women fanned themselves with newspapers and babies bawled in the thick heat.

The young soldier had to make his way through seven coaches to get to the club car, pressing on the airlock door of each one with all his might and trying not to show any sign of the exertion it took before he broke through the sealed barrier with a *foom* of triumph. By the time he reached his destination his arms felt like spaghetti. He determined he would begin the daily push-ups and other basic exercises he had promised himself to continue on his own after basic training but never kept up. Now that he was done with the Army and his real life was beginning, he was going to do those things, he was going to discipline himself.

He ordered a Schlitz and started to undo the button of his collar that was so tight it felt like a string cutting his neck, but then he saw the long tan legs of the blonde. He pulled his tie tighter into place and tried to center it, smiling as he choked. The girl seemed like an omen to him of the phase of his life that was now beginning, a time in which well-tanned and lovely women would be his rightful due. When the Schlitz came, he lifted the cool can to his lips in a private toast, but his trembling hand tipped it too quickly and some of the beer went drooling down his chin, pretty as a madman's spittle.

Mercifully, the girl wasn't looking at him. He wiped fiercely at his chin and the front of his tie and jacket, then calmed himself with a long, carefully aimed draught of the beer. There was an empty seat on one side of the girl, and on the other side was an old guy around forty wearing a shiny suit with one of those diamond Shriners pins in the lapel, obviously no competition. The girl looked cool and athletic—not in a volleyball or field-hockey way, but in something graceful, like swimming. She would glide through the water with long, arching strokes, no thrashing around, just a little foam raised prettily by the rhythmic flutter of her delicate feet. The young man pulled out his cigarettes, trying to devise a good opening line. What do you think about Senator McCarthy and the Red menace? No, that could just start an argument. Never open with religion or politics, that was the oldest rule of all. What do you think of Marlon Brando? Did you like *The Catcher in the Rye?* Is Dave Brubeck really art? Will the mambo last? Have I seen you someplace before? Do you want to fuck?

He could think of nothing witty or original and had almost finished the beer. The near-empty can made a nervous rattle on the circular chromium serving stand. The young man decided to order another and promised himself that when he finished the second one he would go and sit down by the girl whether he had thought of a sharp opening line or not. It took him some time to get the attention of the old colored waiter, and he feared the girl might notice his lack of success. Once she stared right at him and smiled, but he looked away, pretending not to notice. When the waiter finally brought the beer, he gave him an extra large tip, hoping to establish good relations for the future, but the old guy merely grunted when he pocketed the change. No matter, the beer was cold, and the soldier could feel his determination blooming within himself, nurtured by the Schlitz. He would soon be ready. He would stride with casual confidence across the aisle, slip into the seat beside the girl, and say whatever first came to his mind.

Just then a big guy in a wild sport shirt that said "Waikiki" all over it entered the car, cased the scene, and plopped down right in the empty seat beside the girl. The guy had tattoos on his forearms, which probably meant he was dumb. The soldier consoled himself with the thought that the poor guy didn't have a chance.

"Talk about your early summer heat," the tattooed man said loudly to the girl, "I bet it's hot enough to fry an egg on the sidewalk."

How corny could you get? The soldier really felt embarrassed for the poor guy, and he hoped the girl didn't brush him off too bad. But the girl was smiling.

"In St. Louis, I bet you could," she said.

They laughed—together. The guy ordered drinks for him and the girl, and soon they were chattering away like old pals. The soldier tried not to hear them. He tried to think of important things, like the Future, not some silly broad on a train you could pick up just by giving her a stale old line about the weather.

What burned him up most was the guy wasn't even a serviceman. It didn't seem fair. The young man had hoped that when he went in the Army he'd be able to pick up all the girls he wanted, just by being in uniform. As a kid he had seen all those World War II movies where an ordinary GI could go to the Stage Door Canteen and dance the night away with Judy Garland, or maybe just walk down the street and have June Allyson pop out from behind some shrubbery and say, "Hi, soldier," and walk off with him into the sunset. Of course, you could guess what happened in the sunset, even with nice girls like June Allyson. It didn't mean they were bad, it meant they were patriotic. But Korea wasn't the kind of a war that got you laid for being in it. The young man had worn his uniform for two years, and it hadn't done shit for him. The only broad who said, "Hi, soldier," to him was a dumpy old babe around forty at the USO in Kansas City. She gave him some oatmeal cookies that crumbled in his hand.

The war wasn't really a war—a "police action" some of the papers called it—and nobody gave much of a damn about it except for the politicians and the military men and of course the guys who got drafted and all their relatives. Being a soldier during that half-assed war was like being on a team in a sport that drew no crowds, except for the players' own parents and friends. The young man had got a much bigger kick out of World War II, when he served on "The Homefront" as a kid collecting scrap metal and tinfoil and raising a "Victory Garden" of radishes and carrots that nobody ate, and learning to be an "air-raid spotter" so that if the Nazis decided to bomb Indianapolis —thereby knocking out the very heart of the nation—he would be able to stand on the roof of the Broad Ripple lumberyard and spot the Stukas and the Messerschmidts as they dove toward such cultural targets as the Soldiers and Sailors Monument or the world-famous Indianapolis Speedway. World War II had been a fun war, full of glamour and glory, but Korea was just a bore, a national nuisance, drab as olive. His whole generation had been stuck with it, but somehow the young man took it as a personal piece of bad luck. Just the sort of thing that was always happening to him.

"You like the races, huh?" the tattooed guy was asking the blonde. The soldier didn't want to hear about it. He got out the rolled-up copy of the latest *Newsweek* magazine he had stuck in his hip pocket, and plunged into it right at the hardest part, foreign affairs. As well as doing daily exercises in the fruitful, new life that the young man was going to begin, he had also promised himself he would keep his mind in trim, stay up on things, be alert and informed, and as part of this resolution he planned to read *Newsweek* magazine each and every week, not just the sports and entertainment sections but the world and national news and the art and literary parts. Most everyone read *Time,* and the young man figured he might have a little edge by being a *Newsweek* reader, might just be a little more in the know than your average citizen.

The big world news was about the "crisis" of the Fall of Dienbienphu, the French bastion in part of the Commie Orient. It sounded pretty bad. The magazine said that

While it might turn out to be only a heroic incident in the continuing struggle to contain aggressive communism, it might prove to be the cataclysmic event that would trigger a chain reaction culminating eventually in a third world war—this time an atomic war of unimaginable deadliness and devastation.

Fuck it all. More of his kind of luck—the next world war not only wouldn't be any fun, it would probably kill everybody. He often had this feeling that maybe if he ever got settled down, married to a great, sexy-looking babe who was also very tender and motherly—sort of a cross between Marilyn Monroe, Grace Kelly, and old Jane Gallagher of *The Catcher in the Rye*—and he had a great job that paid a lot of money and a couple of beautiful kids and had just moved into a cozy house with a lot of fireplaces and a white picket fence, he would go out to pick up the mail and look up in the sky and see a monstrous mushroom-shaped cloud, and that would be the end. He regarded the H-bomb too as a personal menace, a weapon uniquely and insidiously devised to scare the shit out of him, until it finally blew him to smithereens.

He couldn't finish the article about the latest world crisis, and he flipped through the magazine in search of some less depressing stuff. "Business Trends" said that the Atomic Energy Commission was encouraging colleges to expand their courses in "nuclear studies." Senator Joe McCarthy was fighting with the Army, making more of his famous "points of order," trying to scare everyone about the Reds in government. The first jet transport plane was almost finished. Roger Bannister had broken the four-minute mile. That was something, but the soldier already knew about that. He turned to the book section, hoping to improve his mind. There was a story about some philosopher who a lot of eggheads thought was hot stuff. It said:

Sören Kierkegaard, a melancholy Dane of a century ago, is a triple-threat hero among modern intellectuals. He unwittingly fathered the gloomy philosophy of Existentialism. He anticipated the rise of modern remorse by developing a twentieth-century sense of guilt in the heyday of the optimistic nineteenth. . . .

Shit. The soldier figured he was even born in the wrong damn century. The century of gloom and guilt. Wouldn't you know it? He finished his beer and looked up to see if he could flag down the grumpy, indifferent waiter. A *foom* of the air-compression door announced the entrance of somebody new in the club car, and the young man turned to look.

At the entrance to the car was the soldier whose face had floated up to haunt him from the steam of the hissing train on the platform. He was tall, built in an angular way with broad shoulders that sloped in a V to a narrow waist and hips, and long, slightly bowed legs. His face was lean and dark from the kind of a beard that never quite shaves completely away, leaving a permanent five-o'clock shadow. The face was naggingly familiar to the chubby young soldier who was staring at him, and yet he couldn't quite place it. The tall soldier started walking forward, when the train gave a sudden lurch that sent beer cans skittering precariously over the chrome tables in a general clatter, and something fell and smashed behind the bar. It was the sort of jolt that usually sent anyone who was walking down the aisle reeling into the lap of some stranger, but the tall soldier seemed to catch the very motion of the car with his hips, feinted with it, and continued on, his expression unchanging, his rolling gait with the feet pointing inward moving ahead, ready for anything. It was with the movement that the graceful soldier revealed his identity, for it was the same elusive, flowing sort of move that had so often evaded enemy tacklers, the natural action of the greatest broken-field runner in the history of Shortley High.

It was Gunner Casselman.

After recognizing him, the young soldier buried his head back in the magazine, knowing a famous guy like that would never remember him, even though they were in the same class at Shortley, and certainly wouldn't have anything to say to him. Casselman sat down in the seat next to him and made a pop of his fingers that brought the sluggish waiter to him like a shot.

"Bring me a Bud, please."

"Yassuh, right away."

It was as if the waiter knew, or sensed, who he was, or that he was Somebody. From the corner of his eye the pudgy young soldier could see Casselman was staring at him, almost squinting, his hand raised before him as if it would help him grab hold of the memory he sought. Then the forefinger shot out straight from Casselman's hand, the thumb cocked back, the way kids make like they're pointing a pistol at you, and Casselman said, "Indianapolis. Shortley!"

The young soldier looked up, feeling his ears go hot, and said, "I went there."

That seemed to accurately describe the unsensational nature of his own time at Shortley, as compared to the glorious record of the Gunner.

Casselman thrust his big hand forward and said, "I'm Tom Casselman," and added, "Class of Forty-eight."

For anyone who went to Shortley, it was sort of like having the President come up to you on the street and say, "I'm Dwight Eisenhower," adding, as if you might not know him, "President of the United States." Then you were supposed to shake hands and say, "I'm John Q. Public."

The young man shook the outstretched hand and said, "I'm Willard Burns."

The waiter brought the beer, taking the small coin Gunner left him with effusive thanks, and Gunner stared again at Burns, like he had X-ray vision, and made that pop of his fingers.

"You're *Sonny* Burns."

"That's what they called me."

And, he thought ruefully, it was evidently what they still called him; was what they would continue to call him, the little boy-cherub nickname he would be stuck with into old age, a bearded old coot called "Sonny."

"Sure," said Casselman. "Sure, I remember. You were a photographer. Took pictures for the *Daily Echo.*"

"I did some sports stuff you might have seen," Sonny said.

"Right! Action stuff! Damn good!"

Sonny ran a finger between his neck and the collar of his shirt, looking away as he said, "I got some good shots of you in the Southport game, senior year."

"Right! Hey, this is great. Running into you like this."

Sonny couldn't figure out what Casselman could think was so great about it. Unless there was going to be some reelection of high-school class officers and Gunner was looking for votes, Sonny couldn't imagine what use or interest he could have for the guy.

"Been doing some photography myself," said Gunner.

He pulled out a pack of Chesterfields, gave it a sharp tap, and one of them popped out toward Sonny, just the way it happened when someone offered a cigarette in the movies. Whenever Sonny tried it, either none came out or they spilled all over the floor.

"Yeh," Gunner explained, snapping a lighter in front of Sonny, "I just got back from Japan. Stopped off in St. Louis to see an old buddy at Fort Leonard Wood. Anyway, over in Japan, I picked me up a Nikon. I'm not worth a damn yet—mostly shot a lot of tourist-postcard-type stuff,

Fuji and the temples and gardens and all that—but I really want to learn."

"That's swell," said Sonny.

He noticed that Gunner had several campaign ribbons, including the Korean theater, and a Purple Heart. The only ribbon Sonny had was the one you got for the Good Conduct Medal. He had the sinking feeling that maybe indeed all of life would turn out to be like high school; the Gunners continuing to be heroes, him going quietly on collecting the boring Good Conduct Medals of life.

"You must have been in combat," he said, nodding at the ribbons.

Gunner shrugged. "Caught a little shrapnel in the ass, that's all."

If you really were a hero you never made a big deal of it. You made it sound routine and unglamorous, like shrugging off a ninety-yard touchdown run as "good luck and good blocking," and in so dismissing such feats they came out sounding even more marvelous.

"I got stuck in Kansas City, Public Information," Sonny said, feeling he had to apologize.

Gunner shrugged, like it could happen to anybody. "Only one thing you missed," he said, "but that is one thing no man should miss."

"What?"

"Ja-*pan*."

With just the two syllables, he made it sound fabulous.

"It changed my whole approach," he said.

"To what?"

"You name it. I never really thought about anything before. College, you know, I memorized stuff. But I mean, think, question. There's a beauty there we haven't got—in art, architecture, in food, in philosophy, even religion. Zen. Jesus, it's not that I really know about Zen, but I sort of got like a feel for what they're into, ya know, and it's got the Western religions beat by a country mile."

"Yeh, it sounds pretty great," Sonny said, "from what I know about it."

What he knew about it was mostly contained in a story by J. D. Salinger where one of the brothers believed in Zen. He knew it was a branch of Buddhism and that it had masters instead of ministers and priests. Sometimes the masters hit you over the head with a bamboo stick, to give you enlightenment.

"Say, you ever drink any sake?" Gunner asked.

"I don't think so, no."

Gunner looked quickly around the club car.

"Don't order another beer," he said quietly. "I'll be back."

He came back with a duffel bag that contained a lot of Japanese stuff. Books on Zen. Some No plays. Pictures of formal gardens. A Nikon camera. And a bottle of sake.

"You really should drink it warmed up," he said, "but even so."

He had stopped at the water cooler and shucked off a couple of Dixie cups. Surreptitiously, as if he were fiddling for something in the duffel bag, he poured him and Sonny a cup of the sake.

"Here's to a great culture," he said.

Sonny took a big swallow and it burned going down, making him wince. It tasted sort of like perfume.

"Terrific," he said.

"Can't beat it," said Gunner. "Wait'll you have it warm, like it should be."

"How long were you there, in Japan?"

"Three months. Beautiful. Someday I have to go back. But first I have to find out what I'm doing here. Or going to do."

"Job-wise?"

"Everything-wise. That too, though. I worked at this ad agency up in Chi a couple summers during college. Young bunch of guys, pretty sharp. They said if I came with 'em when I got back, I could write my own ticket."

That sounded just like what Sonny would have expected for Gunner. But the odd thing was, because of whatever happened to him in Japan, Gunner no longer knew if he wanted to go where that kind of ticket would take him. Maybe he had been hit over the head by one of those Zen guys.

"I'm thinking about the GI Bill," Gunner said. "Maybe go back and really study something, instead of horsing around."

"Yeh, it might be nice."

"You going into photography?"

"I dunno, exactly," Sonny said. "I want to sort of get my bearings."

"Yeh, right. No use going off half-cocked. Hey—have some more sake."

"Thanks."

Sonny was getting used to the stuff. It wasn't too bad, after you got going on it.

"Japan," Gunner said. "What an experience. You get outside your own society, it gets you to thinking. You know, you see there's other ways to do things, other ways to look at things."

"I guess."

Gunner said now he wanted to go home and look at everything fresh, reexamine all his old values. What the hell was the good of a damn culture built on neon lights and Hollywood movies, on Sunday church piety and week-day business hypocrisy. He sounded like a damned radical. That seemed kind of unfair to Sonny. He figured a guy like *him* should be the radical, fighting the Gunners of the world who had everything. But he wasn't sure enough of himself, he was too afraid.

They had more sake, and Gunner got going on Japan again, how great it was.

"The greatest thing of all," he said, "is the women. Even the ones that—well, that you'd call whores over here. Over there, those gals are terrific. I guess you'd have to say they're whores, *technically,* in that you have to pay them. But they're not like whores over here where it's wham-bam-thank-ya-ma'am and you feel rotten afterward. They take their time. They treat you good."

He finished off another cup.

"Making love, with one of those Japanese women—it's a whole different thing. It's a whole different kind of experience."

Sonny felt his throat go dry, and when he spoke, his voice cracked. "How?" he asked huskily. "How is it different?"

And Gunner told him.

By the time they got to Indianapolis they had killed the bottle of sake. Gunner's eyes seemed to have receded back into his head, as if he had seen a powerful vision. Sonny was seeing green and purple spots.

"Listen," Gunner said when the train clanked and rumbled to a halt. "Let's get together. No shit."

"Sure," Sonny said.

The sake and the flattery made him almost believe Gunner meant it, believe there was some kind of bond between him and the great Gunner Casselman. He figured he must really be stoned.

The two guys shook hands at the top of the platform, and Gunner asked, "Hey, you gotta ride home?"

"Yeh," Sonny said, blushing. "My mother's getting me. How about you?"

"Mine too," said Gunner.

He made a sort of crooked smile, and Sonny thought maybe there might be some kind of bond between them after all.

2

The great vaulted waiting room of the station, with its
stained-glass windows and dank stone walls, had a massive,
cathedral-like gloom about it. The booming authoritative
voice from the loudspeaker, announcing the arrival and
departure of trains, sounded like it might be the voice of
God, ordering the milling throngs to their appointed
tracks and destinations. They pushed and hurried, obediently, through the shadows and the dust-stained motes of
afternoon sunlight, meeting their appointed trains and
greeting the travelers recently disgorged from the steam-
belching cars on the tracks above. Through the parting
wave of passengers, Sonny saw his mother, rushing toward
him.

"You're *home!*"

"Yes," he said.

Sonny stood almost immobile while his mother hugged
him. He tried to raise his arms to make the return re-
sponse, but they fell back stick-like to his sides. He flinched

and leaned back as her warm mouth brushed his cheek. Behind her, like a shadow, his father stood, tall and embarrassed.

"Welcome home, son," he said, trying for heartiness.

"Thank you, sir."

They shook hands quickly, their eyes not quite meeting.

Mrs. Burns hooked her arm through her son's and pulled him toward the newsstand, where a middle-aged woman he had never seen before was beaming at him, expectantly. She had on a lot of makeup and jewelry, and her eyes looked slightly mad beneath their mascara. Mrs. Burns squeezed Sonny's elbow, pushing him forward toward the strange woman, and said, "I want you to meet Adele Fenstermaker."

The woman placed a hand on each of Sonny's shoulders and looked him over as if he were a gift.

"So this is Sonny," she cooed. "That dear, sweet child I've heard so much about."

"How do you do?" Sonny said.

Adele Fenstermaker's brightly painted face popped toward Sonny with a cat's quickness. He jerked his head away, but felt the sticky imprint of her lips on his right cheek.

"I just *had* to," she said.

Mr. Burns, not quite looking at any of them, nervously cleared his throat. "We're in a no-parking zone," he said.

"Let's go," Sonny said.

He hefted up his duffel bag, slinging it over his shoulder on the side next to Mrs. Fenstermaker. She tripped along gaily beside him, his mother took the other flank, and his father followed behind. As they pushed out the big doors, Sonny got a glimpse of Gunner, striding along with a blonde in tight toreador pants and backless high heels. Sonny wondered if that could actually be Gunner's mother, or maybe some show girl he'd met in Chi who had come down to meet him. The woman's ass moved tantalizingly in the taut pink pants, and Sonny hoped it wasn't Gunner's mother. You shouldn't have those kind of thoughts about a person's mother.

Sonny's mother was wearing a tailored suit of the type she had adopted ever since she had, as she put it, "lost her shape," around the time Sonny went off to college and she started eating so much. She wore silk stockings with flat brown oxfords, like most of the women wore who she met in the Moral Re-Armament Movement, but unlike some of the more devout and stringent females of the MRA, she still applied makeup and regularly went to the beauty shop to have her natural reddish hair twisted into the countless tiny ringlets that always reminded Sonny of electric coils. It seemed to him fitting, somehow, as if the coils were part of some incredibly powerful electrical system that propelled his mother with breakneck speed and energy through her many good works and her dizzy ups and downs of feeling and quick, deep friendships that so often soon turned to misunderstandings and betrayals and outbursts of passionate hurt and rancor. Sonny figured that if somehow those coils of his mother's energy could be hooked up to a generator, her emotions could power the electrical system of the whole city of Indianapolis.

Sonny had hoped his father would be driving the Chevy, but his mother had driven the church station wagon. It was a beat-up old wooden kind, and it said Northside Methodist Church on the side of each front door, and below that was a cross, and under that, in quotation marks, "I am the Way, the Truth, and the Life." Sonny always slouched down in his seat when he rode in it or when he drove it. His mother worked in the church office and had the use of the wagon most all the time.

"You get in back," Mrs. Burns told Sonny, "with Adele."

He did, sitting as close to the door as he could, but Mrs. Fenstermaker slid beside him and grasped his nearest hand. With her other, many-ringed hand she pointed to

Mrs. Burns, who had bustled into the driver's seat, and with a great sigh, Mrs. Fenstermaker said, in a tone of almost sacred gratitude, "If it weren't for that woman. *Your* mother."

"Don't be silly," Mrs. Burns said and started the motor with a gassy, explosive roar.

Mrs. Fenstermaker turned her eyes full force on Sonny, like hot rays, and explained, "When I met that woman, I was on the verge. The absolute verge."

The car leaped forward, rocking the passengers. Sonny felt hot and nauseous, and the sake was doing dangerous things to his head and his stomach. He wished to hell his father had driven so it would at least have been smooth. His mother drove the car like a bronco, pushing it into great bucks and sudden stops. Whenever she shifted, the car made a lurch, tossing the passengers back and forth like riders in a rodeo. Sonny leaned back and closed his eyes.

He tuned out the chatter between his mother and Mrs. Fenstermaker, concentrating on the delicate state of his stomach, as if perhaps he could keep it settled by force of will. The sake seemed to have created a high ringing sound in his head, and he had the sensation he could feel his own teeth. The voices of the women were like a shrill gabble of birds, indistinguishable, until, after a couple of miles, he heard his mother saying, "Sonny? Sonny? There it is. Good old Shortley."

"Mmm."

He knew what his old high school looked like, knew exactly the stern and impressive facade of brick and lime-stone, the wide plaza at the entrance, and the steps rising upward in two long tiers. He knew how scared and excited he was when he first walked up them as a freshman, and in through the massive doors to the clatter and din of the bustling hall. He had thought, back then, that his real life might be beginning, but it hadn't turned out that way.

"It's a shame," Mrs. Fenstermaker said. "About Shortley."

Sonny opened his eyes and asked, "What's a shame about it?"

Though it had given him less than he had hoped, he still was loyal to the old school. It was best in the city, and its graduates were proud.

Mrs. Fenstermaker smiled sadly. "It's getting dark inside. A fine school like that. They say eventually it will be *completely* dark inside."

"Dark inside?" Sonny asked.

He didn't know what the hell the old doll was talking about. Had the lights gone out? Was the electrical system breaking down?

"It's coming," his father sighed.

Mr. Burns turned around toward Sonny, cleared his throat, and his face took on that look of grim intensity that came when he spoke of the wrongs and outrages of the modern, immoral, something-for-nothing, tradition-destroying world—the world that was launched and shaped in America by FDR, and that even Dwight D. Eisenhower seemed powerless to reconvert to its old, decent ways.

"The Supreme Court laid down the law, just this week. The races will be mixed, right in the schools, whether anyone likes it or not."

Sonny understood then how his old school was "getting dark inside." When he went to high school, all the Negroes had to go to Crispus Attucks; no one questioned that, it was part of the natural order of things. But a few years after he graduated, the city saw the handwriting on the wall, the coming tides of socialistic integration sweeping across the country out of Washington, and so had "voluntarily" (before being forced) decreed that colored kids could go to any high school they wanted—that is, if they lived in the neighborhood. And the catch was that colored were slowly but surely spreading north to the neighbor-hood of grand old Shortley.

"I visited school last year," Sonny said. "There weren't many then."

It was a feeble kind of defense and sort of a betrayal of Sonny's own belief that all men were created equal, in-cluding the colored. That was one of the radical notions he had picked up from liberal professors in college, and he didn't like to argue with his parents about it. If you talked about it much, the danger-signal vein of anger would start to show in his father's forehead, pulsing and throbbing, the sign that Sonny most feared as a kid when he did something wrong and his father found out. He wasn't in any condition for an argument right now, of any kind.

"Well," his father said, "it's coming. It's only just be-gun."

"That's right." Mrs. Fenstermaker grimly nodded. "They're up to Twenty-eighth Street now."

Every time Sonny came home from college or the Army he heard the latest report on how far *They* had advanced out of their old small, crowded, rickety bastion. The omi-nous *They*, like some relentless army, crept north past one parallel block after another, destroying real-estate values as they went, as brutally as Sherman laid waste the property of Georgia in his march to the sea. This time *They* were on the march, invading formerly forbidden territories, forcing the retreating whites farther north to the suburb fortresses.

"Thank God you went to Shortley when you did, Sonny," Mr. Burns said.

Sonny sat straighter up in his seat, feeling he had to somehow gather his thoughts and speak out his own posi-tion on the matter, but before he could say anything, Mrs. Burns bolted the car away from a stoplight with a lurch of special force, and then in a loud voice said, "Adele, have

you been to the sale at Ayres? I understand they have some
wonderful things in cotton."

Sonny's mother hated controversy, especially the political kind. Mr. Burns turned around to face the front again
and Sonny sat back, pressing his eyes closed, until almost
ten minutes later the car jerked to a halt in the gravel
drive and Mrs. Burns gaily announced, "Sonny, you're
home," and, in an extra comment that made his stomach
spin even more frighteningly, "Home for *good!*"

Sonny pulled himself out of the car and saw the Colonial-
style two-story house—it looked like a little slice off the end
of Mt. Vernon—waver before him in the afternoon sun.
The house, in a new development that had never quite
caught on, always made him feel guilty, for he knew his
mother had insisted on it being built for the pleasure of
his adolescence, over his father's migraine fears that it was
way out of line with what they could really afford.

"Look, Sonny. There's Winkie!" Mrs. Burns said.

"I see him," Sonny said.

Winkie, the mongrel dog that Mrs. Burns had found
and adopted when Sonny went off to college, came bound-
ing off the porch, his great tongue flapping like a wet pink
flag.

"Good old Winkie," Mrs. Burns said. "Sonny, say hello
to Winkie."

"Hello, Winkie."

Winkie barked, sending waves of pain through Sonny's
reeling head.

"Winkie says hello to you," Mrs. Burns explained.

"I heard him," Sonny said.

"Good old Winkie."

Mrs. Burns knelt down and nuzzled the friendly mutt,
cooing in his ear while he licked and yipped his love. Mrs.
Burns loved to hug and cuddle Winkie, explaining that
ever since Sonny "grew up" and "grew away from me" she
couldn't hug and cuddle *him* anymore, but good old

Winkie didn't mind. It sounded like a reproach, suggesting that Winkie was nicer and more understanding than Sonny. Sonny supposed that was true.

"Ohh," Mrs. Fenstermaker said, "how I love this wonderful home. I can't wait to get inside and kick off my shoes."

Mr. Burns had unlocked the front door, and Sonny went straight upstairs to the bathroom. He loosened his tie, knelt down in front of the toilet like a communicant before an altar, bowed his head in thankfulness at having the bowl there below him, and heaved up a mixture of sake, beer, and breakfast. When he finished he lay down next to the toilet, his head on the cool linoleum floor, which smelled reassuringly of childhood.

There was a soft, tentative rap at the door, and his mother's voice said, "Sonny?"

"Yes."

"Are you in there?"

"Yes."

"Can I come in?"

"Jesus H. Christ," he said under his breath.

"What is it?"

"I'll be right out."

He pulled himself off the floor and splashed his face with cold water. His mouth was fuzzy and sour, but his toothbrush was in his gear and he didn't want to use someone else's. His mother's, for instance.

He took a deep breath and opened the door.

"You're white as a sheet," his mother said.

"I just have to go lie down a minute."

Sonny headed for the door to his bedroom, her following. He flopped down on the lower bunk of his All-American-boy double-decker bed and unbuttoned his jacket. His mother sat down on the bed beside him, and he closed his eyes.

"How do you feel?"

"Fine," he said.

"I hope you'll have an appetite. I cooked a big roast for supper. There's so much of it, I asked Adele to stay. I hope you don't mind."

Sonny said nothing. He concentrated on breathing.

"She dolls herself up kind of flashy, I guess, for a widow. But she's a wonderful person. Very intelligent, too."

Mrs. Burns' voice lowered to a whisper, and she said, "I don't know how she got herself mixed up with that Italian. Remember that little Dominick fellow, works at the little vegetable store in Broad Ripple? The one on Guilford? Well, I don't know what he has, but he sure had her eating out of his hand. And then one day he cut her off just like that. Priest's orders or something. Well, she went to pieces. Slashed her wrists and turned on the gas. A neighbor found her and got an ambulance, and when she got home from the hospital, this neighbor—she's in our church—told Reverend Halverson about her, and he went to call, and I took her some soup and some books I thought might help, and we got to be great friends. That was only two weeks ago, but I feel I've known her all my life. What I *can't* understand is what she saw in that little Dominick. But, you know what they say about the Italians. The men—"

Sonny felt nauseous again and wanted to scream. He knew there was going to be some sex thing coming about Italian men, like they had big pricks or something. His mother wouldn't use that word, she never used words like that, but she had some way of talking about sex in perfectly proper language that got the idea across anyway.

"Please," Sonny said. "I have to rest awhile."

His mother laid a hand on his forehead, feeling for fever. He winced, squeezing his eyes tighter shut.

"I think you're running a temperature."

"I am not," he said slowly and distinctly, enunciating each syllable. "I do not have any temperature whatsoever."

Her hand still lay on his forehead. "There's a lot of it going around," she said. "Some virus, they say."

He said nothing. Her hand felt like a hot weight, and yet it wasn't pressing, just laying there, continuing to touch.

"You always were susceptible to summer colds," she said. "Remember?"

He turned over, away from her, pressing his head into the pillow.

"Al-ma?"

Adele was calling from downstairs.

"Your friend is calling you," Sonny said.

"What is it?" Mrs. Burns called down.

"Are you all right?"

"Yes, dear."

"Is Sonny all right?"

"I think he's running a temperature," Mrs. Burns reported.

Sonny bolted upright in bed and started shouting at the top of his lungs. "I have a fever of a hundred and nine and am dying of a malignant communicable disease contracted in Kansas City from a visiting Japanese exchange-whore please everyone get away or you will get it too please leave me alone!"

His mother ran from the room, sobbing.

Sonny flopped back and buried his head in the pillow.

"Shit," he said to himself, "fuck it all," and, as if falling from a high wall, dropped into a dreamless sleep.

When he woke, there was a tray on a chair beside his bed with a glass of freshly squeezed orange juice, two aspirin tablets, a One-A-Day vitamin pill, and a religious magazine of inspirational thoughts called *The Upper Room*. Sonny looked at the tray and then lay back down, staring up at the slats and coils of the bunk above him, and said in a quiet, deliberate voice, "Fuck you, God; you're a horse's ass, and your only son is a queer."

3

You could have knocked Sonny over with a feather when
Gunner called up and asked if he'd like to get together and
have a couple brews. After Sonny had sobered up from the
sake and thought about the talk with Gunner on the train,
he'd felt his cheeks burn with embarrassment, thinking
what a fool he'd been to imagine a Big Rod like that
would really want to hang around with a nobody like
Sonny Burns. He figured Gunner was just bored on the
train and would have talked to anyone handy. Sonny had
just been handy. It was obvious to Sonny when he thought
about it soberly that as soon as Gunner hit Naptown he
would have a million friends to see, great parties to go to,
all kinds of girls to lay. Gunner was known throughout the
town as a great cocksman. He had probably told Sonny
they ought to get together just to be polite. That was what
you said to a guy—"Let's get together and tip a few
sometime"—and then you forgot all about it. Just a couple

days after Sonny had straightened all that out in his head, Gunner phoned and wanted to meet him someplace.

Sonny was especially glad Gunner called because he hadn't been out of the house yet since he'd been back, and he was really beginning to feel rotten. For three whole days he had mainly sat around in his undershorts, looking at television and reading magazines. His mother had stuffed the icebox with a lot of the rich, sweet stuff that he liked and hated himself for liking—banana cream pie, raspberry revel ice cream, fudge brownies, devil's food cake with lemon icing. He would eat that stuff and drink Pepsis with a lot of ice in them, and belch a lot. He meant to start his program of rigid daily exercise, but the one time he tried he got shamefully diverted. He was all alone in his room with the door closed and he got down on the floor to do some push-ups, but before he even started, while he was lying there preparing to gather his strength, he suddenly thought of the blonde on the train with the great legs and he got a hard-on, and then he started thinking how he might have made out with her, imagined those long tan legs around him, and he jacked off picturing it all in his mind. Then he was too weak to do the push-ups. He went downstairs and had a piece of cake and a Pepsi, feeling sticky all over and worthless as hell. He didn't even get dressed at night to have supper, but sat at the table in his bathrobe. That was his mother's idea, for she felt he deserved a real rest after serving his country for two long years, but he knew his father didn't like it very much. He avoided his father's eyes, as usual. They said things like "Pass the sugar, please" and looked the other way, while Mrs. Burns chattered and told of the sorrowful, tragedy-ridden people whom she met in the course of her day's works of mercy for the church.

Sonny had friends of his own he could have called, even a girl, but he just hadn't seemed to be able to get going. In a way he was afraid that when he did get himself together and do something, it might mark the beginning of his real life, and it might not be any different than the old one. If Gunner hadn't called, God knows how long he would have just sat around feeling lousy and picking his ass. When he actually had a place to go and got showered and dressed, he felt one hell of a lot better. He put on some clean khaki summer pants and his old white bucks and a neat sort of knitted T-shirt he had bought in Kansas City. His mother said she had to use the wagon that afternoon, but she'd drop him off wherever he was going.

"I'm going to the Red Key," he said.

"Where?"

"The *Red Key*," he shouted. "Over on College and Fifty-fourth Street."

"The tavern?"

"It's a bar."

"You're going there in the afternoon?"

"I'm meeting a guy."

"Are you sure they're open—in the afternoon?"

Sonny took a deep breath. "I'm sure."

She drove him there in silence and let him off right smack in front of the place even though he said the corner'd be fine. He would just as soon not have Gunner see him getting out of the car door that said "I am the Way, the Truth, and the Life." He sort of slinked out of the wagon and walked to the bar with his head bent down.

It was cool and dim inside, and smelled very beery. Sonny liked it. The Red Key didn't seem like any special sort of place, unless you knew that Wilks Wilkerson and Blow Mahoney and a lot of the other Big Rod jocks who used to go to Shortley hung out there after work when they had summer construction jobs to make a lot of money and keep in shape. Sonny used to really envy those guys who could casually say, "Yeh, I'm workin' construction this summer." They wore dirty T-shirts and faded khakis slung low on their hips, and they were always whipping out a grimy snot rag that was stuffed in a hip pocket and give the nose a terrific, noisy blow, just like the regular construction guys did. It showed they were real men.

Gunner was already there, and Sonny pulled up a chair at his table. It was still early, and they were the only customers except for one of those old dame lushes in a messy flowered dress, singing to herself.

Gunner had been observing the old gal, and he shook his head and explained to Sonny, "In Japan, you never see a woman drunk."

"No shit?"

"Never. See, the women are there to please the men, and if a woman's drunk, she's not going to be much good to a guy, right?"

"Yeh. I never thought of that."

"They think of everything. Acourse, they've had thousands of years to do it. We think we're so damned advanced, but we're babies compared to them."

Sonny realized you had to go get your own drink at the bar and he got himself a Bud like Gunner was drinking, and came and sat down with it.

"Ours is an infantile, competitive society. Mickey Mouse," Gunner said. "Look, you saw it at Shortley. All that social-climbing shit. The rod system, the jock stuff. You were one of the quiet ones, you just sat back and observed. Watched us run around chasing our tails, a bunch of greenasses. You were a detached observer."

Sonny shifted uneasily and took a gulp of beer. "Well, sort of," he said.

The truth was he had been a detached observer because he was never asked to be an active participant. Now it was like he was getting credit for being something he'd had no other choice than to be. It was sort of weird.

"You were way ahead of us," Gunner said.

"Shee-it."

Modestly denying the credit for having been something he couldn't help being, Sonny realized it probably sounded like genuine modesty, making him seem even nobler.

"Same thing in college," Gunner went on. "All that rah-rah fraternity crap, secret initiation and beating ass and all the rest of it. You saw through that, right? You didn't go Greek, did you?"

"I was Independent."

Sonny didn't explain he was Independent because none of the top houses had rushed him, and he was so much a secret snob that he turned down a second-rate house with a seemingly nice bunch of farmer sort of guys because they didn't have a big name on campus. Instead he moved into a rickety rooming house with a motley assortment of other outcasts—all of them snobs in their own way, trying to take a bitter kind of pride out of not fitting in. You had to have something.

"I knew you weren't the type to fall for that frat shit, Gunner said admiringly.

Sonny shrugged modestly, knowing he was being sort of phony, and yet he began to wonder about that. It was like Gunner had this particular picture of him, and he liked the way that picture of himself looked, and began to even think maybe it was the real picture. Maybe he really had been a shrewd quiet rebel all along, more mature than the others, above their little games. Maybe he just hadn't seen it that way.

"Ya see, I never *observed* anything," Gunner confessed, "never looked at anything and questioned it, till I got to Japan. Then I was a real outsider, for the first time, and I *saw* things. I realized I didn't know anything at all about my *own* society. I just accepted it. The last couple days I've been going around taking pictures. That's one way of seeing things. Ya know? You get something in that lens, you gotta be *looking* at it."

"Right," Sonny agreed, as if he'd thought of it himself long ago.

They had a couple more brews, Gunner talking that way, excited and curious, Sonny just nodding wisely in his new position as the quiet sage.

Around 4:30 Gunner said, "Listen, let's haul ass. Before long the jocks'll be coming in, and I just don't feel like shooting the shit with those guys right now."

"Sure," Sonny said.

He couldn't help wondering if Gunner wanted to go because he didn't want his old jock buddies to see him hanging around with a nobody like Sonny. But maybe it was really that Gunner felt he'd grown beyond those guys and wanted more serious, deep discussion with the sort of guy he evidently figured Sonny was.

Gunner had his mother's wheels—a neat-looking Mercury hardtop—and he said if Sonny had time he'd take him out to the Meadowlark and show him some of the pictures he took in Japan. Gunner was living with his mother in the Meadowlark, a new apartment complex out northeast where a lot of young people lived, couples and groups of guys or girls who had graduated from college and come to Naptown to get a job. It was the first kind of place like that in the city. There was always some party going on in one of the apartments, and in the warm nights you could hear music and laughter. People played records like *South Pacific* and *Call Me Madam*, and the latest jazz, like Brubeck and Chet Baker and the cool guys, and they turned the volume up loud at the parties and nobody complained. It was that kind of place. Everyone was up on the latest thing, right there in Indianapolis.

They had just started looking at Gunner's pictures from Japan when his mother came in. Sonny felt himelf turning red when he saw her. It was the babe he had seen go off with Gunner at the station, the one Sonny thought was probably a show girl down from Chi. Gunner introduced her as "Nina," which was what she liked to be called. You could see why she didn't want anyone to call her "Mother."

It wouldn't have fit. It would have seemed as silly as calling Marlene Dietrich "Grandma" even though she was one.

Nina looked Sonny over like she was annoyed or something.

"I don't think I've seen you before," she said. "What was your name again?"

"Sonny Burns," Gunner answered for him. "He went to Shortley."

That didn't seem to satisfy her.

"I thought I knew all the gang from Shortley," she said. "I don't think I ever heard of you."

"Nobody did," Sonny said, trying to smile.

"Why so?" Nina asked, her eyebrows arching.

"I didn't do much," Sonny said.

"He was a photographer," Gunner said in defense. "For the *Echo*."

"Did you go to DePauw?" Nina asked.

"I.U."

"Oh? What house were you in?"

"The rooming house."

Gunner laughed very loud. "The rooming house," he said. "That's great."

Nina shrugged and stalked to the kitchen. "I guess I don't get the joke," she said.

Gunner looked at Sonny and winked very hard, as if to tell him not to pay any attention. He was showing Sonny a picture of a Japanese pagoda. It was some kind of shrine, on a hill of deep green, with the sunset bleeding behind it. Gunner's pictures were good, they were framed well, they showed a sense of imagination and certainly a competence, and more than that, a flair. It made Sonny a little jealous, it didn't seem right that this guy who was a terrific athlete and all should be good at photography, too, should be able to pick up what it took Sonny years to learn. Some guys were good at anything, which didn't seem fair when most people were just good at one thing or nothing at all. But Sonny felt ashamed for feeling that way. Especially what with Gunner befriending him and all, treating him like he was someone special.

Nina had changed out of her dress and came in wearing another pair of those skin-tight toreadors and a low-cut matching green silky blouse. Sonny tried not to look at her, terrified he would get a hard-on and Gunner would see it and know that Sonny was sexed up by his mother. Jesus. Nina had made herself a highball and was rattling the ice in the glass, so you couldn't not pay attention to her. She had on those backless high heels and was joggling one foot up and down, just holding the shoe on the edge of her toes. Sonny thought her feet were sexy, too, and that made him feel even more ashamed and guilty. He knew a lot of guys thought women's feet were sexy, but it was something hardly any guy admitted or talked about. It was O.K. to talk about tits, and even asses, but not women's feet.

"You fellas want a drink?" Nina asked.

"I was about to get us a beer," Gunner said, and set the photograph box down and went to the kitchen, leaving Sonny alone in the room with Nina. He figured somebody ought to say something, but Nina wasn't any help. She just sat there clinking the ice around in her glass and joggling her shoe and looking sort of haughty.

"It's a nice apartment you've got here, Mrs. Casselman," Sonny said as heartily as he could.

"Call me Nina," she said. "I do like the Meadowlark. I was in a bigger place before, but it was one of those strait-laced buildings down on Meridian with a lot of old people.

The hallways smelled like a hospital. This place is a little cramped, but it suits just fine for a bachelor girl like myself."

Sonny vaguely remembered something about Gunner's father dying when he was a kid, even before he got to high school, but, of course, his mother—Nina, that is—would never think of herself as a "widow" any more than she would think of herself as a "mother." She was a "bachelor girl."

"It's a little cramped with Gunner home, but if he promises to stay I'm going to get us a bigger place, right here in the Meadowlark. Just the two of us."

"That would be nice."

"Has he shown you his pictures of Japan?"

"He has been, yes."

"And the scrapbook?"

"I don't think so, no."

"I kept a scrapbook for him, while he was gone. Of course he doesn't appreciate it—but he will someday."

"Sure," Sonny said.

Nina stood up and went to a bookcase that had the Churchill volumes on World War II, some textbooks, and a row of orange china elephants, linked trunk to tail. She pulled a green-leather scrapbook off one shelf and came and sat down beside Sonny, laying the book on one of his knees and one of hers. She smelled heavily of some woozy kind of perfume, and when she bent forward over the scrapbook, Sonny could see down her blouse almost to the nipple of her tit. He felt dizzy and tried to focus on the scrapbook. There was a page of newspaper clippings, and Sonny read one that said:

> Cpl. Thomas B. "Gunner" Casselman, known to Hoosiers for his gridiron exploits at Shortley and De-Pauw University, is stationed in Japan, where he recently climbed to the top of the fabled Mt. Fujiyama, according

to his mother, Mrs. Nina Casselman, of 3429 East 42nd Street.

"That's something," Sonny said.

"Which?" Nina asked.

"Mt. Fujiyama. Climbing it."

Gunner came in with two cans of beer and stopped short when he saw the scrapbook.

"*Mother*," he said.

That was what he called her when he really was pissed off at her.

"Your friend wanted to see it," she said.

"Whatya think he'd say, no?"

Gunner handed Sonny a beer and grabbed the scrapbook.

"We were *looking* at that!" Nina shouted.

Gunner put it back on the shelf and said, "*Please,* Mother."

Nina let out a heavy sigh and went back to where she was sitting before and picked up her drink.

"He's always been like that," she said to Sonny, "hiding his light under a bushel."

Gunner got that look like he had on the train after all the sake and the deep contemplation, where it seemed that his eyes became glassy and sunk farther back into his head.

Nina put on a Brubeck record and turned it up real loud. Nobody said anything, they all concentrated on drinking. When Gunner was finished he set down his glass on the coffee table and stood up.

"I'm giving Sonny a lift home," he said.

"You haven't forgotten about tonight, I hope?"

"No, Nina."

"I broke two dates for you, sweetie. Not that I wouldn't *rather* go out with you, but you just better show me a good time."

"We'll paint the town, Nina."

"Promise?"

"Absolutely."

"Come give Nina a kiss."

She surged up in her chair, her face lifted high and her tits pressing against the tight silk blouse. Gunner went over and leaned down to kiss her and Sonny looked away. He stood up and went to the door and Gunner was there in a moment, his eyes still sunk back, a lipstick stain on his mouth.

"Good-bye, nice to meet you, Mrs. Casselman," Sonny said.

"Nina," she corrected.

"Nina," said Sonny, not looking at her directly, and hurried out the door behind Gunner.

On the way to Sonny's house, Gunner apologized for Nina's questions about all the social crap, the fraternity jazz.

"She's still impressed by that shit," he explained.

"That's O.K."

Gunner said he was trying to get her to take a broader view of things. He had brought her a real kimono and some incense from Japan, and tried to get her interested in Oriental culture, but she got to suspecting that he was secretly married to a Japanese girl and was trying to soften the blow by making the country sound so great. Gunner got mad once and said, Well, what if he *had* married one, what difference did it make, but Nina went to pieces and he had to drop the whole thing. As Gunner put it, she wasn't too philosophical.

"Most mothers aren't," Sonny said.

"Right," said Gunner. "I can't think of any who are, offhand."

4

The day after Sonny met Gunner at the Red Key he didn't
sleep till noon, like he'd been doing since he got home, but
woke up a little after ten, dragged himself right out of bed,
and did seven push-ups. He shaved, dressed, and went
downstairs humming, thinking of a lot of stuff he wanted
to do. Constructive stuff. Like going down to the darkroom and getting it back in shape again, going out to get
some new chemicals and film, and maybe pick up the latest
Newsweek.

"You're up early," Mrs. Burns said suspiciously. She was
puttering around the kitchen, no doubt making more
tempting pastries to fatten the world with. She didn't just
feed them to Sonny, but to all the sweet-starved people she
met in the course of her work at the church office. She
could pretty much make her own hours, and more than
being in the office itself she liked driving around on
errands of mercy to the sick, the sad, the troubled. It took a
load off Reverend Halverson's back and left him more

time for fishing, which was his greatest passion—next to God, of course. He tied his own flies.

Sonny sat down at the kitchen table and looked at the front page of the Indianapolis *Star*. The main headline was about the Traffic Toll rising. It usually was. If the Reds didn't get you, the highways would, or so it seemed from reading the *Star*. He turned to sports and was happy to see Willie Mays still leading the league in batting. The Indianapolis Indians had dropped a double-header to the Toledo Mudhens. Sonny could never get too excited about the Indianapolis Indians. Not being major league, they didn't seem "real" in a funny way.

"Are you hungry?" his mother asked.

"Yeh, I am."

He felt he could eat one of those he-men lumberjack breakfasts, with smoked sausage, heaps of eggs, and hot black coffee.

"That Casselman boy," his mother said, "you say he lives with his mother?"

"Yes. I mean for now, anyway. He just got home from Japan."

"He looked very familiar."

When Gunner had taken Sonny home the night before, he had come in to use the phone, and met Mrs. Burns. She was gushy with friendliness and please to stay and have a bite to eat, but there was that little edge in her voice, the way there always was before she had sized up any new friend of Sonny and taken her stand on how he or she would aid or hinder her little boy's life.

"He was an athlete," Sonny explained. "His picture used to be in the paper a lot."

"Isn't he the one who was awfully fast? In high school?"

"Damn right. He ran the hundred in ten-one."

"No, dear. I mean fast with the girls."

"I dunno," Sonny muttered, looking at the major-league standings.

"I thought everyone knew. I mean, he had quite a reputation, didn't he? For sowing his wild oats?"

"I dunno."

Cleveland was in first place in the American League. Maybe the Yankees weren't invincible.

"Does he always go to bars in the afternoon?"

Sonny put the paper down. "For Christ sake, what business is it of yours? What if he goes to bars in the morning? What if he sleeps in bars overnight?"

"Don't yell. There's no need to yell."

"I'm not yelling! I'm asking what business of yours is it what Gunner Casselman does?"

"It's my business what happens to my own son."

"What's that got to do with Gunner?"

"If you lie down with dogs, you come up with fleas."

"Listen. That guy is a friend of mine."

"That's exactly what I'm saying."

"Well, it's none of your damn business. For your information, he happens to be a great guy."

He picked up the sports page again and tried to concentrate on the standings, but they blurred before his eyes.

"Really, I just thought maybe you'd want him to come to your party. Now that he's such a good friend of yours."

Sonny looked up, eyeing his mother carefully. She was peeking in the stove.

"What do you mean, my party?" he asked.

"Just a little party. A little dinner for you."

"*What* party? I don't know about any party."

"Well, of course you don't. It's a surprise party. For your homecoming. This Friday night."

Sonny squeezed his hands together and tried not to raise his voice. "Who's coming?" he said.

His mother let out a high, nervous little laugh. "Well, I couldn't tell you *that,* or it wouldn't be any surprise at all."

She set a plate in front of him with a fresh homemade

apple turnover topped with fudge ripple ice cream, and beside it, a large glass of Pepsi with a lot of ice. It was, or used to be, his favorite breakfast, though in college and the Army he had tried to learn to like eggs and sausage and hot black coffee because it seemed more manly. And yet whenever he was home, his mother got him back on the gooey stuff, and he couldn't resist it, even though it made him mad at her and at himself, and after eating those fattening sweets he felt almost as guilty and depressed as he did after jacking off. He often wondered why he couldn't help doing things that made him feel so awful after he did them.

"Would it now?" she asked. "Be a surprise if I told you who was coming?"

"Is it people I know?"

"Some you do, some you don't. But the ones you don't I promise you're going to like."

He had heard such promises before. "Who is it?" he insisted. "Who's coming that I don't know?"

"Well, since you don't know them, you wouldn't know their names anyway."

"Who are they?"

The fudge ripple was beginning to melt down the hot sides of the homemade apple turnover.

"I won't eat till you tell me," he said, laying down the ultimate threat.

Mrs. Burns sighed and said with a fake casual tone, "Oh, just some of the MRA bunch who happen to be in town."

Sonny very deliberately folded his napkin, set it on the table, and went into the living room. He sat on the antique velvet settee and lit a cigarette, trying very hard to be calm. The very initials of Moral Re-Armament made him want to scream. It was a nondenominational (but mainly WASP) religious movement with great appeal for middle-class people who found in its doctrine of "Absolute Purity, Absolute Honesty, and Absolute Love," and in its tearful, wrenching, free-lance confessional sessions, a sort of fulfillment that was lacking in the ordinary going-to-church kind of religion. The adherents to this faith seemed to Sonny a band of smiling, self-satisfied, well-mannered fanatics. They didn't drink or smoke or jack off, or screw anyone unless they were married, and the girls gave up makeup and pulled their hair into knots and tried not to look sexy. They sang cheery, uplifting songs and looked bright-eyed and serene, in a lobotomized kind of way. Some of the full-time salaried members traveled around in "teams" trying to recruit people, and put on shows and plays proving how wonderful it was to be like they were and believe as they did. Mrs. Burns had gone to one of their performances in Indianapolis and seen the happy shining faces of those wonderful young people and felt a great surge of hope that this might be the answer for her troubled, faith-stripped son.

Sonny had been deeply religious as a boy but, as his mother so often explained to people in a trembling voice, "in college he lost his faith." She ascribed the loss to the insidious influence of intellectuals, who were known to be almost all atheistic and who yet were given the task of teaching the young. Her suspicion of the influence of college was bolstered by most of her friends, including some who had been there, like Cousin Harriet Van de Kamp, who was on the Indianapolis school board and told Mrs. Burns on good authority that every college faculty in the country was riddled with Reds. Even the ones in Indiana! Sonny was only one of many innocent young people who had fallen under their atheistic influence and was brainwashed by their Godless doctrines. It was Mrs. Burns' most fervent desire to help Sonny find his faith again, and toward this end she had enlisted an impressive array of spiritual counselors. The fact that none had succeeded in helping Sonny locate what he had lost (his mother seemed to think of it as a tangible object, like a

misplaced car key) did not in the least discourage her but
in fact drove her on to even greater efforts.

Once, on the pretense of taking "a different kind of
family vacation," she had got him to Mackinac Island in
Michigan, the MRA's U.S. headquarters, where whole
teams of firm-jawed young men who all seemed to have
been champion pole-vaulters or halfbacks when they were
in college (which for many was quite some time ago) had
tried to make him see the light. They explained how much
fun purity could be and told Sonny he would feel a lot
better if he told them about some of the dirty things he
had done which most every guy did at some time or other,
like jacking off and thinking dirty stuff about girls (maybe
even *doing* the dirty stuff!) before marriage. Sonny fled
from the island after two sleepless nights, during which he
was terrified that if he beat off, an entire team of former
Ohio State football stars would burst in the room and
demand that he confess and repent, in the name of God
Almighty and the National Collegiate Athletic Association.

Mrs. Burns had to admit that the MRA system "hadn't
taken" with Sonny, but she evidently felt that later injec-
tions might do the trick. Like the bunch who were coming
to supper for Sonny's "surprise party" welcome-home from
the service.

"Fuckin-A," he said to himself. "Fuckin-A John Do."

"It's melting, dear," his mother said.

She had put the ice cream and apple shit on a tray and
brought it into the living room. It sat there before him, a
runny disaster.

"What kind of potatoes would you like for the party
supper, baked or sweet?"

"Either," he said.

"I could make sweet with marshmallow topping."

"Who else is coming?"

"Oh, Sonny, it wouldn't be any surprise at all then. I

wanted it—I wanted it—" Her voice was beginning to quiver.

"O.K.," he said. "But listen."

"Yes?"

"Don't ask Gunner to come."

"I thought it might do him some good," she sniffed.

"Don't ask him."

"All right, dear. After all, it's your party."

Sonny stuck the spoon in the melting goo on the plate and started to eat, so she'd go away. And seeing him eat, she smiled and tiptoed out of the room. A little later, he heard the motor of the wagon burst to a start, like a mortar shell, and gravel churned noisily as Mrs. Burns ripped out of the driveway, hurrying to her missions.

Sonny didn't feel like doing too much stuff now, and he went to the den and flipped through some magazines. *Life* had a story of a nun who had outwitted the Commies. It said:

> The Deliverance of Sister Cecelia
> A resourceful nun who trusted in St. Joseph tells unique story of flight from Reds.

Sonny was getting tired of the damned Reds. He was tired of the damned Christians, too. He wished they'd fight it out and leave everybody alone. They were always "battling for men's minds" instead of minding their own business. The Reds and the Christians both.

They even had it on television. Every day they broadcast the Army vs. McCarthy show. It sounded to Sonny like a trial, but they called it a "hearing." Everything seemed to be called something different than it was anymore, like the war in Korea was a "police action," or a "conflict," instead of a war. Even though they bombed and shot people. It was like they were trying to water things down so you wouldn't get too upset about them.

A lot of people were upset about the Army vs. McCarthy

"hearings" and most of the people Sonny knew around
Indianapolis thought Joe McCarthy was a great hero, hunting down all the dirty Reds in government. The liberal
professors Sonny knew, and some of the guys he met in the
Army who had gone to college in the East, thought it was
McCarthy who was the menace instead of the Reds. Sonny
didn't like the guy's looks, and he liked the defense guy,
old Joe Welch, who was against McCarthy, but he found
the whole thing hard to really follow and he didn't like to
get in arguments about it because if you were against
McCarthy the people for him suspected you of being a
Commie, and Sonny had enough things to worry about
without worrying about whether people thought he was a
Red. Some people in Indianapolis probably suspected he
was already because he didn't believe in God and he
thought colored people should go to school with whites
and he didn't agree that laziness was the only cause of
unemployment.

He picked up a *Ladies' Home Journal*, just to get his
mind off that crap, but even *they* had articles about it.
There was one called "Is American Youth Radical?" and
Sonny couldn't help turning to it to find out the answer.
The article was written by a woman named Dorothy
Thompson, and it said:

> "The high schools and colleges are infiltrated with
> Communists." So goes the argument in some circles. . . .

Sonny was glad to see Miss Thompson didn't go along
with the argument. But what she did say kind of depressed
him anyway. She was trying to say that young people
weren't too bad, and one of the things she said to try to
prove it was that

> There was considerable anxiety in Washington lest the
> GI bonuses would be spent in riotous living. They were
> not. They were spent for education—and the GI was a
> very serious student.

Sonny kind of wished the GI money *had* been spent in riotous living. That's how he'd like to spend his, if he got the bill himself. Actually, he didn't see how you could live too riotously on $110 a month. But at least it could get you away from home. He was really going to look into it. Maybe he could even get a degree in photography, if they had them. It almost seemed impossible, getting paid to learn about something you liked.

He put down the magazine and went downstairs to the darkroom in the basement. He hadn't used it for a couple years, and there were a lot of crates of old clothes piled up in it. His mother collected old clothes and sent them to the Indians. She couldn't see why there was suddenly such concern about the colored when nobody cared about the Indians and they were the *real* Americans.

Sonny picked up his camera and blew the dust off of it. He hadn't used it since his last leave home. He loved the camera, but had just got out of the habit of using it regularly when he went in service. It was a Rollieflex, and he had bought it from one of the photographers at the *Star,* a guy who had helped him learn how to use it. He held it in his hands, and it felt solid and reassuring. He almost felt there was something magic about it, that it was a secret weapon he could use to free himself, to become a person in his own right, to have his own life that was different from his parents'. He resolved to go buy film as soon as his mother got back with the wagon.

5

For the next several days, Sonny and Gunner went on a picture-taking binge. Gunner could use his mother's wheels any day that he got up and drove her to work down at WIBC-TV, and he didn't even have to pick her up because some guy she dated at the station drove her home anytime she wanted him to. After leaving his mother off, he'd come by and honk for Sonny, and they'd go out with their cameras, driving all over town and shooting stuff. They drove to the top of Crown Hill Cemetery, a historic landmark of the city where the famous criminal John Dillinger was buried. From the top you could see almost the whole city spread below, flat and green. They went out to the Speedway and tried getting some action shots of the cars in the Time Trials for the great Five-Hundred-mile race ,hat was held every Memorial Day and known throughout the world. They drove way north to where Gunner knew a guy who had a farm, and shot pictures of the livestock; they even took their cameras inside the

Riviera Club swimming pool and got pictures of guys going off the high dive.

Gunner was restless, always asking questions, and he sort of reminded Sonny of a spy, or maybe a foreign correspondent, prowling the city and looking into little nooks and crannies and snapping pictures and asking people things, like he was trying to get the real scoop on this mysterious city and its natives, the puzzling place where he was born and grew up. He kept asking one particular question that people took as an insult, the question of some kind of nut or subversive troublemaker—*Why?*

When Gunner got an urge to drop in on someone, Sonny just tagged along, listening and smiling. It turned out Gunner wasn't at all ashamed of being seen hanging around with a nobody, as Sonny had suspected he might be, but in fact seemed to want him along, seemed to like hashing things over with him after they'd been someplace, liked hearing what Sonny thought about what was said and what happened, even though most of the time Sonny pretty much agreed with him. Sometimes Sonny felt he ought to disagree more, feared that Gunner might suspect him of just sucking up to him or something, but actually Gunner was so damn convincing that Sonny really did buy most all his ideas and impressions, even the ones that were kind of weird.

One afternoon they buzzed out to Gunner's sister's house to get some shots of her kids. Gunner's sister Peachie lived on Guilford in the forties, one of those blocks of small graying frame houses and brick doubles with front porches, little front yards and occasional hedges to divide one yard from another, a few paint-chipping picket fences, and an alley in back with weather-beaten garages and a few backboards with iron hoops nailed up on them. It was hardly fancy, but nothing you had to be ashamed of; the sort of place a young couple started out in before going farther north to the newer, ranch-type developments.

Peachie was only two years older than Gunner, but it might as well have been twenty years or so; the way she was settled into the niche of her life, it would take a load of dynamite to blast her out of it even if she wanted to. She had two little kids and went around most of the day with a kerchief around her head, mopping and cooking and dusting and washing. She had never been a pretty girl, but was sharp and energetic and fun to be around, and always able to organize things. She had been in some of the good clubs at Shortley and made Delta Gamma at Butler, where she went for a year before marrying Bud Belzoni.

Sonny remembered Belzoni from the teams at Shortley. He was never a star, seldom made first string, and when you thought about it his main talent was in *looking* good on the football or baseball field or the basketball court. There were always guys like that, and Sonny kind of got a kick out of them. In baseball they never could hit worth a damn but were terrific chatter guys—C'mon-babe-c'mon-boy-c'mon-Pete, throw it in there baby throw it past him babe way to go keed. In basketball they weren't good shots but were fancy dribblers and liked to pass behind their backs. In football they were the guys who always patted the lineman on the ass and yelled a lot of defensive warnings and pointed all over the place, but they seldom tackled anybody. But you needed guys like that. They made everybody feel better, and they looked like All-Americans.

Belzoni only went to Butler one semester and then joined the Naval Reserve and went to work at Allison's automotive and airplane plant. He worked the night shift and played on the company's semi-pro baseball team, the Allison Jets, which gave him an extra something every week during summer, though Peachie claimed he put it all back in beer. He was getting something of a belly on him, which was especially noticeable because he wore his pants down around his crotch. He still had a crew cut, and walked in a real pigeon-toed stride, and mostly hung around the house in an old pair of khakis and some sweat socks, drinking beer and scratching his belly and belching a lot. On his nights off he hung out with the boys, hitting the Tropics Club and the Topper and the Red Key. At least he said it was the boys, though Peachie suspected there were some girls, too. She'd confided to Gunner that once last year Belzoni came home with a case of the crabs that he said he must have got off a toilet seat.

"She must have been some toilet," Peachie told him. Peachie was nobody's fool.

The front room was littered with toys and kids. The baby, a little girl named Babs, was squawling in the playpen, and little Bud, Jr., who was around four years old, was playing soldiers with a little towheaded boy named Richard who lived next door. Peachie was in her faded blue jeans and a scruffy man's shirt with the sleeves rolled up, washing the inside of the windows. She said to go on back to the kitchen, she'd be there in a jiffy.

Belzoni was in the kitchen with his sweat-socked feet up on the table, drinking a Weidemann's and listening to a Cubs game on a portable radio. He popped a couple of beers for Sonny and Gunner, and even though they said they weren't hungry, he poked around in the icebox and brought out a bowl of some leftover potato salad, stuck a fork in it, and set it on the table next to where he propped his feet. He turned the ball game down a little so it was easier to talk.

"So," Gunner asked, "how's the ball club doin'? You guys burnin' up the league?"

"Be serious, man. We lost our only pitcher who could get the fuckin ball over the plate. Remember Bo Begley?"

"Pitched for Manual-Tech?"

"Yeh, he even got a tryout with the Dodgers. Well, he got his fuckin pitching hand caught in a fuckin lathe last week. Lost two fingers."

"Jesus," Gunner sympathized, "what a break."

"Put us up shit crick without a paddle," Bud said. "Last night we got our ass cleaned by Link-Belt, fourteen-five." "That's rough," Gunner said. "But what about Begley?" "Like I said, he lost two fingers. No good to us now." Belzoni belched, rubbing his stomach reflectively, and said, "Unless he could work on some kind of knuckle ball. Maybe he could develop a knuckle ball of some kind."

Sonny felt himself rubbing his hands together, checking on his fingers. When he heard stuff like that, he got very nervous and checked to see if his own parts were in place. Peachie came in, got herself a beer, and pulled a chair up to the table with the guys.

"You taking the summer off?" she asked Gunner.

"I dunno. Trying to figure my next move."

"You staying in Naptown?" Bud asked.

"I dunno. Doubt it."

"Nina'll have a conniption fit," Peachie said, "if you don't settle down here."

Gunner got kind of red. "She'll live," he said.

"Man, if I were you," Belzoni said. "Loose as a goddam goose, nothing to tie you down—"

"Don't daydream," Peachie said.

"I was just sayin' if I was Gunner, for Chrissake. If I was, free like that, I'd get my ass to the Coast."

"California?" Gunner asked.

"You bet your sweet ass. Sun and sea, sea and sand. The Good Life, brother. Southern California."

"What the hell," Gunner said, "what's stopping *you?*"

"You bastard!" Peachie said. "My own brother. *I'm* stopping him, that's who, me and those two kids of his in there."

"Hold it, Peach, I didn't mean he should cut out on you. I meant the whole bunch of you go."

"Just pick up and leave?" she asked. "Just pack up and go to California, just like that."

"Why not?" Gunner asked.

"*Why not,*" she mimicked. "Money's why not, for one thing. What're we going to use for money? Sell the kids?"

"Whatya s'pose they'd bring?" Bud asked.

"Shut up, you bastard."

"For Chrissake, Peachie," Gunner said, "you think they don't have money in California?"

"Maybe *they* do, people who already live there."

"Oh, and you don't think they let anybody else earn it?"

"Earn it *how?*" she shouted. "Picking up driftwood?"

"See," Bud said, "you can't reason with her."

Gunner rubbed hard at his forehead, and said, "Listen, Peach, thousands of people go there all the time, they go there and get jobs and buy houses and live in California."

"Hell, yes," Bud said, "it's Opportunitysville. Anyone'll tell you that."

"We live *here,*" said Peachie, "in Indianapolis."

"There isn't any law says you have to," Gunner said.

"There isn't any law says we have to leave, either."

"But why do you have to stay?" Gunner asked.

"It's home," she said. "It's where we live."

"I'd sure like to try that surfing," Bud said.

"I know what you'd like to try," Peachie said. "You'd like to try those blondes on the beach, that's what you'd like to try."

Bud let out a belch.

"Seriously, Peach," Gunner said, "there's nothing stopping you. Why not try the Coast for a while? If you don't like it you can always come back."

"What're you, the California Chamber of Commerce?"

"I just don't like to see people tie themself down when they don't have to."

"Wait'll you get a family, then you tell me all about how free you are."

"I will," Gunner said. "I'll wait. To get a family."

"What're you gonna be, a bum or something?"

Belzoni got up and scratched under his armpit. "Don't listen to her," he said. "Play it loose. Hey, I gotta get dressed. Take it slow, guys."

"We better get moving," Gunner said.

He got up and Sonny followed him to the door. Peachie stood there with her arms crossed, like she had to restrain herself from wringing Gunner's neck.

"Thanks a lot," she said, "for putting that bug up his ass about California."

Gunner started to say something and then he stopped himself and just said, "See ya, Peach," and loped to the car. Sonny hurried along behind him, not wanting to look back at Peachie in the door.

After Gunner started the car, Sonny reminded him they forgot to take pictures of the kids.

"Well," Gunner said, "it didn't seem like the time to do it."

"No," Sonny agreed.

Gunner said he felt like bashing some golf balls, and Sonny said he wouldn't mind watching, so they went out to Little America to the driving range. Sonny really couldn't stand golf. Once, when he was around twelve years old, his father took him out on a dewy spring morning to give him a golf lesson. It was one of those times Mr. Burns was trying to be like a father, but like most of his shy, halting efforts along those lines, it didn't quite come off. Sonny remembered with a vivid embarrassment how his father curled his hands over his, trying to show him how to grip the club, and Sonny could feel his father's hot breath on his neck and smelled the sweet mists rising off the tender early morning grass, and he was dizzy with the sadness of it, the fright of touching, the awkwardness of two human beings of the same flesh and blood who didn't know how to love and were clumsy with fear. Sonny tried, but he never hit one straight ball. His elbows and knees kept popping out at the wrong times, bending when they should have been straight, stiffening when they should have given. After the agonizing hour was over, his father said, "We'll try it again sometime," and Sonny said, "Sure, that'd be great," but neither of them ever mentioned it after that. Sonny wanted to thank his father for the effort, the good intention, but didn't know how. The words, whatever they were, clung to his throat.

Sonny never picked up a golf club after that—except to play miniature golf on dates with girls—but he got a real charge out of watching Gunner drive balls. It looked like pure pleasure. There was the concentration, the brief, nervous flexing of the knees as the stance was assumed, the swing up and back with the eye never leaving the ball, the crack of the club square on the mark, and the graceful curve of the follow-through as the white dot sailed past the hundred-yard mark, the two-hundred yard, the two-fifty, and sometimes clear into the woods beyond.

"*Go* you bastard!" Gunner shouted.

"Great," Sonny said. "You really clobbered it."

Gunner drove three buckets of balls while Sonny looked on. By the time Gunner finished all the buckets, the sky had turned that purple color it gets just before real darkness, and the big floodlights of the driving range had come on. Gunner said he could eat a horse but he didn't feel like going home. Sonny didn't either. They both called their mothers to say they wouldn't be home for supper, and went to the Von Burg's Snack Shop and had the big greasy kind of breaded tenderloins that they seem to make that way only in Indiana, and washed them down with root-beer floats.

Gunner still was restless, and he said he wouldn't mind buzzing by Ray Sheneke's place.

"You remember Shins?" he asked.

"Sure, sort of," Sonny said.

Sheneke wasn't a jock but he was one of the Big Rods who ran around in that gang at Shortley. He was more the

playboy type, a quick, skinny sort of guy who dressed
pretty sharp and carried a churchkey on his watch chain so
he'd always be ready to open a can of beer. He was always
elected Treasurer of everything. Certain guys were always
being elected Treasurer, just like other guys were always
being elected President of whatever it was they were in.
Other guys just voted. Sonny sometimes thought that those
things were decided when you were born, like when Ray
Sheneke came out of the womb, God looked down and
said, "That guy's Treasurer material," and so it would be
for the rest of his life.

"We were lodge brothers at DePauw," Gunner said.
"He was one guy who seemed to have a brain in his head,
when he wasn't partying. You know, if you got him talking
without a lot of guys around."

Sonny wasn't sure if he ought to go along to Sheneke's,
but Gunner seemed to take it for granted, so he didn't say
anything. Sheneke had married Patsi Heppenstall and they
lived way out north on a fairly fancy new street called
Morning Glory Road, off Meridian. The house, a stone
ranch type, was a wedding present from Patsi's folks, and a
lot of people were catty about it. Everyone knew that a
young couple just starting out couldn't afford a house like
that, and some felt they ought to start out like everyone
else in either an apartment or a duplex or one of the older
little houses in closer to town like Gunner's sister Peachie
lived in. The feeling was that a young couple ought to
work their way up, ought to earn their own house, and
that way they'd really appreciate it more. Patsi's parents
took the more controversial stand that you were only
young once and you might as well be able to enjoy it
instead of having to wait till you were old and tired.

A light was on in the big picture window, and a guy in a
chair peered out at the car. The porch light flashed on, and
before Gunner and Sonny made it all the way up the
flagstone walk, Shins was at the door, waving and grinning.

"Gunner, old bastard, home from the wars!"

"Shins, baby!"

Sonny stood with his hands in his pockets while Shins and Gunner pounded one another around in greeting.

"Hey, Shins, you remember Sonny Burns," Gunner said.

Sonny stepped forward and Shins, with an uncertain smile, pumped his hand and said, "Right, yeh, how goes it, man?"

"Swell," Sonny said.

They went inside and Patsi came out from the kitchen, wiping her hands on a dish towel, but when she saw Gunner she dropped it, screamed his name, and threw her arms around him, kicking one leg back in the air like the sexy babes in the movies did when they kissed some guy. She was tall and thin and didn't have much up front, but her long, curvy legs were generally acknowledged to be the best pair at Shortley during her day. When such things were first being judged and appraised by the guys, the accepted fantasy-desire in speaking of Patsi Heppenstall was "How'd you like to have those goddam legs wrapped around ya—*squeezing*," just as the equivalent fantasy for Sandy Simpson, who was famous for the way she undulated down the corridors, was "How'd ya like to have that great little tail on top of ya—*moving?*" These rhetorical questions were answered with moans, wails, grunts, grabs of the cock, and sometimes full collapses to the floor, where the tormented connoisseur would writhe and beat his fists while his buddies howled like mongrel dogs in a midnight alley.

"Hey, Pats," Gunner said, disentangling himself. "You remember Sonny Burns?"

"Hi!" she said, and Sonny smiled.

"Honey," Ray asked, "can you show these guys the Lord and Heir?"

"If you're quiet. He's just gone to sleep."

Led by Patsi, they tiptoed single file into the room of the baby, Ray Sheneke, Jr. It was three months old and looked, at least to Sonny, like the usual small white pudding glazed with red. The room was done in Little Bo Peep wallpaper, and there were enough fuzzy animals to start a small zoo. The baby lay there defenseless and all-powerful, the tiny trophy for which men mated and toiled, raising him up until he could repeat the same process, for another who would mate and repeat it again, making the world turn, making it all go on. Powdered in sleep, the kid knew nothing of all that, sheltered with innocence and love. Overhead, educational birds hung still in his cloudless sky.

"Isn't he adorable?" Patsi whispered.

"Sure is," Sonny dutifully whispered back.

"Whatya think, Guns?" Ray asked quietly, beaming across the crib at his old buddy. Gunner didn't say anything right away, and his eyes had that sunk-back look, like he was staring into some secret void.

"Just think," Gunner said in a quiet, remote tone, "it's just been born—and someday it's going to die."

In the awful stillness that followed, Sonny wanted to die himself, or at least crawl under the crib. It was the kind of terrible silence that comes after somebody lets a fart in church.

"*Gunner!*" Patsi hissed.

She swooped down and plucked up the baby, nestling it against her chest. The baby started to cry. Ray looked like he'd been hit in the face. Gunner, snapped from whatever far place his thoughts had taken him, looked at his friends with panic. His hands reached in the empty air, groping for an explanation.

"He didn't mean what it sounded like," Sonny said, wanting to help.

"I didn't mean," Gunner said, "you know. I just meant, like all of us. We're all going to die, but it hits you when you see a little kid, who has to grow up, and get old, and then—like all of us."

"Stop it!" Patsi screamed. "Shut up!"

The baby squealed louder.

"Oh, Jesus," Gunner said, "I'm sorry."

Ray seemed to have collected himself and he came around and threw his arm on Gunner's shoulder and said, "Let's let Patsi take care of it, O.K.? Let's sit down and have us a drink."

They went in the living room, where one of those elaborate hi-fi sets covered a whole wall. Ray put on a Brubeck LP and quickly brought in some stiff drinks.

"Man, I'm really sorry," Gunner said. "It just didn't come out like I meant it."

"Forget it," said Shins.

He gently poked the ice cube in his glass with one finger, watching it bob back up.

"Guns," he said, "I understand you got hit over there."

"Yeh, once. Nothing much to it."

"It must have been rough. Combat."

"Well, it was weird. I mean, it wasn't all bad. There were times when you felt more alive than you ever do, just because you know you might die. It's—I don't know. Hard to explain. It does something to you."

"I guess it does," said Shins.

His brow pressed into a furrow, and he took a long slug of his drink.

"So how's the life of a family man?" Gunner asked, mustering a hearty tone.

"Old buddy," said Shins, "there's nothing like it."

"How do you mean?" asked Gunner.

Shins looked a little surprised. "I mean it's great. It's the only thing."

"Why?"

"What?"

"Why is it the only thing?"

"Well, you got any better ideas?"

"I don't know," said Gunner.

"Well, what are your plans?"

"I don't know. I'd like to figure things out, first."

"Of course, you just got back. You want to figure who to go with, huh?"

"Or whether to 'go.' "

"To work?" Shins smiled. "That's not much of a decision, is it? Or did you have a rich uncle kick off?"

"Well, there's Uncle Sam," Gunner said. "I'm entitled to the GI Bill."

"But you graduated. You got your degree."

"Yeh, but you can still go back. I could study for an M.A. in something."

"In what?"

"In philosophy, maybe. I don't know."

"But that won't do you any good," Shins said. "I mean, if you wanted to go to law school or something you can use, that's another matter. But that other stuff, you can't use any of it."

"Why not?"

"It won't *get* you anywhere, for Chrissake."

"Where should I get to?" Gunner asked.

Shins finished off his drink and bent his head down, staring at the floor between his legs. "Guns," he said, "a lot of guys get shaken up over there. Jesus, who wouldn't? I mean, it's nothing against a person. But maybe you ought to talk to someone."

"Talk to someone?"

"Someone who understands that stuff. You know. A doctor. I mean, the way you talk. You're all confused."

"About what?"

"See? That's what I mean. You keep asking questions like that."

"But I want to *know*," said Gunner.

"Know *what*, for Chrissake?"

Shins was really getting worked up and Sonny was scared that there would be another bad scene, like with the kid. But Gunner seemed to sense how things were heading, and instead of pressing on with it, he leaned back, took a drink, and said, "I dunno, Shins. I can't explain it too well. I think I'll just relax for a while. Play a little golf, maybe. Get some sun."

Shins smiled with genuine relief. "Atta-baby," he said. "You get a little fresh air and exercise, you'll be ready to run 'em ragged."

Gunner said they better be moving, made a lot of thanks and apologies, and he and Sonny hustled to the car. Gunner drove without speaking for a while, and then he asked, with puzzled impatience, what he obviously had wanted to ask Shins but was wise enough to restrain himself:

"Run *who* ragged?"

"The opposition," Sonny said.

"Wow," Gunner said. "Yeh. The other rats in the rat race."

They went to a little bar called the Melody Inn and ordered boilermakers. Gunner seemed pretty low.

"Hey," Sonny said, trying to cheer him up a little, "I never knew you were a golfer. I mean, that good, the way you clobbered those balls today."

"I used to caddy a lot as a kid," Gunner explained. "The pro over at Meridian Hills took an interest in me. One summer I got real serious about it, and McCardle, he's the club pro, said he thought if I really worked I could make it on the pro circuit."

"That's pretty risky, isn't it? For making a living?"

"Sure it is! That's one thing I like about it. It's a gamble, it's none of that nine-to-five, work-till-you-get-the-gold-watch-and-retire shit."

"Yeh, there's that," Sonny said.

He felt stupid and prudish asking about the risk, just like Shins and all the rat-race guys. But that's what had really come to his mind. Most guys mainly worried about that. When he was stationed in Kansas City, Sonny sat up in bull sessions long through the night with guys in his outfit, college grads mostly, talking about the future and careers, and most guys wanted to know what kind of Security a job could offer. That, and the salary; how much you started at and how high you could go in twenty years.

Gunner was rubbing at his chin, pondering something. "It might not be such a bad idea," he said. "The pro circuit. You'd get to see the whole country, travel a lot, be out in the sun and fresh air. You'd be in shape. You'd have a lot of time to read and think."

"Sounds good," Sonny said.

Gunner poked out a cigarette he'd only half finished and shook his head. "Shit, what am I thinking about? I'd just be a goddam jock again, when you got right down to it."

"Well, there's plenty of other things."

"Yeh."

Gunner was fiddling with a folder of matches. He opened it up and started staring at the inside. It was one of those that had a picture of a woman's head and said "Draw Me." You were supposed to draw the woman's head and send it in to Artists Unlimited, and they would evaluate your talent and see if you had any chance of making it as an artist. If you did, you could sign up for their mail-order instruction course.

"That's something else I used to crap around with," Gunner said. "I did some sketches for the paper at De-Pauw and drew some cartoons for the humor magazine. Shit like that. But I really got a charge out of it."

"I could never draw a straight line," Sonny admitted.

"It's easy," Gunner said. He whipped a pencil out of his pocket and began to sketch the woman's head on a cocktail napkin. When he finished he handed it over to Sonny.

"Hey, that's just like it. You oughta send it in."

Gunner shrugged and put the napkin in his pocket. "Maybe I will."

"Maybe you could study that on the GI Bill," Sonny said. "Art."

"Could be. I dunno. I'm still thinking more of philosophy or something. I'd like to figure things out more."

"Maybe you could do both. Philosophy and art."

"Maybe. What I have to do is, I have to send in for some catalogs."

"Which ones?"

"Colleges, universities. I think some of the big universities. Northwestern, Columbia, maybe even Harvard. See what they have."

"They probably have about everything."

"Yeh."

"You thought about the ones around here? I.U., Purdue?"

"I dunno. I'd like to get away, see something different. Live in a real city. What about you?"

"I haven't really thought, too much. I'd sort of thought of going to work at the *Star*. But the GI Bill—"

"Hell, yes, if the government'll pay you to go any place and study, why not take advantage? Go someplace new?"

"Hell, yes," Sonny said, feeling confident and casual. "Why not?"

"I can't see settling down in Naptown forever. That's for damn sure."

Sonny, who had never seriously thought of anything else, said, "Well, I guess it depends on the person."

Sonny realized, uncomfortably, that he didn't even know which kind of person he was—the kind who stays home or the kind who goes away. He was twenty-three years old and didn't even know that yet. He ordered another boilermaker and tried not to think about who he was. If anyone.

6

On the afternoon of the welcome-home dinner for Sonny, he took a long hot shower and put on his summer cord suit with a white shirt and tie.

"You didn't have to get dressed up," his mother said. "You're the guest of honor, you ought to be comfortable."

"I am," he said.

"You could take off the coat and tie, if you want."

"I *don't* want."

Actually the suit and tie made Sonny feel more protected; it was as if the more formal he appeared, the less chance the MRA bastards had of getting to him with their personal shit. He even wished he had a vest. He sat down in one of the big leather chairs in the den and lit a cigarette.

"Son?" His father was standing in the doorway, blushing a little and rubbing his thumbs across the tips of his fingers, the way he did when he had something personal to say. He cleared his throat. "I thought I'd fix a highball," he said softly.

"Oh, good. Thanks, yes."

Sonny looked away, not knowing how to show his appreciation without embarrassment, knowing his father was trying to help. Mrs. Burns didn't drink at all, and Mr. Burns got terrible temper fits if he drank too much, but occasionally he had a highball of bourbon and soda or bourbon and ginger ale, and since Sonny started drinking in the open from the time of his sophomore year in college, Mr. Burns always offered a highball for him, too, on the rare occasions when he had one himself.

There had never been anything like a "cocktail hour" at the Burnses, or in fact much drinking of any kind at all. When Sonny was a kid growing up, the only drinking he ever saw in the house was at the family Christmas party with his father's few relatives who had come up north to live from Kentucky. On these occasions, at some given signal, the men would leave the ladies alone in the living room and stealthily gather in the kitchen. Mr. Burns would take a pint bottle of whiskey out from its hiding place among the rags and cleaning-fluid cans in the broom closet, and the bottle would be passed from man to man, each one taking a swig from it and then breathing out a warm sigh of pleasure. During this ritual the men would never mention the liquor directly, though sometimes they referred to it by saying, "That's real good Christmas cheer." Mostly they would talk about hunting and fishing and business, manly subjects that the women didn't understand. After the bottle was passed around a couple times to each man, Mr. Burns would replace the cap and slip it back to its hiding place in the broom closet. When the men returned to the living room, the women would giggle and one of them would say what *have* you boys been up to. The men would look flushed and pleased and pleasantly guilty, and the women would click their tongues and shake their heads in mock dismay.

Sonny figured his father needed a drink tonight almost as much as he did, what with the "MRA bunch" coming to dinner. Mr. Burns bore their presence as he did that of all the strangers who came under Alma's wing for a while and were brought into the house like long-lost relatives—the alcoholics, the divorcees, the lonely newcomers to the city, the faith-seekers and faith-propagators, the bankrupt and the suicidal, even the two young homosexual hairdressers who held hands after dinner and said how wonderful it was to be taken into someone's home and treated like people. Mr. Burns sat politely through it all, removing his glasses and pressing his thumb and forefinger on the bridge of his nose until Sonny sometimes thought he would press clear through it.

Mr. Burns came in with the drinks, and after he gave one to Sonny he held up his own glass, coughed nervously, and said, "Well, son, here's more power to you."

"Mmmm," Sonny said, and took a long swallow of his drink. Thankfully, his father sat down.

"Well, you've finished your service," he said.

"Yes, sir. It's nice to have it done."

"Lord, yes."

They both took another drink. The walls seemed to buzz with silence. Sonny figured at least he was lucky that his father didn't try to make him go into his own line of work like a lot of guys' fathers did. Any idea of Sonny becoming an accountant and joining in some kind of business partnership with his father was settled long ago, back in grade school, when it turned out the one subject Sonny could hardly do at all was mathematics. He even flunked freshman algebra in high school, and it didn't work out at all when his father tried to help him with homework. Mr. Burns would get angry when Sonny didn't catch on; he seemed to take it as an insult that his son couldn't under-

stand the field that he made his own living in, the numbers
and ledgers and calculations, the very tools of accounting,
and yet the fact was the very sight of figures and equations
made Sonny headachy and depressed. After the abortive
homework sessions, Sonny and his father never discussed
the subject. Mr. Burns seemed to regard photography as
more of a hobby than a possible career, but he didn't make
any real complaints about Sonny's talk of going into it.

"Well," Mr. Burns said, "your future's ahead of you."

Sonny twisted in his chair, as if he had some kind of itch.
"I guess it is," he said.

He couldn't think of anything to say. That's the way it
was when he and his father were alone together. It was as if
both of them were in a stage play as Father and Son, but
neither one knew his lines and neither was good at im-
provising. They were simply miscast in those roles, and yet
they had to go on pretending to play them.

Sonny wasn't really afraid of his father anymore, like he
was as a kid when Mr. Burns had terrible fits of temper
sometimes, turned an angry scarlet, and cursed and threw
things. Yet it seemed that as Mr. Burns' anger had subsided and he sought for truces with Alma rather than
victories on any issue, his interest and his pleasure in
things subsided too. Sonny had always sided with his
mother as a kid, fearing the angry man who ruled their
lives, but he had come more and more to feel sympathy
and even sorrow for his father, glimpsing "his side of
things." The first such glimpse had come by accident,
when Sonny was home from college one Christmas vacation and found in the basement, among dust-layered relics
of his parents' past, a thin black case that contained a rusty
flute. When he took it upstairs and asked his parents where
it had come from, his father turned pink with embarrassment and said, "Oh, I used to fool around with it, a long
time ago." Mrs. Burns laughed and said, "He used to
practice on it when we first were married, but it gave me

the heebie-jeebies. Ooof. All that high, trilly stuff. It hurt
my head." So his father had once been a music lover.
Sonny also remembered his father getting books from the
library long ago; he liked biography mostly, lives of great
men like Theodore Roosevelt, Billy Sunday, and General
John J. Pershing. When Sonny was in grade school the
family listened to Dr. I. Q. on the radio every week, and
Mr. Burns was very good at the biographical question,
where they gave you hints about the life of a famous person and the contestant tried to guess who it was. Sonny was
sure that Mr. Burns would have won a lot of silver dollars
if he had ever got on the program. Though he didn't get
books from the library anymore, nor did he seem to care
much about having a garden. He used to raise zinnias,
hoeing the beds along the side of the small house where
Sonny was a kid, cutting them sometimes for fresh bou-
quets. Now when he came home he usually sat in the den
and watched television, and on weekends he slept late and
then sat out on the breezeway, leafing through newspapers
and dozing off into fitful dreams that would end with a
sudden snort that shocked him awake, blinking like a
frightened cat.

Sonny wished he could think of something to say to his
father, something to indicate he wished him well, and yet
he didn't know how to do it. He lit a cigarette. His father
sighed. They were saved by the double-dime chime of the
doorbell, a muffled sort of ping-pong sound. Sonny jumped
to answer it.

"Greetings and salutations!"

It was Uncle Buck, Mrs. Burns' half-brother. He was
eight years older than Sonny and had been one of his
childhood tormentors, yet Sonny really got a kick out of
the guy. He liked his tall stories and his wild reputation
with women, which Sonny secretly envied whenever he
heard the family tongues clucking on the subject. He

would gladly take the clucking if only he could get as much tail as Uncle Buck.

"Hey, Unc," Sonny said, knowing it galled him a little to be thought of as anyone's uncle, because it made him seem old.

"Prepare to defend yourself!" Uncle Buck said, putting up his dukes as he had done with Sonny ever since they were kids, doing a little fancy footwork, as he called out, "Look to your God!," and jabbed a quick left into Sonny's gut. It was just hard enough to make Sonny start to double over, at which time Uncle Buck, as always, said, "Sorry, old buddy," gave him a friendly slap on the back, and whispered confidentially, "How they hangin'?," then gave a great gin-aroma laugh and sailed his hat across the room. Mrs. Burns worried herself sick over Buck's drinking and carousing, but she couldn't resist him. Mr. Burns could resist him quite well, especially when he wanted to borrow a little money. Buck was a natural salesman, but he was prone to going off on a toot and having to start from scratch with another company. Right now he was with Federated Siding, which sold brick stuff to put on frame houses.

"Hello, Buck," Mr. Burns said.

"Greetings and salutations, good sir! I trust the world goes well with thee?"

"Fine." Mr. Burns sighed. He stood up and asked Buck, "Would you like to have a drink—or have you already had one too many?"

Buck raised his finger like a schoolmaster and said, "Good sir, there is no such thing as one too many. There is only one too few." Buck roared and then, changing his voice to a quieter, almost sacred tone, said, "Seriously, I'd appreciate one."

Mr. Burns shook his head and left the room.

"So," Buck said to Sonny, "Ya gettin' much?"

Sonny blushed and said, "Sure."

"Way to go," said Buck. "Remember my motto—always choose fast women and pretty horses."

He whooped appreciation of his well-worn line and lit himself a cigarette. The chime ponged again, and Sonny went to answer. He opened the door, and just stood for a moment, staring at the girl. It was Buddie Porter, who had sort of been his girl friend ever since high school. When he hadn't called her on his last leave home, his mother had questioned him about it until he got mad and said it was nobody's business. Buddie was just standing there on the porch, sheepishly, and finally she said, "Sonny? I'm sorry if I shouldn't have come."

"Huh?"

"Your mother called and said it was a surprise party for you, and I told her I didn't know if you'd want to be surprised—by me, I mean. She sort of insisted. You know how your mother is."

"Yes," Sonny said, "I do."

"Well—"

"No, I mean, it's O.K. I was just surprised."

Buddie was still standing on the porch, looking nervous and apologetic. She was holding a straw-basket kind of purse with imitation flowers on it, and she had on a blue summer dress with white flowers, and white flat shoes with a yellow plastic flower on each toe.

"You look like a regular garden," said Sonny.

Buddie seemed puzzled for a moment and then she looked down at her dress, and her purse, and her shoes, and she laughed and said, "Oh," like she might have known he wouldn't like the outfit. Somehow she could never seem to dress in a way that pleased him. He was always pointing out other girls to her when he liked the way they were dressed, but even though Buddie would get the same kind of thing, he wouldn't seem to like it. The more she tried to please him, the more he got annoyed and impatient with her.

"Well," he said, "come on in."

"Are you sure?"

"Sure."

"Hey, Buddie-O, old Buddie," Uncle Buck called out when she came in the room. Mr. Burns came in with the drink for Buck, and he asked Buddie if she wanted one too but just then the MRA people came, and there wasn't any more liquor dispensed.

There were four of them, and Sonny only knew one of them. That was Leona Scholz, a local Jewish lady who had forsaken her faith and her husband of that faith for the Presbyterians and MRA. She offered her lavish home as a sort of hostel for the movement's representatives who were passing through town on their many missions. Sonny had vaguely known one of Mr. Scholz' daughters at Shortley, a dark, sexy thing like her mother had been before she got into MRA and took to pulling her glistening black hair back to a hard bun, eliminating all makeup, and wearing baggy tweed suits and English oxfords with leather tongues. She also wore a permanent expression of satisfaction that seemed to indicate that she either had seen a vision that brought her inner peace or had been struck on the head by a blow that rendered her senseless.

She took Sonny's hand and made the expression at him.

"Hello, Mrs. Scholz," he said.

Mrs. Scholz was able to speak through her serene expression without changing it, and in that manner she introduced the visiting MRA bunch. There was a husband-wife pastoral team from Nebraska, the Reverend and Mrs. Ludlow Darney, and a regular MRA full-time traveling "team" member stationed in Mackinac, Hap Merriman. From what Sonny had seen of MRA people, the Darneys were not typical, lacking as they did the robust good-fellowship aura that exuded from most. The Darneys, in fact, seemed to have been the victims of a vampire attack or perhaps had donated their blood to the YMCA. Hap

Merriman was much more the MRA type that Sonny had met on the island, and in fact, he had a horrible suspicion that Hap might have been one of the clean-cut fellows who asked Sonny to "confess' about jacking off and thinking dirty stuff. Merriman was a big, broad-shouldered guy with a receding hairline who must have been in his early thirties, but he still wore an old varsity letter sweater over a white button-down shirt, along with a pair of summer slacks and sneakers with white sweat socks. He rubbed his hands together a lot, as if he were always about to propose some absolutely madcap scheme, such as everyone going out to the kitchen and cooking up a batch of taffy to pull.

Mrs. Burns came out of the kitchen, where she had been laboring all day long, and said supper was just about ready, they might as well all come in and sit down right now. The kitchen was the largest room in the house, and there was a huge oval table that everyone could fit around. There was, as usual, about three times as much food as anyone could eat, even though there were all those people. Since Sonny had not made a choice between which kind of potatoes he wanted, Mrs. Burns had made both his favorites, the sweet with marshmallow topping and the Idaho baked with melted cheese on top. There was a mammoth roast, done to a brown, bloodless turn (Mrs. Burns couldn't stand "raw meat" the way they ate it in the East, and at fancy restaurants unless you told them different, and then they got snotty about it). There was corn pudding, lima beans, stewed tomatoes, hot rolls, and four kinds of homemade preserves. For dessert you could have your choice of fresh cherry pie with ice cream, or devil's food cake with caramel icing, or both. Most everyone was stuffed by then, and only Hap Merriman had both.

Sonny sat next to Buddie during the meal, and neither of them said anything. They just stared down at their food and tried to eat as much as they could, though neither of them seemed very hungry. There was mostly just small talk, and Uncle Buck told a lot of jokes and amusing anecdotes, so the conversation didn't have a chance to turn to Moral Re-Armament until afterward, when everyone was laid out groaning in the living room. Hap Merriman said how wonderful it was to travel throughout this great land and find wonderful homes and wonderful people like this (and presumably wonderful free meals). What saddened him, though, was seeing how even in the midst of such plenty and among such good people, even church-going people, there seemed to be something lacking.

"So true, so true," Mrs. Scholz agreed in a tone of ultimate calm.

"Hell, yes," Uncle Buck said, "I see it all the time in my own work."

Hap looked annoyed, but turned to Buck with a smile of forced interest. "Is that so?"

"Day in and day out," Buck affirmed. "I go into homes, I see the faces. They're starving for something. Sometimes I try to help. I mean, I don't sell for a *living*. You have to have a real interest in people. I'm no minister, but I do know a little of the Bible, and I do know some of the pitfalls. At first hand." He gave a short, maniacal laugh, then cleared his throat, and said in his deep, meaningful tone, "But seriously, let me say this—"

Mr. Burns took off his glasses and pinched the bridge of his nose. Sonny couldn't look at anyone. He knew that Uncle Buck, as usual, had got the gist of the visitors' concerns and was about to outplay them at their own game. He always did that. Once, when Sonny had a couple Army buddies come and visit, Buck came and took over the whole show telling stories of his combat experience in World War II. Sonny had heard Uncle Buck tell his war stories many times, but they always were fascinating and never the same. If you tried to point out an inconsistency, Buck would get mad and ask if you were accusing him of being a goddam liar. You had to say no, or he might beat the shit out of you.

"We all observe these things," Hap Merriman broke in, trying to get back the lead of the conversation, "and that's why Moral Re-Armament is so keyed to the crisis of our own time, right here and now."

"I believe it," Uncle Buck said. "Did you know this country spends more on liquor than it does on education?" he asked indignantly, not mentioning his own contribution to that statistic. "The pendulum has to swing. It's like Newton's law, whatever goes up must come down."

"Buck, may I speak to you just a minute?" Mrs. Burns asked. She stood up and was glancing nervously around the room, wanting to put it back in the balance it was meant to have.

"Huh? Sure."

Buck got up and followed her into the kitchen, saying to the others, " 'Scuse me, good citizens," and laughing wildly as he disappeared. Hap took charge of the conversation again, and in a few minutes Mrs. Burns tiptoed back in the room, alone, having disposed of Buck in what presumably was a nonfatal method.

Hap was getting to the part about how it was good for the soul to relieve yourself of the sinful things you had thought and done, how it helped to get them off your chest. Often, he explained, folks felt they were the only ones who were dirty and sinful, and that's why in some of these friendly little sessions it was best to have someone begin who had already had the experience of getting these things off their chest in the company of others. That way, the people who had never unburdened themselves in public would feel easier about doing it. Sonny got out a cigarette, and Buddie, who hardly ever smoked, whispered that she'd like one too.

"Take the Reverend and Mrs. Darney," Hap said. "Not only are they good Christians, but their regular work is in the service of the Lord. Yet, when they came to Mackinac, they found in MRA something new and wonderful. They got some things off their chest that they had kept locked up and festering inside for many years."

Sonny had the awful realization that the Darneys were about to speak of those unspeakable matters right now, in this very living room. Hap turned to the drab little couple with a hearty grin. The Reverend Darney crossed one leg over the other and clasped the knee, as if to have something to hold on to. His wife, pale as margarine, fixed her blank gaze on some figure in the rug.

"Even though I am a minister of the Lord," the Reverend Darney began, "I have sinned with the flesh."

Oh God make him stop, Sonny prayed. *Make him save it for You.*

"Before Alberta and I were joined in holy wedlock, we—we knew each other's flesh."

The little woman sat paralyzed. The only thing that moved was a throbbing blue vein in her throat.

"Knowing full well it was sinful," Ludlow continued, "I nevertheless—" There was an awful pause, and then he got out the horrible secret: "I manipulated my wife's breasts."

Somehow the word "manipulated" was what most fascinated Sonny; it reminded him of a man sitting at some kind of control panel, pressing buttons and pulling switches.

There was a shameful silence, and the Reverend Ludlow added, for emphasis, *"Before* marriage."

The thick, embarrassed silence choked the room, and Sonny felt like he couldn't breathe.

"Which only goes to show," Hap Merriman said cheerily, "that the very finest among us, even those in the Lord's service, are not free from sin. I'm sure, for instance, that the wonderful, gracious people who are our hosts tonight, even though good Christians, have done things and thought things that deep in their heart have burdened them for a long time."

There were tears in Mrs. Burns' eyes. Mr. Burns pressed mightily on the bridge of his nose. Sonny was shaking so hard he could barely stand up, and when he did, his head felt light and his knees were uncertain. He turned to the smiling, dumpling face of Hap Merriman and said in a voice so intense it was barely audible, "Get out of here, you lousy turd."

"Beg pardon?" said Hap.

Buddie stood up beside Sonny and squeezed her hand on his elbow. "I think I'd better be going," she said. "Sonny, take me home?"

"I'm taking her home," Sonny said, still gazing at Hap's complacent mug.

"God bless you," Hap said.

"Up yours with a rusty totem pole," Sonny said, as Buddie pulled him to the door.

The night air hit them like a clean bath, and Buddie drew a deep, relieved breath. Sonny was still trembling. Buddie got him into her car and drove north, past many houses, along open fields, not saying anything. Sonny held his head out the window, letting the wind wash him.

Buddie pulled into a driveway at one of the deserted farms where they sometimes parked, and turned off the motor and the lights.

"Do you want to stop?" she asked softly.

"Sure."

He slumped back in the seat, his eyes shut, and Buddie lightly rubbed her fingers over his forehead.

"That son of a bitch," Sonny said. "I'd like to mash his fat face to a fucking pancake."

"Shhh," Buddie whispered. "Don't think about it."

"My goddam mother. Bringing those people home."

"She means well, Sonny. She wants to help."

"Goddam it, how come you always take her side?"

"I'm sorry. It's just I know she loves you, really. So do I."

She leaned against him, smelling of sweet soap and toothpaste. He knew he could do what he wanted with her, which maybe was why he didn't much want to do it anymore.

"When did you get home?" she asked softly.

"I dunno. Last week or something. Are you going to start on that, why I didn't call?"

"No."

"O.K. Thanks, 'cause I don't know why myself. I don't know anything."

"Don't be angry. Please."

She pressed herself on top of him, pressed her mouth on him, hungry and wide open. Her tongue felt sticky.

He moved away. "What do you want me to do, manipulate your breasts?" he said.

"Please, Sonny. Don't think about those people."

"I can't help it."

He lit a cigarette, and Buddie scooted back in the driver's seat. After a while she started the motor and Sonny didn't say anything, so she turned on the lights and backed out onto the highway. They drove without speaking, and Buddie pulled up across the street from Sonny's house. The other cars were gone.

"Well, thanks," Sonny said.

"That's O.K."

She leaned over and kissed him wet in the ear, and he drew away and pushed down the door handle.

"Listen," he said, "I'll call you."

"Will you?"

"Yes, yes, I just said I would."

"O.K. Good night."

He got out, slammed the door shut, and said, "Good night," and she quietly drove away. Sonny stood for a while in the street, smelling the dark green night and wanting to die.

His mother and father were sitting in the den, wearing their bathrobes. Only one dim light was on. It was like they were sitting up for a sick friend. In their bathrobes, they looked older and more vulnerable, defenseless and confused. Sonny felt sorry for them, but he didn't want to sit around and talk. He stood at the door.

"Hello," he said.

"We're sorry," Mrs. Burns said. "We didn't mean to upset you."

"O.K.," Sonny said. "It's O.K. It wasn't you. It was them."

Mr. Burns cleared his throat. "Even so," he said in a weary, grim tone. "Even so, you can't let yourself—fly off the handle. You can disagree without flying off the handle."

"I'm sorry," Sonny said. "But I hate their lousy guts."

"They mean well," Mrs. Burns said.

"Lord, yes," Mr. Burns said. "I don't agree with all their methods, Lord knows, but they're trying. They're trying to help."

"I'm sorry," Sonny said, trying hard not to fly off the handle again. "I just don't want to see them again. Any of them. Ever."

"Sonny, I promise you," Mrs. Burns said, teary-eyed, "I will never invite them here again."

Sonny didn't mention she had promised that once before. He just wanted to go to bed and not think about anything. He wished he could lift the aura of gloom, the religious hangover. He could see his parents were suffering from it too.

"Hey, what happened to Uncle Buck?" he asked. "Did you send him to the movies or something?"

"I asked him to do an errand," Mrs. Burns said. "And he was glad to," she added with defensive pride.

"An errand?"

"I got some leftovers together and had him take them over to a new family that just moved into the parish neighborhood. They haven't got settled yet."

"Huh," Mr. Burns snorted. "Buck probably ate it himself."

"Oh, Elton."

"Maybe he shared it with them," Sonny said.

His mother sighed. "Buck *means* well," she said.

"I guess we all do," said Sonny.

"Lord, yes," Mr. Burns agreed.

While they all were in general agreement on something, Sonny hurriedly said good night. He wanted to get safely to bed before anything could spoil the temporary harmony.

7

The day after his welcome-home party, Sonny woke up around eleven, but he didn't get out of bed. He was sorry he woke up at all. You could tell it was one of those steamy hot days outside, and he didn't want to do anything. His hand was gently fondling his prick. It had been about half-erect when he woke, the sort of condition that the guys at Boy Scout camp used to call "a semi." He wanted to beat off, but he couldn't think of anything that got him charged up. He tried to remember the blonde on the train coming home, but she had already faded from his mind. He closed his eyes and tried to squint her back into focus, but the memory of how she really looked ran together, like a photograph left in the rain. He tried thinking of stuff he had done in the past with Buddie, when he still was hot for her, but it just didn't get him going.

There was a soft rap on the door, and he quickly drew his hand off his cock.

"Sonny?" his mother said.

"Yes?"

"Are you up?"

"No."

"I have to go the office now."

"O.K."

"I left you a tray. Outside your door."

"O.K."

"Are you all right?"

"Yes."

"I'll be back around two."

"O.K."

"You don't have to get up if you don't want."

"I will. In a minute."

"If anyone calls, I'll be at the office."

"I know."

There was a pause. He could still hear his mother's breathing, and he lay motionless, both hands innocently lying under his head on the pillow.

"I love you," she said.

"Me too," he answered.

He couldn't make himself say, "I love you," to his mother anymore, and when she said it to him and waited for reply, he said, "Me too," which he realized was ambiguous. It might either mean he loved her too, or it might mean he loved himself, too. That was probably closer to the truth. He heard her tiptoe away, down the stairs. Then the car boomed and skrcaked from the drive. His prick was limp; he had even lost the semi. He got up and opened the door, and took the tray in and set it on his desk. There was a white-meat chicken sandwich with the crusts cut off, a big glass of Pepsi with ice, a piece of lemon chiffon pie, two brownies, and the morning *Star*. He took a sip of the Pepsi, and then went back to bed with the sports section. He might have never got up at all if Gunner hadn't called.

"How 'bout that film we shot?" Gunner asked. "I thought we were going to have a big developing bash."

"Oh, yeh. Right. We ought to do it," Sonny said.

"How's about right now?"

"Sure, I mean, like an hour or so would be O.K. I have to finish something up first."

What he had to do was get dressed and get himself together, but he wouldn't have dreamed of admitting to Gunner he was still lying around the house just vegetating, halfway through the damn day.

Sonny got a real lift from just being in the darkroom, and having Gunner there to watch and to learn made it even better. Him, Sonny, able to teach something to a guy like Gunner, able to give him some bit of knowledge he sought, that was really something. It was like being able to bestow a gift on someone you liked, and it was really the best kind of gift, much better than the kind you could wrap in a package.

Gunner was really absorbed and eager to know. Like everything he did, he wanted to dive right into it and find out everything he could about it, and his questions and admiring comments at Sonny's knowledge of the developing process made Sonny actually feel like Somebody.

The most exciting part was when you put the blank paper in the chemical bath that would bring the picture to life; the forms taking shape, the gathering of the darks and shadows and outlines until the actual picture came forth in its full detail. That was a kind of creation, a kind of magic. It always gave Sonny goose pimples, and he had the feeling Gunner felt the same way about it.

Sonny had got some good action stuff, but most of Gunner's was fuzzy and blurred. Sonny told him about how you corrected that with shutter speed and all, and assured him he'd get the hang of it soon. He figured he really would, too, but it was nice to be able to reassure him.

Afterward they had a couple cool brews, and Sonny felt clean and strong.

"You really got it down cold, all that stuff," Gunner said admiringly.

Sonny smiled and looked down at his brew. "Shee-it," he said. With appropriate modesty.

They planned to go out and shoot some more film real soon. But when Gunner called the next day, he had plans of a more exotic nature.

"We're choppin' in tall cotton," he announced.

"Yeh?"

"No shit. Nina's got a date to go to Churchill Downs for the races. She'll be in Louisville overnight and the place'll be ours."

"Hot damn."

"Can you line up something for Saturday night?"

"Sure, I think so."

"One of us can have the bedroom and the other the couch."

"Great."

"Remember DeeDee Armbrewster? Shortley girl I used to be pinned to and all that crap. She just got home from I.U. graduation and gave me a buzz. Sounds like she's hot to trot."

"Great."

"Yeh. I'm a little on the horny side."

Gunner was used to getting it regular. Sonny said very casually he'd line up something for himself and be ready for action. When he hung up, he felt a little panicky, and he went to his room and bolted down the lunch his mother had left. Then he put on a pair of undershorts and lit a cigarette. He didn't like to smoke in the nude, for fear a hot ash might fall on his dick and damage it beyond repair. He was always thinking of things like that.

The problem now was who to get for Saturday night. If only this was happening back in Shortley or maybe even in college, he could get a lot of girls who'd just want to go on a date if they were going to be doubling with the great

Gunner Casselman. Maybe some still even felt that way. Maybe that sexy Phyllis who Sonny saw at the Riviera. She used to go to Northwood Methodist, but now she was at nursing school, which probably meant she went all the way. Nurses were supposed to do everything. Sonny had meant to call her but for some reason he had put it off, and now it was too late. If he wasn't absolutely sure she did the big trick, he didn't want to take her to Gunner's and feel like a greenass, just sitting out in the living room playing records while Gunner was humping away on DeeDee Armbrewster right in the next room. The only girl he was sure of was Buddie, and so, even though he didn't really want to screw her anymore very much, he knew he had better take her. What the hell would Gunner think of him if he couldn't produce a girl he could lay?

Gunner had been getting his ever since high school, everyone knew that, even Sonny. Even if you weren't on the inside, the word got down to you somehow. Gunner did it right in the school building. He did it with Patty Mandrake on a table in the biology lab, he did it with Sissy Glisson down in the boiler room, he did it with DeeDee Armbrewster in the bushes by the side entrance of the building between the acts of the Annual Shortley Variety Show. He even did it in the back of the auditorium when they showed free movies at lunchtime. There were teachers snooping around sometimes but Gunner had Blow Mahoney for a lookout. Blow got his name because the thing he liked most in life was getting blown, and he talked about it all the time and greeted people by saying, "Hey, blow!" Sometimes he used to drive around the block at lunchtime in his old Model T, and when he first went around, you'd see Sandy Masterson sitting next to him, but then by the second time around you wouldn't see Sandy at all, you'd just see Blow himself, driving along with a look of incredible ecstasy. When he didn't drive to school he and Sandy would go to the lunchtime movies and do it there in the darkened back of the auditorium; and since Blow always sat upright in his seat while Sandy was giving it to him, he was happy to keep a lookout for Gunner at the same time, while Gunner was making it with DeeDee behind the last row of seats. Blow was happy to help out a friend, as long as it didn't interfere with his own pastime.

Maybe because not many guys made out as much, everyone talked about the ones who did. Everyone in the whole city seemed to know what happened to Gunner when the night before the opening round of the state basketball tournament his senior year he twisted his ankle jumping out of the second-story bedroom window of Alison Mac-Adoo, whose father had come home unexpectedly early from a concert of the Scottish Rite Chorus. When Gunner hobbled onto the floor the next afternoon, his ankle all taped, the whole fieldhouse let up a roar, and everyone cheered, "We Want Gunner," even the kids from other schools. He was a hero even though he didn't get to play. It was like that in college, too, and even though Sonny was down at I.U. and not even in a fraternity, he heard stories of Gunner's exploits at DePauw, like the time he got caught naked with a Theta on the roof of the Sigma Chi house by Mother Simmons and lost his scholarship for a full semester. And Gunner himself said Japan was the best he ever had.

Buddie, of course, was glad to accept Sonny's invitation to "a party over at Casselman's place," which is how he had described the evening to her. Sonny consoled himself that even though he'd rather have a sexy new babe to go with, it would be a relief to have a comfortable private place to make out. Usually he and Buddie, like most everyone else they knew, had to do it in cars and on golf courses and fields of deserted farmhouses, where you were always getting caught in barbed wire or rolling onto old cowshit or worrying about getting bushwhacked. It seemed like unless you were married and had your own place, you had to be a combination acrobat, woodsman, and stud to ever make out. Which is why some kids got married, so they could fuck when they wanted without getting thorns in their ass or find themselves putting on a show for a bunch of bushwhackers. Sonny used to go bushwhacking himself when he was in high school, driving around with a carload of guys and sneaking up on some poor couple making out and then flashing a goddam spotlight on them and hooting and jeering and yelling a lot of dirty stuff and running away after spoiling things. It was a favorite sport.

Sonny really was hot for the idea of having Gunner's place to do it in, without being bothered, but the trouble was, when the evening of the "party" came, he wasn't at all in the mood. He'd have much rather gone out boozing with Gunner, or developed some pictures, or even just stayed home and watched television. That was always happening to him. It seemed like the need for sex came in waves, and for some reason whenever the sex was available the need was at its lowest ebb. The times when he seemed to be drowning with desire there was never anything around. Now with this great setup he couldn't have cared less. If it just was a date he had with Buddie, he'd have made some excuse and got out of it, but he wouldn't dream of backing out and letting Gunner suspect he wasn't a regular guy who took it whenever he could get it.

Gunner came by and honked for Sonny after supper, and they went to pick up DeeDee.

"Listen, ole buddy, would you mind coming in?" Gunner asked him when they got to the Armbrewsters'. "DeeDee's old lady'll talk my ear off. She's one of these amateur patriots, ya know?"

Sonny was afraid he knew all right—his mother was friends with some of those ladies—but he was happy to make things easier for Gunner if he could by going along. It was like talking to religious people, you felt more comfortable if you had a buddy with you.

Mrs. Armbrewster was a large woman with combs in her graying hair and a pair of rimless glasses that hung on a velvet ribbon around her neck. Mr. Armbrewster wasn't around, and Gunner said later he seldom was; he worked long hours at his office and bowled a great deal.

"DeeDee isn't quite ready," Mrs. Armbrewster said, "and I'm so glad to have a moment to talk with you young men. *Veterans,* I should say."

Gunner had introduced Sonny as a friend who had also just got out of the service, which was the biggest kind of buildup you could give to Mrs. Armbrewster. She pinched her glasses onto her nose and asked the young men to step into her study for a moment if they would. As she turned to lead them, Gunner gave Sonny a nudge with his elbow and rolled his eyes up into his head.

The study was a dim, secretive little room with a desk, a large metal office file, a silk American flag on a gold tripod stand, and a Statue of Liberty lamp with a lightbulb in its hand instead of a torch. On the walls were a framed Preamble to the Constitution, a certificate of membership in the Daughters of the American Revolution, an aerial view of Mt. Vernon, a bearded Jesus kneeling under a heavenly spotlight, a photo of General MacArthur smoking his corncob pipe, and a homemade sampler that said "The Price of Liberty Is Eternal Vigilance." Catherine Millbank Armbrewster had committed herself to that vigilance, clipping items every day from newspapers and magazines on the latest Red activities and maintaining her own private file (though private, it was always at the disposal of the proper authorities, as she had written in a confidential letter to J. Edgar Hoover himself) of state and local communist subversion, ranging all the way from the teaching of the Robin Hood story in public schools (with the help of Mrs. Armbrewster and other patriots, this Marxist text with its message of rob-the-rich-and-give-to-the-poor was successfully banned from the Indiana state school system), to the brazen attempt by the local branch of the pinko American Civil Liberties Union to secure the hallowed halls of the Indianapolis War Memorial for a speech by the left-leaning industrialist Paul Hoffman. With the American Legion leading the way, this plot was also nipped in the bud, rasing howls of protest from what Mrs. Armbrewster thought of as the International-Jew editorial writers of the Eastern Commie Inner Circle rag, *The New York Times.*

Mrs. Armbrewster pulled out a drawer of her file, and Gunner and Sonny sat down on a little two-seater couch, trying not to look at each other.

"You men have served," she said. She took Gunner's hand and said, "You fought. You bled."

Gunner squirmed. "I caught a little shrapnel," he admitted, omitting the location of the wound.

"And your friend?" she asked, turning her gaze on Sonny.

"I was stationed in Kansas City," he said. "Public Information."

She patted his hand. "*Some*one has to do the paper work," she consoled him.

"Absolutely!" Gunner chimed in.

"And now what?" Mrs. Armbrewster asked. Her eyes glimmered meaningfully behind the spectacles.

Sonny looked to Gunner.

"Now?" asked Gunner.

"It isn't over," Mrs. Armbrewster darkly announced. She picked a book off her desk and handed it to Gunner, saying, "You were there. You must read this."

Gunner gingerly took the book in his hands. It was called *From the Danube to the Yalu,* by General Mark Clark.

"The Yalu River," Gunner said, by way of a comment.

"Turn to the opening," Mrs. Armbrewster instructed.

Gunner flipped a few pages and came to an underlined part that said:

In carrying out the instructions of my government, I gained the unenviable distinction of being the first U.S. Army commander in history to sign an armistice without victory.

But when I signed the armistice, I knew, of course, that it was not over—that the struggle against Communism would not be over in my lifetime. The Korean war was a skirmish, a bloody, costly skirmish, fought on the perimeter of the Free World.

Gunner coughed and said, "Well, it was bloody all right."

"You go on reading that—you were there, you deserve to know the real meaning of it," Mrs. Armbrewster said.

"And you"—she nodded to Sonny—"you were in Information here at home. We need more information like this—"

She handed him a copy of the new *Saturday Evening Post,* folded to the editorial page, which she had marked in red:

All over the country nowadays the Communists are busy in a vast and silent infiltration, moving skillfully into a wide variety of local, regional, and national groups. No pro-Moscow orations bubble from their plausible lips. They appear to be sincere, hard-working liberals, eager for the success of the organizations in which they have become active, including unions, parent-teacher organizations, Democratic clubs, and in a few cases even Republican clubs.

There was no one you could trust, Sonny figured. The editorial went on to say:

And yet this insidious operation is a part of the Communist Party's effort to re-establish the popular front. . . .

"Oh, *Mother.*"

Sonny looked up and saw DeeDee Armbrewster standing at the door of the study. She had her hands in fists on her hips, looking as if she'd caught her mother showing her personal diaries to the guys or baby pictures of her in the nude. DeeDee wasn't too political, herself.

"Hi, Deeds," Gunner said, standing up and going toward her.

"Gunner." She smiled.

He kissed her the way you kiss a girl in front of her mother, and said, "You remember Sonny Burns, don't you?"

"Oh—of course," she said, looking at him blankly.

"I must talk with you young men again soon," Mrs. Armbrewster said as they started edging from the room. "Every day counts."

"Right!" Gunner affirmed with great gusto, taking DeeDee's arm.

"Yes, ma'am," Sonny said.

They all three piled in the front seat of the car, DeeDee in the middle. She had on a sleeveless summer dress and Sonny felt nervous, touching her brown bare arm. She was one of those cool, confident girls who always seemed to be beyond his reach. She wasn't any great beauty, but she had a firm little body and a fine-boned face with perfect teeth and brown eyes that seemed to look right into you, not afraid of anything, and that rich kind of dark chestnut hair that was thick and clean and caught the sunlight just like the hair of girls in those advertisements for diamonds.

"Were you snowing my mother this time?" she asked Gunner. "Or was she snowing you?"

Gunner laughed and said, "Listen, I'm in like Flynn with your old lady now."

"I bet. Big War Hero. God, if she only knew."

"Whatya mean?"

"Nothing," she said and leaned up and gave Gunner a little nip on the ear.

Buddie was wearing a peasant blouse and a full skirt and those black flat Capezios that always reminded Sonny of boats stuck on the feet. In Buddie's case, he noted, pretty big boats, at that. She looked very homey, like one of those healthy Dutch girls carrying pails of milk. She reminded him of the sort of girl you'd like to have for a sister.

When they got to Gunner's place, the girls went right to the bathroom to comb their hair and fix up, although they had presumably been doing just that before the guys picked them up. Gunner took Sonny to the kitchen, where he had made a whole big thermos of seabreezes. He poured one for Sonny to taste, and Sonny gulped about half the glass and pronounced it just right. It tasted almost like straight grapefruit juice; you hardly even noticed the gin. That was the beauty of the seabreeze. You could load a hell of a lot of gin into the grapefruit juice and still barely taste the gin, so a girl would drink it down easily and not feel like she was really boozing it up, and before she knew it she was happy. And friendly. It was a favorite drink for taking on picnics and blanket parties.

Gunner poured drinks for the girls when they came out, and put on a record of Chet Baker and Strings. The new cool jazz was very soothing, very relaxing. And yet it wasn't too obvious, like putting on Frank Sinatra love songs right away. DeeDee said she wanted to hear all about Korea and Japan, and Gunner got out his photographs. DeeDee and Buddie and Sonny sat on the couch and Gunner sat cross-legged on the floor and passed up the photos, which went from hand to hand. Sonny kept sneaking glances at DeeDee's pointy boobs. The left one had her diamond Theta pin right on the tip of it. Buddie had a pretty nice pair, but you couldn't see them through the baggy folds of her peasant blouse. Sonny poured another seabreeze and let his mind float off with the music. "Love Walked In."

"What a Difference a Day Made." That soft, sexy trumpet.
Cool to make you hot.

Gunner was telling the girls about Zen and pouring
more drinks. These weren't the kind of girls you could
just take into an apartment and lock the door and turn the
lights off, even if you'd been screwing them for years. They
were Nice Girls. You worked them up to it, got them in
the mood, so they could be sort of surprised when it
happened, let it seem like they didn't have any idea what
was coming at all.

For all of Sonny's problems he at least was thankful he
wasn't a girl. Some of them really got the short end of the
stick, if you really thought about it. The ones who made
out with guys and weren't in the right clubs and came
from big, poor families usually got the reputation of being
sluts. But you take a girl like DeeDee, she was always in
the in group, and in the top clubs and sororities, and she
wouldn't do it with a guy unless she was going steady or
pinned or chained to him, and that made it all right, that
wasn't being whorish or anything, even though if you
counted up, she had gone steady and been pinned and
chained to a hell of a lot of guys, ever since she'd been a
freshman in high school. But getting laid by all those guys
didn't count against her. Also, it didn't count against her
to do it with a guy she *used* to go steady with or be pinned
or chained to; after all, if you were once in love, who could
know when the old spark might not be rekindled? All in
all, if you figured it out, DeeDee Armbrewster had probably fucked a pretty fair number of guys between the ages
of fourteen and twenty-one, but there wasn't a guy or girl
in town who would have thought her promiscuous. She
wasn't a slut; she was a Theta.

Buddie was a nice girl too. She and Sonny had gone
steady for a while in college. They couldn't get pinned
because Sonny didn't have a pin, and while some of her
Sisters in Tri Delt frowned on that (they were always

trying to fix her up with Greeks), she was such a swell kid
that it didn't really hurt her reputation, her standing as a
Nice Girl who it was O.K. for anyone to marry.

Sonny noticed that DeeDee was laughing a lot, louder
than normal, and he realized everybody must have had
four or five seabreezes. Gunner turned out the big overhead light and put on a record of Frank Sinatra songs for
lonely lovers. They were songs by the new "mature"
Sinatra, but as far as Sonny could tell, the main difference
was that the old, immature Sinatra songs were good for
getting teen-agers hot, while the new "mature" ones were
good for getting people hot who were already out of
college. That was O.K. with him.

Gunner pulled DeeDee up to dance with him, and she
slipped off her shoes and put both arms around his neck, so
she was kind of hanging on him, pressed tight against him,
and they barely swayed. You could just see their hips
moving, against each other. Sonny took Buddie's hand, and
she stood up and cuddled right into him. They did the
same swaying thing, and she pressed her box against his
dick, but he didn't have any kind of hard-on. By the time
the record was over, Gunner had danced DeeDee into the
bedroom. Sonny turned the record over, poured himself
another drink, and led Buddie to the couch. He knew he
had to get a little more stoned to get sexed up.

He drank down the new drink very fast, almost in two
gulps, and then pulled Buddie down on the couch and
started kissing her fiercely, almost frantically, hoping to
get himself worked up.

"Isn't anyone home?" Buddie whispered.

"Whatya mean? Gunner's here, and DeeDee."

"I mean his mother."

"No. She's in Louisville, at the races."

"Oh."

Buddie started tugging at her blouse, and she sat up and
pulled it over her head, and then shucked off the big,

ballooning skirt. He liked her a lot better in her underwear, even though it was white and sort of wholesome
looking. Buddie never wore the black, lacy kind that really
sexed him up. But even the wholesome white kind was still
underwear, and that was a lot sexier than the healthy sort
of Dutch-girl dresses and skirts and blouses she wore. She
started unbuttoning his shirt and giving him little kisses
on the chest as she went. When she got to his stomach, he
held his breath, so it wouldn't be so fat. He stood up and
took off his slacks, but left his shorts on. He didn't like to
take off his shorts till he had a real good hard-on. It was
embarrassing, having a girl see his dong when it was limp.
He started kissing her and reached around for the hooks
on the back of her bra. No matter how many times he
undid those damn things, he could never do it smoothly.

"Let me," she whispered, sitting up and with one quick
motion releasing the mechanics of it, then sort of slumping
her shoulders forward so it slid down. Sonny pulled it off
the rest of the way. She really did have nice tits, and when
he first saw them a long time ago, touched them, kissed
them, he got tremendously excited, but now they didn't
affect him much more than seeing her elbows. And yet
they were the same tits. He lay down beside her and
started kissing them, trying to get himself aroused. She
pulled one of his hands down to her panties and slipped it
inside. He felt along the fuzz and probed with one finger
for the slit. It was already wet. He put the finger in and
worked it around and she started to moan, that pleasurable
moan. With one hand she was fondling his cock, and it was
responding. She slipped off her panties, and Sonny
propped himself up on one elbow, to deal with the
damned inevitable problem.

"Is it a good time?" he asked.

That was the code.

"Yes," she said. "I ought to be getting it this week."

Her period, she meant. That meant he didn't have to

fumble and fight with the hateful rubber. Sure, it was taking a chance, but it had worked for him so far. If you weren't too sure, you could always pull out. That wasn't really safe either, but most guys preferred it to using the damn rubber. He heard that some girls who went East to school got diaphragms, but mostly the girls in town didn't get those until they got married, if even then. It was like an admission of guilt, or something. And besides, you couldn't very well go and ask the family doctor unless you were getting married could you? A doctor Sonny knew in the Army said someday there'd just be a pill the girl could take and she wouldn't get knocked up! That'd be the day. Imagine fucking and not having to worry about pulling out or putting a damn rubber on or what time of the month it was. Sonny figured they'd probably invent it after he was too old to do it anyway.

Buddie was stroking his cock, and it was nice and hard and ready for action. He scrambled on top of her and she guided it in for him. He always had trouble finding the right place. She moaned as it went inside, digging her nails in his back. He felt weirdly removed from what was going on, like it was him just watching these people do this. He didn't feel much of anything at all, except a kind of annoyance at himself that he could get a real good hard-on now with Buddie when he didn't really care much one way or the other, but when he first knew her and really creamed for her, his prick would start sagging on him as soon as he tried to stick it in, or if he got it in, it would shoot off right away. That same thing had happened to him with an older woman he dated in Kansas City, a secretary he met who was almost thirty years old and not too bright but nice and sexy. He would get all charged up and then, when the time came, his cock would start to shrink, and if he managed to worm it inside her he'd shoot his wad right away. She was very nice about it, but Sonny got so embarrassed he stopped calling her. She called him a couple times to see what the matter was, and he acted real nasty and irritated and never saw her again.

Sonny was sitting on top of Buddie, with his prick going in and out, like it could go on forever, when the record ended, and he could hear the voices of Gunner and Dee-Dee coming from the bedroom. They were kind of shouting in whispers, and you could hear everything.

"Dammit, we're not in school anymore. We're supposed to be *adults*," DeeDee said.

"So? You mean adults don't fuck?"

"No!"

"Are you crazy?"

"No! I mean, I didn't mean what you said."

"Which?"

"That adults don't—don't do it. I wish you'd stop using that word."

"What word?"

"Fuck!" she shouted.

Gunner laughed, and DeeDee said, "Dammit, I'm serious."

"You used to like me to say it," Gunner insisted. "You used to like to say it yourself. While we were doing it, you used to say, 'Know what we're doing? We're fucking.' And I'd say—"

"Stop it!"

Sonny had stopped moving his prick and was just sitting on top of Buddie, straining his ears.

"What's wrong?" she said.

"Shhh."

"You shouldn't listen," Buddie whispered.

"Shhh."

"What I mean is," DeeDee was whisper-shouting, "I don't want to be like some teen-ager, hiding out and finding secret places to do it, and parking and going on golf courses and all that."

"Who's on a golf course? Does this look like a goddam golf course to you?"

"We're hiding out, like criminals."

"This is my own apartment, for Chrissake."

"It's your mother's apartment."

"She's gone, I told you."

"She might come back, you never know. We'd have to hide and sneak around like criminals."

"She won't come back till late tomorrow."

"It doesn't matter."

"For God sake, what is it you want?"

DeeDee began sobbing. "I want to do it in my *own* house."

"In *your* house? Are you nuts? With your parents there upstairs?"

"*No,* you idiot, I mean my *really* own house. Goddam it, I want to get married!"

Gunner didn't say anything, and DeeDee started sobbing again. Sonny heard Gunner walking around, and a match was struck.

"Look," Gunner said. "I just got home. I don't even know what I'm going to do. Here, take a puff."

Sonny had withdrawn himself from Buddie and lit a cigarette of his own. With the talk of marriage, his prick had gone soft. He had been through that with Buddie, but she knew better than to bring it up anymore. She picked her blouse off the floor and spread it over her chest, like a blanket, huddling beneath it like an orphan out in the cold.

"Listen, Deeds, I love to do it with you. That's all I know right now. You like it, and I like it, and we'll worry about the rest later. Come here."

DeeDee sort of moaned, then it was quiet, and then there was giggling and hard breathing and sounds of thrashing around, and after a while the turmoil settled into the steady, hard, rhythmic creak of the bedsprings.

Sonny mashed out his cigarette, pulled Buddie's blouse off her chest, and went at her hard and fierce again. Soon he got his own rhythm going with her, pounding up and down as hard as he could, trying to make it as loud and as long as possible. It wasn't that he'd got so terrifically aroused by Buddie. He wanted Gunner to hear him doing it, wanted his friend to know that he was really quite a fucker himself.

8

Even though Gunner had gone over the apartment with a fine-tooth comb to remove any traces of evidence of what he called the "fuckathon" of Saturday night, his mother found some long strands of dark chestnut hair in her bed. She was plenty pissed, and wouldn't let Gunner use her wheels for a while. Sonny talked to him on the phone and Gunner said he was doing a lot of reading and was into a really deep book called *The Lonely Crowd* that really had a lot to say. Sonny had heard of the book but hadn't ever got around to it, and it made him feel guilty and a little bit jealous that Gunner was reading it. He couldn't get over this nasty little feeling that a guy who had all that Gunner had shouldn't be brainy, too, and know a lot of stuff that Sonny didn't know. He was ashamed of feeling that way, but he did.

After talking to Gunner he got a sudden urge to read something really worthwhile, like he promised himself he was going to do on a regular basis when he got out of

service—just like the regular program of daily exercise—
but he hadn't got around to it yet. He poked around the
house, looking at the bookcases in the den, but he couldn't
find anything that appealed to him. His mother kept
buying the popular new religious books so many people
were reading, and planted them around the house, in
Sonny's path, like landmines. She had Norman Vincent
Peale, of course, just about everyone had a copy of *The
Power of Positive Thinking,* and she also had *The Greatest
Faith Ever Known,* by Fulton Oursler; *A Man Called
Peter,* by Catherine Marshall; and *The Robe,* by Lloyd C.
Douglas. There was one she'd tried to lure Sonny into
reading with the promise that it wasn't "religious" at all,
called *TNT, The Power Within You,* but it sounded too
much like the *Positive Thinking* of Norman Vincent
Peale. Those kind of books were about the only ones they
had except for real old ones that his father had inherited
from his family, like *Ben Hur, Lorna Doone,* and *The
Works of Lord Tennyson.* Sonny had never seen anyone
reading them, but they looked good on the shelves. In his
own room Sonny had some of his old college textbooks; a
bunch of photography manuals; some novels he liked such
as *Look Homeward, Angel* and *The Sun Also Rises;* a few
intellectual paperbacks he had never finished, like *Human
Destiny,* and *Philosophy in a New Key.* He had often tried
to read philosophy, hoping it would answer some of the
riddles of life, but he always got bogged down in it and felt
himself lost in a thick, sunless swamp. He would give up in
order to breathe and clear his head. Among his father's old
books he found a collection of essays of Ralph Waldo
Emerson, and he read a couple of them or at least skimmed
them, but he really couldn't concentrate. Little fears and
doubts and memories of embarrassing things he had done
and said, of mistakes he had made, buzzed and flitted in his
mind like annoying little gnats, scattering his attention.

He started sleeping late again, hanging around the

house in his undershorts, eating sticky pies with whipped cream and watching television quiz shows that burst into trilly organ music when anyone got the right answer. He was really glad when Gunner called that Wednesday afternoon and said he really had to get out of the house and wondered if Sonny could borrow some wheels. Sonny said he would. He showered and shaved and put on a clean sport shirt and the slacks of his summer seersucker suit. He felt clean and light.

He heard his mother roar into the driveway while he was dressing, and he went downstairs and found her sitting on the couch in the den, her legs spread wide apart, fanning her skirt up and down. It was something she did in hot weather a lot, and it made Sonny queasy. He didn't say anything, but tried not to look at her.

"Well," she said brightly, "you're dressed up fit to kill."

"No I'm not."

"Come here a sec," she said.

Looking down at the floor, he walked over to her. She reached up and patted back the wave of his hair, getting it in place. He winced and backed off.

"Can I use the wagon?" he asked.

"I guess. Where are you going?"

"Just out. Around."

"With Buddie?"

Sonny clenched his fists, then worked them open and shut, open and shut. "No," he said.

"Who's the big date then?" she asked cheerily.

"There isn't any big date! There isn't any kind of date! I'm going to pick up Gunner and go have a beer or go to a movie or something!"

"There's no need to yell. I just asked."

He let out a deep breath. "O.K. I'm sorry."

Mrs. Burns opened her purse and fished out the car key. It dangled from a chain with a bright plastic daisy on it.

Sonny started to reach for the key but then pulled his

hand back, not wanting to grab. Instead of handing him the key, she held it in her open palm, staring down at it.

"Sonny?"

"Yes."

"I know you're in real thick with that Casselman boy. I just hope you influence *him*, instead of letting him—"

"For Christ sake! He's not a 'boy.' I'm not a 'boy.' Don't give me that crap!"

Mrs. Burns bit her lip and her head jerked to the side, as if she'd been slapped. Her eyes squeezed shut so hard it contorted her whole face. Sonny fought back a scream. He wanted to tell her to mind her own fucking business and keep her goddam nose out of his life.

But he needed the car.

"I'm sorry," he said.

Tears slid down from her squeezed eyes.

"Don't," he said. "Please."

Her hands fumbled blindly in her purse and came up with a wadded Kleenex that she dabbed at her eyes, without opening them.

"Go ahead," she said. "Take the wagon."

The key was lying in her lap, and Sonny reached down and plucked it out, the way you would reach in and pick a coin from a fire. He stuck the key in his pocket and shifted his weight from one foot to the other.

"Thanks," he said.

Sniffling, she dug in her purse again, pulled out a wadded bill, and pressed it into his hand. He stuffed it in his pocket, not looking at it. Almost every time he went out, she gave him a five- or a ten-dollar bill. They never spoke about it, and Sonny tried not to think about it. He just took it.

"Thanks," he said.

He stood for a moment more and then walked to the door. When his hand touched the knob, his mother's voice, not quite steady yet, called, "Sonny?"

"Yes?"

Sniffing and sobbing, she called through her still-trickling tears, "Have a good time!"

"Thanks," he said and walked out.

Gunner said he really had a thirst on him and suggested they go tip a few at the Topper, down on Illinois Street. The Topper had a combo but it didn't come on until around nine, and in the early evening the place was pretty quiet. Gunner told Sonny all about *The Lonely Crowd,* and how he realized he had always been "other-directed" most of his life, and hoped now he was getting more "inner-directed," doing what he believed in himself and not giving a shit what the crowd thought. He said Sonny had probably been more of an "inner-directed" kind of guy right from the start, and he wished that he had too, he wouldn't have wasted so much time on Mickey Mouse crap like fraternities. Sonny accepted the compliment, just as if it were the truth. He really figured he wasn't any kind of "directed," he just got blown along by things.

Sonny tried to remember something deep from the couple of essays of Emerson he had skimmed, just to throw something into the conversation to show he read intellectual stuff himself, but the few phrases and thoughts he could bring to mind were wispy and fleeting, nothing you could really grab hold of. Gunner ordered them another round and lit a cigarette. It had suddenly gone dark outside, and one of those quick, drenching showers came that splattered on the plate-glass windows and pummeled the sidewalk and street with streaks of silver and then, with a grumble of thunder, passed on. The guys didn't say anything for the three or four minutes of the rain, but just watched and listened to it. They were sitting at a table by the open door. No one had bothered to close it during the shower, and the fresh smell of the rain drifted in through the stale, beery air of the bar. It was like some deep, poignant perfume mixed of elemental things. Both guys shifted restlessly in their chairs. Gunner stabbed out his cigarette, half finished.

"Man," he said, "what I wouldn't give for a nice, new piece of ass."

"Yeh," Sonny said. He had felt it himself with the furious rain and the moist, lingering odor it left.

"Something real soft and tender," Gunner said.

"Ooooh, baby."

"I'd give my left nut to be in Kyoto right now."

"God," Sonny said. He imagined a sweet, gentle Japanese girl, slowly and artfully removing a silken robe, beckoning to him as she spread her sweet-smelling body over a golden divan. A flickering lamp, throwing long shadows. A soft rain, washing the exotic emerald foliage outside the window. . . .

"But the fact is," Gunner said, "we're at Thirty-fourth and Illinois Street, in the Topper, in Indianapolis, Indiana, U.S.A."

Sonny's dream disappeared with the very sounding of names that identified his present location. He took a drink of beer and said, "How about DeeDee?"

"No thanks. Not till she gets off that marriage kick." Gunner poured his glass full again. "Besides," he said, "how about Buddie, for you?"

Sonny shrugged. "I dunno."

"See? That's what I thought."

"What?"

"It's not just getting laid we want. A guy can get laid anytime. It's something—*extra*. More. At least new. Different."

"Yeh, you're right."

Gunner was always saying stuff that Sonny felt himself but never said, fearing it might sound wrong or that other people wouldn't know what he meant and would think he was a little weird or something.

"Maybe we ought to go hunting," said Gunner.

"You want to?"

"No harm in trying."

"Hell, no," Sonny said and waved at the waitress to bring more beer. He had spent more evenings like that than he cared to remember, cruising around with another guy and trying to pick up some tail, getting drunker and hornier as the prizes eluded them, or scorned them, or were won by others, right in front of the eyes of the losers. Long, muddled evenings when the need filled you up like a horrible pressure that wiped out everything else and was finally relieved at home in the shameful unworld of fantasy under the covers, in the lonesome dark, shot. But maybe with Gunner it would be different. Gunner had guts and lean good looks, and success was a habit with him. That was the most important thing of all, that aura of success; the cunts could smell it on you. They could sniff a loser from here to South Bend. With their eyes closed.

"Remember Donna Mae Orlick?" Gunner asked, rubbing his chin. "Waitress at the Ron-D-Vu?"

Sonny laughed. "Who doesn't?" he said, just as if he'd fucked her himself. It seemed like everybody else had. Donna Mae was famous. She mostly liked jocks, though. Even in a literal sense. Sonny heard that Donna Mae had done it once for Rip Stolley, who was "Mr. Basketball" of Indiana in his senior year in high school and went on to be All-American at Purdue, and Donna Mae had got him to give her one of his old jockstraps. She carried this moldy old jockstrap around in her purse for a couple years, and was always whipping it out to impress somebody, though the sight of a cruddy jockstrap—even when it came from "Mr. Basketball"—was enough to make most guys toss their cookies. Some of the other waitresses swore that it wasn't Rip Stolley's jockstrap anyway, but that might have just been because they were jealous.

"I don't even know if she's around anymore," Gunner

said. "Jesus, I haven't been back in a year and a half. We could buzz the D-Vu, though, and ask around."

"Why not?" Sonny said, trying to seem casual. He was shaking a little bit, excited by the prospect that something might really happen.

They settled up the tab and walked to the car. As they neared it, Gunner laughed and said aloud the words on the side of the wagon, "I am the Way, the Truth, and the Life."

"It was easier to get this one than my old man's car," Sonny apologized. "It's a real bitch having that shit on the side, though, especially for tonight."

"Hell, no," Gunner assured him. "That might help us to score. We can say we've come to save their soul."

That fuckin guy can always see the bright side, Sonny thought admiringly.

They rolled down the windows in the front and Sonny drove with his right hand, the left arm slung out the window in a V-form, casual-like. As they drove north, toward the D-Vu, the sharp, green smell of wet grass grew stronger, an earthy intoxicant. The tires made a licking sort of sound on the soaked streets.

"Donna Mae Orlick," Gunner said. "What a pair of knockers."

"Tree-mendous," Sonny said. He wasn't speaking from what might be called, in a factual sense, "first-hand knowledge," but he wasn't really lying, either, since he often *saw* how tremendous her boobs were, pushing against her light silk waitress blouse. She didn't wear a bra and you could really see the nipples and the little bumps around them. What did you call those things? Niplets, maybe.

"You rubbed the tips of those babies," Gunner was recalling of Donna Mae's knockers, "they stood up hard as pencils. Then she was ready to go."

"Mmmm," Sonny commented.

His prick had begun to crawl forward along his left

thigh. He pulled his arm in from outside the window and gripped the steering wheel with both hands, hard.

"Shit, though, she's probably long gone from the D-Vu," Gunner said.

"Well, ya never know."

Dear God, Sonny thought, *let Donna Mae Orlick still work at the Ron-D-Vu.* Then he added, *Forgive me, oh, Lord.*

Even though he hated God and religion, sometimes words and phrases like that, sounding like prayers, broke into his mind uninvited and without his consent, as irresistible as intruders who force their way into your house.

"Donna Mae, Donna Mae, do it with me in the hay," Gunner sang, making up his own tune.

Ron-D-Vu was spelled out in purple neon letters on the roof of the drive-in. It was made in a cement circle, painted white, with an oblong hole cut out where the waitresses picked up the orders. The car crunched up on the black cinder skirt that spread out and around the building, and Sonny drove slowly, looking for a spot. Cars nestled up around the place like puppies feeding off a giant tit, and there always were others patrolling the outer edges, looking for a good slot. It wasn't any good for a couple of guys to pull in next to a car with other guys, or guys with dates. What you wanted was to slide in next to a car with a couple of sexy babes who were hot to go.

"Take a lap," Gunner said.

Sonny eased the car around the circle, peering for something good.

"There!" Gunner said, spotting a convertible with two blondes. Sonny had just gone past and he stopped and looked to see if he could back in, but as he stared in the rear-view mirror, a two-tone Ford gunned into the space with a squeal of tires and a shower of cinders.

"Shit," Sonny said apologetically.

"Ah, fuck it. Pull in anywhere."

Sonny eased the car into the next big space he saw. On one side was a car with a guy on a date, the girl leaning on his shoulder. On the other side was some old guy and his wife.

"We might as well chow down," Gunner said, "if we're gonna be boozing the rest of the night."

"Right," Sonny agreed, but he had no appetite. He knew he should eat because you get smashed faster on an empty stomach, but when he was thinking about sex he was never hungry. He ordered a plain hamburger and a Coke just to get something inside him so he wouldn't get woozy or sick right away when he started drinking. Gunner asked for two cheeseburgers with everything, an order of fries, an order of onion rings, and two chocolate shakes. The waitress was a scrawny, bored-looking girl with no tits at all, and food stains on her blouse.

"Say, Good-looking," Gunner asked her when she finished writing the order down. "Does Donna Mae Orlick still work here?"

"Not that I heard of," she said and flicked away, turning her nose up.

"Maybe she's just new," Sonny said hopefully.

Gunner shrugged. "Let's case the joint," he said and got out of the car.

Sonny got out of his side, blinking in the neon glare. He wasn't used to parading around the drive-ins on foot, like the Big Rods always did, strolling along like they owned the place, peering into cars and banging on the hoods of cars whose drivers they knew, or sometimes just if the driver was a cute girl. Sonny tried to feel casual. He shoved his hands in his pockets, kicked a little at the cinders, and followed along behind Gunner.

A bunch of guys were gathered around a Ford that was cut down and painted like a stock-car racer with a big, scrawly number "77" on the side. The hood was up, and the guys were looking in at the motor, which was no doubt

very souped-up. Sonny recognized some as old Cathedral
guys, who had gone to that Catholic high school. Mainly
people from Shortley and Butler University went to the D-
Vu, but some of the Cathedral guys went there looking for
North Side snatch, guys who didn't want to go out with the
girls from St. Mary's. Sonny had always been a little afraid
of those Catholic guys, with their silver religious medals
hanging on chains outside their T-shirts; swarthy, dark
guys with big muscles who figured they had God on their
side, too. And Sonny believed it. A couple of the guys in
this bunch around the car were in Naval uniforms, but the
others were in slacks and sport shirts, and there was one
really big guy wearing Levis pressed like iron and a fancy
orange-silk cowboy shirt. As Gunner and Sonny ap-
proached, the group began looking up from the hood and
checking them out. One guy spit a big hocker into the
cinders, and Sonny began to slow down, but Gunner
sauntered right on and said real loud, "Who is that fancy
mothering cowboy? Tom Mix or Roy Rogers?"

The guy in the cowboy shirt whipped around with his
eyes looking like tips of knife blades, and Sonny stopped
dead in his tracks.

"Big Quinn!" Gunner shouted.

The big guy relaxed, straightening up from what looked
to Sonny like his karate position for instant murder, and
tipped back his cowboy hat. "Gunner, you ole bastard," he
said with pleasure.

The two guys met and whacked the hell out of each
other in greeting. Sonny remembered, when he heard the
name, "Big Quinn" was one of those Cathedral guys who
was supposed to be a great athlete but was always dissipat-
ing and never made his grades, so he never got to play
varsity ball, but in the sandlot games and the alley-ball
games he outplayed all the big stars from around the city,
and in a funny way they had more respect for him than for
the heroes everyone knew about. Only the other jocks

knew about Big Quinn; he was something special. Instead
of going to college, Big Quinn served a four-year hitch in
the Navy, and now he was driving stocks in the dirt-track
races and working part time in the Herman Cohen Men's
Attire Shop on 38th Street. He always dressed real sharp.

Gunner and Big Quinn shot the shit for a while and
Gunner got around to asking him whatever happened to
Donna Mae Orlick.

Big Quinn hooted and slapped his knee. "Married," he
said. "Settled down. Can ya picture it?"

"How'd it happen?" Gunner asked, in the tone of a man
inquiring about a great pianist who had lost his fingers.

"Some guy from Terre Haute knocked her up. She had a
pie in the oven, and the guy married her."

"Shit," Gunner said, "couldn't he have got three witnesses to testify?"

It was said that if a girl got pregnant and you could get
three other guys to testify they had fucked her, too, there
was some law that said you didn't have to marry her because she was a loose woman or something. It was one of
those things that everyone seemed to know about, but
nobody was too clear on. If you asked a lot of questions
about it, that showed you were green, so everyone just
accepted it, as far as Sonny could tell.

"Buddy, you talk about *three*—he could of got three
hundred," Big Quinn said. "But the guy was from *Terre
Haute*. He didn't *know*."

"Oh, my achin' ass," Gunner said.

"*His* achin' ass," Big Quinn said, and both of them
laughed. Gunner said he had to get back to his chow, and
both guys biffed one another on the arm and said they'd
see each other around.

"Well, no more Donna Mae Orlick," Gunner said as he
and Sonny went back to the wagon.

"Son of a bitch," Sonny said.

Somehow he figured it was *his* bad luck, that it was just

to torment him that Donna Mae had got knocked up and married some Terre Haute guy. The waitress came with the food, and Sonny made himself swallow the Coke and hamburger even though he didn't feel like it. Gunner chowed down like a starving Armenian. When he finished he let out a satisfied belch, clapped his hands together, and said, "O.K., team, let's go get 'em."

Sonny gunned the motor, pecled the old wagon out of the lot and into the street with confident purpose, and then slowed down. "Where to?" he asked.

"Well, what say we check out the East Side. Maybe we can find us some Tech babies."

"Right," Sonny said, feeling a shiver of fear and excitement.

They were on their way to what was for them, North Side guys, foreign and often hostile territory. Looking for "Tech babies," girls who went or had gone to Manual-Technical High School. Manual-Technical! The name itself conjured up in Sonny's mind images of vast machinery; lathes and pistons, turbines and diesels, great groaning gears and belching smokestacks, sooty air and greasy rags, Bessemer steel, spontaneous combustion. That was the sort of thing Sonny figured you learned about when you went to Manual-Technical. The massive school was housed in an old armory, a spread of gray, dungeony buildings on a grassless, sooty campus by the clanging streetcar tracks, in sight of the factories where its graduates would file into line after graduation to grind out their living. The school's colors were black and red—most brutal of hues, most basic and bestial, red of the workingman's blood and black of his heavy industrial machines. Their athletic teams were called "The Black Riveters" and were known for their hulking, grinding efficiency. Their line could mash enemy quarterbacks to scrap; their fullbacks were trucks wearing uniforms. Manual-Technical stood on the opposite side of town from Shortley, and though there were other schools scattered between and beyond, these were the two giants, the natural archrivals, the poles of human opposition—the Manual-Technical Black Riveters versus the Shortley Blue Barons. The Shortley colors were robin's egg blue and cream ("whipped cream," the envious rivals called it and sneered at the Barons as "cream puffs") and yet their rivalry over the years was evenly matched, it ebbed and flowed back and forth like the very forces in the world itself that the two schools seemed to represent.

As they neared downtown, before turning east, Gunner spotted a colored woman on a streetcorner, crooking her finger at them.

"Dark meat for sale," he observed.

Sonny glanced up at the street number, to file in his memory. Just in case.

They headed out East 10th Street, and Gunner asked Sonny to stop at a dim little park where some kids were clustered on benches, talking and giggling.

"I'll check it out," he said.

Sonny didn't want to watch as Gunner sauntered right up to the kids and struck up a conversation. There were some louder giggles, and Gunner came back and said to move on.

"Jail-bait," he explained.

They stopped again when Gunner spotted a couple of girls in toreadors hanging around outside a little rundown drugstore. Sonny pulled up at the opposite corner and Gunner went back to talk to them. Sonny lit a cigarette, trying not to let his hand shake. He snuck a look in the rear-view mirror and saw Gunner gesturing, turning his powers of persuasion on them. Sonny wondered what the hell he'd do if Gunner actually got them into the car. He was almost more afraid that Gunner would succeed than he was that Gunner would fail. When Gunner came back alone, Sonny felt a secret relief.

"Just little teasers," Gunner explained when he came back empty-handed. "Listen, let's hit the Tropics Club. It's farther out on Tenth."

The Tropics Club had a jazz combo, and the place was heavy with smoke and people. Burly guys with T-shirts and tattoos on their biceps, sharpies with flashy sport shirts and ducktail haircuts, babes in tight skirts and flouncy hairdos. The combo wasn't bad, and Sonny and Gunner ordered boilermakers and started tapping the table in time with the music. A couple of babes came in by themselves and sat down about three tables away, but they were real dogs.

After three boilermakers Gunner glanced at the two broads again and said, grinning, "Funny thing, later it gets, the better they look."

"The dogs, you mean?" Sonny asked.

Gunner raised a palm, as if protesting. "Think positive," he said. "Look for the good in people."

"Like what?"

"Well, take the blonde, for instance. Her face'd stop a clock, but see if you can't find some 'good points' about her."

"Yeh," Sonny said. "She's built like a brick shithouse."

"If I ever saw one," Gunner said. He bolted his shot, chased it with a long gulp of beer, and looked a little glassily at Sonny. "But I never did see one, come to think of it. Did you?"

"What?"

"Ever see a brick shithouse? I mean a real one."

"I guess not," Sonny admitted. "Just the wooden kind."

"Yeh, me too. And yet all our life we go around saying a woman is built like a brick shithouse if she has big knockers. What have big knockers got to do with a brick shithouse? Nothing sticks out on a shithouse, does it?"

"Not that I ever saw."

"Man," Gunner said, shaking his head. "It's weird. We

say all kind of stuff we don't even know what it means. Or how come we say it."

"There's probably a lot of stuff like that. We say."

"Fuckin-A there is."

The combo had finished a set, and there was loud giggling from the two broads.

"They're hot to go," Gunner said.

"I guess," Sonny said without much enthusiasm. He figured if Gunner actually got the girls, he would be stuck with the one who was not built like a brick shithouse. This one who was not had red hair that looked dyed, piled on top of her head, and enough lipstick to paint a wild Indian.

"Let's go get 'em," Gunner said.

Sonny felt faint. "Listen," he said, "I gotta take a leak first."

Gunner looked him straight in the eyes and Sonny coughed and looked away, hoping he didn't seem nervous. "Look," Gunner said understandingly, "maybe I oughta go make the first move myself. Then, if it looks like action, I'll call you over."

"Good plan," said Sonny.

Gunner finished off his beer and started ambling over to the two broads. Sonny hurried to the head. It was one of those moldy kind of crappers with only one toilet and no pissing trough. The toilet didn't flush too well and there was a pretty bad mess in it. Sonny took aim and then looked away from it, up at the wall. There was a picture of a cock, and underneath it said "Eat Me." Under that someone had scrawled in pencil, "I did—Kilroy was here." Under that somebody else had written "Kilroy Sucks." In another place was a phone number and the message "Call Susie—she likes to blow." Sonny read this stuff while he pissed, then shook the last drops off and tucked his prick back in. It seemed especially small, as if already retreating from the war-painted redhead. On the wall beside the door was a rubber machine, and it said in big letters "For Sanitary Purposes Only," like you weren't supposed to use them for fucking. The brands were obscure ones you didn't ordinarily hear of, like Varsity Tip, King O' Hearts, and Kamikaze. Sonny pulled out his wallet and checked to see if he still had the single Trojan in the secret pocket of it. It was there, getting pretty rumpled and beat-up-looking. Anyway, Trojans were best. Everyone knew that. Sonny wasn't sure how everyone knew it, but it was something you just knew, like you knew that whores didn't kiss on the mouth, and Nice Girls didn't do it when they were riding the rag, and drinking too much gin in hot weather could make you blind.

When Sonny came out of the crapper, Gunner was sitting at the table with the broads, gesturing a lot. Sonny thought maybe he ought to go over, but he sat down at his own table instead and drank what was left of his beer. The combo came out to start the next set, and after another few minutes Gunner returned to the table.

"What happened?" Sonny asked.

"They're married," Gunner announced.

"No shit? Where's their husbands?"

"Night shift at Allison's."

"Oh, brother."

Those were the kind of guys who would beat the shit out of you if they caught you messing around with their women.

Gunner ordered another round for him and Sonny.

Sonny felt bloated and sticky from the beer, his throat burned from the whiskey shots, and the music made a rhythmic ache in his head. It would have made sense to give up the idea of getting any pussy and go home to bed, but the quest seemed even more urgent, more all-consuming now. The thing about hunting for pussy was that once you started you couldn't give up trying until you passed out or something. No matter how many things fell through and how late it got, it became all the more important to do it then, that very night. The future didn't count.

Gunner popped his fingers. "I got it," he said.

"Yeh?"

"Maybe. If she's still around. Broad I picked up in this neighborhood once. She dropped out of Tech and was working at Curtis-Wright."

A factory girl! That was almost as good as a nurse, or so they said. Gunner made his way through the tables to the one telephone. It was on the wall, without any booth. Gunner looked a long time through the phone book, and then Sonny saw him put a coin in. The combo was going like crazy, and it must have been hard as hell to hear anything. But Gunner came back grinning.

"We can pick her up in fifteen minutes," he said.

"Does she have a friend?"

"She must have," Gunner said.

Gunner bought a pint of whiskey off the bartender, and they drove to this seedy old apartment house not far from the bar. There was a figure in the shadow of the doorway. Gunner whistled, and this girl came flouncing out. She was wearing tight black toreadors and high heels and had on a tight, low-cut blouse. A little gold cross dangled in the start of the crevice between her tits. Gunner got out of the car and the girl got in.

"Terry, this is my buddy George," Gunner said.

"Glad to meet you, Terry."

"Likewise," she said without looking at him.

"Let's take a little drive," Gunner said.

"Hey, what is this?" Terry asked. "You said we was havin' a date, Ron."

She thought Gunner's name was Ron. That was for safety, so if you ever knocked up one of those broads, they couldn't track you down. That's why Gunner introduced Sonny as "George."

"Yeh, well, we are," Gunner said.

"Two fellas and one girl ain't *my* kind of date," she said huffily.

"Sure, but you gotta friend, don't you? A friend for George?"

She looked at Sonny and a pink bubble appeared on her mouth, expanded to the size of an egg, then burst.

"Maybe," she said.

"Well, let's go get her," Gunner said.

Terry wiped her mouth with the back of her hand and said, "I'd have to call and see."

"O.K. Listen. We'll go back to the Tropics and you can call."

She blew another bubble, and Sonny started the car. They were having the last call for drinks at the Tropics, and Terry said she wanted a Singapore sling.

"O.K., we'll order it for you," Gunner promised. "You call your friend."

Her friend said it was too late, but she would be happy to go some other time. Sonny and Gunner downed their last boilermaker and Terry chugged her Singapore sling and then gulped the fruit. When they got in the car, Gunner offered her a swig from the pint, but she wouldn't take it. Gunner took one and passed it to Sonny.

"Hey," Terry complained, "this ain't no real date. You take me home."

Gunner put his arm around her, and his hand dangled down onto her left tit.

"You're lookin' real great, Terry."

"Don't give me none of your bullshit, Ron."

"Whatya mean, bullshit? I'm telling you, you look like a million."

"Keep your hands to yourself, you North Side cocksucker. This ain't a real date, and I'm goin' home."

Sonny started the motor. He drove real slow, and Gunner did his best to warm her up, but she wasn't having any.

"O.K.," he said when they got to her place, "I'll give you a call, and you get your friend, right, and we'll have a real date."

"Yeh, and I mean a real date, like a movie and all. Not just fartin' around in a car."

"Sure, sure," Gunner said, "that's what I mean."

She primped at her hair, straightened her blouse, and said, "O.K., when is it?"

"Huh?"

"The date?"

"Oh, well, real soon," Gunner said. "Look, I'll call in the next couple days."

"Yeh, and my Aunt Minnie is the Queen of Spain."

"No shit, I mean it," Gunner said.

"Seein's believin'."

"You'll see."

"Lemme outa this heap."

Gunner got out and Terry switched her tail up to the apartment, her heels clicking on the sidewalk. The door slammed, and she was gone, like they had only imagined her. She really was sexy-looking, though, and Sonny was perspiring as he thought of fucking her while she yelled a lot of dirty stuff at him. Gunner took a gulp from the pint and passed it to Sonny. He took one too, and it scorched his raw, churning stomach.

"Well, we can always take Terry and her friend," Gunner said. "They put out, but you gotta treat 'em right first."

"Yeh," Sonny said, but it wasn't much consolation for the moment. Even a sure thing for the future didn't help the need right then, it was only a dream, bringing no immediate relief.

They finished off the pint and then went to the Toddle House for breakfast. It was glary and noisy, and Sonny's head was throbbing. Gunner had a stack with sausage and Sonny had a piece of icebox chocolate pie and a Coke.

Gunner was still hungry and he ordered a pecan waffle. In the middle of it, he put down his fork and clutched at his head. Sonny thought maybe he was sick. In a way he was, but not in the stomach.

"This isn't it, man," Gunner said. "Chasing tail and boozing ourselves blind. Shit, this just isn't it."

"How do you mean?"

"I mean," Gunner said emphatically, "there's got to be more in life than pussy."

"Yeh, I guess you're right," Sonny said.

Gunner finished off his waffle with a vengeance, like a man inspired and determined. Sonny felt better too, like maybe it was one of those points in life when things were going to change, going to begin. Finally. When they got outside, Gunner stretched and pointed at the pink streaks in the eastern sky.

"Fuckin dawn," he said.

Sonny took it as an omen. "Right," he said. "A new fuckin day."

PART TWO

1

As part of Gunner's plan to find more in life than pussy, he announced to Sonny they were going down to the Herron Art Museum and look at the art. Sonny had never been to the Herron before—never been inside, anyway, even though he had passed it thousands of times driving home from downtown. It was a gray, square building that reminded Sonny of a mausoleum, maybe because it looked like one or maybe that was secretly how he felt about museums. Housing for the dead. It had never occurred to him to go inside the place, nor had he imagined that anyone except art students who studied at the Herron school had any reason for going inside.

"Are you sure they'll let us in?" he asked Gunner on the way down.

"Sure they will, it's a mu*seum*, for God sake."

"I thought maybe you had to be a student at Herron or something. To get in."

"It's for the public," Gunner explained. "All you have to be is one of the public."

"Oh."

Gunner was right. You just walked in and moseyed around, going from one room to another, looking at the paintings and pieces of sculpture they had. But it wasn't as easy as it sounded. For Sonny, at least. There was a certain technique for standing and looking, for tilting your head in just the right way, for shifting around to get another angle on the thing, moving in closer and then farther back, squinting a little bit, and knowing the right time for leaving one painting and going on to the next. Gunner, of course, got the hang of it right off, as if it were a new kind of sport and he picked up the moves with his natural ability. Sonny felt awkward as hell and was sure that anyone could tell he didn't know a damn thing about art and was just pretending. One of the hardest parts for him was sticking with one picture for the right length of time. After he had looked at the damn thing for five or ten seconds, he figured he had seen it, and yet he knew that if you moved on that quickly it meant you weren't serious. You had to hang around and keep ogling the damn thing.

Gunner even knew how to make the whispered comments. Rubbing reflectively at his chin, he would squint at a picture and say something like "Interesting, yeh, I think he's on to something," or "I'm not sure he got what he wanted there." Sonny just nodded agreement to everything.

Some of the paintings were by native Indiana artists who showed pictures of hills and trees and brooks and the usual crap in pretty places like Brown County. Then there were others by people from New York that didn't have anything you could make out exactly, but consisted of lines and splotches and bursts of color, without any actual thing you could identify like a house or a cow.

It was in the room of some of these paintings without any actual pictures in them that both guys found something of genuine interest to view. It was an art object all right, but a living one, dressed in hip-hugging tomato-colored toreadors and a tight silk blouse, contemplating the paintings with absorbed intensity. Of course, in a case like this, when there was something you would really like to clap your eyeballs on for a long time, from all different angles and distances, you had to pretend not to really be looking at it—or her—at all. She carried a pair of big sunglasses and gnawed at the stems as she stared at the paintings, making Sonny want to gnaw on something himself. Every so often her tongue would come out and move speculatively over her lips in a slow, lolling sort of way. She wore no lipstick, and somehow that seemed even sexier. There are certain kinds of girls who can get themselves up in a way that is opposite from what is supposed to be sexy and come out looking even sexier. Maybe it's because they weren't supposed to do it that way but obviously didn't give a damn, or maybe because there was something offbeat about it, Sonny wasn't sure. The girl wasn't what you'd call pretty; her nose was long and had a kind of bump in the bridge of it, her lips were very thin, and her eyes were set a little too close together, but the whole effect was somehow attractive, exceedingly sexy. Maybe it was the aura about her, the stuck-up air that she didn't give a damn what anyone thought, she knew she was pretty hot stuff.

Sonny saw the girl catch Gunner giving her the once-over, and she shot him a glance that would have staggered a charging bull. Then she strolled out, sliding on her sunglasses, her tight little ass twitching sassily.

Talk about Art.

Gunner was watching her with the studied appreciation of a connoisseur, and as she went out of sight, he started moving after her, as naturally and unhesitatingly as if he already had a date to meet her. Sonny drifted along behind, digging his fingernails into his palms. It not only terrified him to try to pick up a girl himself, it even made him nervous to see another guy try. If the other guy failed, it somehow seemed to Sonny like a slap in the face of all men, himself included, and he cringed to see it.

Gunner was halfway to the sidewalk, pursuing his prey, but Sonny stopped as soon as he got outside. He leaned back against the door, looking down at his feet and trying to blank out his mind. In moments like that he was tempted to pray, but since he had lost his belief he resorted to repeating scraps of nursery rhymes, which was almost as good. If you didn's really think about the words they sounded a little like prayers, their rhythm supplying the comfort of incantation.

> Little Jack Horner
> Sat in a corner
> Mumbledy-mumble pie . . .
> Stuck in a thumb
> Pulled out a plum
> Blackberry juice in the eye.

Taking a deep breath he sneaked a glance toward the sidwalk and saw Gunner casually standing with the girl, talking, as if it was the natural thing. He motioned to Sonny, impatiently, as if Sonny should have known all along it would be all right. Feeling his heart accelerate to high, Sonny walked up to them, not looking directly at the girl. Gunner introduced Sonny and said he had just asked Marty—that was the girl, Marty Pilcher—to have a cup of coffee with them over at the drugstore across the street. Sonny fell in on the other side of the girl, but a little behind her and Gunner, like a kid who was tagging along.

The drugstore was one of the old-fashioned kind that had big wooden booths and was sort of dark and musty inside, with an odor of camphor and cough syrup. There was a tall electric fan that buzzed complacently but didn't affect the temperature. It was hot as blazes, and Sonny didn't feel like drinking any coffee, but he knew that was what to order.

You didn't invite a sophisticated girl to go have an ice-cream soda with you. Coffee sounded more mature and worldly.

Marty scooched into one side of the booth, next to the wall, and Gunner moved in opposite from her. Sonny sat down next to Gunner, sort of on the edge of things. It really was discouraging being so nervous when it wasn't even him who was trying to operate with the girl.

"I thought you looked familiar," Gunner said to the girl and explained to Sonny, "She went to Shortley, too. Couple years behind us."

"Oh," Sonny said, adding his sparkling bit to the conversation.

"I don't think we actually met," the girl said pointedly to Gunner, "but then we wouldn't have. You were a Big Rod."

She blew a stream of smoke from her nostrils and with a mocking sort of smile said, "Isn't that what they called you Golden Boys?"

Gunner shifted uncomfortably and stared into his coffee. "That was high school," he said, like it didn't really mean anything.

"And college, too," the girl said in the same mocking tone. "DePauw, wasn't it? Football star. Big Man on Campus."

Gunner winced, and scratched at the back of his head.

"B.M.O.C." the girl said with a grin.

"Come on," Gunner said, sounding like a kid who was being picked on. Marty just smiled and delicately picked a little fleck of tobacco off her bottom lip.

It really was something. There was Gunner having to be embarrassed about all the stuff that had made him a hero, a star, a rod. But it was obvious that those things were the opposite ones to anything that would impress this particular girl. She was playing it cool and a little bit mean.

Sonny thought how great it would be to fuck her, and he suddenly felt dizzy and weak.

"Weren't you in the Annual Varieties at Shortley?" Gunner asked, desperately trying to throw some prestige thing back at *her*. The Annual Varieties, an elaborate, original show put on by the students, was pretty big stuff at Shortley. It was said that you never could tell when scouts from Broadway or Hollywood might be in the audience.

"Sure I was in the Varieties," Marty admitted; then added, "Jews were allowed."

"Hey!" Gunner said, like he'd caught her in a foul. "Don't give me any discrimination stuff. Jews were in everything at Shortley, even the best clubs, even in—well, the Big Rod cliques. In every class, all the time I was there, anyway. In my year there was Sue Ann Glick, and Sammy Katzman."

"Sure." Marty smiled. "And in my year there was Roberta Tallon and Norm Siedenbaum."

"So?"

"So, in every year, in every class, one male and one female Jew are taken in at the top. That's what the quota allows."

"*What* quota?" Gunner demanded.

Marty sighed and then said, as if she were only repeating the obvious, "The quota that allows two Jews, one of each gender, to be among the top social caste at Shortley in each new class."

Gunner snorted. "That's crazy," he said and turned to Sonny, looking for help. "Tell her, will ya? You're an objective observer. Was there a 'quota,' did you ever hear of any 'quota' like that?"

Sonny chewed at his lip. "Not that I ever heard of," he said.

That was true, but the funny thing was when he started thinking back, it seemed like Marty was right. In every class there turned out to be a dozen or so boys and a matching number of girls who were really the top, the real rods and roddesses, and in each group there was just one boy and one girl Jew. Sonny had never really noticed it before, but when he thought about it, damned if it didn't seem to be the case.

"Well?" Marty asked.

"It seems like that's what happened," Sonny said.

Gunner slapped a hand on his forehead and looked from Marty to Sonny. "But *how?*" he insistently questioned them. *"How* did it happen?"

Marty blew a neat little smoke ring at him. "Natural selection," she cooed.

Gunner's hand tightened on his forehead, pressing the brow.

"No, but really. How did each top group in each class always have two, no more and no less? Always one boy and one girl who were—" his voice trailed off—"Jewish."

"To show that all men are created equal," Marty said brightly, "regardless of race, creed, or color."

"But listen," Gunner pleaded, "nobody ever said that. I mean, I was on the inside of that stuff, and I swear to God, nobody ever sat down and said, 'O.K., who'll be the two Jewish kids to make it this year?' You don't believe that happened. Do you?"

Marty shrugged. "Probably not. That would have been embarrassing."

Gunner looked to Sonny, but he wasn't any help. "Son of a bitch," Gunner said softly. He kept holding his hand pressed to his forehead, as if he was keeping his brains from falling out. Finally he let out a long breath and said, almost like he was talking to himself, "Wow. The stuff people do. And don't even know they're doing it."

Marty reached over and touched his hand, not so much with affection, but rather, consolation, as if she were comforting a little kid.

"We did it too," she said. "The Jews had their own

vicious social thing going, their own clubs and in groups and nasty little hierarchies."

"Besides," Sonny found himself saying aloud, "you didn't have to be Jewish to be on the outside."

Marty gave him a sympathetic smile that made him look away and wished he hadn't said it. It would have sounded even more like asking for sympathy if he added the thing he so often thought about, the feeling he had that it might in a way be lucky to be a Jew or something so you'd have a real reason for being shut out of things and it wouldn't really be your fault, the fault of the actual person you were. It seemed to Sonny to be even more humiliating to be a regular WASP and still be left out, because then the only reason for not being accepted was yourself, the way you were. You got to wondering whether you had B.O. or something, like in the ads where even your best friends wouldn't tell you.

"I was a snob," Marty said, "in my own circle. I was in Hadassah Debs. That was very big for the Jews."

"Hadassah Debs," Gunner said. "Yeh, I remember that. Did you join a Jewish sorority? In college?"

"I went to Wellesley. At least the cliques there didn't have badges."

"You went East, huh?" Gunner said with that certain edge of awe that the fact commanded from those who got their higher education nearer home.

Marty nodded and mashed out her cigarette with a determined jab. "I'm going back, too."

"When?" Gunner's question had a note of urgency about it.

"When I serve my time here. Daddy'd let me go now, but Mother thinks if I stay a year I'll meet a nice boy at the country club and grow up to be just like her. So I'm taking courses at Herron and painting, and if I stay a year I get my freedom. This time next year, I'll be gone."

"Where?" Gunner asked, leaning forward a little.

Marty looked puzzled, as if he ought to know. "New York, of course."

"Oh, right."

"Is there any place else?"

Gunner shrugged. "I might end up there myself," he said casually. "I've got the GI Bill coming. I could use it anywhere. Columbia, maybe."

"Oh? What would you study?"

Gunner shifted uneasily in his seat. "I dunno, exactly. Philosophy, maybe. Maybe something in art. Something to do with art."

"Oh," Marty said, obviously unimpressed. Sonny felt embarrassed in Gunner's behalf, something he would never have imagined could happen. Marty yawned and said, "Well, thanks for the coffee. I have to run."

She slid from the booth, a set of keys jangling in her hand, and started off.

"Wait!" Gunner almost pushed Sonny onto the floor as he scrambled out of the booth. Marty turned and looked at him with her eyebrows slightly raised, questioning, as if she couldn't imagine what in the world Gunner might have to say to her. Sonny thought she looked exotically arrogant.

"Well," Gunner said and cleared his throat. "Why don't we, uh, get together sometime? I mean, you know, I'd like to talk to you again. There's some stuff I'd like to talk to you about."

"Oh?"

She damn well wasn't making it easy. Sonny felt downright sorry for Gunner.

"Do you have a phone?"

"My father does. It's in the book."

She turned again, twitching off in that teasing walk. Gunner stood watching, in a kind of trance.

"Some girl," Sonny said.

"It won't be easy," Gunner said, mostly to himself. Then, as if snapping awake, he looked wildly at Sonny and said,

"Holy shit! What's her father's name?"

"She didn't say."

"Come on!"

Gunner dug in his pocket, pulled out an assortment of coins, and flung them all on the table. He ran out the door and looked desperately up and down the street. Then he started running and Sonny trotted behind, wanting to help. A new Chevy convertible was pulling out into traffic, and Gunner spotted Marty at the wheel, ran out in the street dodging a truck, and caught up to the convertible just as it halted for a stoplight on the corner.

"Hey!" he yelled.

She turned her big dark sunglasses on him.

"What's his name? Your father?"

"Solomon," she said, and with just one corner of her thin lips curling almost imperceptibly upward she added, "As in the Old Testament."

The light greened, and she gunned off with tires screeching, leaving Gunner in a gassy cloud. He turned and trotted back to the sidewalk, noticeably limping. Sonny figured he must have twisted an ankle dodging the truck in his rush to Marty's car.

"What's wrong? You hurt your ankle or something?"

"Hell, no," Gunner said quietly, sweat beads showing on his brow, "I've got such a goddam hard-on I can barely walk."

2

Sonny walked around the block with Gunner—slowly, of course, like you'd walk with a guy who was just getting over a leg injury. Gunner kept slamming his fist into the palm of his other hand and saying, "Son of a bitch." Sonny suggested they might have a nice cool brew somewhere, but Gunner didn't feel like sitting still. He was nervous as a cat. He lit a cigarette and threw it into somebody's yard after just a couple puffs.

"C'mon," he said, "let's roll out to Little America and bash a few balls."

Gunner didn't say a word on the way. Sonny was thinking it was sort of funny—not funny ha-ha, but funny strange—how their good intention to get some real first-hand culture turned out. It seemed like everything led to pussy, even Art. He didn't mention that to Gunner, though.

Sonny looked on and chain-smoked while his buddy took things out on an innocent bucket of golf balls.

"She thinks I'm a stupid jock," Gunner kept saying, and then he'd wind up and knock another ball to hell and gone.

"No, she doesn't," Sonny would answer, but it didn't sound very convincing, probably because he wasn't really convinced of it. Besides, he felt silly, trying to reassure one of the town's great cocksman about a broad!

Gunner was sweaty after just one bucket, and he said what the hell, they might as well go tip a few. They went into Broad Ripple to the Melody Inn, which had the virtue of being the closest place to get a beer. It was getting on toward five and there were some businessmen already gathered—not big businessmen, but guys who probably sold roofing or air-conditioners or some other door-to-door kind of thing. Sonny figured that must be a real bitch of a way to make a living. It wasn't bad for college guys on summer vacations, but these were guys with thinning hair and spreading waistlines, guys with slack, puffy faces who wore wingtip shoes with ventilation holes and white-silk socks with arrows up the side. A couple of them had broads along, probably gals they picked up in an office, the kind with those big, shellacked hairdos and double chins and laughter that was loud without being happy.

"Order me a Bud," Gunner said suddenly and headed for the back of the bar. Sonny figured he was going to the head. Maybe he even had to puke, poor bastard. His face had a faint green tinge to it. Sonny ordered Buds when the waitress came, and they were there when Gunner got back to the table. He looked in a little better shape, and when he sat down he said with relief, "It's there. It's in there."

"What is?"

"Her phone number."

"In the *head?*"

Gunner looked plenty pissed off. "Hell no, it's not in the head, it's in the phone book! Under her father's name. What the hell kind of girl you think she is? The kind that guys write her phone number in the head in a crummy bar?"

"Jesus, no, man. I'm sorry. I didn't get what you were talking about. No shit. I thought you went to the head."

That was a terrible thing to say about a girl, that her phone number was written in the crapper. You often saw girls' phone numbers written on the wall of a head, especially in bars, but they were numbers of whory broads that a guy would write down for general consumption, with an explanatory comment under the number like "Stella Wants to Fuck" or "Connie Eats Cock," something like that. Sometimes Sonny wondered if they were real girls' phone numbers and if the girls really did the stuff it said on the wall. Once when he was pretty loaded he took down one of those numbers, but he threw it away when he found it in his billfold a couple weeks later, written on the back of an old university ID card. The truth was that if he ever called a number like that and some sexy babe answered the phone and said to come on over, he'd be scared shitless, so there wasn't really much point in calling. The number might be phony, or it might not, and either thing would end up depressing him.

"Listen," Gunner said, "I've got to convince her I'm not a dumb jock."

"Oh—right."

Sonny had got so wrapped up in his own imagined troubles he'd forgot about his buddy's real problem. "Why don't you tell her about Japan?" he suggested. "The stuff about Zen."

Gunner stroked his chin. "Maybe," he said.

He brooded over another round of beers, and Sonny reminded him they probably ought to get home for dinner. Gunner drove him back without saying anything and almost passed the house.

"Well," Sonny said when he got out, "good luck, man. Lemme know what happens."

"Right," Gunner said, sounding a million miles away.

Sonny walked slowly to the house, his thoughts sunk deep in his friend's dilemma. He wondered if Gunner had ever failed before and whether the Jewish girl really didn't like him or was just putting on an act. Maybe she didn't like him because he wasn't Jewish. Sonny knew a lot of the Jewish people felt that way, and at first it had surprised him; he had figured a Jewish person would be flattered that a regular person would be hot for them, and then he realized that was prejudice on his part and he felt lousy for thinking it. He walked in the front door wondering if maybe Gunner could argue with the girl that she was discriminating against him if she didn't fuck him. There was more than one kind of discrimination, after all, and surely one was as bad as another. His head was filled with those vital questions as he wandered into the living room, and he didn't even notice anyone until his mother's voice broke his concentration.

"Sonny, I want you to meet a wonderful man."

A big, craggy-faced fellow was sitting across the room, and he stood up and came toward Sonny. He was one of those carved-out-of-mountain sort of guys, with iron-gray hair and a jaw that could stop a crowbar.

"Hello, sir," Sonny said.

The man took his hand with a grip that would have turned an orange to instant juice. "Happy to meet you, son. I'm Luke Matthews."

The name sounded familiar, but Sonny couldn't quite place it. Maybe he was some famous guy.

"Mr. Matthews wrote a book," his mother said.

"Oh. You're a writer?"

"I wouldn't say the literary art is my true vocation," Matthews said with a craggy smile. He had a couple of bright gold teeth.

"Well," Mrs. Burns said quickly, blocking further questions, "maybe you'd like a cold beer, Sonny? There's some beer cold in the icebox."

Sonny looked at her very hard and she coughed and looked away. He figured something was up. His mother putting cold beer in the icebox was a sure tip-off. He went to the kitchen and opened the refrigerator door, cautiously. Sure enough, there among the cakes and pies and brownies was a six-pack of Weidemann's. It wasn't his favorite, but it sure as hell was beer.

"I think Mr. Matthews would like one, too," his mother called in cheerily.

The plot thickened.

Sonny punched open two cans with the churchkey and, because there was company, poured them into glasses. After he gave Luke Matthews his beer and sat down, he stared at the guy and asked, "What was the book you wrote?"

"I'll just leave you two alone for a while," his mother said. "I have some errands to run."

She scurried out of the house, and Sonny looked back at Luke, waiting for a reply.

"My book is entitled *And the Heavens Answered.*"

"Oh," Sonny said, "I get it."

He should have known. The beer had thrown him off, but you couldn't tell about the new religious guys, some of them smoked and drank just to show they were One of the Boys. They were the kind who told you that Jesus was a regular guy, a real sport.

"Give it a chance, boy," Matthews said. "Give it a fair chance."

Luke stood up and plucked a book from the coffee table beside him and handed it to Sonny.

"I don't even ask you read it all," he said, "although many have found some interest in its pages. I merely ask that you note from the jacket what it is really about, rather than make your own prejudgments."

The cover had the title and showed a man in a prison outfit kneeling in the prayer position, with the sky opening up to throw down the heavenly spotlight on him.

On the back was a picture of Luke at his craggiest, and an explanatory blurb:

Luke Matthews is the pseudonym of a hardened convict whose evil deeds as a young man struck terror into the hearts of many citizens and communities in the area where he was reared, somewhere west of the Mississippi River. At nineteen he was sentenced to forty years in federal prison on a variety of counts, and was judged untreatable by prison psychologists, a hard-core case of criminal personality. However, at the age of twenty-four, while working on the rockpile, he experienced a personal religious revelation that sent him for days into a coma during which the only words he muttered, over and over, were "Luke—3:24." Witnesses claim that Matthews had never read a Bible in his life and was totally unfamiliar with the scriptures. Yet, when he recovered and asked for a New Testament, and saw the message, he knew that God had spoken to him, and he gained an inner calm and strength that changed his entire personality. He became assistant to the prison truck gardener and developed a new breed of hardy carrot that can be grown even in the soil of the desert. At age thirty-nine, after twenty years in prison, he was released on good conduct. Despite his flair for horticulture, Matthews felt that he was called to a vocation of spiritual guidance, not limited to any denomination. He founded and organized the movement known as "Retreats Away in the Woods" (popularly known as "RAW"), which has become a source of inspiration and healing for growing thousands. On leaving prison, Matthews shed his old name with his old life, and has since walked in the steps of his Master, under the new name by which he has counseled and inspired so many— Luke Matthews. This book is the story of his life and quest.

Sonny took a couple of swigs from his beer. "I read what it was about," he said.

"So you see, son, I am not exactly naïve about the ways of the world."

"I guess not," Sonny said.

"So then, perhaps I can be of some service to you. As a friend. A man who has experienced much and found the Light after years of darkness."

Sonny took a deep breath. "Mr. Matthews," he said, trying to keep his voice steady, "I'm afraid there's been a misunderstanding."

"What's that?"

"My mother."

"Your mother understands that you are troubled, and she wishes to help you."

"My mother does *not* understand that I am sick of hearing about God. I don't believe in Him. I don't even like Him."

"Well." Luke chuckled. "You can't dislike something—or someone—who doesn't exist. Now can you?"

Sonny closed his eyes. "Mr. Matthews, I have to work things out for myself."

"Every man does, son. Every man does. But a man can be helped by his friends. Conversely, he can be led into harmful pathways by his friends, if he does not choose them carefully. Sometimes the most magnetic people, people of great personal charm and influence, do not use that gift for good works. They may not be evil in themselves, yet they may walk in evil ways and lead others with them on the downward path."

Sonny began to see Mr. Matthews' mission more clearly. He had evidently been commissioned by Mrs. Burns to "save" her precious little boy from the evil influence of Gunner Casselman. Sonny tried to keep calm. He counted to twenty-five.

"Sir, I'm afraid my mother doesn't understand about my

friends either," Sonny said with slow, precise emphasis. "I am afraid she will let me have to choose my own friends. I'm—I am no longer a little boy."

He hadn't quite been able to bring himself to say, "I am a man," for fear it might not sound convincing.

"You are at a turning point," Luke Matthews said gently.

"Well then, I'll make the goddam turn myself!" Sonny shouted.

"I know how you feel, son."

"You do? That's fine! Because I have just one favor to ask you."

"Anything that's in my power, son."

Sonny stood up. "Leave me alone. Leave me the fuck alone."

Matthews folded his big hands together, cracking the knuckles like a volley of shots. "I will respect your wishes," he said. "However, if you change your mind, if you wish to discuss with me any matter at all, I will be at your service as long as I am here."

"Here?" Sonny asked. "You mean here in town?"

Matthews cleared his throat. "To be more specific, here in this lovely home, where your mother has so generously extended me your family's hospitality."

Purple spots began to float before Sonny's eyes like bright balloons. He turned without saying anything and went upstairs to his room. There was a battered little black valise with the initials "L.M." printed in gold, lying at the foot of the bottom bunk bed. Fresh towels and a washcloth were laid out neatly beside it. The purple balloons drifted out of Sonny's sight, and his whole mind focused on a single stark fact.

He was rooming with Luke Matthews.

Sonny marched out of the house without even saying a word to his new roomie. He walked down to 59th Street and headed west, toward College Avenue. There was a Standard station there, with a phone booth. He was so mad he didn't even want to use the telephone at home. That probably didn't make sense, but somehow it matched the way he felt. He didn't want to have anything to do with the goddam place. They ought to hang a goddam cross on the door and turn it into a mission. That's almost what it was anyway.

He walked with a very determined pace along 59th Street, noting to himself that he was obeying the traffic law that said, "Where there are no sidewalks, walk on the left-hand side of the street, facing traffic." Back in grade school you had to memorize the traffic laws, and Sergeant Hackenthorpe of the city police force came around to talk to the kids in the auditorium and told them all the horrible stuff that happened to you if you didn't obey the traffic laws. The main thing Sonny remembered about the talk was Sergeant Hackenthorpe telling in a very sad voice about a kid who ran out into the street after his ball without looking both ways, and was hit by a car and killed. The boys had to try like mad to keep from laughing, and Richard Armitage got to giggling so hard that some snot came out of his nose and then everybody on his row cracked up and the principal had to quiet them down. What broke the guys up was the part about the kid running into the street after "his ball," which they took to mean his testicle. The boys were just learning the words that had sex meanings as well as clean meanings and they went into fits when anyone said those kind of words you could take in a dirty way. But maybe Sonny figured, the whole uproar over the "ball" part of the story was what made him remember it, and made him remember the traffic laws. A person's mind was really weird. Sonny found himself picturing one of his balls dropping off and rolling into the street and him running after it and getting hit by a car. Jesus, he was really in a stew.

By the time he walked the mile or so to the Standard station he was soaked with sweat, and he could feel his heart thumping like crazy. Sometimes when he got mad he thought he might be having a heart attack. Maybe that's how he would die—of having a heart attack. It might not be so bad. It would sure as hell be better than having one of your balls drop off and roll out into the street, and then having a car hit you when you ran out to retrieve your ball. Sonny stepped into the phone booth and reached in his pocket for a dime to make a call, and while he was fishing around he just sort of checked on his balls to make sure they were safe inside there. His balls seemed to be O.K., but he only had a quarter and a nickel and some pennies. He walked up to the station and went inside, where a couple of grease-smeared guys in coveralls were horsing around. He hated to just ask them for change, which he thought might piss them off since he wasn't buying anything, so he put his quarter in the Coke machine and got a bottle of Coke and a dime and a nickel back. He gulped down about half of the Coke, which was warm and acidy tasting, and went back out to the phone booth. He called up Gunner, but his mother answered and said he wasn't home. She sounded very snippy about it, and Sonny just thanked her and hung up. He still had two nickels left, and he put them in the phone and dialed Buddie Porter's number.

Her mother had to call her, and Sonny was afraid she might not get there before his time ran out. It was probably only a minute or so, but it seemed a long time to Sonny while he stood there waiting in the lighted phone booth, and he got more edgy. When Buddie finally answered, all out of breath, he was kind of mad at her. He told her without any explanation to come and pick him up at the Standard station.

"Do I have time to change?" she asked.

"No!" Sonny shouted.

"All right."

She drove up about five minutes later in her mother's station wagon. She was wearing a pink party dress made out of some stiff, frilly material, and she had a gardenia corsage on the left shoulder.

"What the hell are you all dressed up for?" Sonny asked when he got in the car.

"I'm sorry," she said. "I was going to a dance."

"A *dance?* What dance?"

"At Meridian Hills. One of those summer dances they have."

"With a date?"

"Harry was taking me."

Harry Stapler was a very nice, serious guy who had a good position at the Indiana National Bank and was madly in love with Buddie. As Sonny's mother so often and ruefully summed up the situation, hinting at her son's own lack of appreciation, "Harry Stapler worships the ground that girl walks on." His mother knew all the gossip about Sonny's friends.

"You mean you broke the date with him," Sonny asked with irritation, "at the last minute?"

"He understood," Buddie said.

"What the hell did you tell him, for Chrissake?"

"I told him something came up."

"Oh, my achin' ass."

Sonny chewed her out something awful for breaking the date with Harry, but all the time he was doing it he secretly somewhere felt this little twinge of pleasure that she'd done it, broken a date for a dance at a country club just to come and meet him at a goddam filling station.

After Buddie said how sorry she was, Sonny told her to drive to the Topper, he had to have a drink real quick. It was too early for the combo and the place was fairly quiet. The few people in the place stared at Sonny and Buddie, probably trying to figure out what a girl all dressed up was doing with a guy in a T-shirt and dirty khakis. Sonny felt like rum and Coke, and Buddie had that too.

"Is anything the matter?" she asked.

Sonny said he didn't feel like talking till he finished at least one drink. He sat in glum silence, swallowing the stuff like medicine. When the second round came, he lit a cigarette and told all about Luke Matthews and how pissed off he was at his mother. He said he felt like taking off for some place, just getting the hell out. He didn't want to go back and sleep in his room with that religious nut. They had more drinks, and Sonny said he was running kind of low so Buddie opened her purse and slipped him a ten-dollar bill under the table.

"Maybe I'll hitchhike to Michigan," he said after his fourth rum and Coke. "I could sleep on the beach. Bum around."

"Oh, Sonny. Don't do that."

"Why *not?*" he demanded.

"Something might happen to you."

"Who gives a shit?"

She reached across the table and touched his hand. "I do," she said.

He pulled his hand away. "I don't."

"Oh, Sonny."

"What?"

"I wish you were happy. I wish I could make you happy."

She sounded so syrupy sweet it made him sick.

"Fuck it," he said and ordered another drink. Buddie didn't have any more drinks. She had only another three dollars after the ten and didn't want the money to run out if Sonny still felt like drinking. The combo came on around nine, and the place began to fill up and get real smoky. That made Sonny cheer up a little; the hazy darkness and the booze and the music. The colored guys in the combo played fairly good jazz, the kind Sonny liked where you could pretty much always figure out what the melody was, the way Brubeck did it. After the second set Sonny had lost count of his drinks and he was feeling a lot less pain. He had one more and then figured he might just go home and sack out instead of hitchhiking up to Michigan and bumming around on the beach until he got arrested or starved to death or was carried away in an undertow or something.

Buddie drove him home and parked across from the house, turning the lights and the motor off. Sonny really just wanted to go on in and hit the sack, but he felt like he owed her at least a kiss, for being a good kid. He put his hand on the back of her neck and she scrambled all over him. Her mouth was open so wide he thought she might fracture her jaw. She was hot as a furnace. He tried to mess around a little, but he didn't really feel much like it. Her crinkly pink party dress didn't sex him up at all, and it scratched the hell out of him. He started thinking of Marty, the stuck-up Jewish girl at the museum, and imagining how great it would be to have her get hot with you. He closed his eyes, picturing how she looked, but he knew it was good old Buddie sprawling all over him. He pulled away.

"What's wrong?" Buddie asked in a hoarse whisper.

"We can't really do anything here," he said. "We better just stop."

"We could do *something*," she said and pulled his hand down, placing it inside her panties. "Please," she whispered.

Automatically, trying not to think about it, he felt around with his longest finger, rubbing it in the soft part between her legs. She was already wet. The finger probed inside, like a trained animal that didn't really have anything to do with Sonny. It moved itself around, obediently, performing its task. Buddie shivered and squirmed and panted, digging her fingers into Sonny's neck and then let out a frightening gasp as a sudden stream made Sonny's hand warm and sticky wet. Buddie rested her head on his shoulder and he sat perfectly still, thinking how great and exciting this had been in high school. The next day, when the guys asked you what you got the night before, you could say you got finger action inside the pants. That wasn't as good as really fucking but it rated right along with dry-humping and was much better than just the necking stuff like frenching and getting covered-tit or even bare-tit. It was really pretty much of a failure if you parked with a girl and got only covered-tit, and sometimes when Sonny just got covered-tit he actually lied if anyone asked and said he got bare-tit.

"Oh, darling," Buddie sighed.

Sonny took his hand away and wiped it on the upholstery of the car seat. "Listen," he said. "I really got to go."

Her crinkly dress was all scrunched around and tangled up, and her hair was a mess. She looked like she'd been through a wringer. "Call me," she said. "Please?"

"Sure. I promise."

He gave her a little peck on the cheek, got out of the car, and walked straight up to the house without looking back.

Most of the house was dark, but the porch light was on, and a light in the downstairs hall. Usually his mother kept the light in his room on for him—a torch burning in the window, "Make my bed and light the light . . ." but tonight it was dark because of the sleeping guest. Sonny felt his way into his room and to the desk, where he turned on a small lamp with an imitation antique shade of dark-green glass. He looked around the room, and sure enough, there was old Luke Matthews sacked out in the lower bunk. Sonny took off his shoes and socks and pants, and was ready for bed. Ever since he'd been old enough to get ready for bed by himself—his mother still put his pajamas on him until he asserted his independence at around twelve years of age—he mostly wore the shirt and undershorts to bed that he'd worn during the day. It was easier than taking everything off and getting into pajamas.

He climbed up the cunning little stepladder to the top bunk and rolled onto it. Luke Matthews made a sleepy snort and tossed below him. Maybe he was dreaming of his old, evil days. The book hadn't said exactly what the horrible shit was that Luke had done, but it must have been pretty awful to get him all that time in jail. Murder, maybe; rape, at least. Maybe old Luke had been a sex fiend. Maybe even a queer one, you couldn't be sure. A lot of the religious guys went in for that sort of stuff. There was one guy Sonny's mother brought home to save him during a college vacation who supposedly healed people by faith, but Sonny didn't go for the method of treatment. The Reverend Brownlow, who traveled with a mannish-looking wife and spoke often and glowingly of his young son who went to Florida State on an athletic scholarship, took Sonny into the bedroom and told him wonderful things would happen if Sonny would only kiss his white little flittish hands and say, "I love you," three times. Sonny didn't want to find out what the wonderful thing was and the Reverend Brownlow, shaky and perspiring, prayed that God would love him anyway. For all Sonny knew, Luke Matthews might favor similar methods of treatment, given the opportunity. Just because a guy was craggy-looking didn't mean he wasn't queer.

Sonny tried not to think about it. He tried to shut his mind and go to sleep, but he found that his hand was moving with a homing pigeon's habit-formed aim toward his prick. It was soft, and that only made him feel more urgently the need to make it hard. He thought of Marty the Jewish girl, remembering the way she carefully picked the little fleck of cigarette ash off her lower lip—that thin and sensuous, cool and arrogant lip. Sonny felt excited and yet, even though he coddled and stroked and massaged his prick, he couldn't get it hard, and that made him frantic. He had started to jounce around a little in the effort to coax his cock to attention, and telltale squeaking sounds began to escape from the bedsprings. He heard Luke Matthews stir below, and held himself perfectly still, barely breathing. Jesus, you couldn't jack off in the top bunk of your All-American-boy double-decker bed when a goddam professional Holy Man named Luke Matthews was sleeping in the bunk underneath! Or maybe the craggy old God-peddler was only pretending to be asleep, lying in wait to catch Sonny in the awful act and make him repent for his sins.

Sonny took his hand away from his uncooperative cock and put both hands under his pillow in the form of prayer. He concentrated hard on thinking of healthy, unsexy stuff. The courageous battles of World War II, Flying Fortresses raining vengeance on the evil enemy. Comin' in on a wing and a prayer . . . crisp autumn afternoons, and football. Knute Rockne, All-American. The Fighting Irish of Notre Dame. "Outlined against the blue-gray October sky, the four horsemen rode again." The Four Horsemen of Notre Dame. Most people could only name you three. The hard one was Miller. Don Miller. Most anyone could name you Stuhldreher, Crowley, and Layden. Elmer Layden, the fullback. When Sonny was a kid he had a game called "Elmer Layden's Official College Football," one of those board games painted like a playing field, a little metal football you moved back and forth and a tube with three dice you shook after calling a play to see how much yardage you made. Elmer Layden's Official College Football . . .

Oh, God in heaven. Sonny remembered something about the Elmer Layden game that he didn't want to remember at all. It was just the opposite of the healthy-crisp-autumn-afternoon sort of thing he was trying to concentrate on. After he got to high school he never played the Elmer Layden game anymore but it still sat around in his closet, along with Monopoly, Chinese Checkers, Photo-Electric Football, and Champion Ice Hockey, which consisted of a long metal plate with a little goalie at each end that you could turn around real fast with a knob and have them slam a marble back and forth with their sticks. He had outgrown them all, but found a new use for the Elmer Layden football game—a use that would have probably made Elmer Layden, All-American, puke with disgust. The cardboard "playing field" of the game was hollow underneath, so if you lifted it out there was a secret kind of box, a hiding place that no one was likely to discover. Sonny had used that innocent-seeming, All-American-appearing place to hide the dirty sex magazines he started buying in high school whenever he worked up the nerve to go downtown to the stores that sold them, stores that reeked of guilt and filth, where no one except the lewd old bastards at the cash register looked anyone else in the eye; those smutty, gray-faced perversion profiteers who sneered at you as they put the magazines you bought into the telltale plain brown paper sack. The magazines Sonny bought had names like *Titter* and *Wink* and *Peek,* and inside were pictures of impossibly sexy babes wearing black-silk stockings and elaborate garter belts and skyscraper heels, lolling their tongues in their luscious mouths, kicking their shapely legs in the air, adjusting the strap of their lacy brassieres that could barely hold in those pointed boobs. They promised the most unusual sort of evil erotic excitement and stimulation. Sonny would flip through the paper with a feeling of unslakable thirst, imagining what he'd like to do and have done to him by the different women, deciding which one he'd jack off to after he had sized up the whole gallery, playing out the scene in his fantasy, speaking the fake name of the woman in the picture that the magazine gave them to help you pretend they were real, and then setting his hard cock against the inside left part of his thigh so he could lie on it and rub back and forth without having to use his hand (a technique that seemed in its pretense more nearly like actual fucking). He would feel himself swell with a throbbing, incredible ecstasy that grew so intense it was almost unbearable until it burst, blotting out his mind in an ultimate blind moment of release, leaving him spent and limp, sprawled on the sticky result of his fantasy.

Afterward the magazine would seem sickening to him and he'd hide it away, as quickly as possible, under the green-cardboard football field, and stick the Elmer Layden game box underneath the Monopoly set in the closet. When it was over he felt lousy and dirty, and the magazines that only moments before had displayed the pictures of a paradise prized above everything else suddenly seemed ugly, shabby, shameful, embarrassing, and sick. In his nauseous revulsion he would sometimes stick them back in their plain brown paper sacks and and sneak down to the basement and shove them in the furnace, watching them burn to the black crisp oblivion they deserved. Then usually after a couple of weeks he would wish he still had them, feel a need for their pictures as deep as the urgent thirst that comes with a hangover, and he cursed himself for destroying the magazines, knowing he would have to put himself through the humiliating ordeal of going downtown to those smelly stores and forcing himself to do it all again.

Sonny hadn't used the Elmer Layden game ever since he went into service; when he got out of basic and PIO school he and some other guys got an apartment off the base in Kansas City and Sonny kept his girlie magazines in an old college notebook that had a zipper on it. He had thrown the notebook and the magazines inside it away just before he got out of service, though, as part of the abolition of his past, of wiping the slate clean and starting fresh. He could have kept the zipper notebook and used it for something else, but he didn't even want to be reminded of what he had used it for before. He felt sure that when his real life began he wouldn't feel the need for those magazines of sexy fantasy, not only because it was an adolescent kind of thing but because he thought he wouldn't need to pretend things then, he would actually *do* them, he would fuck sexy babes whenever he felt like it; until of course he met the just-right Rodgers-and-Hammerstein sort of girl across a crowded room and would fall in love forever and enjoy pure, legalized, clean, moral sex with his wife and be free of dirty thoughts and desire for the rest of his life. Actually, he originally thought that jacking off was just something you had to do until you fucked, and once you started fucking you didn't feel the need for masturbation anymore. It surprised and depressed the hell out of him when after he fucked for the very first time, struggling and slipping and panting on a moonlit golf course with Buddie Porter, he came home and jacked off twice. He figured that must have been because he wasn't madly in love with Buddie, maybe it was only when you started fucking girls you were madly in love with that you didn't have to beat off anymore.

Sonny's head ached from the rum, but he felt completely wide awake and terribly horny. He wondered if maybe there were any old girlie magazines left in the Elmer Layden game. He could take it into the bathroom and lock the door. As quietly as possible, he creaked down the wooden bunk ladder to the floor and stealthily made his way to the closet. The door whined when he pulled it open. He stood stock-still for a while, listening for Luke Matthews' steady breathing, then reached his hand into the right-side shelves of the closet where his old games were stacked. He tried to feel the right box by its size and started pulling one out that began to rattle. It must have been the Monopoly set, and the little metal pieces were making the noise. He shoved it back in with slow care. He felt the box below it and was almost sure it was Elmer Layden's Official College Football. He slipped it out little by little, holding the box above it with his other hand so he could let it down quietly when he pulled the Elmer Layden out.

Luke Matthews tossed a little and made a honking kind of snore sound. Sonny stood perfectly still, then after a minute or so of silence he tiptoed out of the room, holding the game steady so the dice wouldn't make any noise. He stopped outside the bathroom door, listening for sounds from his parents' bedroom right across the hall. All was quiet. He went in the bathroom and closed the door before switching on the light. Then he flipped the little lock on the door handle. Settling himself on the toilet seat, he carefully lifted the top off the Elmer Layden Official Football game box and set it on the floor. His heart was starting to beat a little faster in anticipation of the possible trove of erotic treasure just below the playing field. He reached his finger between the bottom part of the box and the cardboard playing field, lifting it off to reveal—nothing.

The secret storage place was empty. He must have burned the last batch of magazines in one of his fits of nauseous, self-hating zeal. He put the top back on the box and held it on his lap, trying to think of something. He was hornier and more frustrated than ever now. He set the game on top of the toilet bowl and eased himself onto the floor. There was a little round mat that was dark-green and probably wouldn't show the jizm too badly if he managed to get his rocks off. He lay down with his cock out on the mat and pressed his body over it, moving back and forth, picturing again the way Marty the Jewish girl picked the little fleck of ash off her arrogant lip. He imagined licking it off for her with his own tongue, thought of eating her tight little arrogant cunt until it got wet and inviting, then ramming in the full throbbing head of his cock. But nothing worked. He couldn't even get up a semi. After a while he realized it must be because he felt guilty, imagining that stuff with a girl that his good friend was hot for. Marty was Gunner's girl, or at least he wanted her to be, and Sonny felt like he was betraying his friend by imagining all this sexy stuff with his buddy's girl. What a shit he was.

Exhausted and guilty, Sonny tucked his cock back in his undershorts, picked up the game, and crept back to his bedroom. When he opened the door, the little reading light above Luke Matthews' bed was on, and Matthews was propped up in bed on one elbow, blinking and staring at Sonny.

"What's going on?" he asked.

"Nothing," Sonny said. "I'm going to bed."

"What's that thing—that box you're carrying?"

Sonny let out a long breath and said flatly, "It's a game."

"A game?" Luke asked, rubbing at his eyes. "What kind of a game?"

"It's Elmer Layden's Official College Football Game," Sonny explained, and stuck it back in the closet.

"Oh," Luke Matthews said, "I see."

Sonny climbed up the little ladder and flopped on the bunk, burying his head in the pillow. Luke turned off the bed light and said, "Well, good night, son."

"Good night," Sonny murmured into the pillow.

Aching and sweaty, his mind was tormented by the mouths of beautiful women that pursed to a kiss and then faded into blackness, sudden glimpses of silken thighs that crossed themselves into his consciousness with a whisper and then were gone, breasts that burst at his brain through the lacy constriction of their tight brassieres and suddenly evaporated. . . . Thrashing and scratching, he became uncomfortably entangled in the sweaty sheet, too tired to extricate himself, too dispirited to care, until finally, as a gray dawn turned the flat sky the color of soiled linen, he passed to the blessed void of a dreamless sleep.

3

Sonny woke up around one o'clock in the afternoon, feeling as if he'd been drugged and beaten on. Everything ached, especially his head. The only consoling fact was that Luke Matthews had taken off, probably in pursuit of more salvageable souls. Little wonder. The craggy old bastard wasn't any dunce, and he no doubt decided that a college-grad Army vet who kept bad company and played kid football games in the bathroom late at night was a more complex spiritual problem than his convict-holy-man training had prepared him to deal with. He could probably make more headway with your simple, ordinary murderer-rapist. Sonny at least respected him for realizing when he was out of his depth.

Mrs. Burns didn't mention Luke Matthews anymore, and Sonny accepted an unspoken truce on the matter. The only reminder of the departed Holy Man was his book, which still lay on the coffee table like an unexploded bomb, a dud of the salvation-literature armory. Though Sonny resisted the temptation to bitch about Matthews' visit, he became even crabbier and more irritable with his mother, and she became busier baking and cooking, turning out an orgy of cream-filled pastries, butterscotch rolls, and fresh berry pies. Sonny sat around the house stuffing in the goodies and despising himself, becoming more flabby and sullen all the time. He had quit calling Gunner in the evening for fear of getting Mrs. Casselman and having her snap at him, and nobody answered anymore when he called Gunner's place in the afternoons. He stopped getting hopefully excited when his phone rang because it usually turned out to be for his mother. Once when his mother answered the phone and said it was for him, Sonny quickly licked some butterscotch icing from his fingers and rushed to the upstairs phone where he could talk in private, figuring it must be Gunner. It only turned out to be Buddie Porter, though, calling, she said, just to see how Sonny was. Sonny said he wasn't feeling too well, but crossly refused her offers to take him for a ride or bring him some new magazines. He promised to get in touch with her if he thought of anything at all she could do for him.

When almost a week went by without any word from Gunner, Sonny began imagining all kinds of things that might have happened to his pal. He might have been turned down flat by the sexy Jewish babe and rolled up to Chi to take the job with the advertising agency. He might have decided to leave Indianapolis without even saying good-bye to anyone, even his friends. Or maybe, worst of all, he didn't think of Sonny as a real friend after all; maybe he'd got bored with Sonny and gone back to his old crew of big-timers, wondering how he'd ever got mixed up with a nobody like Sonny Burns.

Sonny's moping around got so bad that his father came into the den one evening while Sonny was watching TV and drinking a Pepsi, and rubbed his thumb against the

tips of his fingers in an awful, discomforting sign that he
was about to "have a talk" with his son.

"You ought to get out of the house, get some sun," Mr.
Burns said.

"Yes, I will," Sonny mumbled.

Mr. Burns cleared his throat and made the little nervous
forward motion of his knees, as if trying to make sure of his
stance. His face was flushed and frowning. "You can't let
yourself get *down*," he said.

"No, sir."

The terrible, pulsing silence fell between them, and Mr.
Burns let out a deep, despairing sigh and left the room.
Sonny wished himself dead.

The next afternoon Gunner called, sounding as casual
and friendly as if no time had passed at all, and said he'd
come by to pick Sonny up in an hour or so. When Sonny
got dressed, his clean khakis were so tight in the waist he
didn't know if he could even get down a beer.

Gunner wasn't in the brooding mood that Sonny last
saw him in, and in fact seemed on top of the world. When
they settled at a table over at the Key, Gunner explained
the whole thing. He'd been seeing Marty every night, and
he hadn't been home in the afternoons because Marty was
giving him painting lessons. She even had her own studio,
a top-floor room in a crumbling old apartment building
down by the Herron, equipped with an easel and all the
crap you needed to paint with, and even a hot plate so if
you got inspired you could keep right on going and heat
up some coffee or something and not even have to go out
until the fit of creativity had passed. Gunner said that
even though he'd taken an art course and messed around
with sketching, he had never painted with real oils, and
that's what Marty was showing him.

"I doubt I'll be any good or anything," he said, "but I
get a charge out of it. Just holding the brush, mixing the
paint on the palette. The whole bit."

Sonny felt even more loggy and good-for-nothing, sitting around all that time on his dead ass while Gunner was out mastering a whole new field of artistic activity. The bastard seemed to give out waves of enthusiasm when he talked about painting, almost like one of the religious nuts giving you the Christ line. But even though Sonny was impressed and curious about Gunner's progress in art, he couldn't help wondering how he'd progressed in other areas; like, for instance, the area between the luscious thighs of his new art teacher.

Not wanting to come right out and ask about it, Sonny just made the subtle observation that "I guess she didn't think you were a dumb jock after all, huh?"

Gunner grinned. "Well, who knows," he said modestly. "The whole problem was, I was playing defensive ball. When I first met her. You remember. Jesus." Gunner grasped at his head, embarrassed for himself. "I played it all wrong. Even when I first took her out. You know where the hell I took her?"

"Where?"

Gunner laughed disparagingly. "To a goddam foreign movie. At the little art movie theater they got now, down around Thirtieth and Capitol." He shook his head at what he obviously felt was his own stupidity.

"What was wrong with that?" Sonny asked.

"Shee-it, man. A truly bad call. I was trying to play her own game, you see? I was trying to be more intellectual than she was, worrying about whether I was coming off like a dumb jock. It was awful. She kept putting me down, naturally. But I was hooked, and when you're hooked you can't think straight. I could feel what was happening—I knew I was playing the loser, but I couldn't snap out of it. Like when you're trying to wake up from a dream and can't do it."

Sonny swigged anxiously from his beer. "So what happened?" he asked.

Gunner popped a cigarette out of a pack of Chesterfields and struck a match from a folder using only one hand. "I got pissed off," he said.

"At her? You mean at Marty?"

"Right. It's the only thing that saved my ass."

"How?" Sonny asked, feeling stupid as hell.

"Well, she invited me in for a drink after the movie, and we're sitting in this little den kind of room they have, and some serious music is on the record player, and she's being bitchy as hell. Just like the way she was that day at the drugstore. Remember?"

"Yeh, yeh."

"I was trying to talk this big game, a lot of intellectual shit, and she kept shooting me down. Every now and then she'd yawn, which was getting me more and more pissed. Then she made some crack about how boring the people were in the Midwest, and that's when I flipped my lid. Thank God. I just didn't give a damn anymore, and so I said what I really thought, not giving a shit if she liked it or not." Gunner sipped at his beer, smiling.

"What was it," Sonny asked, "that you said?"

"I said to her, 'Look, bitch, I didn't go to college in the East, and I'm no intellectual. I'm just a big dumb jock, but I know a couple things you don't know, or don't want to know, like I know I want to fuck you and I know you want it too.'"

"Jesus, what happened?"

Gunner made the sharp, popping snap of his fingers. "She was jelly," he said.

"Goddam," Sonny whispered in awe.

Sonny couldn't imagine himself ever doing anything like that, except with a girl like Buddie, who he already was sure of and thus didn't care too much about. But he knew that the mean, tough-guy approach really worked, and not just for Gunner. Sonny had avidly studied an article in a recent *Life* that explained how different movie

actors appealed to women. It said there was a surprising
number of women who were hot for Richard Widmark,
the guy with the madman grin who made this crazy little
laugh whenever he hurt someone. Sonny had seen the
movie where Widmark knocked off a poor old lady in a
wheelchair by pushing her down a long flight of stairs,
which sent him into a real peal of his crazyman laughter.
Life's analysis of why so many women were attracted to the
fiendish little actor was that "cast in his first movie in a
sadist role, Widmark appeals most to women who want to
be treated cruelly. This may be a larger group than is
recognized. . . ."

You bet your ass, Sonny thought. He figured he would
never be able to appeal to women that way and consoled
himself by *Life*'s analysis of why so many women creamed
over Frank Sinatra: "According to considered Hollywood
judgment, Sinatra's popularity is based on his appeal as a
mixed-up character whom women want to take care
of . . ."

Sonny felt that was his own best hope.

"I even brought home my first canvas," Gunner was
saying, having lost interest in the trifle of his sexual con-
quest. It seemed like now that he'd found some nice new
pussy he could afford to be interested in higher things, like
art. Sonny felt guilty for thinking that but he couldn't
help it, even though he knew he was probably just jealous.
He said, of course he'd like to see the canvas, and Gunner
drove them out to the Meadowlark, steering with one hand
and beating a little jazz rhythm on the outside of the car
with his other hand.

It was really hard to find much to say about the canvas,
and Gunner helped out by explaining, "It's more like an
exercise, a way of getting the feel of paint."

It was mostly just swatches of blue and green, laid on
very thick, and all Sonny could think of was the finger

paintings you did in grade school, but he didn't mention that.

"It looks like the real thing," he commented.

"Well, it's the real material, anyway," Gunner said and leaned the small canvas against a lamp on an end table. He put on a lively Brubeck LP and got them a couple cans of beer. Just as Gunner settled on the couch, the doorbell rang and he got up to answer.

"Is that your mother?" Sonny asked, hoping it wouldn't be.

"Don't know why she'd ring," Gunner said. "Maybe she forgot the key."

After the buzzer from downstairs there was a knock at the door, and Gunner opened it. Instead of his mother there was a middle-aged guy in a rumpled light-blue sport coat and slacks that drooped down in folds around the tops of his canvas rubber-soled shoes.

"Mr. Thomas Casselman?" he asked.

"That's me."

"I'm Mr. Libby, from Artists Unlimited." He edged his way into the room and asked, "May I come in?," after he already had.

Gunner looked confused, but asked the guy to sit down. "Are you a friend of Marty's or something?"

"Beg pardon?" The man smiled.

"Marty Pilcher. She's an art student, down at Herron."

"Oh, no, we're not connected at all with Herron. Or any other *local* group." He made *local* sound very small-time. "We're a national organization," he said.

"Well," Gunner asked, scratching at the back of his head, "can I get you a beer?"

"Oh my, no, not on the job."

He pulled a big portfolio onto his lap and cleared his throat. "I'm sure that you are just the sort of person who can benefit from our kind of personal, professional guidance," he said.

"I don't get it," Gunner said. "Who are you?"

"Mr. Libby, from Artists Unlimited. Here, I should have given you my card."

He handed a little printed white card to Gunner, who looked at it blankly.

"Yeh, I see, but I still don't get it. I mean, how did you get *here?* How do you know me or anything?"

"From your talent," the man beamed. "A small sample, of course. Yet enough for a professional eye to detect the kind of rough talent that can be sharpened and honed into—who knows? A true artist."

"What sample?" Gunner asked. "What are you talking about?"

"The little challenge in the matchbook cover—the drawing of a woman's head that you were able to reproduce with enough skill to bring me here today."

"The matchbox," Gunner said. "You mean the one that said 'Draw Me?' "

"I remember!" Sonny volunteered. "Yeh. It said 'Draw Me,' and you drew the woman on a napkin, at the Red Key. Remember?"

"I remember drawing it," Gunner said, "but I sure as hell never sent it in. I'd have had to send it in, for them to give you my name, wouldn't I?"

"Of course"—Mr. Libby smiled—"of course you sent it in."

"Goddam it, I didn't send anything in!"

"Well, someone must have," Libby said. "I'm here, aren't I?"

Gunner turned to Sonny, staring at him suspiciously. "You were there, when I drew the damn thing. Did *you* send it in?"

"Me? I wouldn't send anything in for another guy. Besides, you put it in your pocket. I saw you."

"Well, it's really academic," Mr. Libby said. "Perhaps you should simply accept the mystery as a further sign, pointing your way to a career in art. The important thing is, Artists Unlimited can start you up the ladder of that career, with a series of home instructions that *you* work on and send in to our staff of master artists for a personal, professional critique of each and every lesson you complete."

Gunner looked dazed. "Who the fuck," he said almost to himself, "could have sent it in?"

"It's as if you were sitting at the feet of one of our contemporary masters," Libby went on, "benefiting from his own genius, the secrets of his art applied to *your own work*. Within five days after sending in your completed lesson, you receive in the mail—"

The door opened and Nina Casselman walked in, pulling a big white floppy summer hat off her head and shaking her thick bright blond hair out with one hand in a way that Sonny thinks of a woman preparing for bed—but not for sleep.

She put one hand on her hip and asked, with her eyes wide, "Am I interrupting anything?"

"Not at all, I'm sure," Mr. Libby said, rising.

"Nina, this is Mr. Libby," Gunner said. "You know Sonny Burns."

Nina dismissed Sonny with a glance that was suitable for brushing off a gnat and swiveled over to extend her hand to Mr. Libby.

"I'm from Artists Unlimited," he said.

"Oh, really?" Nina asked with interest.

"There's been some kind of mistake," Gunner said nervously.

"On the contrary"—Libby beamed—"this young man, Mr. Casselman, has great talent in the field of art."

"Of course he has," Nina said. "He has ever since he was a little boy."

"Oh—then you're—his sister?"

"Thank you." Nina smiled. "He's my son."

"*Really,*" Mr. Libby said, "I'd have never—"

"Few people would," Nina said and sat down on the couch beside Mr. Libby.

"Nina, I was just explaining to Mr. Libby there's been a misunderstanding. Somehow this coupon got sent in to his company, with something I drew, and he thinks—"

"I think your son has great potential," Libby confided to Nina.

"Well, of course."

"Listen," Gunner said, "I swear to God, I don't even know who sent the damn thing in, it was just a thing on the inside of a matchfolder and—"

"The woman's face?" Nina asked. "The one you were able to draw so beautifully on a rough old napkin?"

Gunner's mouth opened and he pointed at his mother. "You," he said accusingly, "*you* sent it in."

"I certainly did."

"But I didn't mean to send it in! I never intended to send it in!"

Nina sighed and got out a cigarette. "Of course you didn't," she said, "you're so painfully modest."

Mr. Libby lit her cigarette, smiling with understanding.

"*Mother!* It was a joke!"

"Talent is no joke," Mr. Libby said reproachfully.

"Indeed it's not," Nina agreed. "When I saw that little coupon, and the way he had drawn such an exact reproduction of the woman's face—in fact, it seemed to me his was a little better than the face they showed—I just had to do something about it."

"Where did you find it?" Gunner demanded. "How did you get the damn thing?"

"I was going through your pockets."

"What the hell were you doing in my pockets?" Gunner shouted. "You haven't got any business in my pockets."

"I was only getting some things of yours together for the

cleaner!" Nina shouted back. "Doing you a *favor,* seeing you're taken care of, and what thanks do I get?"

Gunner slapped the palm of his hand at his forehead and was quiet for a moment.

"Your son may not appreciate it now," Mr. Libby said quietly to Nina, "but I assure you that in a matter of weeks, after he has completed Lesson Number One—"

"Look," Gunner said very quietly, "I'm sorry for the misunderstanding, but the fact is, by coincidence, I *already* am taking art lessons."

"What kind of 'art lessons?' " Mr. Libby asked.

"Private ones," Gunner said, looking away.

"Well, *this* is news," Nina said.

"I just started," Gunner explained, "recently."

"From whom, may I ask, are you taking these lessons?" Libby inquired.

"From an art student. She's an art student at the Herron, studying art."

"You mean that little Jewish girl you've been running around with?" Nina asked indignantly.

"What's 'Jewish' got to do with it, for God sake?"

"Well, she is, isn't she?"

"The point is," Mr. Libby said soothingly, "no student, of any kind, is able to give instructions as competently as a professional, accomplished professional artist. That goes without saying. You see, Mrs. Casselman, our course is designed by the leading artists of the land, and the lessons your son completes will be personally criticized by professionals in their field."

Mr. Libby no longer addressed himself to Gunner at all, but poured his soupy pitch entirely toward Nina.

"That sounds marvelous," she said.

"Imagine, being able to study under the masters of contemporary art."

"What 'masters?' " Gunner asked.

Mr. Libby smiled benignly. "Men like Orville Lockwood. Himself. He is on our board of directors."

"Really?" Nina said.

Lockwood was the guy who drew all the famous covers of *American Life* magazine that were so beloved by all. Or at least by most everyone. Secretly, Sonny got depressed by them, all those pictures of happy families with good old white-haired Grandma and overworked Pop and long-suffering Mom, and the mischievous kids, all around the Christmas tree or the Thanksgiving dinner table, the way everything was supposed to be. The worst things that ever happened in those pictures were little Spot the dog having to get a bandage on his paw or little Junior getting caught stealing from the cookie jar. The pictures always made Sonny feel that's how things were supposed to be and the fact that his own family wasn't like that at all made him feel worse about everything. He wished that fucking Lockwood would come and spend a Christmas at *his* house, with everyone sullen and on edge and disappointed, his father with a holiday migraine headache and his grandmother having hysterics because Uncle Buck had disappeared after the Christmas Eve office party, and his mother wringing her hands because she forgot to put the stuffing in the turkey. He wished the bastard would draw a picture of *that*.

"Orville Lockwood!" Nina said. "*The* Orville Lockwood?"

"The only one," Mr. Libby said proudly.

"Did you hear that, darling?"

"Yes, Mother," Gunner said. He had sunk into an armchair, staring at something far away.

"The entire course can be begun with only a thirty-dollar deposit," Mr. Libby said quietly to Nina, "the rest paid in installments after each of the twelve lessons."

"Only thirty dollars!"

"Mother, I haven't got it," Gunner said.

"Well I have!" she said and fished into her purse, bringing out a checkbook.

Gunner jumped up and shouted, "No, please! I don't want to. I don't want to take the lessons. I'm already taking lessons."

"I know what kind of lessons you're taking," Nina huffed.

"Don't you pay. Don't take her money!" he shouted at Libby.

Gunner had a big principle about not taking his mother's money or letting her pay for things for him after he got out of college. He had explained the theory about it to Sonny, about how a guy had to really be independent and if you took from people you owed them something, even relatives, maybe even especially relatives, because a lot of times what they wanted in return was more than money and more than you could pay. Sonny agreed wholeheartedly and knew that was right, but didn't mention to Gunner how he still got almost all his spending money from his mother. It was too embarrassing. He promised himself that when his real life got underway he would refuse any money that his mother offered him. He would stand on his own two feet.

Gunner ended up paying the down payment for the Artists Unlimited course and enrolling himself in the twelve-lesson plan, which came to a total of $120. Mr. Libby assured Nina that Gunner would never regret it. He didn't even try to assure Gunner, who was fit to be tied by then.

When Mr. Libby left, Nina mixed a batch of martinis for everyone, saying they certainly had something to celebrate. The beginning of Gunner's artistic career.

Gunner's eyes had begun to move back in his head, and he had a sort of blank, zombie expression.

"Now that you're having *real* art lessons," Nina said,

"you won't have to spend so much time with that little Jewish girl."

"Her name is Marty," Gunner said wearily. "You could just call her Marty. You don't have to put in the 'Jewish' all the time."

"Oh. Does it bother you? That she's Jewish."

"No, Mother. It bothers *you.*"

"Are you trying to accuse me of being prejudiced?"

"I'm not accusing anybody of being anything."

"I better get going on home pretty soon," Sonny said, but no one seemed to pay any attention to him. He was mainly trying to give Gunner an excuse to get out, but Gunner seemed in some stage beyond really being bothered, like he had switched off a whole set of nerves, or injected Novocain into his mind. Maybe it was some kind of Zen trick he'd learned in Japan. The Japs seemed to know the answer to everything—fucking and turning your mind off.

"I never said a word when you took out those little Jewish girls in high school, and even in college," Nina went on. "I'm as broadminded as the next person. But now, it's a different story."

"Why?" Gunner asked, out of the depths of his trance.

"For heaven sake, you're a *man* now. You'll be getting married."

"I will?"

"Well, won't you?"

"I don't know."

"Of course you will. You're at the age when any girl is a potential wife. You know that as well as I do. Don't play dumb."

"I'm not."

"Not going to marry her?"

"Not playing dumb."

"Then you *are* going to marry her, is that what you're

saying? You're telling me you're going to marry a Jewish girl?"

"What if I am?"

"Listen to him!" Nina said frantically, looking to Sonny for consolation. "Do you hear what he's saying?"

"Well, I'm not sure," Sonny said, swallowing what he hoped was enough martini to get him to the place where Gunner seemed to be.

"Of course, you're playing dumb, too." Nina said. "I forgot, she's a friend of yours. You introduced her to Gunner, didn't you?"

"No, ma'am," Sonny said.

"We all met at once," Gunner said. "At the museum."

"That's beside the point! Don't you know what it means, marrying a Jewish girl? Don't you know what they do, before they get married?"

"What do they do?" Gunner asked with real curiosity.

Nina started sobbing. "I hope she has a handsome father. I hope that much."

"Why?" Gunner asked. He sat forward, as if waked from his coma, still calm but now genuinely curious.

"Don't you know?" she sobbed. "Don't you know what they do before a daughter is married? Oh, God."

"What do they do?" Gunner asked.

"The father, the night before the wedding. He does it with his own daughter! It's part of the Jew religion—they make them do it!"

The tears were streaming down Nina's cheeks and dropping into her martini, which she clutched with both hands.

"Where did you hear that, Mother?" Gunner asked quietly. "How did you happen to come by that little nugget?"

"Everyone knows," she screamed. "It's common knowledge!"

She rushed to the bedroom, sobbing, and slammed the door.

Gunner ran a hand over his forehead and then slugged down the last of his martini. "Well," he said. "You learn something every day."

"Jesus, where do you suppose she got that?" Sonny asked.

"I dunno. Sunday school, maybe. Wherever it was she learned that Catholic priests charge two hundred dollars for praying the soul of a sinner into Purgatory."

"Two hundred?" Sonny asked.

"That was when I was a kid," Gunner said. "It's probably gone up, like everything else."

4

Sonny was relieved to know that Gunner was still his friend, but he realized there wouldn't be as much chance to hang around with him now, what with the sexy Jewish girl providing him with afternoons of art and evenings of lustful abandon. Or so at least Sonny imagined Gunner's schedule—a full life if there ever was one. Sonny determined once again to fill the long, hot days of his own existence with something more than whipped-cream desserts and television, swore he would try to "pull himself together," as his father put it. The summer was melting away like the unfinished ice cream Sonny left on his plate at breakfast, running out in a soupy mess.

To help himself get in a better mood, Sonny went out and bought a record of *Victory at Sea*. It was written by the great Richard Rodgers to go with a TV documentary about the glorious Battle of the Pacific in World War II, and when Sonny saw a rerun of the program he found himself closing his eyes and just listening to the music. It gave him gooseflesh and made him feel like a different kind of person. He played the record in his room on the portable Victrola he got for high-school graduation, and felt transformed. The music stirred him, made him aspire to finer things; as he lost himself in it, let it take him, he seemed to feel his mind and soul expand, as if they were getting oxygen. He imagined himself in a spotless white suit, doing noble and dangerous things, at considerable sacrifice to himself. Immersed in that music, he was cleansed of all desire for pussy, and he felt if he could just keep the music playing in his head he would never again be plagued by dirty thoughts. He would never even have to jack off anymore if he could just keep the lofty spirit of the music in him. Da-da, da-*da* dumm-dumm; da-da, da *da* dum-dum. . . . The sun on the water. Salt spray of the sea. Clean winds, whipping banners of Right and Justice. Men standing tall; chest out, shoulders back, stomach in. A sense of pride and honor. The best in man. A man who lived with that melody, who moved with that rhythm, would never be caught eating late-morning breakfasts of fudge ripple ice cream; such a man would never loll around the house all day, letting his life slip by, rotting his teeth with Pepsi-Cola.

After Sonny brought the record home and played it alone in his room, twice over, he did five push-ups and ten sit-ups. Even that much had him sweating and breathing hard, and he took a long shower, making it as cold as he could stand it at the end, gritting his teeth and feeling frozen but proud.

He put on clean, fresh clothes and sat down at his desk with a pencil and a piece of lined notebook paper. At the top he printed "Things To Do." The lettering looked rather faint, and Sonny went downstairs and sharpened the pencil with a paring knife. When he came back up he crumpled the paper and printed the title on a new piece. He stared at the paper awhile and then lit a cigarette.

After a while he wrote under the heading:
  —Job, career
    —Photography?
      —Talk to Biff Barkely, Indianapolis *Star*

Instead of writing more "Things To Do" he called up Biff, who said to come on by, he didn't go to work till four that afternoon. Mrs. Burns had the car, but Sonny figured it would do him good to take a brisk walk to the Barkelys' house, they only lived five or six blocks away. It was one of those cloudless days of glaring heat where you saw what looked like puddles of water on the street that disappeared when you got up close. Not a single leaf stirred. People were sheltered inside behind curtains and blinds, and nothing moved except the cars that slipped by, blazing with sudden reflections of sun. The discomfort hardly even bothered Sonny, and in fact made him feel tough, like a Foreign Legionnaire.

The thought of going to see Biff Barkely affected him almost like listening to *Victory at Sea;* it added a little bounce to his walk. Biff had been his first boss at the paper when Sonny was just a high-school kid submitting pictures of the principal handing a certificate to the winner of the American Legion Oratory Contest, or the home-ec teacher showing her girls how to operate a new sewing machine, stuff like that. Biff had taken an interest in Sonny, got him a summer-replacement job at the paper after his junior year in college, and became a kind of mentor to him. Mrs. Burns was always telling people that "Sonny thinks Biff Barkely hung up the moon," saying it with a grudging sort of amazement, as if she didn't quite understand it but supposed it was O.K. Sonny had noticed, even as a kid, that when he got to like someone a whole lot his mother sort of got mad at them, in a funny way. She would try to get to know them herself and treat them extra nice, but there was always a certain edge in her voice when she talked about them.

Biff was almost old enough to be Sonny's father, but he didn't seem that old. He was actually almost forty, but he wore a crew cut and sport shirts and seemed so damned active and alive that you thought of him as being a young guy. He talked like a young guy, too, not in what he said but in the way he said it—quick and to the point and often funny. Watching him moving along the sidelines shooting a football game was to Sonny a beautiful thing to see, like a complicated dance performed with grace and agility. Beside him, Sonny felt waterlogged.

Biff could shoot anything at all but he mainly liked working sports, probably so he could use up some of his wiry energy running back and forth and getting into weird positions and bolting out of them to scoot down the sidelines and catch the next bit of dramatic action. He had won some top awards and twice had pictures in the Best Sports Photography Annual, which wasn't just an Indiana thing but the best in the whole country. Sonny would have followed Biff into trenches or flaming walls, and maybe because his devotion was plain and simple, Biff confided in him sometimes about the intrigues and bureaucratic baloney at the paper and how things got screwed up by management guys who didn't know their business and tried to tell other people how to do their job. It was maddening. It was like that in life. Unfair.

Biff had a couple little kids and a good-natured, pretty wife whom he liked to tease, but not in a mean way. Sonny was very impressed that Biff never cussed or used dirty words in front of his wife. When she was around, Biff would come to the part for those words and just pause, like leaving a blank space, and then go on. Sonny really liked that. He wished he would meet some girl he felt that way about. And live happily ever after, never again dreaming of sexy whores in filmy black underwear. All he had to do was find a girl to marry who was soft and pink and smelled like a nursery—no, smelled of cologne, one he could call his own.

Sonny was humming love songs, thinking the words to himself, as he got to the Barkelys' house. He stopped then, feeling a little embarrassed, not wanting to give anyone the impression he was covetous of Biff's wife, in case anyone was reading his mind at the moment. Someone like God. Even though Sonny didn't believe in Him, he sometimes feared that God might be reading his mind at any given moment, trying to catch him thinking something wrong. That wouldn't be hard.

Biff's wife answered the door, wearing a sundress, a flowered apron, and her usual cheery smile. She made Sonny think of daisies.

"Welcome *home*, Sonny. Come in."

"Hi, Carolyn."

He had always called her and Biff by their first names, even when he was a high-school kid. That's the way she and Biff were, like friends instead of older people. Biff came hustling downstairs, shook hands, and said, "Coffee's on."

They went to the kitchen, where the coffee was on. It was always on. Black and strong. Biff consumed it with a nervous sort of hunger, morning and night. Coffee and cigarettes were his vices.

"Well," Biff said, "you're free, white and—twenty-two?"

"Three in October," Sonny said.

"So now you seek your fortune."

"I guess," Sonny said. "Soon, anyway."

"One generation riseth, and another generation passeth away."

"Not *you*," Sonny said with some alarm, not wanting Biff to think of himself as old or passing.

Biff bit on his cigarette, making it tilt upward, like FDR. "Not yet," he said.

"Naw," said Sonny. "Hey, I liked your Speedway stuff."

"Yeh? You go to the race this year?"

"No."

"Mr. Vukovich did right nicely."

Biff always called sports guys "Mister," maybe because most other people called them by their first names even when they didn't know them.

"I saw he did," Sonny said.

Biff bent his head down and sipped at his coffee. He smacked his lips and said, "So, you ready to come to the paper and make a nice, dishonest living?"

"Well, I don't know. I mean, I don't even know if they'd hire me. Regular."

"Only trouble is those pinch-penny"—he looked in the front room, where Carolyn was doing some darning, and instead of saying the word with which he would have described the management, he paused, making the blank space, and continued—"probably won't hire anyone new till one of our speed-graphic grandpas kicks off. We got enough deadwood around there to build a raft."

"Well, it might be a long time," Sonny said, "till there's an opening."

Biff shrugged. "Might. But we're not the only paper in town. Not to say in the country. Ever think of getting out?"

"Well, I *have* been thinking about the GI Bill. I could get a masters in something."

"Ah-ha! And Uncle Sam foots the bill."

"Most of it, anyway."

"What're you waiting for? You could go to Chicago, New York, even Paris. Pick yourself up some free-lance work with the camera."

"Well, I don't know. You'd have to be awfully good, in a big city."

"Phhhht. You're young. Now's the time."

"Well, maybe."

"Just remember, if you want to move up and out, don't wait till it's too late." Biff tightened his lips on the cigarette and sucked in hard. "Take it from yours truly," he said.

Sonny took a hot swallow of his coffee and asked, warily, "How do you mean?"

"The time to talk to the Big Boys is when you're young. I waited till just a year ago. Went to New York and made the rounds. Showed 'em my stuff."

"What happened?"

Biff made a kind of snort. "They patted me on the head and sent me back to the farm, where I belonged."

"But how? How could they do that?"

"Easy."

"But you've won prizes!"

"So've a lot of other hayseeds."

Sonny hated hearing Biff talk that way about himself; it depressed him in an embarrassing way, like hearing your own father cry.

"Aw, come on," Sonny said feebly.

"Them's the facts," Biff said. "The big city's full of bright young men."

"You're not old."

"Pressin' forty."

"That's not too old."

"It's too late."

Biff mashed out his cigarette, popped from his chair, and led Sonny down to the darkroom. He had some prints drying of some action stuff from an Indianapolis Indians game with the Toledo Mudhens.

"They're great," said Sonny.

"Minor league," Biff said. "Triple A. Just short of the majors. That's my league."

"You shouldn't say that."

Biff didn't answer, but started talking about what shutter speed he'd used to get the shot of a guy stealing home. Sonny tried to listen, but he wasn't really hearing it. When they went back upstairs, Sonny said he had to be getting

home, and Biff said he'd give him a lift. They didn't talk
on the way, and when Biff let Sonny off in front of his
house, he pointed a finger at him and said, "Remember,
you're young. Now's the time. You're one of the special
ones. You could really make it out, you could really get
out of here. Don't wait till it's too late."

Sonny nodded and turned away. There was something
in Biff's alert, lean face he had never seen before. It was
like he'd turned sour.

Sonny went straight to his room and turned the record
on, hoping to regain his high spirits. Seeing that sour part
of Biff made him feel pretty low, and Biff saying he had
the stuff to get out, to make it as a photographer in some
big city, scared him more than it made him feel good. It
meant he really had choices, which meant he might have to
choose. And he didn't know how.

He thought of other, less scary stuff to worry about.
That morning, in the general mood of his effort at self-
mastery, he had stunned his mother by accepting without
any argument her plea that "just the three of us" go out
and have supper at a nice restaurant. Ordinarily Sonny
shied from any situation that put "just the three of us"
together, alone—for it often seemed that their alleged
family was lonelier in one another's company than any
other situation. They always seemed to get locked into
straining silences and awkward formalities; a kind of embarrassed gloom would settle over them until, many times,
tears would start to form in the corners of Mrs. Burns' eyes
and Sonny would frantically find some excuse to escape.
Today, though, he wanted to face responsibility, to play
his rightful part like a man. Besides that, he'd begun to
feel guilty about always being so grumpy and farting off
his mother all the time. He even began to feel that maybe
she wasn't much different from other mothers. Watching
Gunner's old lady go to pieces about the Jewish girl had
somehow been a comfort to Sonny, made him realize he

wasn't the only guy whose mother got crazy. He sometimes wondered if perhaps there wasn't something that happened to a woman's head when she became a mother, like some of the screws getting loose up there. Maybe it was something they couldn't even help.

Mrs. Burns came home a little after five and said she and Sonny were supposed to pick Mr. Burns up at work and they'd go on from there to the restaurant. She drove the church station wagon in her usual jolting style, but Sonny tried not to let it get on his nerves.

"I talked to Biff Barkely today," Sonny said, which for him to volunteer to his mother was a regular gossip column of information.

"How nice! Did you talk about a job?"

"Not exactly."

"Well, no need to rush. You're only young once." She sighed and said, "It goes so fast. It's gone before you know it."

Sonny hated to hear his mother talk about her youth; it was one more treasure that was lost, like her shape, like his faith. It was actually hard for Sonny to imagine her being a young girl. The albums with snapshots of her wearing the bobbed hair and long beads and funny dresses of the flapper era seemed to him like pictures of another person. And yet she had been that person. He suddenly wondered if she had felt like a different person then, if she had been different on the inside as well as the outside in the days when she posed for those old, smiling pictures. He wanted to ask her about it, yet it was hard to put in words, the thing he meant.

"Do you still feel the same now as you did then?" he asked. "When you were young?"

"How do you mean?"

"I mean, do you feel like it's still the same you, right now, that you are the same person as when you were a young girl?"

She coughed, and the car bumped to a halt at a stoplight. "Yes," she said. "If I know what you mean. You
mean, am I the same inside, only older on the outside?"

"Yes," he said, "that's it."

"Yes. That's why it's so hard to look in a mirror. You are
looking at yourself, but you don't recognize yourself. It's a
shock. The person you see is older, and heavier, and has
wrinkles. But you don't feel that way inside, and it's hard
to believe that's how you really look now, how other
people see you."

"It must be very hard."

"Sonny? I tell you. It's the hardest thing in the world."

It was something that Sonny had never really thought
about before, and he felt a sudden, sharp sympathy for his
mother, not as "his mother" but as Alma, a person, a
woman who was growing old. He looked away from her,
out the window, at the stores on Broad Ripple Avenue.
Hardware. Five and Ten. Drugs. And there was nothing in
the stores, nothing in any of the stores, that would help.
There was nothing you could buy that would help; no
monkey wrench from the hardware store, no toys from the
Five and Ten, not even any drugs from the drugstore that
could change anything, really. Maybe just looking at the
things, though, and buying a few of them now and then
helped take your mind off the thing that you couldn't
change at all, which was that you were getting old, that very
moment, everyone everywhere, turning into the person
who would finally die and not be a person at all, no matter
how hard that was to believe. Sonny knew it was true of his
own mother; she had said it in a way, and he could see it.
He was sorry, and yet it didn't really make him sad down
deep, because he couldn't really believe it was happening
to him, too. He believed it in his head, but not in his
feelings inside. Even when he tried to grasp the fact, he
felt that it wouldn't be happening to him for so long that
by the time it did he wouldn't really care, it wouldn't

matter very much. Of course, maybe his mother had felt
that way too once, back when she lived in the snapshots
before they got curly and yellow.

Mr. Burns was waiting for them on the sidewalk outside
his office, and he insisted on getting in the back, leaving
Sonny up front with Mrs. Burns.

"Have a good day, folks?" he asked.

"Mmmm," Sonny murmured.

"So-so," Mrs. Burns said. "How about you?"

"Just fine."

Any day that went along pretty much as it should, without any major upset or unexpected catastrophe, was just
fine with Sonny's father. Somewhere along the line, some
years back, Mr. Burns seemed to have turned his emotions
down to low, like the barest flame you could get on a gas
burner before it went out altogether. That way you didn't
feel much, one way or the other; the decrease of joy was
maybe compensated by the decrease of pain. It was a kind
of bargain you made; a pact with neither God nor the
Devil but some gray, purgatorial mediator who fixed your
spirit with Novocain.

"Where we going?" Sonny asked.

His mother was driving far north on Meridian, and he
couldn't think of any restaurants out that way.

"We're going someplace first, before we eat," Mrs.
Burns said.

"Where?"

Sonny's father reached from the back and patted him on
the shoulder, smiling mysteriously. "You'll see," he said.

"It's a surprise," Mrs. Burns said.

Sonny was afraid of that. He started chewing at his
thumb.

"Sonny," his mother said. "Your thumb."

He took his thumb away and stuck a cigarette in his
mouth.

The car turned off Meridian onto a dirt road, and they

were in a flat, scrubby area with most of the trees cut down. A big white wooden sign said in flourishing scroll letters:

Rolling Hills Estates
For gracious modern living.
E. T. Garnisch, contractor

There was no hill, rolling or otherwise, as far as the eye could see. The goddamn place was flat as a pancake. There was a series of dirt roads laid out, like a grid, and wooden stakes that evidently indicated the subdivision of the lots. The pretend streets all had little street signs, wooden ones with hand-painted names. They turned on one that said "Wildbrook Lane." There wasn't any brook, but maybe there would be later. It would be easier to make a brook than a rolling hill.

Sonny wondered if his parents were about to go through the awful agony of housebuilding again, perhaps this time constructing a special wing on the place to serve as a bachelor suite, with personal den and private entrance. Then Sonny would be ungrateful as hell not to live in it after they had gone to all that trouble and expense. His mother was always mentioning Randolph Marbury, a nice, very shy fellow who worked at the Medallion Men's Wear on 38th Street and helped Mrs. Burns pick out presents for Sonny. The thing that his mother found so marvelous about Randolph Marbury was that even though he was thirty-something years old he still lived with his parents and claimed to be crazy about the arrangement. Randolph was always telling Mrs. Burns stuff like "Alma, I know some people think I'm funny or something, but I love my parents and I don't see why I shouldn't live with the people I love." Mrs. Burns would report Randolph's sentiments and add her own comment, such as "Personally, I think it's a wonderful thing for someone to love his parents and not be ashamed of it." Sonny would make a noncommittal grunt, understanding all too clearly the moral of the story.

Mrs. Burns stopped the car and said, "Well, here we are." They all got out and stood on the edge of an empty field, staring into the distance. There wasn't any grass in the field, just dirt and weeds.

"You tell him," Mrs. Burns said. "You tell him what it is."

Mr. Burns cleared his throat. "It's your lot, Sonny," he said.

Sonny looked at him blankly. "My lot?"

"We had a little something saved up," Mr. Burns said, "and we bought you this lot. Someday, when you're ready to build, you'll already have the lot."

"We know you won't be our little boy forever," Mrs. Burns said, forcing a smile that looked like someone was choking her. "Someday, sooner or later, you'll find the right girl, and you'll settle down. We want to help all we can, but of course we don't want to interfere. Do we, El?"

"Lord, no," Mr. Burns said.

"We just want to help. We manage to save a little now and then, and we get more pleasure out of doing a little something for you than we would for ourselves. We only want your happiness, isn't that right, El?"

"Lord, yes."

Sonny wished desperately that they wanted something else; it would make it easier for him to breathe.

"That's what we live for," his mother said. "Your happiness."

He couldn't look at them and he wanted to start running over the grubby fields, into the woods, as far as possible. The silence was smothering, and Sonny felt like screaming, but instead he said, "Well, thanks. Thanks very much."

Mr. Burns tentatively put a hand on his shoulder, which

was the sort of thing a father should probably do at such a time. "Well, it's your lot," he said.

Sonny looked out on the flat, dusty stretch of land and said to himself, *This is my lot. My lot in life.*

Far off, beyond a scruffy stretch of woodland, the sun collided with the flat horizon and began to bleed.

5

There was going to be a party of some art-student friends of Marty on Saturday night, and Gunner fixed it so Sonny could come, too. Sonny was really excited about it, figuring something might happen that would open up new possibilities for him, serve as an entry into real life. The problem was Gunner said he could either come alone or bring a girl, and Sonny couldn't decide whether or not he should take Buddie Porter. Taking her might be best because it would show the other girls there that he could get a girl if he wanted, that he wasn't some poor shlunk who couldn't get a date for Saturday night. On the other hand, there might be some fabulous girl at the party who he'd see across a crowded room and know was for him, and they'd madly embrace and live happily ever after. In that case Buddie would just be in the way, and he'd wish he hadn't taken her.

The more Sonny thought about the idea of a girl art student, the more aroused he got. He pictured her as

having long, flowing hair and a very thin, bony body fitted
out in black leotards. This girl would probably believe in
free love and scoff at all convention. She might have
studied in Paris and learned a lot of things there—not just
things about art. The more he thought about the imagi-
nary girl, the less he wanted to be saddled with Buddie,
and even though he'd made a date with her for Saturday
night, he called and explained he had to go to a party but
wasn't allowed to take anyone. He said the party was being
held in a very small house and there just wouldn't be room
for one more person. Buddie said that was all right, she
understood. She always understood. It annoyed the hell
out of Sonny.

It was hard to figure what to wear to the party, especially
since Sonny didn't know the people, but he knew they
would be artistic and therefore different. He wanted, as
always, to fit in and be approved of by everyone, but it was
extra hard to do that if you were trying to fit in with
people who didn't want to fit in themselves. If he knew
they would all wear gunnysacks, he would gladly have
gone out and got him a gunnysack. But he didn't know at
all, and that was the worst thing. Finally he settled on his
summer seersucker suit, which was pretty plain and neutral, but he wore with it his old white bucks, for a casual
touch, and an orange, satiny sport shirt for dash and color.
The shirt wasn't really like him, which is why he'd bought
it, hoping to add a little flavor to himself. The satiny
material had some sort of electric quality about it and kept
sticking to his skin in different places. The arms were way
too long, and he had to keep nipping at the sleeves to keep
the cuffs from bagging down over his wrists almost to his
knuckles. It was especially hard to keep nipping up the
sleeves when you had a coat on. You had to reach your
hand in under the coat and tug up the shirt from around
the shoulder. Keeping the sleeves up that way under a coat
made it look like Sonny had some kind of terrible itch that

he couldn't lay off of. Still, it was the only shirt he had that
was kind of flashy, and he settled on wearing it.

He got all dressed and splashed some Old Spice on him
right after supper, but the party didn't begin till nine, and
he didn't want to just hang around the house and let his
mother try to sniff out a lot of information from him about
where he was going and who he was going with and why he
wasn't taking Buddie. He closed the door to his room and
played *Victory at Sea* over once to get in the right mood of
confidence and positive thinking, and then he got the keys
to his father's car and took off.

Sonny just drove around for a while, the way you do
when you're killing time, turning here and there with no
particular purpose, gliding along and letting the people
who were going some particular place zip past. Just driving
could calm you down sometimes. The wheel gave you
something to hold on to, your mind could switch off everything but signals and traffic and your body sort of went on
automatic, working the clutch and shifting gears, pressing
the brake and nudging the accelerator just right. Sonny
was glad of cars. Not just because they got you someplace,
but more because they gave you something to do. Even as a
little kid who wasn't old enough to drive yet, cars had
helped Sonny that way, filling time, like when him and
Dicky Bishop or Bobby Sturdivant would sit on the front
steps of somebody's house on the block on those long early
evenings of summer after supper when the sky was gray
pearl and got dark so slow you barely even noticed it
happening. The way you played "Cars" was to have each
person guess what kind of car would be the next one to
pass—Ford or Chevy or Buick, or maybe a long shot like
Studebaker. For each right guess you got a point, and the
kid who had the most points after it got too dark to see
what kind of car it was for sure won the game. Actually
there wasn't much traffic on the block and you could win
by scores of 3–1 or 2–0. There were enough cars that

passed to make it possible to play if you sat for a couple hours, but few enough so that it was kind of exciting when one came by. When you guessed a lot of them right, it made you feel kind of spooky, like you had the power to see into the future.

Sonny drove around for almost an hour but it still was only twenty after eight, so he fell by the Topper to have a couple drinks. The place was just warming up for a big Saturday night, the smoke and the voices getting thick, and the colored guys of the Rhythm-Airs combo breaking out their instruments and plugging in the electric organ. Sonny took a seat at the bar and ordered a seven-and-seven. He had just started to take the first sip when some joker slapped him on the back so hard he jiggled the glass and spilled a little bit, hearing at the same time the unmistakable, maniacal laugh of Uncle Buck.

"Kilroy is here!" Buck said in greeting, and Sonny turned around and shook hands with him.

"How about stepping over to a dark little booth and joining me and a charming little lady for a drink?"

Sonny didn't really feel like hearing Buck's latest stories, it wouldn't help the confident, positive mood he was trying to build, but he couldn't see any way out of it.

Buck's girl for the evening was a bright-dyed redhead with a tremendous set of knockers that you got a pretty good view of through the wide cleavage of her tight, V-necked purple-cotton blouse. Buck just introduced her as "Gerry." His girls never seemed to have last names. They were always named something like Gerry or Flo or Stell, and they always looked wild and hard, like they'd had a lot of experience and were out to get some more.

"Hey, where'd ya get that fancy shirt, cowboy?" Buck asked, reaching across the table and fingering the satiny material.

Sonny could feel himself blushing, fearing maybe the shirt looked silly after all.

"I donno," he said. "Somewhere or other."

"Must of got it off one of the rodeo riders at the State Fair," Buck said with a laugh. "Hey, where ya headed all spruced up like that? Got a heavy date?"

"Not exactly," Sonny said.

He was terrified that he might let something slip about the party and Buck would insist on going along. God, Sonny could picture it. Buck would find out it was an arty crowd and start telling stories about his days in Paris studying with Rembrandt, and if anyone pointed out Rembrandt was dead, Buck would get pissed off and claim it was Rembrandt's grandson or something.

"Gotta meet someone in a while," Sonny said.

"Aha! A clandestine rendezvous!"

Gerry looked at Buck like he was a little wacky, or maybe was speaking a foreign language.

Buck nudged her, gave her a big lecherous wink, and said, "My esteemed nephew here is one of the silent types—but don't be fooled. Confucius say, 'He who talk little, get much!' "

Buck roared and slapped the table. Sonny bolted a slug of his drink, feeling his ears go red.

"I think he's kinda cute," Gerry said, looking at Sonny in a way that made him press his legs together.

"See there, I told ya! The silent ones get 'em every time!"

"Shee-it," Sonny said, finishing off his drink.

"Hey, let me fill that glass for you, friend and neighbor."

Before Sonny could say anything, Buck had called the waitress and grandly ordered another round. When Buck bought you a drink, he made it seem like Diamond Jim Brady had just ordered champagne for the house.

"And how's your good mother, my God-fearing sister?" Buck asked.

"O.K., I guess."

"You may tell her," Buck said with a flourish, "that her

ne'er-do-well little brother has just secured himself an
enviable position as sales manager of an up-and-coming
new corporation. A group of young go-getters have recently purchased a franchise for a new type of Infra-Ray
sandwich-heater that will revolutionize the concept of the
hot lunch. You don't need an oven, don't need a grille,
just set 'em up on the counter of a drugstore, what have
you. And yours truly will head up the management of sales
for the entire Midwest."

Sonny translated that to mean that Buck would be
selling sandwich-warmers on the East Side of Indianapolis.

"Seriously," Buck said, switching from his fun tone to
his serious, radio-announcer voice, "there's a mint in this
thing. It's there for the taking."

"Great," Sonny said.

Buck laughed and put his arm around Gerry, telling her
in his fun voice, "Stick with me, baby, and you'll be fartin'
through silk!"

"Mr. Big Bucks, huh?" Gerry said suspiciously, but she
didn't move away when Buck's hand slid down and gave
her a friendly little pinch on the right boob.

Sonny slugged down the drink as quick as he could and
said he really had to take off. He was sweaty and nervous,
and wanted to be alone, wanted to try and collect himself
before the party. It was almost nine.

Buck shook hands and gave him a knowing leer for good
luck, and Sonny said good-bye and headed for the door.
Just when he got about halfway there, in the middle of the
goddam bar, he turned back around as Buck yelled, "Hey,
Sonny"—everyone looked up from their drinks and talk—
"remember my motto, 'Work like a Trojan, especially at
night!' "

Sonny tried to grin, hearing snickers and giggles all
around him, and ducked for the door, frying inside.

The party was at a guy's named Oliver Shawl, who lived
on Talbott Street around 21st. Although the advancing

They had already crossed 21st Street on their long march north, *They* had left some pockets of whites still hanging on, as in this area. The whites who still lived there either couldn't afford to move or didn't care about *Them* coming in and lowering all the property values. That was the reason many whites retreated from the black wave, not because of prejudice but because of property values. It was strictly a practical matter, and it saddened many of the liberal whites who wanted to live next to coloreds but couldn't afford to because of property values going down, but did have enough money to afford moving to a nice new neighborhood farther north. So the whites who were left were either the ones who were so poor they couldn't even afford not to be able to move because they couldn't afford to stay in a mixed neighborhood, or the impractical dreamers like artists and oddballs who didn't even care about property values.

The block that Shawl lived on was still not all one color or the other. The colored were there, though, you could see it because they sat around on their porches, the way the colored do. It was the way they had of sitting around on their porches that seemed to annoy many white people, as if they did it in some colored sort of way that made whites cluck their tongues and say, "Look at them, sitting around on their porches," like there was something wrong about the way they did it.

Right next to Shawl's place there was a porch full of colored people, kids and grown men and old ladies, all mixed up together, sitting around talking and being colored. Sonny didn't look straight at them, but he tried to smile, sort of at an angle, hoping to show them he was friendly and supported the Supreme Court Decision, so they would be less likely to slit his throat with a gleaming razor. He had grown up hearing how niggers would just as soon slit your throat with a razor as look at you, and though he had learned in college there were many educated colored who didn't do that stuff, the razor thing always came to his mind when he saw one.

Shawl lived on the ground floor of a rickety old duplex badly in need of paint, and rented the upstairs out to students. As soon as Sonny walked in, he knew he had worn the wrong thing because nobody else had on a coat or jacket, everyone was much less formal than that.

Sonny hung around inside the door, afraid to plunge on in, but luckily Gunner spotted him and came right over. Gunner, of course, was dressed just right for the occasion, wearing his go-ahead sandals, a rumpled khaki shirt with the sleeves rolled up, and a pair of faded blue jeans that even had some splotches of paint on them. Already. You'd have thought old Gunner was born with an easel in his mitt.

Gunner looked Sonny over real quickly, probably wondering what the hell he was doing in a goddam cowboy shirt, but he didn't mention anything about it. He led Sonny to the kitchen, which was pretty moldy-looking. There was an old table with no cloth on it, and some gallons of wine, a few stacks of paper cups, and a giant box of Cheez-Its. There was a big old washtub on the floor with ice and beer in it, but Sonny said he'd like some wine. He figured that was more of an artistic kind of drink than beer. Gunner poured him a Dixie cup full of what looked like some dago red.

They went out to what must be the living room, though it didn't have any furniture except for a couple Salvation Army chairs and a kind of mattress on the floor with a bedspread over it that people were sitting on. Gunner told Sonny he wanted him to meet the host, and Sonny glanced around the room, looking for some tall, gaunt guy with haunted, artistic eyes. Gunner couldn't seem to spot him either, although there were only ten or so people in the room, but then there was a new, strange sound, a mechanical kind of whirring noise, and a guy buzzed into the room riding a motorized wheelchair. He was a neat, serious-looking guy who had evidently had one of those diseases that leaves your arms and legs as thin as curtain rods and pretty near useless. When Gunner introduced Sonny, Shawl just nodded and gave him the once-over with an expression Sonny hoped was a smile but looked much closer to a sneer.

"Join the festivities," he said, then whirred away, back toward the kitchen.

"Shawl is pretty cynical," Gunner said.

"I can understand."

Marty was there in a pair of her skin-hugging toreadors and a low-cut blouse knotted at the waist. She was sitting cross-legged on the floor with her shoes off, wiggling one foot in time to the music. It was a record of a guy singing and playing the guitar, but it wasn't hillbilly music exactly. It sounded to Sonny more like old English folk songs but it was about America. Something about This land is your land, and it's my land. . . . The words seemed a little communistic.

Marty smiled and nodded at Sonny but didn't interrupt her foot-wiggling concentration on the music. Sonny tried bobbing his head a little to the rhythm and looked around the room. There were four or five guys, most of them older-looking, and only two other girls besides Marty. One of them wasn't really a girl but an older woman around thirty-five or so. She sat on a chair in a corner all by herself, sipping a Dixie cup of wine and staring at nothing special. She was the only person sitting in a chair, unless you counted Shawl in his mobilized wheelchair. The only other female was a fairly young, arty-looking girl wearing sandals and Levi's and a man's white shirt. Her hair was long but more stringy than sleek, and to put it most generously the girl was rather hefty. The ravishing girl that Sonny had counted on seeing across the crowded room

wasn't anywhere to be seen. He should have brought
Buddie after all.

It didn't take long to finish the wine in the Dixie cup,
and Sonny went to the kitchen for a refill. He got talking
to a tall, skinny guy with glasses named Donald Hoskins,
who was a real painter, although he taught art to support
himself. Unless you were great like Picasso or somebody,
that's what you had to do to make a living, if you were an
artist. Hoping he didn't sound stupid, Sonny asked Hoskins how people got to see his paintings.

"You have a show," he said.

"Where do you have it?"

"Well, anyplace you can. In an art gallery, mostly. I had
one last year in New York. In an art gallery there."

"Hey, that's great. New York."

Hoskins smiled rather painfully. "I guess it's nice to
have had it," he said.

"Did you sell a lot of your paintings?"

"Two—or one, really. Maybe you could call it one and a
half."

Sonny wasn't sure if the guy was pulling his leg. "Can
you sell half a painting?" he asked.

"No, not actually. What happened was, one painting
was bought by a cousin of my mother who lives in New
Jersey. Another one wasn't exactly bought by anyone, but
it was damaged when the paintings were shipped back and
I collected insurance on it."

"Oh."

"I did get paid for it, anyway."

"Well, that's something."

Hoskins shrugged. He didn't look bitter, just sad. Sonny
couldn't think of anything consoling to say, and he eased
out of the kitchen, wandering back to the living room.
There was a smaller room off of it that was full of books
and magazines and papers. Sonny didn't exactly mean to
peek in on Shawl's private stuff, but he couldn't help

noticing that some of the magazines were those little egghead weeklies that were printed on rough paper and didn't have any pictures on the covers, just names of articles. Magazines that looked like that were usually pretty pinko, and Sonny wondered if maybe Shawl was actually a Commie. They said it was people who were bitter and down on everything who joined the Commies, and God knows Shawl had a right to feel that way. Maybe the whole place was a secret communist cell; with the magazines and the folk music and everything, that's about all you'd need. It was hard to tell, though, and Sonny was kind of ashamed of himself for being suspicious. Jesus, there were even some friends of his mother who thought *he* was one, so he shouldn't go around suspecting other people, not unless he really had the goods on them. . . . Even then you didn't always know. McCarthy claimed to have the goods on all kinds of people, but other real proven Americans, even United States Senators, said he was full of baloney.

Sonny went back and sat down beside Gunner. There was a cool jazz record on now, one of the ones with a soft, moany trumpet, and Marty had her eyes closed, all absorbed in the music. Sonny asked Gunner in a whisper, "Is Shawl an artist himself?"

"No, he works on the *Times*. He edits stuff, on the copy desk."

The *Times* was the only paper in town that supported Democrats sometimes, but that was probably because it was part of a national chain, and maybe because of that it wasn't as widely read as the *Star* and the *News*. Some people didn't quite trust the *Times,* maybe because it supported Democrats sometimes or maybe because it was owned by outsiders.

"Shawl likes artists, though," Gunner explained. "They're more in line with his own views about things."

"His views?"

"Yeh, you know. Against the status quo and all."

"Oh."

Gunner said it casually, as if there was nothing to worry about. Sonny just hoped old lady Armbrewster never got a load of Shawl and his crowd. She'd have J. Edgar Hoover on them in nothing flat.

Besides Shawl himself there was another guy there who wasn't really an artist but was pissed off at the status quo. His name was Eddie Messner and Sonny remembered him because he used to play ball for Shortley. When Sonny was a kid only eight or nine years old, he started reading everything in the sports page and he knew the names of all the Shortley players, who seemed like remote gods to him, even the reserves. Messner hadn't been a star but he fought his way into the starting lineup in his senior year. He was what the sports pages call a "watch-charm guard," which meant that even though he was only a little bastard, the coach had stuck him in the line with the monsters who slogged around and battered the shit out of each other and were trampled all over by the backs and never got the glory. Sonny had also seen Messner officiating some of the football games at Shortley when Sonny was taking pictures for the *Echo*. Officials made a little money for working a game but mainly they were old jocks who liked to do it just to have an excuse to wear a uniform again. Messner didn't like his real work very much, which was selling vacuum cleaners, but it gave him time to knock off when he wanted and officiate a ball game. Sonny remembered once before a ball game Messner was in the locker room talking to some of the guys about his crummy job, telling them they better get their glory and enjoy it now 'cause soon enough they'd be peddling some damn thing just like him. It really depressed Sonny, hearing an older guy talk like that to a bunch of young guys.

Sonny's dislike for Messner got even worse because of the way he was acting at the party. He was flirting around with the fat girl art student, just like she was his own age or something. Sonny thought it was pretty crummy for old bastards in their thirties to horse around with young girls like that. Messner seemed pretty drunk, and Sonny wondered if he was Irish. He looked like he might be. He was small and wiry and had the kind of thin red hair that showed the freckles on the top of his head. He was sitting on the mattress thing on the floor in a corner of the room, practically trying to feel up the fat girl right in public. Sonny wished if the guy had to fool around he'd pick on the blond gal in the chair, who was more his own age. She looked real lonely and probably would have liked the attention, even from Messner.

Just when Sonny was thinking all that stuff about the guy, Messner suddenly yelled out real loud, "Hey, Casselman—are you the great Gunner?"

Everybody turned to look, and Gunner just said, "I'm Casselman."

"Didn't reck-a-nize ya at first. Didn't expect to see a Big Rod out slumming with us oddballs."

"What do you mean slumming?" Gunner said.

Messner laughed, but it wasn't a funny laugh. "They had the same system back when I was at Shortley," he said. "I know all about the Big Rods. They stick together, they don't give a tumble to the peasants."

"Jesus, man," Gunner said, "that was *high school.*"

"Once a Big Rod, always a Big Rod."

Gunner shook his head, disgusted like, and took a swig of his beer.

But Messner wouldn't let up. "I played ball, too," he said. "Even started my senior year. But that's not enough to be a Big Rod. You gotta come from the right background. Your old man has to belong to the country club and have a big house set back on Meridian Street or Washington Boulevard."

Gunner looked like he couldn't believe what he heard.

He raised his own voice for the first time. "You're fulla shit, man."

Gunner was right. There were plenty of rich kids who never made the In Group, yet some of the Big Rods—Gunner himself, in fact—were from families that seemed to barely scrape by, and the kids had to work part time.

If they played ball they had to work on weekends or nights or get up at five in the morning and carry *Star* routes with a couple of hundred customers, or maybe do all that stuff. Just being rich couldn't make you a Big Rod, but evidently that's what Messner had made for his own excuse. It must have made him sore as hell to beat his brains out making the football team and *still* not get In, so he had to blame it on something that wasn't his fault, like his family not being in the bucks. At least Sonny never fooled himself that way. He knew damn well you didn't get to be a Big Rod just by being rich, or even good-looking, or even a good athlete—you had to have some quality that was hard to pin down, a certain kind of confidence, a little swagger but not in a boastful way, an easiness, a style, an air of casual good nature, of leadership that wasn't sought but seemed to come natural. You couldn't pin it down but you could see it in a person.

"You're telling *me* I'm fulla shit?" Messner said, pointing a thumb at his chest, as if to make sure.

"You are if you believe that crap about money," Gunner said. "My old man traveled for Goodyear and he kicked off when I was ten. My old lady got a job as a saleslady at Ayres, I got a morning *Star* route and set pins at the Broad Ripple bowling alley. In the summer, when I got old enough, I worked construction and caddied on the weekends. We lived in a double at Thirty-ninth and Winthrop and the Monon railroad went right in back of the house and the whole place shook like an earthquake had hit whenever a train went by. You call that a big social country-club background?"

"Whatya want us to do, cry in our beer?" Messner said.

"No, man—just quit crying about what happened to you in high school. For Christ sake, man, how old are you now? How long have you been out?"

"I'm old enough not to have to take any bullshit from a punk like you."

Messner got to his feet and hitched up his pants. He had on a pair of old brown slacks, a moldy-looking T-shirt, and tennis shoes without any socks.

Without planning it or thinking about it, Sonny found that he was standing up too, facing Messner. He was scared shitless of fights, but something deeper than fear was moving him now.

"He's my friend," Sonny said. "He isn't any punk. You shouldn't say that."

"You gonna stop me, you little suck-off?"

"For God sake, Eddie, sit down!" yelled the lady who was sitting all alone. Messner didn't pay any attention to her, didn't even act like he heard. Sonny stood rooted in his place, ready for whatever had to happen.

"You shouldn't say terrible stuff to people," Sonny said. He heard his voice from far away, like it was coming from someone else.

"You trying to suck off the Big Rod, huh?" Messner said.

"Hey, Messner, just take it easy, man, O.K.?" Gunner said evenly. He didn't move from his place on the floor.

Marty put her arm around Gunner and said, "Go have a beer, Eddie."

That seemed to make Messner even madder, and little red splotches came out on his cheeks, like a disease.

"So, your suck-off buddy has to protect ya, and even your hot little piece of tail has to protect ya, huh?"

Gunner stood up. "I said you better take it easy, man."

The lady who had yelled for Messner to stop was leaning forward in her chair, twisting her hands together. "Please, young man, don't hit him," she said to Gunner.

Gunner turned to her and held up his palms. "Jesus, lady, you think I *want* to?"

"Just keep your mouth clean when you're talking to my wife," said Messner.

Gunner did a double-take on the woman, and so did Sonny. Christ, if it wasn't Mrs. Messner, sitting all by herself while her husband got drunk and fooled around with a young girl art student right in front of her face.

"I'm sorry," Gunner said to her.

"You damn well better apologize," Messner said. He took a couple steps closer to Gunner and Sonny, hitching his pants up again with a sort of James Cagney move. He was a good four or five inches shorter than Gunner, and probably thirty-some pounds lighter. If the dumb bastard really started something, Gunner would clean his ass. Sonny figured Gunner didn't really need his help, but he wanted to help anyway, he wanted to be there when it counted.

They all stood there staring and then there was a whirr into the room and Shawl buzzed up between the potential combatants in his jazzy wheelchair.

"There will be no primitive combat," he said. "You are guests in my house, all of you. You will have to make the apparently difficult effort to comport yourselves like civilized human beings."

"I'm sorry," Gunner said. "I don't want to cause any trouble."

"Ah, how heroic, how chivalrous!" Messner taunted.

"Mr. Messner," Shawl said in the tone of a stern professor, "if you can't control your hostility, I shall have to ask you to leave."

"Who's hostile?" Messner challenged.

Mrs. Messner had stood up and gone to the front door. "Let's go home, Eddie, please," she said. "I'm going home."

Messner turned away, deflated, and mumbled, "I'll be along in a while."

Mrs. Messner took one last look as her husband settled back down next to the fat girl. It was like she was turning her cheek for one more slap before leaving.

Someone put on one of those brassy, blasting Kenton records, and everything seemed to settle down.

Gunner let out a long, tired sigh and rubbed at his temple. "High school," he said quietly. "Fuckin high school. Doesn't it ever get over with?"

Sonny was wondering that himself, and his suspicions didn't cheer him up too much.

"Let's go," Marty said. "Let's get out of here."

She turned to Sonny with a look of real concern and affection. It seemed like the first time she had really looked at him.

"You come with us," she said. "You oughtn't to stay around here by yourself. That Eddie's liable to get crazy again."

"Right," Gunner said. "We'll meet you at the Key."

They managed to get one beer down before closing time, and even though they were pretty low after the Eddie scene, there was a warmth among them that was nice.

When they left to go home, Gunner biffed Sonny one on the arm and said, "Thanks, buddy."

"Yes," said Marty and squeezed his hand.

"Shee-it," Sonny said.

He felt very glad that he had acted in a way he never had before, that he had shown where he stood. It almost made up for the absence of the beautiful girl art student he had expected to meet at the party and fall madly in love with.

He went home to bed and jacked off thinking about her, the way he imagined she'd be. Maybe he would really meet such a person and really get married to her. Gunner would be the Best Man.

6

The day after the party was a stifling summer Sunday, and
Sonny woke up around eleven, bleary and slightly nauseous. His parents were at church, and he went down to the
kitchen and had a couple aspirin, a Pepsi-Cola, and a
peanut-butter sandwich. He took the Sunday *Star* out onto
the breezeway and experienced the soothing relief that
came with the anticipation of sinking into the sports
section and the funnies, those magic parts of the paper that
at least for a while had the power of pushing the everyday
fears and fuming thoughts of the future clear out of his
mind. He hadn't even finished the funnies, though, when
his parents came back, blessed for another week, and Mrs.
Burns reminded him today was the day they all had to go
to Grandma Lee-no's for one of her big Sunday meals.
Sonny had put this occasion off ever since he'd been home
but there was no getting out of it any longer. Grandma
Lee-no had called a few days ago and said that she knew
nobody loved her anymore and she was just a worthless old

woman, but anyhow she was cooking up a real big Sunday meal and if everyone didn't come and eat it she was going to kill herself.

Not wanting to have his grandmother's blood on his conscience, in addition to all his other guilts, Sonny made himself go get dressed. Grandma Lee-no was his mother's mother, and Sonny had "named" her when he was a little boy who couldn't pronounce her real name, Leona. Like everything he did then, Grandma Lee-no thought the name he gave her was the cutest thing in the world and cherished it as a special gift from her "little angel-child," which was what she called him then and in fact still did, insisting, "You may be all grown up but you're still *my* little angel-child."

Grandma Lee-no lived in a little house up on Guilford that Sonny and his parents had lived in until they built their own place and gave the old house to Lee-no, who had just retired about then from a lifetime of service at the Indiana Gas and Utility Company, where she worked one of the switchboards, raising her children without any help from that fly-by-night no-good Johnny Haspel, who had left with some floozy for parts unknown when Alma was just a little girl and Buck was still a baby. Oh, yes, he came back and visited every few years when the kids were growing up, bringing them toys and trinkets and buttering up to them with his old snaky charm, making them think he was wonderful—until they were old enough to understand he was nothing but a two-bit liar with a slick tongue, all promises and no delivery, just like most men. They were so cute when they were little boys, but then they all grew up to be—*men.* Even little Sonny had gone and done it, just like the rest of them, but Lee-no still loved him anyway.

"Oh, my lit-tul *angel*-child," she cried when Sonny came in her front door. "Kiss your pore old ugly grandma."

Sonny leaned down and bumped his lips dutifully and

dryly against her slack, parchment cheek. Her wiry little arms squeezed his waist, and he pulled away.

"Hello, Lee-no," he said.

"Oh, I know you don't want Lee-no to squeeze you anymore," she said. "Nobody loves an ugly old woman."

"I love you," Sonny mumbled and sat down on the couch.

"Sonny loves you," Alma assured her, "We all love you, Mama."

"Lord, yes," Mr. Burns said.

"Well, you all just sit down by the fan there. I'm still a-cookin'."

The whole house was like an oven, and the little oscillating fan on the floor buzzed bravely but only sent out enough of a breeze to sort of tickle you. Alma went to the kitchen and Sonny and Mr. Burns picked Lee-no's Sunday paper apart, trying to find something to distract them. Not even the funnies and the sports could work their magic on Sonny in Lee-no's house, though; there was an oppressiveness about the place, a sort of invisible gravy of despair that clogged your senses. The many mementos and photographs and figurines that cluttered the mantel and the marble-topped table and the knick-knack shelves didn't brighten things but seemed to Sonny like little symbols of sorrow and betrayal; a picture of Sonny as a cute little boy in a sailor suit, his cheeks tinted with rose, smiled from a heart-shaped frame; a grayish picture of Alma as a fair young maid, circled with silver; a model airplane curved and painted by Buck as a boy, a plaster Jesus kneeling in prayer, a silver reindeer Sonny had liked to play with long ago, a gold Statue of Liberty that Johnny Haspel had sent from the 1939 World's Fair (it turned out to be the last thing anyone heard from him), a snapshot of Buck with some Army buddies just before he was sent overseas, a pincushion that looked like a tomato, a souvenir plate with a picture of the White House that Miss Verbey from across the street had brought from her trip to Washington.

The house grew smokier and hotter as mealtime neared, and when everything was done, Grandma Lee-no came out with tears in her eyes, wiping her hands frantically on her apron, and said, "I guess we'll have to go ahead. Buck's not here, wasn't here all night, never called. The Good Lord knows if he'll ever come back."

"Now, Mama," Alma said, following Lee-no into the living room, "you know Buck, he's all right."

"He never tells me anything," Lee-no whined.

Mr. Burns cleared his throat and reddened. "He'll be back, don't worry. When he's hungry or out of money, he'll be back, I'll guarantee you that."

Uncle Buck, having been recently divorced for the second time and "between jobs" again, had moved back with Lee-no, who still feared every time he went on a toot and didn't show up for a few days that he had come to a bad end, been murdered or kidnapped. It was not clear to Sonny who would wish to kidnap Buck or from whom they might expect to extort any ransom money. Certainly not from Mr. Burns. Sonny didn't mention that he had seen Buck in the Topper only the night before and that he was probably right now humping away on that sexy redhead he'd been with. Sometimes Buck had the nerve to take his girls home to Grandma Lee-no's and fuck them right on the rollaway bed in the dining room. If Lee-no discovered Buck in the bed with a woman she would scream and holler and pound her fists on the wall and threaten to call the Army, the Navy, and the Marines. Lee-no didn't seem to have too much confidence in ordinary police.

Everyone gathered around the dining-room table, which steamed like a caldron with gravy and potatoes and a monster chicken stuffed with dressing. All bowed their heads while Grandma Lee-no said grace:

"Dear Heaven-ly Father, we ask thee to bless this food,

in the name of thy Son, Jesus Christ. And bring Buck back home safe again."

The grace-prayer seemed to have relieved Lee-no, and she turned to her joking mood, saying, "Good-bread-good-meat-good-God-let's-eat!"

"*Ma*-ma," Mrs. Burns said, as if she were shaming a naughty but lovable child.

Grandma Lee-no banged her fork on her plate and said, "If that bad boy isn't home by dark, I will call the Army, the Navy, and the Marines!"

Mr. Burns sighed and asked, "You want me to carve, Lee-no?"

"Oh thank you, Ellie. You're *sech* a gentle-man!"

Mr. Burns stood up and attacked the great, stuffed bird.

"You can give me dark meat, as long as it's *that* kind," Lee-no cried. "Don't want any that *other* dark meat, though, that what's taken over." She held her nose and said, "Pee-yue!"

"*Ma*-ma," Mrs. Burns cautioned.

"Well, I don't care, Alma. I wished my daddy was alive now, he said way back then in the Depression the Jews and the niggers were a-gonna take over, and the good old Klan was the only thing'd stop 'em, by golly!"

"For God sake, Lee-no," Sonny said and stood up from the table.

"An-gel child!" she whined.

"Sonny! She doesn't mean it," Mrs. Burns said.

"Why, Alma, I mean every word," Lee-no insisted. "Just like Daddy use to tell us: 'We're KKK and we mean what we say!' *Whoo*pee!"

Sonny headed blindly for the door, hearing behind him the sudden sobs of Grandma Lee-no, crying through the fumes of food, "Let him go, he hates me anyway, I might as well die."

Sonny stood for a while on the front porch and then

came back in and shoved himself up to the table. He crammed himself with the food so purposefully and indiscriminately that by the end of the meal Grandma Leeno was no longer threatening to die. In fact, she felt good enough to sing "Moonlight and Roses," which she claimed Sonny used to love to hear when he was her little baby angel-child and she rocked him in her arms at night until he went off to "seepy-time."

He said he remembered.

The next day Sonny felt worse than if he'd been boozing all night. His stomach was stuffed and his head glommy. He tried to do push-ups, but could only make five of them. He took a shower, drank an Alka-Seltzer, and sat in the den leafing through magazines. He hadn't kept up with his plan to read every new issue of *Newsweek*, hadn't even bought one for almost a month. He had already read most of the *Life*s and other serious magazines in the house, and about the only thing he hadn't gone through already was a June issue of the *Ladies' Home Journal*. He flipped through it and came to an article called "Young Home-Builders." It was about a young couple who had built their own terrace, and told how to do it.

> When next-door neighbors George and Mary Mallen drop over, or we give a dinner for relatives, the terrace gives us elbow room. Breezeway door opens on back yard; so does kitchen door, for food transporting. Plastic dishes are kept in barbecue shed; it also holds a handy grill on wheels.
>
> Breezeway's coffee table matches window seat; Don topped both in green plastic, smoothed over adhesive with a rolling pin. That magazine holder on the wall? Bright cotton—with pockets!

There was a picture of a young guy in a sport shirt sitting at a little table reading a newspaper, while his wife sat on the other side, watching him read. Sonny wondered if he would be doing that in a couple of years, on his own clever little terrace. Maybe it wouldn't be too bad, if you had some wife you were madly in love with. What the hell else were you supposed to do?

Sonny didn't really feel like thinking things out, at least by himself. He wished to hell Gunner would call, and they could tip a few cold ones and philosophize about stuff. Sonny sat around the house all day, and the next day too, but Gunner still didn't call. Maybe he had gotten in thick with the arty crowd, but Sonny kind of doubted it. They were obviously suspicious of him because he had been a Big Rod, just as his old Big Rod friends were suspicious of him because he was going out with a girl from the arty crowd and was always asking those weird questions, asking people why they did or thought what they did. There was even a rumor around that Gunner had been shell-shocked in the war, which explained the change in his personality. His old friends were relieved to know he couldn't help the way he was acting, and they figured he'd snap out of it sooner or later. Sonny guessed it was probably the first time in Gunner's life he had been on the outside of things. Still, he had a sexy girl and he had his art, so you couldn't feel too sorry for him.

Sonny was frankly more concerned with himself, his failure to get his real life started. He felt himself slipping into the same old nonlife of sleeping through half the day and eating through the rest of it, and he figured anyway the more he just waited for Gunner to call, the less chance there was of it, like the watched pot that never boils. He couldn't depend on Gunner or anyone else to get him off his ass, he had to take the bull by the horns himself.

> I am the master of my fate
> I am the captain of my soul. . . .

He repeated that over and over in his mind, a litany that left out God but still was inspiring. He started getting up around ten, taking a shower, doing his push-ups, and playing the *Victory at Sea* record. He did that three days in a row and worked up from seven to nine push-ups by the third day. He bought himself a copy of *The Caine Mutiny,* and reading it made him feel that even if he still was sitting around a lot he at least was improving his mind with literature. Besides it was a good story and blanked out his mind almost as well as the funnies and the sports page.

One day he called up Buddie and got her to take him down to the Herron so he could get another look at the art. Maybe he was partly hoping they might run into Gunner and Marty, but they didn't, even though they went for coffee at the drugstore across the street. Sonny found himself getting very irritated at Buddie. She didn't seem to know what to say about the art they had seen, any more than Sonny did, and she was wearing a little-girl-type sundress that was about as sexy as a paper bag. He kept thinking of Marty in her skin-tight toreadors, and getting more grouchy. He refused to go swimming with Buddie and got pissed off as hell when she noted he was white as a sheet even though it was the middle of summer. He made her take him home and went to his room to work on another "Things to Do" list. He wrote on it:

Take more pictures
    —Send for university catalogs
        Graduate schools
            —photography?
    —Get some sun

He was tapping the pencil against his teeth, thinking of other constructive things to do, when the phone rang. It was Gunner, sounding very mysterious. He said he had something to show Sonny but it wouldn't be quite ready for another few days. He'd call him when it was.

Sonny felt much better after the call. He was sure the phone had rung at that particular time because he was already going ahead on his own with constructive plans, not depending on his friend. That's the way things worked —if you sat around waiting for something to happen, it never did, but if you forgot about it and made yourself get on with things, what you wanted to happen would happen. Sonny felt rather pleased with himself and wondered if his insight might not make a fine, memorable essay, the wise sort of thing that Ralph Waldo Emerson wrote. Maybe he would try it sometime.

In the meantime he got on his bathing suit and snuck outside, behind the breezeway on the side away from the street, where he spread out a blanket and lay down to get some sun. Buddie's remark had gotten to him. He hated to go to a pool or the lake or any place white as a sheet when everyone else was already tan, and he figured maybe he could get a secret little coat of coloring by making himself lie out behind the house for an hour a day.

He wondered what the secret thing was Gunner wanted to show him, and suspected it was probably a painting. It would probably show great promise and mark Gunner as a rising young Picasso. That was the kind of luck that guy had. Sonny tried not to feel resentful about it. He turned over from his stomach onto his back. His feet stuck out over the blanket and the grass tickled them. The sun was uncomfortably hot, and Sonny had to squint, even behind his dark glasses. He looked at his watch and found that only seven minutes had passed. Son of a bitch. He rolled back over on his stomach, closing his eyes and trying to keep his mind from falling into memories of old frustrations and failures, but it was hard to control the damn thing. It seemed like there was a movie running in his mind all the time, a movie that showed all kinds of terrible shit he had done and had happened to him and that he might do and might happen to him in the future, and Sonny couldn't seem to stop the movie when his mind didn't have other things to distract it, like talking or reading or watching TV. After a while he felt some per-spiration on the back of his legs and decided it was time to go on. He had only been out twelve minutes, but he couldn't lie there anymore. He went upstairs and took a long, lukewarm shower, sitting down in the stall and closing his eyes so that the water made a safe, enclosed world.

Gunner called a couple days later and said he was ready to show Sonny what he'd been working on and would like to meet him at the Key that afternoon around three. That seemed a funny place to look at a painting, a bar that was dark even in the brightest part of the day, but Sonny didn't ask any questions. He put on a short-sleeved sport shirt, the kind you didn't have to tuck in, and he let it hang out over his khakis so no one could see that the top button was open. He couldn't get it buttoned anymore.

The day was bright hot, and as usual it took a little while to get your eyes focused to the bleary afternoon darkness inside the bar. There was an old guy sitting near the front, wearing a checked shirt and suspenders and an old felt hat. He was muttering to himself. Aside from the old guy and the bartender, there only seemed to be one other person in the place, farther to the back. Sonny walked toward him, blinking and squinting. Even when he got right up to him, staring him right in the face, he had to ask, "Gunner?"

The man smiled. "It is I, Agent X-Twenty-seven," he said.

It was only his voice that affirmed his identity for sure. Sonny fumbled a chair out from the table and sat down.

"You betray a certain shock," Gunner said, sounding pleased.

"Yeh, that's right. I do, I am," Sonny said, which was putting it mildly.

Gunner had a beard.

Not the kind of beard he used to grow by just not

shaving a couple days before a football game so he'd look more tough and mean. This was a real, honest-to-goodness beard, bristling out of his cheeks and chin, a full-scale bush of a beard like the ones that Lincoln and Jesus and the Smith Brothers had.

It was one thing for guys like Jesus and Lincoln and the Smith Brothers to have beards. They were dead. Besides, they lived in times when other people had beards, too. But this was not such a time, not by a long shot. Having a beard in the summer of 1954 was like running around without any clothes on or passing out copies of the Communist Manifesto or reading a dirty book in a crowded bus. It was asking for trouble. As far as Sonny knew, the only *living* people who had beards were poor bums who couldn't afford a razor and the guys who lived at the House of David, which was some kind of religious sect up in Michigan. People didn't mind the House of David guys having beards because they were obviously harmless crackpots, and sort of funny. The House of David had a baseball team and it was quite a big attraction because people couldn't imagine how guys could have beards and also play baseball at the same time.

"What'll ya have?" Gunner asked.

"Huh?"

"You want a beer?"

"Oh, yeh. I'll have a Bud."

"Bring the man a Bud, would you please?" Gunner called to the bartender, just as if nothing was wrong. When the bartender brought the beer, he looked gloweringly at Gunner and then suspiciously at Sonny, as if they were some kind of criminals, or worse, maybe Commies. It made Sonny nervous. Being a friend of a guy who had a beard was the next worse thing to actually having one yourself.

"How does it look?" Gunner asked.

"The beard?"

"What else?"

"Well, it's a swell beard, all right. If you want to have a beard."

"What's wrong with having a beard?"

"I didn't say anything was wrong with it. If you want to have it."

"Well, since I have it, that must mean I want to have it."

"Yeh, but how come you want to have it?" Sonny asked.

Gunner swigged some beer from right out of the bottle. It was evidently easier to drink from the bottle if you had a beard. Less chance of spilling.

"It's a theory I got," Gunner said. He was always getting theories. "The beard itself is neutral," he explained. "There's nothing good or bad about a beard by itself, right? It's just a lot of whiskers. Anyone could grow them."

Sonny nodded, but suddenly wondered if he could grow a beard himself, even if he wanted to. Not that he'd ever dream of doing it, but he feared that if he actually tried it might just come out fuzz, little-boy fuzz, instead of real manly bristles.

"The thing is, not many people have them anymore," Gunner went on. "So if you have one it makes you different. It makes people treat you different even though you're the same person. It's the closest thing a guy like me could come to being a foreigner, here, in my own home town, knowing what a foreigner would feel like here, how he might be treated, what it would be like."

"What do you think you'll find out?"

"I don't even know yet," Gunner said, and then he smiled. "But I will."

It kind of gave Sonny the creeps, though he didn't want to let on. It seemed like just his luck, Gunner growing a goddam beard right when Sonny got to be his friend. Hanging around in Indianapolis with Gunner Casselman made you feel special, like you were somebody, but now

that he had gone and grown a beard it could only make
you feel silly and a little bit scared. Sonny was afraid that
Gunner could tell he felt that way, and he didn't want to
show it. In a way the beard was a test of their friendship,
and Sonny was determined to pass. He was damned if he'd
let himself fink out like he usually did when he was worried about what "everyone" thought.

They had four beers apiece, talking about other stuff,
just as if nothing was wrong, and Sonny had the guts to ask
Gunner to come on in the house when he drove him home,
even though he knew his parents would probably be there.

Mrs. Burns jumped back like she'd seen a vampire.

"What is it?" she asked.

"It's me," said Gunner.

"It's Gunner," Sonny explained, "with a beard."

Mr. Burns came into the den, carrying part of his newspaper, and stared at Gunner. "Name of God," he said.

Mrs. Burns laughed nervously and asked Gunner, "Did
you join the House of David?"

"No, ma'am," Gunner said cheerfully, "just grew a
beard."

"Is that the new fad?" Mr. Burns asked.

"No, sir, I don't think so," Gunner said.

"Well," Mrs. Burns said philosophically, "to each his
own."

She really wasn't that philosophical about it, though.

After dinner, Mr. Burns went upstairs with a migraine,
and Alma asked Sonny to come sit with her in the den. She
took her purse from off the end table, put it on her lap,
and opened it, drawing out a folded-up bill she kept in her
hand. Sonny wondered if she was going to try to get him to
tell her something. A sawbuck for your thoughts. When
Sonny was a kid, she was always asking him, "A penny for
your thoughts," and if he told her something, she really
gave him a penny. Once he told her he thought Mr. Burns
treated her mean, and she gave him a nickel. When he told

her something she didn't like, some thought that was critical of her, she'd grudgingly give him the penny but add unpleasantly, "You're getting more like your father every day."

"Your friend is quite a character," she said, trying to smile.

"Who, Gunner?"

"I guess he's a real individualist."

"I guess."

Sonny shrugged, trying to stay calm.

"Are all the kids growing beards now?"

Sonny took a deep breath. "We're not 'kids,' Mother. And I don't know. I don't know what anyone's doing."

"Are *you?*"

"Am I *what,* for Chrissake?"

"Please don't swear at me," she said, her voice beginning to quake. "I know you don't love me anymore but—"

"Stop it! Stop it! Stop saying that stuff!"

"Just tell me then," she sniffed, "if you're going to do it."

"Do *what?*"

The tears started down, and she gulped out the awful question. "Are you going to grow a big dirty scratchy old beard like your friend!"

"No, Mother. Please. Please don't cry."

She took a wadded piece of Kleenex from her purse and dabbed at her eyes. "Do you promise?"

"No!" Sonny shouted. "Goddam it, I *don't* promise. I'm just not going to grow one, that's all. I'm not a kid anymore. I don't have to promise anything."

"You don't have to yell at me."

Sonny closed his eyes. "I'm sorry," he said. "I'm going up to my room. I'm not mad, I just want to go up and read."

He started for the stairs, and his mother said, "Wait—here."

She was holding out the folded-up bill. Maybe it was supposed to be a bribe for not growing a beard, and he wanted to tell her to take it and cram it. He knew he was getting low again, though. After the afternoon's four beers he only had some change left. He walked over to her, not looking straight at her, and grabbed the bill. He stuck it in his pocket without looking at it or unfolding it.

"Thanks," he said.

"I love you, Sonny."

"Me too," he mumbled.

He went upstairs and shut the door. Flopping down on his bunk, he closed his eyes and tried to turn his mind off, tried to stop the tortuous movie from starting to roll in his mind.

> Jack Sprat would eat no fat
> Wife would eat no lean
> Together diddle diddle
> They licked the platter clean

He sat up on the edge of the bed and pulled the wadded bill from his pocket. It was a ten. It would buy a lot of beers at the Red Key.

7

A couple days later, on one of those real July scorchers, Gunner called and told Sonny to get on his swimming trunks, he'd buzz by and pick him up in about a half an hour. Sonny had been in the den with the blinds closed and the air-conditioner on, spooning up an improvised Black Cow he had made by putting fudge-walnut ice cream into a Pepsi because there wasn't any plain vanilla in the house. The fudge-walnut didn't go too well with the Pepsi, but still it was frothy and cold and soothing.

"It's pretty hot out," Sonny said.

"Huh? That's the point. Only thing to do on a day like this is hit the water."

"I guess," Sonny said.

"Fuckin-A. See ya."

When Gunner got a plan in mind, there wasn't any stopping him, you had to go along. Sonny slurped up the last of the Black Cow and shlunked up to his room to get his trunks. He had only lain out on the blanket behind the

house two days, once for twelve minutes and once for seven-
teen, and he didn't even have a tinge of pink. He looked
white and bloaty in his bathing suit, like some kind of
medical specimen. That was one reason he never liked to
go swimming. The other thing was that, even though he
could swim all right and wasn't afraid of drowning, he had
never been able to learn to dive. He always had to sneak
into the pool, when no one was looking, or horse around
with someone until they pushed him in or he could fall in,
pretending he'd lost his balance. Once he'd managed to get
in the pool, he had to do all his swimming then and there,
because if he got out he would have to go through the
whole complicated ruse of getting back in respectably, and
it just wasn't worth it.

Gunner, of course, was one of those guys who was in and
out of the pool all the time, running along the edge and
diving straight and flat with just enough of a knife edge to
cut the water instead of slap it, taking a couple of laps,
then hauling himself out, dripping and snorting, invig-
orated by the water; he would sooner or later saunter up to
the diving board, test it with some springy bounces, and
soar up into an arc and a clean dive, hardly making a
splash as he slipped through the surface of the water.
Everyone knew the story of how Gunner entered a city
swim meet the summer after college and took second place
in the hundred-yard free-style, without any real practice or
official training. The guys who had worked out all winter at
the Y were plenty pissed off.

Sonny pulled on his khakis and a T-shirt over his bathing suit, put on his bucks without any socks, slung a towel
over his shoulder in a way that he hoped looked casual,
and went out to the front porch to wait for Gunner. The
heat was awful and he could feel himself perspiring after
only a couple of minutes. Gunner pulled up across the
street, his left arm hung in a V-shape over the side of the
car, and gave a honk. All the windows were down, but the

car was still like a furnace. Sonny got in and slung his own arm casually out his window, but the side of the car burned him and he pulled the arm back in.

Gunner said he thought they'd buzz out to Meridian Hills and see if anyone was there. Gunner didn't belong, but he had a lot of friends who did, and if you were a friend of a member they would let you go ahead and take a swim. Sonny knew a few people who belonged but he never went out like that, just figuring he'd find someone he knew and be able to use the pool. He didn't think he knew them that well, and there was always the chance they might say no and he would have to slink away in shame, so he never even tried it.

As far as you could see, everything around the stately brick Colonial clubhouse at Meridian Hills was a bright, shimmering green—the golf course, the gently rolling lawns, the thick lush trees. Gunner pulled up in the parking lot near the pool, where a dozen or so cars were parked. You could hear yelps and giggles and the spraying sound of splashes from the pool. Gunner got out and started ambling up to the poolside, with Sonny following behind him, trying to amble.

"There's Wilks Wilkerson," Gunner said. "We're in."

Wilks had been a Big Rod at Shortley, a hulking sort of awkward guy who made his natural clumsiness seem stylish and entertaining, so that whenever he got in a ball game everyone would laugh and cheer, "Go get 'em, Wilks." He got in a lot of reserve basketball games, and he'd give a little salute to the crowd when he'd come on the floor and everyone would go wild, and he'd bound around fouling guys and getting into trouble. When he ever made a basket, the place would go berserk. He was very popular and had a famous greeting for everyone, "Hey-Hey-Say," that was his trademark. He was a Beta down at I.U., and the few times Sonny had seen him on campus Wilks would give him the old "Hey-Hey-Say" even though he didn't really know him, he just looked familiar. Old Man Wilkerson had a tool-and-die shop and he made his pile in the war—the real war. Lots of guys made a pile in that one, but Korea was such a half-assed war Sonny didn't even know of anyone who'd made his pile in it, though some probably had and some who'd made it in the real war probably built their piles higher during Korea.

Wilks was grinning and talking to Mitzi Harmengast, who was lolling on one of the poolside lounging chairs, being sexy. Wilks had on a ratty old brown bathing suit that looked like someone's discarded underwear. If your family was loaded and you had it made, you could wear stuff like that and it was O.K.—in fact, it was a big thing to do.

"Hey, Wilks," Gunner called.

"Hey-Hey-" Wilks automatically started his greeting, but as he turned and saw Gunner, it stuck in his throat and the last word came out long and low instead of perky—"Saaaaaay."

Wilks' jaw dropped about a mile, but he got himself quickly together and clapped his hands, like it was some kind of borass Gunner was pulling, a stunt to shake people up or something.

"Hey, man," Wilks said, "where's the cough drops?"

"Wha-say, man. You remember Sonny Burns."

Wilks turned to Sonny and pumped his hand, staring at him with a blank smile and saying, "Hey, yeh, sure, how's it go, man?"

"Hi," Sonny said.

Wilks slapped Gunner on the shoulder and laughed. "I heard the word, fella, I heard the big word on you, but seein's believin'. Gunner grows a beard. You goin' out for a big part in the Christmas play? Like the *lead*, I mean?"

Wilks guffawed, and Gunner smiled and said, "Might do that. Just might do 'er."

"Too much." Wilks laughed. "Truly, truly."

Mitzi Harmengast raised up out of her loll and removed her sunglasses to look at Gunner.

"Say, Mitz," Gunner greeted her.

"What're *you* supposed to be?" she asked coolly.

"Be?" asked Gunner.

"He's a Smith brother," Wilks explained. "One of the original Smith Brothers. You know, Mitz, the cough-drop guys. All he needs is the other brother and he's in business, huh, Guns baby?"

"Sure," said Gunner.

"I don't get it," Mitzi said and slipped her sunglasses back on.

"There isn't anything to get," Gunner said. "It's just a beard."

"Just a beard," Mitzi said skeptically and eased back down on the reclining chair, her big boobs heaving up inside the Jantzen so you could see the beginning of where they were still white, which was getting pretty close to the old nipples.

"O.K., Wilks," Gunner said, "you in shape or not?"

Gunner had his trunks on under his faded jeans and he shucked off the pants and drew the T-shirt over his head, dropping it beside him.

"I'll race you four laps and winner buys the brews," he said.

"Hey, hold on, man," Wilks said.

His jolly Hey-Hey-Say expression was gone and he looked confused and suspicious, like Gunner was trying to pull one on him.

"Whassamatter?" Gunner teased. "You been dissipatin' again? O.K., make it two laps."

"You gotta be pulling my leg," said Wilks.

"And I'll give you a full second to start."

A couple kids around twelve or so had cautiously come up to stare at Gunner. Their eyes bugged out and their mouths were ready to catch flies, but Gunner didn't seem to notice anything.

"Be serious, man," Wilks said.

"O.K.," said Gunner, "if you're that bad off, you go free-style, I'll go breaststroke. You can't get a better deal than *that*."

Wilks frowned and shook his head. "You can't go in the water like that," he said.

"Like what?" said Gunner. He looked down at his faded navy-blue trunks with a line of white piping up each side and an old red-and-white lifeguard medallion sown on the left leg. The whole place had gone suddenly quiet. A girl at the end of the diving board stopped springing and simply stood on the edge, watching Wilks and Gunner. A guy in the deep end was turned toward them, treading water and arching his head up to see what was happening. Mitzi had risen up again from her lounge chair, her mouth a straight red pencil mark. On the other side of the pool a little girl in a flowered bathing suit ran along the cement lip above the water, her wet feet making a tiny splat-splat that was the only sound you could hear.

"Ole buddy," Wilks said in a low voice, "you can't go swimming with a frigging beard."

Gunner laughed and said, "If you think it'll slow me down, that gives you better odds."

"Be *ser*ious, man," said Wilks. His shaggy eyebrows bunched into a painful expression of distress.

Gunner raised his palms up and said, "I am serious. What's the beard got to do with it?"

"This is a *pool*, ole buddy. I mean, if it was the ocean, it might be different. Or even Lake Michigan, maybe. But this is a *pool*."

"I know it's a goddam pool," Gunner said.

"So, you can't contaminate it. Be reasonable, man."

"Contaminate it! Who's con*tam*inating it?"

"Nobody is, right now. And I'm gonna keep it that way.

It's plain common sense you can't go into a swimming pool with a beard. You'll get the water dirty."

"Dirty! You saying my beard is dirty? Is that it?"

"I'm just saying it's a beard."

"But it's clean! There's nothing dirty about it."

"A beard is a beard," Wilks insisted.

Mitzi stood up and raised the straps of her suit back over her shoulders. "I'm not swimming in any pool that's had a beard in it," she said and turned away, walking toward the clubhouse.

"You're crazy," Gunner said. "You're all crazy or something."

He started walking past Wilks toward the edge of the pool, but Wilks put a hand on his shoulder and stopped him.

"We been ole buddies," Wilks said. "I don't wanna have to stop you. I don't even know if I could, but I'd have to try and I don't wanta do that."

Wilks kept his hand on Gunner's shoulder, and the two guys stood glaring at each other, neither one moving a muscle. The little girl had stopped running, and the splat sounds were gone, leaving no noise at all. The sun was a silent blast over everything, cooking everyone where they stood. Sonny had the weird feeling that they all were being baked into place, that they'd all be immobilized there forever, forming a strange tableau called *The Swimming Pool.* He prayed to hell there wouldn't be a fight. But his friend Gunner was being challenged, and if he chose to fight, Sonny would have to fight with him. It would be the two of them against the whole population of the pool, including Mitzi and her big boobs and even the little girl in the flowered bathing suit, not to speak of Wilks and every other guy around the place. He wondered what it would feel like to crack your head on cement.

Gunner let out a long breath and said quietly, "O.K., forget it, man."

Wilks took his hand away and Gunner picked up his T-shirt and khakis, wadding them into a ball.

"Still ole buddies, Guns?" Wilks said as heartily as possible.

"Sure, man, sure," Gunner said and started for the car. Sonny went beside him, feeling all those eyes like hot little suns boring into his back. Then suddenly the air was filled with splashes and splats and yelps and whistles as the pool unlocked into life again.

Sonny didn't say anything when he got in the car, and neither did Gunner. He drove back to his mother's place at the Meadowlark, and Gunner took a cold shower and then mixed up a batch of seabreezes, pouring two tall glasses full and handing one to Sonny.

"Once when I was a junior at Shortley," he said quietly, "the first hot day of summer, me and a bunch of guys piled into Andy McGovern's old thirty-eight Buick and went to the Riviera for a swim. You know the damn Rivvy, it's no damn country club, it's ten bucks a year or something and you don't have to be anybody to join. There were about six of us, and Sammy Katzman was with us and he said he didn't belong, but, hell, you can take a guest on your card and all the rest of us belonged, and so we piled out and we start walking up to the pool building, the bunch of us, and out comes old man Barlow, that bald old fart who used to be the manager, and he stands on the steps with his legs apart and points a finger right at Sammy and he says, 'You kids can't bring that Jew-boy in here.' Maybe he knew Sammy from someplace or had seen him play ball and knew his name, or maybe he just had a Jew-detector or something. I don't know, but it was like getting hit in the face with a wet rag, I was that surprised, I guess we all were—except maybe Sammy, who hadn't really wanted to go all along—and we stopped dead in our tracks and then Blow Mahoney started yelling and cussing at the old bastard and us joining in saying, 'Yeh, you prick, this guy's our friend, he's better than you any day, you old turd-head,' and the old bastard gets beet red and starts yelling he's going to call the police and Sammy keeps saying, 'Come on, you guys, let's go, let's get the hell out of here,' and finally we pile back in the car and felt like shit, and Sammy kept trying to make a joke of it like he always did about that stuff, he kept saying, 'I wish you guys would get the word around that *I* didn't kill that character, maybe the Jews killed him but *I* didn't kill that guy and hang him up on the cross, not me, it was some other bunch of Jews.' Finally we all got horsing around and tried to forget about it, but we all still felt like shit. It was the first time I'd seen something like that happen, and it wasn't like some story you read about a Jew getting discriminated against, it was our buddy, it was Sammy Katzman. He was one of *us*."

"Yeh," Sonny said.

Gunner got up and started pacing the room, rattling the ice in his glass and munching on his lips, and then he suddenly stopped and wheeled around toward Sonny, his face alive with some discovery.

"You know the only goddam person who didn't even mention the beard when he first saw it, who acted like I was the same guy and nothing different had happened?"

"No," Sonny said, knowing it sure as hell wasn't him and feeling ashamed of that. "Who?"

"Marty's father."

"Yeh?"

"Bet your ass. You oughta meet that guy. Man, what a guy. I could sit around and shoot the shit with that guy for hours."

"Yeh, I'd like to. Meet him."

"We'll fall by there sometime."

"Great."

Gunner poured them each another seabreeze and put on a Brubeck. He was getting back in his regular spirits after the swimming-pool business, and Sonny felt a lot better himself. He was really relieved that there hadn't been a fight and was secretly glad that he didn't have to go swimming after all. Maybe he could make it through the whole damn summer. By October, everyone else would be white, too, and he wouldn't have to worry about it again till the following June.

Gunner's mother got home unexpectedly early; they had let people off because of the heat. She kicked off her shoes, flopped down on the couch, and said to Sonny, "What do you think of my fine-feathered friend here?"

"Oh. The beard?"

He took a long sip of his seabreeze, hoping he didn't have to get into it with Mrs. Casselman. He didn't want to let Gunner down by sounding as if he disapproved, but he didn't want Nina to think he was a far-out guy who liked beards. She wouldn't let it drop, though.

"Do a lot of your friends have beards?" she asked.

"No, ma'am," Sonny said, twisting in his chair.

"Well, don't you think it looks a little weird?"

"For God sake, Nina," Gunner said, "what do you expect him to say?"

"I expect him to say what he *thinks*."

Trying to sound both loyal to his friend and patriotic, too, Sonny said feebly, "Lincoln had one."

"Oh, so you approve, then," Nina said, as if her worst suspicions had been confirmed.

"He didn't say that, Nina."

"I heard what he said."

"Let me get you a drink," Gunner said and went to the kitchen.

"I suppose his girl friend likes it too," Nina said.

Sonny cleared his throat and said, "I really don't know."

"You're a friend of hers, aren't you?"

"Well,—yes, I guess."

"Of course, a beard is more common to the Jews. Their rabbis have to have them."

"I don't know," said Sonny.

Gunner came in with the drink for Nina and said, "Please, Mother, let's not get on the Jews again."

"I'm not 'on' them. I just made a statement."

She turned to Sonny and said, "My son believes I'm prejudiced. His own mother."

"Please, Nina."

"Actually, I've become very interested in their religion and history. They have quite a long history, you know."

"Yes," Sonny said, "I understand they do."

"I've been reading up on it."

"Oh?"

"She took out a book," Gunner explained.

Nina got up and handed a library book to Sonny. It was called *Judaism from Ancient Times*. Sonny turned it over in his hands, not knowing what to say.

"Must be interesting," he finally commented.

"Fascinating," Nina said. "But there's still a lot I haven't come across yet. Gunner, you say Marty's father's so smart, would you ask him something for me? About one of their customs?"

"What is it, Nina?" Gunner said evenly.

"Well, when they have their funerals—"

"Yes?"

"Is it true that they bury their dead standing up?"

Gunner grasped at his forehead and stared at Nina out of eyes that seemed to have looked at an atom blast without dark glasses.

"No, Mother," he said in a dry, flat tone. "They lay 'em down, just like the rest of us."

A few days after they didn't go swimming, Gunner took Sonny to see Marty's studio. It was in an old three-story house in a dingy block down around the museum. A commercial artist and his wife owned the building and rented

out rooms for studios and also for living quarters for
students who studied at the museum school. Marty's room
was on the top floor, and it had one of those curving
windows that protrudes like a turret. The room was completely bare except for the art stuff—canvases, paints,
buckets of turpentine, a huge easel, a table smeared with
colors and cluttered with brushes and tubes and jars.
There was also a hot plate with an old coffeepot on it, and
a hunk of cheese that looked a couple centuries old. And
yet, Sonny felt charged up, just being in the room. There
was an excitement about it, a feeling of purpose and
creation. Something was happening here. Someone was
making something. Sonny felt a tingle that went through
his shoulders and his arms, down to his fingers.

"Yeh," he said, nodding his head.

"The real thing, huh?" Gunner asked proudly.

"Yeh."

"Would you like to see some of my paintings?" Marty
asked.

"Sure."

Marty seemed different in the room, more relaxed and
friendly even. She moved around in it with a kind of
authority that was different from the sexy, feminine as-
surance of her social self, freer in a way, free in the way of
a seaman on the deck of his ship. She was wearing a pair of
paint-splattered jeans and a raggedy man's white shirt with
the sleeves rolled up.

"Here," she said. "Gunner, give me a hand."

She had gone to a corner of the room where a dozen or
so canvases stretched onto frames were propped against the
wall. Gunner helped her as she moved them out, one by
one, and placed them against another wall, in the best
light. Sonny felt silly because he didn't know how to make
the right comments, and he just sort of made sounds, like
"Mmmm" and "Yeh" and "Ahhh." Some of them had
people in them, but they weren't the jolly All-American

folks of Orville Lockwood's homey magazine covers; they were misshapen, elongated, puffed up, twisted, their heads on wrong and faces distorted in pain and surprise and fear and confusion. They weren't pictures of how people looked but of how people felt. Some of the canvases had no pictures at all, just colors, swirls and patches and planes of color, thickened and lumped, like hunks of emotion.

"I feel like a dumb ass," Sonny said. "But I know you're doing something real."

"She has it, all right," Gunner said.

"I'm learning." Marty smiled. "I'm learning what color is. God. You take green. Have you ever really thought about green?"

Sonny bit at his lip and then grinned foolishly. "Lucky Strike green has gone to war. That's about all, as far as thinking about it. That I can think of."

"Or yellow? *God.* Yellow."

"Cowards, I guess," Sonny said.

"The sun," said Marty. "Heat. Energy. Life. Van Gogh's sunflowers."

"I never saw them," Sonny admitted.

"They'll knock you out," Gunner said.

"And goldenrod," Marty went on, "growing wild."

"I've seen that, as a kid," Sonny said. "Does it still grow around here?"

"Sure. You just stopped seeing it. You stopped looking. Most people do."

"Hell, yes," said Gunner. "You go stale. You have it as a kid, that way of seeing things, and you lose it. That's what they call 'growing up.' "

"I guess, yeh," said Sonny.

"Going back, going back to seeing it fresh, like a child, that's art," Marty said. Her face had a real glow of excitement. Gunner put an arm around her and hugged her against him.

"This kid's got it," he said. "She can teach it, too."

"Better than Artists Unlimited, I bet." Sonny grinned.

"Oh, man! Wait'll I show you the letter I got. When I didn't do Lesson Number One and didn't send the next fee."

Gunner went over to where he had slung a khaki jacket over a chair, and he pulled out this letter and handed it to Sonny.

"All over America," it said, "the lights are burning late at night in the homes of those who are getting ahead. Ambition is burning, while others sleep. We don't think you're the kind of sleepy soul who wants to let opportunity and fortune pass him by. We know you want to complete this course and be right in the forefront of the kind of creative people who will emerge as the great talents and geniuses of their generation. Please send the $10 fee for your next lesson—not for our sake, for yours."

"Wow," Sonny said.

"See, they're worried about *me*," Gunner said. "It's not the bucks they want."

"Of course not, dear," Marty said mockingly. "It's your future they're worried about."

"I bet Orville Lockwood himself is worried," Sonny said.

"Maybe he'll paint a magazine cover showing me staying up late, burning with ambition."

"Is that what you burn with, dear? Ambition?"

Marty squeezed Gunner and he gave her a kiss on the forehead.

"Sometimes," he said.

Sonny looked away, imagining Gunner and Marty burning up with lust every night, their bodies tangled in bizarre positions never before imagined. Gunner moved away from Marty and said why didn't they all go out for a nice one. Sonny appreciated that; he felt Gunner must have sensed that he was feeling kind of out of it. Some guys seemed to delight in lording it over you when they had a girl, nuzzling up to her in front of you and sort of looking like "See what I've got and you haven't?" but Gunner was good about that kind of thing. He didn't go in for showing people up, even though he could have if he was that kind of guy.

They had a round of Buds at the Key and then went to Marty's house. She and Gunner were going out again that night, and they asked Sonny to join them but he said he was busy. He just figured it would depress him to be out with them when he didn't have a girl he was hot for himself. They insisted he stop by the house, though, to meet Marty's old man and he said O.K. to that.

The house was one of those imposing brick jobs set way back from the street on Washington Boulevard. It looked like a small castle, with vines running all over it and casement windows. While Marty got dressed to go out, Sonny and Gunner went and sat in the den and had a drink with Mr. Pilcher.

Solomon Pilcher was the first man Sonny ever met in person who could genuinely be described as *suave*. Not slick, not slippery. Genuinely suave. When he made you a drink, he didn't just slosh some booze in a glass and plunk a couple of ice cubes in it. He measured; he poured; he stirred. He proffered the drink to his guests with a manner that made you feel special, like an honor was being bestowed, a bond established. But for all this there was nothing stiff or uncomfortably formal about the man, and Sonny not only felt at ease with him, he felt more sophisticated himself, as if Mr. Pilcher's charm was a kind of light that brightened his guests as well as him. He treated you as a gentleman, and so you felt like one.

The room itself made you feel good, too. Wherever you sat—on the pillow-fattened sofa or one of two matching easy chairs—you sank, softly, into a downy ease. Quiet, intricate music came from a pair of speakers whose parts were all hidden except for a pair of speakers that were

blended among the books. The books were fine and old,
yet they didn't just seem like decoration. Sonny felt sure
Mr. Pilcher really read them, returned to them like hon-
ored friends, and chose just the right one to suit his
particular mood. Gunner got talking about Japan, and Mr.
Pilcher asked interested, interesting questions; he was con-
versant, of course, with certain aspects of Japanese culture—philosophy, art, the theater. Warmed by the drink
and the conversation, Sonny would have been happy to sit
there the rest of the evening.

When Marty came down, Mr. Pilcher stood up and
Sonny and Gunner scrambled to their feet. Mr. Pilcher
asked Marty if she cared to join them in a drink, ad-
dressing her like a visiting princess instead of his young
daughter fresh out of college. Marty looked tan and cool in
a white summer dress that was cut low enough to show the
beginning of her cleavage. She wore several interesting
rings and a gold sort of band in the form of a serpent on
the upper part of her left arm. She had no makeup on
except for the dark accentuation of her deep brown eyes.
Sonny felt himself getting a hard-on, and he felt crude and
uncivilized.

"You look lovely, dear," Mr. Pilcher said.

"Terrific," said Gunner.

"Yeh, I'll say," Sonny added and quickly shut up, his
bumbling compliment sounding raw and awkward in the
perfumed air. He drained the last of his drink and the ice
cubes made a clicking noise against his teeth.

"Let me freshen that."

Mr. Pilcher was across the room and had the glass before
Sonny could decide if it was the right thing to have a
second, so he just settled back to enjoy it. Marty mainly
talked to her father while Gunner looked on admiringly,
and Sonny's concentration floated pleasantly off as he enjoyed the voices, the pleasant tone and feeling of what was
being said, without really hearing the words. The com-

fortable mood, the serenity of the room, was broken by a
brittle voice that said curtly, "We're late."

In the door was a small, sharp-faced lady who was
browned in that leathery way that comes to middle-aged
women who are serious about their golf.

Mr. Pilcher stood up and said, "You know Mr. Casselman, dear; this is his friend Mr. Burns. My wife, Lilly."

"Evening," said Gunner, snapping to attention, and
Sonny stood and said, "Pleased to meet you."

Mrs. Pilcher gave each of the guys a quick glance, almost
like a slap, and turned to Marty. "Just remember you have
to be up early tomorrow," she said.

"Yes, Mother."

"Let's go," she said to Mr. Pilcher. He smiled, set down
his drink, and came over to shake hands with Sonny and
Gunner.

"It was pleasant to talk with you. I hope we'll meet
again."

"Thank you, sir," Sonny said.

"Great," said Gunner. "See ya soon."

Sonny was glad his parents weren't home when Marty
and Gunner dropped him off; he wanted to be alone and
think. He went to his room to put on his favorite thinking record, *The New World Symphony*. It was the only
symphony record he owned, and he guessed maybe he
liked it because there was a popular song made out of the
tune of one part of the symphony, a song called "Going
Home," which was sad and yet somehow sweet and nostal-
gic. The whole symphony reminded Sonny of wide open
spaces, autumn campfires, and wild, strong rivers. America past and pure, still clean and uncluttered. He put on the
record and lit a cigarette, thinking what a great guy
Marty's old man was, the great way he made you feel just
talking to you. Sonny wondered if it was the thing people
called "Old World charm," and whether there was something Jewish about it, some quality they had. Most people

thought of Jews as talking too loud and trying to Jew you down, out of your money, but Sonny had several professors who were Jewish and had that special aura of culture and grace that Mr. Pilcher had.

The only other person he knew who had that, though, wasn't Jewish at all. It was Mrs. Hullen, the mother of a girl who Sonny had a real crush on when he was a sophomore at Shortley. Mrs. Hullen came from one of those families where everyone went to the fancy Eastern colleges and all of them had swanky jobs like being presidents of banks and Episcopal bishops and headmasters of expensive little schools, and she married a man from the same sort of clan who graduated from Harvard Law School and was a leading attorney. But Mrs. Hullen didn't seem to Sonny like a snob; she had that way of treating you as a gentleman and so making you feel like one even when you only were a moldy sophomore in high school. She offered you tea and liked to have real conversations, talking about world events and books, not in a dry, schoolmarm way but so it was really interesting and fun, and her eyes were fantastically alive, as if taking everything in and getting a big kick out of it all. Sonny loved just seeing the way she sat in a chair, her back perfectly straight, without seeming stiff or uncomfortable, her hands resting in her lap, occasionally making a graceful gesture but never fidgeting. He could simply not imagine her ever crying or yelling at anyone or going to pieces, and yet she was a mother, with a son and two daughters. Mr. Hullen was polite enough, but he hardly ever said anything and seemed a little scary to Sonny. If it came to picking an All-Star parent team, Sonny would choose Mrs. Hullen and Mr. Pilcher. But that was something you couldn't choose, at least for yourself. You took what you got and made the best of it. Or the worst of it.

Sonny went out taking pictures by himself the next day, feeling very proud and manly that he was getting off his ass and doing something constructive without anyone else's help or urging or companionship. He went to a little playground about a half-mile from his house, nearer to the old neighborhood he'd grown up in. There was a wading pool and swings and teeter-totters, and Sonny really got a kick out of watching the kids and getting what he thought were some good shots. He stopped off and had a cherry Coke at Binkley's Drugs on the way home, and came in hot and tired but feeling a nice satisfaction with himself. He even noticed a little stirring, an almost physical sense of the small, fluttery feeling of a kind of hope.

He walked in the den and found his mother wiping her eyes with a wet washcloth. Her face was pink and puffy.

"What's the matter?" he asked.

"That woman," Mrs. Burns said. "I am going to give that woman a piece of my mind."

"*What* woman?"

"Your *friend's* mother. That Casselman woman."

"What the hell are you talking about?"

"That woman had the nerve to call me and go on and on about *you* being a bad influence on *him*. Can you beat that? *Her* son is just perfect, of course. God's gift to the universe. Innocent as a babe in arms. My foot, he is. *I* know what he is. And I know what he's done to *you*."

"For God sake, we've been all through that stuff. It's none of your business."

"Oh, I suppose it's *her* business, though?"

"No, it's not anyone's business."

"I'd have gone to see that woman long before this, except I knew you'd hate me even more."

"*Please* don't say that stuff. I don't hate you. I don't hate anyone. Please don't do something awful."

"You see," she started sobbing. "Whatever I do is awful."

"I didn't say that!"

"You think it. You think I'm awful. My only son. When

you were a little boy you loved me so, and now you hate me."

"Stop it!" Sonny shouted. "Stop saying that stuff or I'll shoot myself! I swear to God I'll find a gun and shoot myself!"

Mrs. Burns began screaming. Then great, horrible sobs came out of her, as if her insides were being wrenched out. Great spots were exploding in Sonny's eyes, and he thought he was going to heave. He groped for the door and went outside, blinking as he propped one hand against a white square wooden pillar of the porch. He closed his eyes and tried to settle his mind.

> Hi Diddle diddle
> Cat with a fiddle
> Cow jumped out into Noon
> Little dog laughed to see the port
> And the Prince ran away with a goon

He stood on the porch until he stopped shaking so bad and then went back inside. His mother was pressing the washcloth on her forehead, sniffling and breathing hard.

"I'm sorry," she said.

"I'm sorry," said Sonny. "Are you all right?"

"Yes." She managed a little smile that looked like it hurt. "I've got to fix my face. I've got to see that woman at six o'clock."

There wasn't any way he could argue her out of it, so he insisted on going with her. He went upstairs and called Gunner from the little telephone alcove. Gunner had already talked to his own mother, and he sounded a hundred years old.

Mrs. Burns got all dolled up in a pink suit and matching pillbox hat. She looked like she was going to a PTA meeting. Maybe that's sort of what it was, except the children were grown. All they needed was a teacher to chair the meeting.

Gunner greeted them at the door, wearing a fatigue camouflage suit he'd brought home from the Army. Sonny wished he had one too, even though he knew that kind of camouflage wasn't going to help much. It was designed to keep you safe in jungles from enemy gooks, but it couldn't protect you from wild mothers. Nina Casselman was arranged on the couch, wearing one of her slinky silk-blouse-and-toreador outfits and the backless white heels, one of them dangling from the toes of a crossed leg. Sonny felt a flush of excitement and looked away. It seemed like betraying his own mother to get sexed up by her enemy-mother. Mrs. Burns sat down in an armchair and Sonny stood beside her, as if taking up a required position.

"Would you care to have something cold to drink, Mrs. Burns?" Gunner asked politely.

"I don't drink, thank you," she said as curtly as possible.

"I meant a Coke or something. Orange juice?"

"Nothing, thanks."

Gunner and his mother already had drinks themselves, and without even asking Sonny, Gunner brought him a martini strong enough to curl the hair on your chest.

Nina dipped a finger in her martini, sort of stirring it around, and said haughtily, "It's too bad this had to happen."

"I agree with you there," Mrs. Burns said. "If your son hadn't influenced Sonny the way he had—"

"My son," said Nina, "is a leader, always has been. Frankly it's beyond me how he got mixed up with your son and his radical, antisocial ideas, but—"

"*My* son has always been a good boy, a normal person, until he met—*him*—that playboy with a beard."

"He never had a beard before he got mixed up with *your* son."

"That's ridiculous," Gunner said.

"It's true," Nina insisted.

"It doesn't have anything to do with anything," Gunner said.

"No," Sonny said. "It really doesn't."

Neither of the mothers paid any attention.

"I can understand," Nina continued, "how a boy like your son, who never pledged anything, who wasn't in any house at all in college much less a *good* house—I can understand how a bitter boy like that would be attracted by Jews and Communists, but—"

"Jews! It's your son who's out lalligagging around with a Jewish girl day and night, everyone knows about *that,* let me tell you—"

"My son was never involved with any Jew girl until he started running with *your* son and his crowd."

"What crowd?" Sonny asked, startled at the notion of his being the leader of a crowd of any kind, which is what Nina made it sound like.

"There isn't any crowd, Nina," Gunner said.

"Don't lie for him, he's got you all confused," Nina said.

"I really don't have any crowd, Mrs. Casselman," Sonny said.

"Don't try to brainwash *me,* young man!"

"Brainwash!" Mrs. Burns shouted. "My boy's the one who's been brainwashed. It's your son who has the communistic beard. My Sonny shaves, like a good American."

"Of course!" Nina said. "He wants to be safe himself, he wants to talk *other* people into beards and let *them* take the consequences."

"It's *my* goddam beard!" Gunner said. "Nobody talked me into it."

"They have their ways," Nina insisted. "You don't even know how they do it, how they talk you into doing their bidding."

"Are you implying my Sonny is a Communist?" Mrs. Burns asked in a trembling voice.

"If the shoe fits, wear it," Nina said. "If you lie down with dogs you come up with fleas."

"You can say that again, but it's my son who got the fleas!" Mrs. Burns yelled.

"Please," Sonny pleaded, looking helplessly at Gunner.

Gunner went to the middle of the room, pointing his hands at each mother, like a referee, and made an announcement.

"Listen," he said. "I'll shave off the beard. Will that make everybody happy? Is that what it's all about?"

"It's what's on the inside that counts," Mrs. Burns said, sobbing.

"It sure is, sister," Nina said sharply. "And let me tell you—"

"Cut it, Nina, just cut it," Gunner ordered. "I'm shaving the beard and that's all she wrote."

Sonny put a hand on his mother's quaking shoulder and said firmly, "Come on, let's go. We have to go home."

Sonny drove the car back while his mother sat sniffling and crying, leaning against her door as if she were trying to press so hard she'd fall out. When they got home she washed her face and had two aspirin and a Pepsi.

"Are you still going to see that boy, after what happened?"

"After what happened!" Sonny yelled. "What happened was you and his mother acted like crazy people, that's what happened!"

"See!" Mrs. Burns cried. "He's turning you against me, he's making you take his side!"

"Jesus Hannah Christ," said Sonny. He was too tired to scream or even to argue. He went to his room and slammed the door, flopped on his bunk, and tried to shut his mind off.

Help me, God, God help me. I hate your ass, but help me if you can. Help me lie down beside the still waters.

8

Shaving the beard off seemed to make Gunner look older—maybe just having the damn thing had aged him, what with all the crap he had to take about it. His cheeks looked hollower and whiter than before he had the beard, and his skin was a little raw, making him appear as if he'd just recovered from an illness. A couple days after the Great Mother Meeting, he picked up Sonny and they got a six-pack of Bud and went up to Crown Hill Cemetery, picking a high, shady spot where you could look out over the city and no one was likely to bother you. They just sat and sipped for a while without saying anything, and then Gunner started talking about how Marty's mother was hounding her about seeing so much of a *shaygetz*—that was the Jewish word for a guy who wasn't what Marty called "O.O.T.T.," One of the Tribe—just as Gunner's mother was on his back about dating a Jewish girl.

"We're getting it from both ends," Gunner said. "What a lot of shit."

"Are you really serious about Marty?"

" 'Serious about?' What does that mean? How the hell do I know? I like to fuck her and I like to talk to her—that's a pretty rare combination, you know?"

"Hell, yes."

"But we both have things to do. She doesn't want to get locked into a picket fence, like DeeDee's so hot to do. She's got her own stuff to do, her art. And I don't even know yet what the hell I've got to do. Except try to find out what it is."

"Are you still going up to see the ad agency? In Chicago?"

"Yeh, I figure I owe 'em that. And myself, too. I really think I'll get on the GI Bill train, but I at least could tell 'em that, maybe they'd like the idea of a guy doing that before he settles into a regular job."

"Yeh, right. Might as well keep it open."

"The pay ain't hay, I'll tell you that. They were talking seven thousand as a starting salary."

Sonny whistled and said, "Shit, that's as much as Biff Barkely makes over at the *Star* right now, and he's been with 'em—Jesus, maybe fifteen years."

"You talked to him, huh? About a job there?"

"Yeh, but I don't know. He's kind of bitter, it seems like. He kind of encouraged me to go to New York or something, try the big guys."

"Why not? You can always come back here, you might as well see what it's like in the big city. Hell, you could get the bill and do some work on the side."

"Maybe. I guess maybe I ought to go talk to the guys at the V.A. About getting the bill."

"Yeh, I was down there once, but I have to go back and get the forms and shit. I think I'm going to try to get into Columbia. I was talking to Marty about it."

"Man, that'd be great. Having a girl there, right there in New York."

"Yeh. New York."

New York City.

Just hearing the name or saying it to himself gave Sonny a kind of tingly feeling, exciting and scary at the same time. The flat, familiar town stretched out below seemed tamer but also safer. He just didn't know if he had what it took to survive in a real big city, much less the biggest and toughest of them all. Of course, if he had a friend there, a friend like Gunner, who'd make out anywhere in the world, it might be easier, might even be some fun.

"I've had it with Naptown, anyway," Gunner said. "I know that much."

"Maybe so," said Sonny, who didn't really know.

They left the cemetery at dusk, the long straight rows of streetlights started coming on, laid out orderly and predictably, the way the city was. There was something dull but reassuring about it.

On the way home Gunner mentioned casually that Marty had a girl friend from college coming in for the weekend, and wondered if Sonny'd like to be fixed up with her. Marty said the girl was pretty sexy-looking and wasn't short on brains, either. Sonny said sure, very casual, just as if such opportunities came along all the time. Gunner said the date would be for Saturday night, and then if Sonny liked the girl, they could all do something on Sunday, too. If *he* liked the girl. Sonny could only think about whether the girl would like *him*. He didn't even know her but he was already worried.

Sonny tried to work himself into a casual mood as he got dressed for the date on Saturday night. In the shower he sang "Bye, Bye, Blackbird" at the top of his voice, and after he got out and dried he slapped Old Spice After Shave Lotion all over himself with stinky abandon. Casual him. Devil may care. But beneath the loud, jaunty singing and the smell of Old Spice, he was terrified by the thought that his date might really be a great sexy girl and he would ruin everything. He tried to comfort himself with the thought that she wouldn't really be smart or sexy at all and there wouldn't be anything to be nervous about. But it wasn't usual for a girl to describe another girl as "sexy-looking" to a guy she was fixing her up with. Marty, of course, was sophisticated, and there was the possibility she really meant it and the girl was really sexy-looking. There was always that possibility. You knew there was no possibility at all when a girl tried to fix you up with a friend and described her by saying she had "real personality" or, even worse, was "loads of fun." If there was one thing Sonny couldn't stand, it was a girl who was "loads of fun." That meant she was homely and plain and hated sex and tried to make up for it by talking a blue streak and faking a lot of laughs and suggesting "fun" things to do like why don't we all go to the zoo and feed peanuts to the polar bears. Girls who were loads of fun always loved to go to the zoo. You couldn't lay a hand on them in the fucking zoo.

The deal for the evening was that they all were going to have dinner at the Italian Village Restaurant, and then go dancing out at Westlake. That was a very sexy plan if you had a good date; it showed you could have a real sophisticated evening in Indianapolis. Sonny put on a new sport coat his mother had bought him at Medallion Men's Wear —a plaid number—and a pair of white-linen slacks that were tight in the waist but looked debonair as hell, a sharp, thin black knit tie, and his old white bucks. He looked himself over in the mirror and judged the whole outfit to be pretty damned sharp, but goddam if he didn't have a pimple on the end of his nose. It seemed like whenever anything important was going to happen he sprouted a big ugly pimple on the end of his nose. He squeezed it, but instead of breaking, it just became redder and more clownish-looking. He put some of his mother's pancake makeup on it, and that helped a little. It wasn't so red then, it just looked flaky and cruddy.

The pimple really depressed Sonny, because that was one thing he thought would stop happening when his real life began—getting a goddam pimple on the end of his nose at a crucial time. But there it was again, blooming right on the end of his nose, even though he was a college graduate and a veteran of the U.S. Army. He guessed he would probably have a fucking pimple on the end of his nose the day he died, and they would have to spread pancake makeup over it when they fixed him up for the casket display. People would pass by and say, "My, he looks natural—he even has a pimple on the end of his nose." Sonny suspected he'd be able to hear them say it, too, even though he wouldn't be able to talk back. They probably had it rigged up that way for you in hell, so you could hear the last shitty comments and not be able to reply.

Sonny was getting himself in a terrible state, and he was thankful that Gunner picked him up early so they had time to stop at the Key for a drink. Sonny had two seven-and-sevens while Gunner drank a beer, and he wished he had even more when Gunner told him the unexpected good news.

"We got the house to ourselves," Gunner revealed. "Marty's folks are gone for the weekend."

Sonny had to take his hand off the drink to keep the glass from rattling. "Terrific," he said.

"Here's the plan. When we get back from Westlake, we'll hit the den and shoot the shit there for a while. Then Marty 'n I'll slip upstairs to the bedroom. You and the babe'll have the den. You know—I mean, if you want to make out with her."

Gunner said it as if it would be Sonny's decision to make, according to his own whim. He said it so matter-of-factly that Sonny actually felt a little cocky, like he was a regular make-out artist.

"Great," he said, nodding at Gunner. "That couch in the den looks real nice and cushiony."

Gunner slapped him on the back and said, "I recommend it highly, ole buddy," and both of them broke up laughing, just like a couple of cocksmen planning to knock off their piece for the night. The movie in Sonny's mind showed a couple of hooded, desert marauders riding down on the tents of the frightened, waiting women. He even forgot about the pimple on the end of his nose.

Marty's college girl friend was Gail Thayer, from Cincinnati. To Sonny's astonishment and terror, she was a goddam dream. Maybe not everybody's dream, but Sonny's. She was tiny and dark, with glossy black hair and big greenish-gray eyes and perfect white teeth circled by a lush little mouth with lipstick that was deep dark red. She had on a plain gold sleeveless dress with an emerald pin that looked like a bug, crawling up her tit. She wore white heels and sleek, seamless nylons. Sonny loved to see women in stockings, but it depressed the hell out of him when they had the seams crooked or were loose and all wrinkled up around the ankles. That ruined everything. But Gail's were just right, glistening tight against her legs, like a shiny second skin that could be peeled off.

Marty proposed they all have a drink before taking off for dinner, and Sonny silently blessed her. The carefree, cocksman feeling he had worked up before over drinks with Gunner had completely crumpled when he got a load of Gail. His date. Oh, God, *his* date. Holy shit. He couldn't speak or think, but luckily Gunner had sparked a nice casual conversation as he mixed a batch of martinis. Sonny was only vaguely aware of Gunner smiling and handing him a glass, but after a couple of deep slugs he was able to tune in to the story his buddy was telling. Evidently when Gunner heard Gail was from Cincy he had launched into a hilarious account of how Shortley had played Withers High of Cincinnati in his junior year and got their ass racked.

"We were undefeated going into that ball game," Gunner was explaining. "But we knew Withers had been the state champs of Ohio the year before and had fourteen returning lettermen. We were scared shitless, but tried not to let on. The coach could tell we were shaking in our goddam cleats, though, and he gave us this fiery pep talk, you know, like in the movie of the Big Game. Our coach was this guy Herman E. 'Nails' Nedrick, and he talked like Pat O'Brien playing Knute Rockne, you know, and he finished up the talk saying 'Men—'" Gunner stood up and pointed a menacing finger, imitating Herman E. "Nails" Nedrick, making his voice deep and bellowing just like "Nails" used to do it, and said, 'Men, you may have heard a lot about how tough these Withers guys are, but *Men*, I'll tell you something right now and I want you to re-member it. . . .'

"Well," Gunner said in his regular voice, "we're all holding our breath and waiting for the big scoop, and 'Nails' says"—now Gunner made the deep imitation voice again—" 'Those Withers guys put their pants on the same as you do—*one leg at a time!*' "

Everybody broke up, Gunner included, and he sat back down, holding his stomach. He was great at telling those old high-school stories and making them sound funny as hell, like they were funny kid stuff that everyone had grown out of years ago, so everyone liked to laugh not just because Gunner told it funny but because it made you feel more mature and sophisticated to see how funny all that kid stuff had been. The girls laughed beautifully, throwing their heads back, and Gail asked in a tinkly, light voice, "What happened? What happened *then?*"

"We got slaughtered," Gunner said, smiling, "fifty-two to nothing."

Everyone laughed again, and Marty rubbed her hand on the back of Gunner's neck, scruffing up his hair a little.

"My hero," she said, making a fake sigh of awe. She was sort of pulling Gunner down to her, but he straightened up, pointed to Sonny, and said with great interest, "Hey, man, did you go to that one, the Withers game?"

"Not that one," Sonny said.

"Sonny was our ace photographer," Gunner said, turning to Gail, making it sound like a very big deal.

"Oh?" she asked, raising her eyebrows and looking fascinated as hell.

"Hell, yes, he shot all the action stuff of the games. Great stuff."

"Well, I made some trips," Sonny said modestly, "with the team." Catching Gunner's conversational lead, tossed like a perfectly pinpointed pass, Sonny grinned and said, "Hey, Gunner, you remember the trip to South Bend, senior year, to play South Bend Central, when the bus broke down and Herman E. 'Nails' Nedrick had everybody change into their uniforms on the bus and gave his pep talk about how 'The Game Must Go On,' and guys were getting their gear all mixed up and climbing all over each other like a Laurel and Hardy movie?"

Gunner gave a great guffaw and said, "Hey, that was fabulous, but I can't remember it all. You tell it."

"What happened?" asked Gail, as if she were totally enthralled.

Sonny told the story, making it as good as he could and throwing in some stuff that didn't even happen to make it funnier. Everybody laughed—led by Gunner—at the right places, and when Sonny finished telling it, he felt like a million. He wasn't clutched up at all, even with that sexy little babe fixing her misty, greenish-gray eyes on him like he was someone terrific. He hadn't even got tongue-tied or showed he was nervous, and it gave him the light, floating sensation that maybe now, maybe at last, his real life was actually beginning. The way it was supposed to be.

When they all piled into Gunner's car to go to the Italian Village to eat, Gail sat sort of in the middle of the back seat so that when Sonny got in he was right next to her, and it made him feel tremendous. He really hated it when a girl hugged the door. The loads-of-fun girls always did it, and the sexy ones did it if they didn't like you. It was a way of telling you without using words, "O.K., Buster, you stay on your side and I'll stay on my side, just keep your distance." When they did that it really depressed the shit out of Sonny. It made him feel like a fucking leper. But here was this great little sexy Gail, so close that her bare, sun-tanned shoulder was touching him, and he could smell the sharp tang of her perfume.

At the Italian Village, where they had red-checked table-cloths and drippy candles, Sonny drank a lot of wine and talked with great ease, but he only picked at his food. Whenever he was sexed up he didn't feel hungry; it was like the two things didn't go together. He just ate enough to make it look as if he were eating like a normal person, but he didn't actually taste anything.

It was a fresh, starry night and the roof was rolled back at the Westlake dance pavilion, which made for a great make-out atmosphere. There was a roof that they could roll over the dance pavilion if the weather was bad, and there were imitation clouds and stars set up in the roof, but it wasn't as good as the real job. Everyone ordered drinks, and the first time Sonny went out on the dance floor he put his right arm around Gail's tiny waist and she melted right into him. None of that stiff, plenty-of-space-between business that the loads-of-fun girls gave you. This was the real thing, the thing that made it worthwhile for a guy to go through all the crap of taking a girl to a dance. There was a good band that played a lot of slow, sexy stuff, and they even had a vocalist, a guy named Harry Henneman who used to play a little ball at Shortley but never made the team at Butler University and dropped out of school to become a crooner. He would never replace Frank Sinatra, but he sang good, sexy ones like "My Foolish Heart."

He threw in a lot of warbly effects and did the whispery numbers with his eyes closed and his head bent back like he either was shooting his wad or had wrenched his spine. Sonny had a hell of a hard-on and Gail was moving her thighs against it so blatantly and beautifully that Sonny was afraid he might come right there on the dance floor, spoiling his debonair white-linen slacks. Once in high school that actually happened to him—his wad had blasted off right when he was dancing that way with Penny Sampleton, who was crawling all over him and secretly licking him in the ear. After the dance they parked and Penny cried and said she felt dirty for having such dirty feelings, and Sonny took her home. Later he heard she became a nurse and married a guy from Manual-Tech who drove stock cars and played the vibes.

Luckily the band broke into a mambo just when Sonny was afraid he was about to shoot it, and he said they'd better sit down. He confessed to not knowing the mambo and Gail said she didn't mind, but while it was playing, she snapped her fingers and wiggled her head to the rhythm, like she really wanted to be doing it, and that got Sonny a little depressed, but he tried not to let on and ordered another drink. Gunner said he didn't know the mambo either, but he and Marty got out on the dance floor and tilted around, looking to Sonny like a couple of experts. Around midnight Gunner said he thought they ought to shag the place, which was fine with Sonny, not only because he was tired of dancing but also because he'd about run through the last of the money his mother had given him buying seven-and-sevens for himself and Tom Collinses for Gail.

In the car going back Gail leaned her head against Sonny's shoulder and he put his arm around her with firm manliness but didn't try to kiss her. That was kid stuff, just kissing, when you had a house to go to where no one was home and there was plenty to drink. Sonny felt as confident as Roger the Lodger, the guy in the limerick who did it with the Old Lady from Cape Cod. By God.

Everyone went to the den when they got back to Marty's, and Gunner made drinks while Marty put on one of those hot Spanish gypsy records—the kind where they're all stamping their feet and it sounds like everybody's getting their rocks off about every two minutes. Sonny figured maybe that's why the Spanish were known as a "hot-blooded" people, the way they sang and danced like they all were shooting their wads.

Sonny sat down on the couch and Gail settled beside him, pulling off her shoes and tucking her feet in underneath herself. She leaned back, not touching Sonny, but making herself touchable. He casually slung his arm up on the back of the couch, not actually touching her but getting himself in position. After Gunner passed the drinks around, he flopped in one of the easy chairs and Marty curled up on his lap. Gunner told a couple good stories, a nice mix of high-school football and Japanese religion, and then Marty nestled down closer to him, pressing her mouth on his ear, and Gunner cleared his throat and said he and Marty were going upstairs for a while and everyone should make themselves at home. He gave a little look to Sonny, a look that said, "O.K., man, do your stuff," but wasn't too obvious or embarrassing. A lot of guys would go out of the room with some cornball wink or terrible joke like telling the girl, "Be careful, that guy's horny!" or something that would ruin everything for you, but Gunner wasn't like that, he made Sonny feel like he really did hope he made out.

Sonny was alone in the dimly lit room with Gail, and the passionate gypsy music was building to another climax. He got up and poured more whiskey in his glass, then sat back down and tried to think of something to talk about for a while. He wanted to talk some more before trying anything, so he would feel more sure of her wanting him to do it. They had already, at dinner and at the dance, got through the usual crap about what did you major in and what are you going to do (she majored in English and wanted to get an Interesting Job), plus the kind of extras you throw in like Do you remember what you were doing when you were a kid and Franklin D. Roosevelt died, and how older people didn't understand *The Catcher in The Rye* either because things had changed so much since they were kids or else they didn't remember, and how Adlai Stevenson was a brilliant man but seemed too wishy-washy for most people to trust him being a great leader; all the preliminary shit.

Sonny had really enjoyed the preliminary shit with Gail, though, because she seemed so feminine and sexy and impressed by his opinions, and looked him right in the eyes, and ran her tongue over her lips a lot, and laughed whenever he said something he meant to be funny. He gulped the hot solace of his new drink, thinking, Oh, God, oh, Jesus, maybe this is It, The Answer, the Great Girl who will make everything O.K., the perfect combination of sex and intelligence that every man is supposed to find, that is his rightful due, as stated by the United States Constitution itself, which promised Life, Liberty, and the Pursuit of Happiness, making it an actual law that was right on the books! Sonny sometimes wondered if the catch was in the word "pursuit" of happiness; suspected that the acquisition of it wasn't really promised, just the chase, and that you might have to keep pursuing it until you keeled over and couldn't even sue the government for your rightful share.

"Do you really think you might go to New York?" Gail asked. Sonny had been talking big about the GI Bill and him and Gunner maybe going to Columbia and getting interesting jobs in New York. Gail had said she was going there herself in the fall, maybe to look for a job in a publishing house, which her background in English qualified her for, and so Sonny had been more positive about the possibility of New York than he actually felt; but with the saying it he began to believe it. A whole life had bloomed in his mind, with him and Gunner and Marty and Gail having a youthful, sexy, fascinating life in New York, skipping hand in hand as a foursome down the Great White Way, like in those color musical movies about backstage life on Broadway, where people from little towns lived on spaghetti and wine in the basements of the big city until they were discovered and became great stars with their name in lights.

"New York is really the only place, when you get right down to it," Sonny said. "Don't you think?"

"Well, there's San Francisco, they say."

"I guess. But it's not New York."

"No," she sighed, "it's not," nestling closer against Sonny. He guzzled down the rest of his new drink and got up to pour some more.

"You like some more?" he asked.

Gail shook her head and got out a cigarette. When Sonny sat back down, she put her hand on his knee and whispered, "You won't drink too much, will you?"

"Oh, no," he said and laughed. "I got a large capacity."

"I'm having such a wonderful time," she said.

Sonny gulped so much from his glass that he almost choked.

He rubbed at his eyes and said, "Jesus, me too."

"I'm glad."

Sonny took another burning swig of the whiskey and said, "You know, really, I'd like to tell you something."

"Yes?"

She looked up into his eyes, and inhaled her dizzy perfume.

"Well, what I want to say is, you're—" He took another

fiery gulp, then set down his glass. "Fantastic," he said. "I
mean, Jesus, you're everything, you're incredible, I never
knew anyone. I'd do anything for you. I'd—"

She drew her head back off his shoulder and said, "You
don't even know me."

"Yes I do! No kidding, I mean, I know what I feel, I
feel—I don't know how to explain it. Everything."

"Shhh," she said and put a finger very gently on Sonny's
mouth. She moved her own mouth up to about a hair's
distance of his, and he leaned down just a little and tasted
her lipstick, like some wonderfully sour jam, and then he
put both his arms around her and they were kissing, really
kissing, her sharp little tongue flicking at his teeth and in
between them, and he started mashing his left hand all
over her firm little tits and then reached down and felt her
ass and she cuddled into him, biting at his lips, digging her
nails in the back of his neck, and he suddenly pulled away.

"What's the matter?" she asked, her eyes searching.

"I have to go to the bathroom," he said.

He had been scared shitless he was going to come, and
he felt if he could only take a piss he could get a new start.
Gail moved back and primped some of the hair into place
that was falling in her eyes.

"Oh," she said coolly.

"I didn't mean—"

"Go ahead, for God sake!"

Sonny got up and went to the downstairs bathroom.
After he pissed he looked at himself in the mirror and
brushed his hand through his messed-up hair. Most of the
pancake stuff was rubbed off his nose, leaving the pimple
red and sore-looking, with awful brown flakes from the
makeup around it. He figured anything he did would only
make it worse, and he just washed his hands and tried not
to think about his nose. When he went back to the den he
poured more booze in his glass and sat down. Gail had

turned the gypsy record over and the fucking Spaniards were stamping and yelping again.

"I'm sorry," Sonny said.

"About what?"

"That I had to go to the bathroom."

"Don't be *sorry*," she said, kind of disgusted.

Sonny felt panicky, like he was in a bad dream where he did and said all the wrong things and couldn't stop. He had done all this before with girls he liked, practically slobbered over them until they demanded to be taken home, and he couldn't understand what had happened, why they didn't accept his trembling declarations of love, but now it was worse because he knew he was doing the wrong thing, saying the wrong thing, but he couldn't stop, couldn't break out of the nightmare he was making for himself on the spot. He wanted to explain but it was too complicated, and he reached out and took Gail's hands in his own.

"Listen," he said, "I wish I could make you understand. I love you. I am hopelessly and madly in love with you."

She closed her eyes and said, "Get me a drink."

Sonny jumped up and fixed the drink, and when he placed it in her hands, he said, "Here, darling."

He sat down and lit a cigarette, trying to steady himself. He knew he should be like Richard Widmark, or at least like Gunner, and say he wanted to screw her whether she liked it or not and hump her like a goddam maddened stallion, fucking her senseless.

"I'm sorry I said that stuff," he whispered. "I shouldn't have said it. About being in love with you and everything. But it's true. I'm sorry, but it's true."

She took a healthy swallow of her own drink, which Sonny had made strong as hell, and said in a very even, quiet tone, "If you don't stop being sorry, I'm going to scream."

"I'm—" He stopped himself and wavered up to slosh

some more booze in his glass. He spilled some, and it dripped down his debonair white-linen slacks.

"You're drunk," she said.

"I'm not!" Sonny shouted, and he felt that was true, or partly true. The part that made his hands shake and made the room waver and her face go fuzzy right before his eyes was drunk, but somewhere, below all that, some part of himself saw everything soberly clear.

"Listen," he said, trying desperately to talk from that sober clear center of himself, "I love you, but I want to go to bed with you."

As soon as he said it, he realized the two things sounded contradictory, which maybe in awful fact they were, in his own body and mind.

"To bed?" she asked, with a mocking wide-eyed imitation of innocence. Her hand that was holding the drink dipped and some of the whiskey dripped in her lap.

Sonny wanted to say yes, to fuck, but what he said was "So we can have sexual intercourse."

She giggled, and he stared down into the warm brown hell of his drink.

Gail finished off her own drink and stood up, wobbling a little.

"All right," she said, and reached her hand in back of her neck. There was the sound of the zipper being glided down, and she pulled the dress up over her head and dropped it in a lump to the floor. She stood there looking at Sonny in her bra and panties and seamless stockings, just like the sexy babes in the jack-off magazines, but she was there, real, in the flesh, reachable and—oh, Holy God—fuckable. She burped, giggled, and then unhooked the stockings from the garters and rolled them down and off, teetering and swaying, flinging each stocking away with an ironic, stagy flair. They fell slowly, like punctured, long balloons.

"Well," she asked with a sour smile, "Sexu-all Inter-course?"

Sonny started ripping at his shirt, like he was blind and crazy, tearing at himself as well as the cloth, trembling and yanking down his pants, wrenching off his shoes, pulling the socks off his feet, and in only his light-blue jockey shorts lunged at her, wrestling her down to the plush carpet. They rolled and grabbed and bit, clawed and scratched, tearing off what flimsy stuff still hid them until, panting, Gail reached between his legs and said, "Oh, God."

His cock was limp and useless.

"Listen, it'll be all right," he promised in a panting desperation. "You'll see, it will be, just wait—"

"Oh, God," she said again.

Sonny rolled away from her, mashing his face in the carpet and cursing Buddie Porter, who could make him get hard when he didn't even care, and cursing himself for not being able to get hard when he cared so much he felt it would kill him. He shut off a scream that was rising from his chest, rolled over, grabbed the girl, and pressed himself on her, biting and fumbling in a messy mixture of fear and desire, and he felt down to his unresponsive cock that was growing just a little, tauntingly halfway there, and tried to work it inside her, but it shrank back, receding inside him, and she rolled away, muffling herself face down on the carpet, her creamy little ass heaving up and down in spasms against the floor. Sonny reached out and tentatively touched the back of her neck and she jerked away in a scooting motion across the floor, lying still, and then after a while, in a flat, dry final-sounding voice, said, "Leave me alone."

Sonny thrust his right hand inside his mouth and bit down as hard as he could. He wanted to kill himself, he wanted to die.

"Please," she murmured, "go away."

Sonny jumped up in a furious, gripping panic and wrestled his clothes on, relentlessly, tearing and pulling, shoved his ridiculous feet in his shoes without any socks and blindly started for the stairway, looking for Gunner, but after he grabbed the banister he heard the steady rhythmic thump thump thump of real sex, flesh pounding on flesh, and the place where the terrible movies ran through his head lit up with a neon sign that said *Don't ruin it for everyone else,* and he turned away and fled, out of the house, into the crickety night.

He never really knew how he got the mile or so back home; only remembered falling and starting again and clutching at fences and lightposts and throwing up in somebody's yard and tossing his shoes with a dumb, quick clatter on the stone apron of a filling station, and running a barefoot, mindless, nothing-headed one-man race in which each step on anything sharp or hurting brought relief out of punishing pain, and falling, somehow, falling and finding his own single bunk of a hunk of an empty bed.

He hit the pillow and slept for a fragment of uneasy time, knocked out the way you would be if your head hit a stone. He woke with a start, wondering where he was, and much worse, who, and worse than that even, why. He reached for his cock to see if it still was there, and it was, but withdrawn, unfunctional, defeated, for all purposes dead, and Sonny came coldly awake, with a single-toned hum in his head like a note struck on a pitchfork.

He stepped quietly to the bathroom, switched on the light, and closed the door behind him. Despising the face he saw in the mirror, he yanked the mirror door open and surveyed the bottle-crammed jumbled insides of the medicine cabinet. He slipped out a packet of Gillette Blue Blades. Sponsors of sporting events. Well, there would be an event all right, he didn't know how sporting. Some said bullfighting wasn't a sport, but a ritual. A ritual of death.

Kill the bull and spare yourself. Spare the rod and spoil the child. Here's the church and here's the steeple, open the doors and here's the people. Sonny unwrapped the blue-paper jacket with a picture of Mr. Gillette on it and pulled out the naked blade, flat and black. He held it in his right hand, admiring the efficient, cold beauty of it. Be razor-sharp, with Gillette. He brought his left hand toward his face, palm up, and stared with fascination at the faint tracks of the veins in his wrist. They were supposed to be blue, but they looked more like turquoise. He had never really examined them before. They seemed too delicate and small to carry the blood of a person's life. Maybe if they were severed, the rest of the blood in your body came rushing to the opening, like water flooding through a hole in the dike. Hans Brinker held his finger in the dike and saved a city. What city was it? Amsterdam, Rotterdam. Who gives a damn?

Sonny took the blade and made a slight, tentative scratch on his wrist. Enough to make blood come. Not a lot, but still real blood, surprisingly red and real. Sonny made a braver scratch, and then two or three in a row, quickly, so that little rivulets of blood began to flow together, forming a thick little puddle. It looked very beautiful, and Sonny started crying, not with any noise, just feeling the warm run of tears down his cheeks, and yet he was smiling at the same time. He started smearing the blood over his face and over the front of his torn shirt, like an Indian painting himself to prepare for a ceremony—a battle, a blessing, a death. Sonny sat down on the seat of the toilet, making a few more cuts and watching the new blood. He hadn't really hit any vein that he could tell, but the blood came sliding out, pooling, running down into his hand, and Sonny watched it with a growing sense of calm, a deepening, cleansing relief, such as he had never known. He felt it was easier to breathe, easier to live; a horrible pressure in his head had subsided.

When he understood that he was not killing himself, that he didn't intend to do that—right then, anyway—the first thing he thought of was that anyone who found out about it would think he was a chicken, a showboat searching for sympathy. He had always thought that himself about people who cut their wrists but didn't really kill themselves—they were objects of pity and contempt, poor bastards so botched that they couldn't even succeed at their own death, or so mulingly sick for attention and love they could think of no way to gain it except to fake a suicide attempt and have the scars to show it. Sonny knew a guy in college who cut his wrist a couple times and always went around afterward with a lot of Band-Aids so everyone could tell what happened, and everyone laughed at him and thought him a coward and a fraud. But now Sonny understood that cutting yourself might not have anything to do with suicide or even sympathy, that it was a very private act, a thing of its own; a self-treatment, perhaps, like the lancing of a wound—the lancing of the wound of living. And it really had helped. Maybe that's why they really did it in the Middle Ages, the bloodletting cure, administered when they didn't know what else to do. As Sonny had administered it to himself. He felt cleaner and freer than he had in a long time, but also very much afraid. He vaguely understood there were forces in him, powers and impulses he couldn't control, that might kill him yet.

He went to the sink and ran cold water on his wrist, then wrapped a lot of gauze around it and slapped big strips of adhesive tape over it, making a bulky, awkward bandage. He tiptoed to his room, closed the door, and had a cigarette. The windows were tinted with gray, the morning beginning to open and spread. Sonny was dog-tired but he didn't want to sleep. He crawled into bed and stuck his wounded arm way down under the blanket so if his mother looked in she wouldn't see. He wanted to get out of the house without running into his mother or father, but didn't want to arouse suspicion by sneaking out before they got up. They'd be going to church. He waited it out until they woke and took their turns in the bathroom and scurried off in the half-conscious, helter-skelter manner in which they drove themselves into another day. They didn't eat real breakfast; his mother would have Pepsi with ice, his father a cup of black coffee, each one standing as they poured down the individual fuel they required to begin.

When Sonny knew they were gone he quickly dressed, putting on some khakis and the satiny orange shirt with the sleeves that were too long—at last the baggy-sleeved shirt had a purpose; it would hide his bandage. He called Gunner at Marty's, waking them both from their long night of lovemaking, telling Gunner that he had to meet him somewhere, quick, somewhere they could talk alone. Gunner said his mother had gone to church and was going to a picnic afterward, so they could go to the Meadowlark.

Gunner honked outside about ten minutes later. He hadn't had time to shave and he looked gray and bleary. Sonny didn't say anything and Gunner didn't ask any questions. When they got to the apartment, Sonny said he needed a drink, and Gunner poured him a whiskey, straight.

"What is it, man?" Gunner asked gently. "What's up?"

Sonny set his drink down on the coffee table, unbuttoned his left sleeve, and rolled it back, exposing the bandage. Gunner saw what it was, and he reached out and held Sonny's hand, squeezing it hard. His eyes got that look of staring into an atom blast, and he started shaking his head and saying softly, "No, man, that's not it, that's not the way. It isn't, man, it really isn't. I tell you, no, it's not."

He stood up and started pacing back and forth, clutching his temple, saying, "We gotta do something, we gotta figure something out. We gotta get outa here."

Sonny just sat and watched him, unable to speak or think.

Gunner suddenly stopped and made the pop of his fingers. "We'll take off," he said. "We'll go on a trip. I gotta go to Chi sometime anyway, and we can stop at the lake. We'll hit the road, get some fresh air, a little sun and water."

"How?"

"I'll get the car. I told Nina I had to borrow it sometime to go to Chi, and I'll tell her I have to go now, the agency called me. We'll get the hell out of here."

"What'll I tell my folks?" Sonny asked.

"Nothing. Anything. Leave a note. Say you'll be back in a week, you went on a camping trip. They're at church now, aren't they?"

"Yes."

Gunner hustled Sonny back down to the car and roared off to the Burns' house. No one was there. Sonny sat down in the den, feeling dizzy, not sure what he was doing.

"Listen," he said, "no shit, Gunner, what'll I do?"

Gunner popped his fingers and pointed one at Sonny like a gun, and then, making it an order, he just said one emphatic, clear, irrefutable word, said it so there wasn't any question or confusion:

"Pack!"

PART THREE

1

Sonny sat in the shade with a can of beer, trying not to be noticed. The hot bright life of the lake was playing out all around him, in the yard of the Beemer's cottage and on the old white-painted wood pier that pointed out into the water. Chris-Crafts buzzed and bounced farther out, racing and riding or towing water-skiers; a couple of little kids shrieked and cried as they played with their buckets and shovels on the short strip of yellow-gray sand, and Gunner and the Beemer boys and some others cavorted all over the place in a game of keep-away with a beach ball, sometimes spilling the action over into the yard, up the steps of the cottage, across the road, anywhere. The only other stationary person except Sonny was Old Man Beemer, who sat in a big wooden lawn chair, sipping at a can of beer and grinning, occasionally shouting taunts or encouragement to the keep-away players, surveying the whole scene like some old, benevolent king. In a way that's what he was, and the scene was his creation, the family cottage and the pier and the boat, all bought by the sweat of his enterprise, his charm, his continual long hours for so many years building up the business, expanding it from a single hole-in-the-wall bakery in a little side street in Broad Ripple to a main plant with huge expensive ovens and branch stores all over the city supplied by the spanking white trucks that bore the blue slogan "Beemer's Is Better!" At just about the point that Old Man Beemer had brought this to its peak, had set up a flourishing business ready for his sons to take over and carry on in the best Beemer tradition, ready himself to sit back and reap a little fruit of his labor in the form of leisure and gardening and fishing and the fine new home he had built out in the swanky new Millbank section, at about this time he had his heart attack. He could still enjoy things, but he had to be careful, of course, had to really watch others enjoy what he had built, but that was in fact true reward for him, that's what it all was for anyway. The Boys. And Ruth, of course. But mainly the Boys. So he sat every day of summer at the lake, in that same chair, as if he had been placed there, an old king set on his throne, holding for a scepter the glistening can of cold beer.

Sonny envied him in some weird way. At least it seemed like he was supposed to be there, was part of some pattern that made sense, had done things right and well and been paid off not just in money but in the two fine young boys who would carry on and do things right and well themselves and earn their own chair on the lawn someday. In one way it seemed kind of boring, like reading about the Life Cycle of the Hummingbird or something, but in another way it seemed safe and solid and secure and orderly in a way Sonny's life was not at all. Mr. Beemer belonged in that chair, but what the hell was Sonny doing under that tree, on his lawn, trying to keep away from the sun and the happy sport of the lake? He had on his bathing suit because Gunner insisted. He said it was no use coming

to the lake and sitting around in your street clothes, and
Sonny argued that he couldn't go around with his left
wrist all bandaged up and no shirt sleeve to hide it (everyone knows what has happened if a person has his left wrist
all bandaged up) and have to answer a lot of questions.
But Gunner popped out the solution to that, running
down to the general store and buying an ace bandage that
ne expertly wrapped and clamped securely on Sonny's
whole left forearm from wrist to just under the elbow,
explaining that Sonny could say now he had a sprain. It
was perfectly all right to have a sprain and an ace bandage
—in fact, it was sort of a mark of honor, the sort of thing
athletes were always having happen. It also gave him an
excuse to not have to water-ski or anything too strenuous,
or even go swimming, though he still could wade out from
the sand where the kids played, edging into the water until
it got up around his waist, holding his left arm up so the
bandage wouldn't get wet. He could also lie on the pier
and "soak up some sun," which Gunner, in fact, had made
him do for several agonizing hours early that afternoon.
He tried counting sheep, reciting to himself the Gettys-
burg Address, and going through his nursery rhymes, and
that helped hold off the daymares but it also made his
mind tired as hell.

It was better in the shade with a beer and a newspaper.
He could memorize batting averages and standings, which
was another way of keeping the bad shit from taking over
your mind, and also he could watch the guys playing their
games and horsing around, which was especially active and
funny because there were always some good-looking girls
around the Beemers and the guys got a charge out of
showing off. There wasn't anything wrong with that,
Sonny would have done it himself if he knew how and
wouldn't just look silly instead of agile and tough and
daring.

In the keep-away game it ended up that everyone was

chasing Jocko Beemer with the beach ball and he took the damn thing up a tree and Gunner climbed after him and knocked the ball out of his hands and there was a big pile-up on the grass with everybody diving in, a mass of arms and legs and screams and friendly curses, healthy young guys in the open air having themselves a ball. Old Man Beemer and Sonny looked on and smiled.

After everyone untangled from the pile-up, dirty and grass-stained and breathing hard and laughing, Kings Kingley let go a big belch and said it was beer time. Kings was five years or so older than the rest of the guys and he already had quite a gut on him, but he still wore his bathing trunks low, so the gut slopped over the elastic waist. He still hung out with the guys just like he was still fresh out of college himself, fresh from winning his varsity letter in football at Wabash. It seemed stranger because he looked even older than he was; he was one of those guys who get the very thinning hair and the big gut early in life. He had married a Theta from DePauw who hailed from somewhere in Illinois, but he was always leaving her and the kid and running up to the lake, hoping to find a big bash, maybe even some action. At night he wore his old white sweater with a block W, but he wore it backward, the W on the back instead of front, as if to show it didn't mean a damn thing to him it was just a sweater to wear, that's all.

Some girls from a couple cottages down wanted to go water-skiing, and so the Beemers and Chuck Berback and a couple of buddies of Jocko Beemer's from the Phi Delt house at I.U. took their beers and went out to the Chris-Craft with the girls. On the back of the boat, in those gold letters formed in an arc, it said, "Beemer's Better," and you didn't know whether it meant the bakery stuff or the boys or everything Beemer, but it probably was true. Jamie Beemer was the oldest brother, he was in Sonny and Gunner's class. He was never a star but he played reserve

ball and everyone admired his guts because he got right in
there and mixed it up even though he was a skinny and
fairly frail-looking guy, and he was in all the best clubs and
everything. Jocko Beemer was two years younger, and he
was a star all the way around, not so much because of his
actual physical ability but because he was one of those
natural-leader guys. He was fairly short, but he had this
chin that sort of jutted out and very clear blue eyes, and
you just had confidence in him. You saw him walk out in a
field, and you said, "There's my quarterback." He was the
kind of guy Sonny always wanted to be; maybe every guy
does.

Gunner didn't go out in the boat, even though he liked
to water-ski and, of course, was damn good at it. He could
do the trick where you shake off one ski while you're
actually skiing, and balance yourself so you keep standing
up and riding on the other ski, even though the boat is
going like hell and making turns so you have to go over
the waves that are stirred up. Gunner stopped and asked
Old Man Beemer if he wanted another can, and Mr.
Beemer said no he was fine, thanks, and Gunner said,
"Way to go!" and clapped a hand on the old guy's shoulder. The guys all treated him like that, like one of the
boys.

Gunner had brought out new beers for Sonny and
himself and he sat down under the tree and said, "How
goes it, man?"

"Fine, I'm fine," Sonny said, feeling like shit.

"Nothin' like a little fresh air and sun," he said, pleased
his remedy seemed to be working. "How long were you
out today—in the sun?"

"Couple hours."

"Tomorrow you can do three."

"Great," he said, like it was a real treat. He really
appreciated how Gunner was trying to help, and didn't
want to act like it wasn't doing any good. He had felt

guilty about Gunner leaving town and leaving his girl behind just to try to help Sonny out, but Gunner had insisted he wanted to do it, that in fact it was a good thing for him to get away, too. He said Marty's mother was making life miserable for her about spending all her time with a *shaygetz,* and they might as well take a break, try to let the old lady cool off a little. Besides, Gunner said the last letter from Artists Unlimited didn't seem so worried about his wasting his talent as about collecting his dough. It had ended by saying, "You may hear a knock on your door anytime; our representatives will be dispatched immediately if you don't honor the enclosed debt by return mail." A knock on your fuckin door! It was the Mail Order Gestapo after his ass, Gunner said, and he was taking it on the lam.

Gunner popped him a cigarette and took one for himself.

"You gotta learn to enjoy things more," Gunner said.

"How do you mean?"

"I mean, you must think you're a real prick or something. Shit, man, you got a lot on the ball."

"Shee-it."

"Shee-it me no shee-its, buddy. I mean it. You got your photography. You got a way of explaining it to other people, too. Like you did with me. You got guts, even though you're no big jock. You stuck by me, even when you might have got clobbered a couple of times. And Marty thinks you're an attractive guy. No shit. Christ, so maybe you're not Joe Stud, you're a good guy and you'll find a good girl. There aren't many Joe Studs anyway, mostly there's a lot of guys with big mouths who *think* they're Joe Stud. You got to be able to like your*self.* Ya know?"

"Sort of," Sonny said. He felt embarrassed and wondered if he could ever feel that good about himself.

There was suddenly a loud series of honks, the three

longs and three shorts, that was sort of like a signal back at
Shortley, among the Big Rods mainly but then copied by
almost everyone—there wasn't any law against honking
that way, even if you weren't in the big clubs or anything—
and this old red Studebaker came charging right into the
yard like it was plunging right into the lake. It stopped
with a screech, just past Old Man Beemer's throne-chair.
On the side window of the car was a Budweiser sticker that
said, "Y'all come—Bring Bud."

Sonny was just as glad of the distraction; he hadn't
known what to say about Gunner's advice.

Gunner cupped his hands and called, "Heeeey, Wheels
baby!"

Wheels Conzelman had come to Shortley after getting
kicked out of some military academy, and he didn't know
anyone and was too small to be a jock and not very coordi-
nated, but his old man was an executive with some big
national firm and had a lot of bucks and bought him that
red Studey for his sixteenth birthday, with the hitch that if
Wheels flunked out of Shortley or got kicked out or didn't
graduate, the car got taken away. Of course, he was known
to his old man as Richard, which was his real name, but he
got known around school for the car. At first the Big Rods
made fun of him, but then he started letting them use the
car and taking them places and also driving them on dates,
which was very useful because not many guys had their
own car and couldn't get the folks' car *all* the time and so
they sort of took Wheels in even though some of them
joked about his having a "four-wheel personality," but
Wheels didn't give a shit, he even said it about himself,
and he didn't seem such a bad guy at all. Just like Sammy
Katzman joked about being a Jew, Wheels joked about his
four-wheel personality, and if you joked about something
like that, people accepted you more. He did flunk out of
college his freshman year, but that wasn't part of the deal
about the car, and besides right away he enlisted in the

Marines and you could hardly take the car of a U.S. Marine away from him.

The Marines had shaved off Wheels' curly blond hair, and even though he'd been out for almost a year, he still kept it shaved, just as he kept wearing his old Marine fatigues and T-shirts that said, "Camp Lejune," the way some guys wore their old athletic gear even after they got out of college. There was another guy with Wheels, a guy who Sonny liked a lot, even though he hardly knew him, a guy called Sparky Mackenthorpe. They called him Sparky the way you would call a fat guy "Slim," because he was the most relaxed, easygoing guy you could ever meet. He never went out for ball, but everyone liked him. He was the sort of guy people asked for advice and went to when they were in trouble. It was soothing just to be around him, his easygoingness calmed other people down. He was always dressed nicely, not sharp or fancy, but casually right, like his personality. He had on some plaid bermudas and loafers and a nice-looking blue T-shirt, one of the kind with an alligator on the tit.

The newcomers gave a big greeting and clapping on the shoulders to Old Man Beemer and then came over to Gunner and Sonny. Gunner gave the quick introduction-reminder he always did—the "You remember Sonny Burns," said so the person would think he *should* remember the guy, and they always said, "Yeh, right, sure, man, wha-say." Wheels and Sparky didn't have any place lined up to stay, and Gunner told them to come on over to the Sargent with him and Sonny.

The Sargent was an old hotel that used to be hot stuff on the lake a long time ago, but it had gone to seed and the summer before they took all the beds and crap out and it was just standing there, so you could go over with a sleeping bag and pry open one of the windows and have a room at the lake, even though it was an empty dilapidated old room, dusty as hell, decorated with spiderwebs and peeling paint. They said the owners were trying to sell it and in the meantime they evidently didn't give a damn if people sacked out on the floors. Some of the windows were broken out, by guys who couldn't pry them up and get in any other way. It wasn't exactly vandalism, no one threw rocks to break the windows for the hell of it, they just couldn't get into the room they wanted any other way.

They found an empty room and then Wheels went out to the car and brought in a couple of six-packs and a fifth of Echo Springs bourbon.

"Don't you wanta go back to Beemers and hit the water?" Gunner asked. "Before the sun goes down."

"It'll be there tomorrow," Wheels said and cracked open a can with a churchkey he had hanging from his belt on a little chain.

"Ole Wheels," said Sparky with a little chuckle, "he puts first things first."

Everyone got beers and Wheels opened the Echo Springs and offered it to anyone who wanted to take some jolts from the bottle, but he was the only one who felt like it, at least yet. He would take a little gulp and then chase it with some beer.

"So what's up with you, Wheels?" Gunner asked. "You been out long?"

"Almost a year. Already lost three jobs."

"No shit?" said Gunner.

Sparky clapped Wheels on the back, affectionate like, and said, "You'll be O.K., buddy. You'll do 'er."

"Fuckin Sparky." Wheels grinned. "He believes in *any-body*."

"What is it?" asked Gunner. "Getting back to civilian life?"

Wheels took a gulp of the bourbon and wiped the back of his hand across his mouth. "Fuckin Marine Corps," he said. "They ruin ya for anything, except for *them*. They only teach ya one thing, and then, goddam it, you can't forget it."

"What's that?" Sonny asked.

"*Kill,*" Wheels said.

"Time," Sparky said. "It takes time, ole buddy."

"No, man. It's not like the Army. Or the Air Force, or anything normal. I mean, they don't just teach you how to do it, they put it in your goddam *brain* to kill. They put it in there deep, so it's what you think about doing, and you can't stop thinking about it. I remember in boot camp at Lejune, some guys couldn't take it, and the DIs spit on 'em and kicked their ass and told us they were fags and goddam mama's boy queers. Maybe they were the goddam healthy ones."

"I've heard guys say that," Gunner said. "About the Marines. I knew some guys."

"It's great for combat," Wheels explained, " 'cause they make you good at it. You *want* to kill and know how to do it good. But what the fuck do you do when you get home? It doesn't just go out of your head, when you get back home. It's in there, all the time, man. I wake up with it at night."

"Jesus," Gunner said. He reached over and took the Echo Springs bottle and had him a slug.

"Well, now," Sparky said in his drawl—not the Southern kind but the special Indiana kind, slo-o-o-o-w and nasal twangy—"you can't just brood on it all the time, you gotta get your mind off it, little by little."

"Sure, Sparks," said Wheels, like it wasn't so easy, like he didn't believe it would go away.

"Hey, Sparks," said Gunner real bright, trying to change the subject for Wheels' sake, "I heard they made you a fly-boy."

Sparky said, yeh, he had enlisted in the Air Force, a four-year hitch, and he was about to go to some isolated place in Alaska, some base stuck up there in the middle of nowhere.

"Where it is," Sparky said, "they don't even have any *Es*kimos."

"What'll you do for snatch?" Wheels asked.

"Penguins, I guess."

"That's shitty, putting guys up there like that," Gunner said.

"Well, they try to make it up to you in advance, before you go. I just got back from my three weeks of it."

"Of what?" Sonny asked.

"Well, just before they send you up to nowhere to freeze your ass for a year, they send you to what's supposed to be this special flight training in Florida. You get extra pay for the three weeks, and what it's really for is so you can have a ball down there, live it up real big, to sort of tide you over."

Sonny noticed that although Sparky had a good tan, he had the deepest, purplest circles under his eyes he had ever seen.

"Great," Gunner said. "How was it?"

Sparky made a little chuckle and took the Echo Springs bottle himself and nipped some. "You really wanna know?"

"Sure, man."

"Well, I tell you. And I'd only tell my friends. I was there for three weeks. I spent seven hundred dollars. And I never got laid."

Wheels let out a shriek, and Gunner clutched at his head.

"That's terrible, Sparky, that's terrible," Gunner said.

Sparky just grinned philosophically, and he said with resigned acceptance, "Gunner, it's the American Way."

2

Hearing other guys' troubles made Sonny feel a little bit better, though that made him feel ashamed and guilty, feeling better because other people were in bad shape. He didn't really wish anything bad on anyone, but it was nice to know he wasn't the only miserable bastard. Another shitty thing, though, was that he still secretly felt he was the *most* miserable.

That night everyone went over to Beemers, but the Sargent Hotel group waited till after dinner because the Beemers already had three guys there, one on a spare cot and two sacked out on the porch in a hammock and a wicker couch, and Gunner said he didn't want to give Old Lady Beemer four more mouths to feed, so they got some ham and cheese and four quarts of milk and a couple loaves of Wonder bread and made sandwiches. They ate in Wheels' car and then rolled over to the Beemers. Even if you weren't actually staying there, it was headquarters, and Old Man and Old Lady Beemer didn't mind at all; in fact, they liked it that way, having a mob of young people coming in and out all the time. Old Lady Beemer had gray hair, but you could tell she'd been a great-looking girl, she had that sweet-pretty kind of face, and damned if her legs weren't even too bad, except the old veins were beginning to show up on them, violet-colored and crawling.

There was a full moon and everyone was outside, on blankets, and the Beemer boys had hauled the big cooler out there so you could grab a beer without having to go all the way to the house. There were some cute girls, a couple Sonny recognized from Shortley, and some others from around the lake, summer girls. Jocko was dating this blonde from Logansport, supposedly a real hot number and plenty stacked. He always had the cute ones. Everyone was just horsing around and drinking. The four guys at the Sargent had killed Wheels' bourbon, though he had done most of the damage on it himself. One of the girls Sonny knew of from Shortley was Hildie Plummer, who had short-clipped strawberry-blonde hair and a lot of freckles and wasn't any queen but wasn't a dog either, the only trouble being she was one of those "personality" girls, one of the kind who was loads of fun. She spotted Sparky and squealed his name like she was about to come in her panties, and ran over and hugged him, not sexy but with loads of fun in it.

"Well, Hildie," he said real nice and put his arm around her, just being friendly, knowing it wasn't any use as far as making out, but being nice anyway. It got Sonny depressed, thinking how this really good guy was about to be shipped off to some ice cap or something for a year, what was supposed to be one of the best years of his life, and he was horny as hell and had spent that seven hundred bucks for nothing in Florida, and how much he needed a piece and how easy it would have been for Hildie just to go off with him somewhere and let him have it, and yet she would have probably rather have been shot by a firing squad, keeping her precious cherry for some poor bastard who would marry her and settle down for a life loaded with fun. It got Sonny hating all the women, all the goddam bitches tossing their little tails around and then acting like it was a federal case if a guy wanted in. And yet he had been offered the best he had ever seen in many ways and yet couldn't do anything about it, which was the worst thing, the scariest thing of all. He had told Gunner the truth about what really happened—and worse, what didn't happen—and how scared shitless he was. It wasn't the sort of problem Gunner was familiar with himself, but he said he was going to set his mind to it, he was going to figure something out, and in the meantime for Sonny not to worry until he came up with something. Somehow that relieved Sonny a little, like knowing a great doctor has taken your case. You have to give him a little time to come up with the cure.

Even that couple hours in the sun had got his body pink and sore, not really painful but touchy enough so that just having a shirt on was kind of irritating. Gunner was out in it most of the day, but it just deepened his tan. Sonny figured you could make a good case for the idea that the world is basically divided into two kinds of people—the ones who tan and the ones who just burn. The healthy and the messed-up. Show him a guy who just burns, and he could show you a messed-up guy.

A couple of the girls started singing "In the Evening by the Moonlight" and everyone joined in, doing it the slow way first and then the jazzy way. After that Kings Kingley sang the Wabash song, and hardly anyone could join in because the words went on so long and there were so many verses you had to have spent four years at Wabash to know the damn thing. Sonny figured if you went to Wabash and learned that damn song it probably took up your whole time. That got 'em started on fraternity songs, "Phi Delta —Phi Delta Thay-ay-ta," and "Pass the Loving Cup

Around for Beta Theta Pi" and then the anti-Beta song, "Up in the Air Beta Bird-man, Up in the Air Upside Down," and the sorority songs like "Remember the Golden Arrow of Pi Phi." Hearing those songs depressed Sonny, made him feel it never ends, they'd be singing that stuff when you're eighty and you'd still feel outside of things, not good enough to belong. He knew almost all the damn words to all of them but didn't join in, like that would have been cheating or pretending he was part of all that when he wasn't. Wheels sang along with the rest, even though he couldn't pledge because he was on probation because of low high-school grades his first year and then flunked out, but the difference was he *could* have pledged, he knew that some of the big houses would have asked him, so you could see why he didn't mind singing the songs and why it seemed all right that he did. Of course, no one would have minded if Sonny had sung either, it was him who would have felt funny about it.

After one of the songs Hildie chirped, "Hey, gang, speaking of Kappas, did you know that Sandy Masterson got engaged?"

Sandy had been a Junior Prom Queen at Shortley and a Kappa at I.U. and was always being voted this and that for being so beautiful. She was one of those dumb but nice sort of beauties, always walking around like she was in a daze, hypnotized or something. Sonny wondered if she was like that even when she screwed or whether she really got hot and active. He had a feeling she'd just lie there in the daze, letting the guy go about his business.

"Who to? Who's the guy?" several people asked at once.

"He's a Phi Gam," Hildie revealed, "from Michigan State. She met him at a wedding."

"Way to go, Phi Gams!" yelled Kings Kingley, who had been a Phi Gam.

"Phi Gams always were lucky," said Jamie Beemer, who had been a Sigma Chi. "Not good, just lucky."

"Shee-it," Kings said, "tell it to the birds."

"Shee-it," Jamie answered back.

"Hey, Hildie," Gunner asked, and he had that curious edge in his voice, like he was about to pop one of those questions that got people nervous. "How come when they asked you who Sandy married you said 'a Phi Gam?' "

Hildie didn't get what he meant. "Because that's what he *is*," she explained.

"But isn't he anything else?" Gunner persisted. "Is he a jock, is he a lawyer, is he a veterinarian, is he rich, is he handsome? Does he have green eyes and red hair, or walk with a cane, or sing opera in Italian?"

"Well, I'm sure he's *cute*," Hildie said, kind of miffed.

"How do you know? Just 'cause he's a Phi Gam?"

"Goddam right," said Kingsley, and some other guys hissed and booed.

"No, really," Gunner went on, "I mean, you tell about a girl we all know getting married, and you describe the guy just by saying what fraternity he was in."

"What's wrong with that?" said one of Jocko's lodge buddies from Bloomington who didn't know Gunner and might have thought he was some wildeyed, nutty Independent or something.

"Nothing's *wrong* with it," Gunner said. "It just seems funny, when you think about it. It seems especially funny when you realize after Hildie described the guy that way, nobody even asked anything else about him, like that was all anybody needed to know, what fraternity he was in."

"So what do you want, the guy's life story?" asked Kingsley, kind of grumpy.

"No, man, I just mean it tells a lot about us, about what kind of values we have, that's all," Gunner said.

"Oh, Jesus, we gonna have a sociology class or something?" asked Jocko Beemer. "*Val*ues, for Chrissake."

"Gunner's turned real egghead on us," Jamie said.

"What's with this guy?" asked the big lodge brother from Bloomington.

"He's O.K.," said Jamie. "He's just gone a little egg-head on us since he's been to Japan and seen the world."

"Sounds kinda pinko to me," the Bloomington guy complained.

"Pinko!" shouted Gunner, and Sonny's stomach got that queasy feeling, the one like he had at the swimming pool that day when he thought Gunner was going to get into it with Wilks Wilkerson.

"Now, now, here we are at the *lake*," drawled Sparky in his best soothing voice. "The *lake* is no place for politics and arguments, the lake is for fun. Now I'm about to go someplace where if they had a lake at all the damn thing'd be frozen solid, and I'm here to get me some lake time in before—"

"Hey, Sparky, is that true, you're goin to Alaska?" Jocko asked.

"Alaska!" gasped Hildie, and everything got around to that, the Bloomington guy cooled down and Sonny could see Gunner kind of felt bad for stirring things up and he just guzzled at his beer and kept quiet. He saw what he'd meant, though. It reminded him of this minister's wife his mother got in thick with for a while, she always described a person by what religion they were, like "Did you know the young Sampler boy married a Baptist?" which was a little weird to her, she being a Presbyterian.

Jamie unloaded some more beer into the cooler, and Sonny had another one too, and then everyone got to singing again, this time the old campfire sort of songs, the ones you sang on blanket parties and hayrides and on summer nights at the lake, ones like "I Been Workin' on the Railroad," "Good-bye, My Coney Island Baby," and then slower, sadder ones, like "My Gal Sal" and "Over the Rainbow" and "Home on the Range."

How often at night when the heavens are bright
With the light from the glittering stars
Have I stood there amazed and asked as I gazed
If their glory exceeds that of ours. . . .

Sonny leaned back, lying down all the way so his body
was still on the blanket but his head was on the grass. You
could see about a million stars up there. On a clear night
in town you could see about a half million, but you got out
to the lake and you could see twice as many. The songs
were making him sad as hell, and when they started singing "There's a Long, Long Trail A-winding, Into the
Land of My Dreams," he really felt choked up. He guessed
the deal was he felt scared and sorry for himself, like he
was on the wrong damn trail and that it wasn't winding to
any land of dreams, that he'd always be on the outside
listening to other people sing about their dreams, ones that
would come true for them but not for him, that he'd
always be just listening and watching, waiting for his life
to begin, waiting until the damn thing would be over and
nothing would have happened. Jesus. He started thinking
like that and it was like falling, falling deeper and deeper
into some pit you couldn't climb out of. He made himself
sit up and finish his beer, and even sing some. He sang
along with "Down Among the Sheltering Palms," and
after that one Jocko and his girl got up, quietly, and
walked off hand in hand, down along the lakeshore, no
doubt going somewhere to make out, and the Bloomington
lodge brother picked up on one of the lake girls and they
wandered off someplace, too. The thing started breaking
up. Wheels had passed out, quiet and calm, like he'd been
conked on the head. Sparky asked if Gunner and Sonny
would help get him back to the Sargent, and they carried
him out to his red Studey, Gunner holding him under the
shoulders and Sonny and Sparky taking a leg apiece.

They got him into the blanket on the floor in the room

he and Sparky had thrown their stuff in at the Sargent, and offered Sparky some candles but he said no thanks he was bushed and he just wanted to crap out so they said good night and went down the creaky hall that smelled like somebody's old attic, Gunner with the flashlight, and got to their room and lit a candle.

By the light of it, Gunner had his prophet look.

"Pinko," he said, shaking his head. "Anything different is pinko. Anything you ask, if you really want to figure things out, that's pinko too."

"Yeh," Sonny said, "it seems like it."

"Maybe we ought to move on," said Gunner. "I'm restless as hell."

"Sure," Sonny said. "Me too."

"There's other lakes."

"Hell yes."

They each had a beer and then Gunner blew out the candle and got in his sleeping bag. Sonny's sunburn was hurting and so he just lay on top of his bag. It seemed like hours getting to sleep, hours of fighting off thinking of Gail and what had happened, and he drank another beer in the dark. Finally he must have flaked out because he woke up out of a mixed-up dream, sitting straight up, blinking into an early-morning sunless light.

A voice was yelling, "No, goddam it, no, no!"

Gunner was sound asleep, and Sonny started to get up and then he heard Sparky's voice saying, "Wake up, wake up, you're O.K., buddy. It was only a dream."

It was poor Wheels Conzelman's dream. The one the Marines had given him.

When they got up, they went to a Shell station to shave and brush their teeth, and then went by Beemers so Gunner could have one more swim, and Sonny did his wading act. The little kids on the sand stopped shoveling and stared at him, and he tried not to notice them. Finally this little girl asked how come he couldn't swim, and he

said he could but not right now because of his arm, waving
the bandage at them. They just stared some more. Sonny
figured that little girl would grow up to be a real bitch.

They took off around eleven and Gunner just drove due
north, on 421, and they just talked about this and that,
nothing special, just flapping their lips in the breeze.
Sonny was eager to know if Gunner had figured out anything about his cure, but he didn't want to press it. It was
hot as hell and Gunner stopped at a gas station and took
off his shirt and drove on, saying he'd like to hit another
lake. Around three o'clock they began to see a lot of signs
advertising cottages and dances and shit at Lake Bold
Eagle, which was only twenty miles or so off the main
highway. Gunner said that might be a good place, they had
a public beach and bathhouse. Bold Eagle was the lake
where most of the Manual-Technical people went if they
could afford to go to the lake at all. It was sort of chintzy
and had a roller rink and tacky little cottages and most of
the boats were just outboards, the people who went there
could never have bought a Chris-Craft.

Sonny was tired of wading and he just sat on the beach
while Gunner went in, and then, when he'd swam and
dived himself silly, he seemed even more full of pep than
ever and said they ought to go by the roller rink and see if
there was any stuff. In fact, there were some pretty sexy
Manual-Technical babies, or at least that type, ones with
tight skirts and toreadors and low-cut blouses so you could
see the line between their boobs. Some of them were roller-
skating alone, some with guys, and some were with other
girls, crossing their arms and holding hands while they
skated and twirled to the recorded organ music. Sonny and
Gunner didn't go in, but it was sort of an open-air rink
and they stood leaning on the fence and watching, just like
you'd lean on a corral fence and look over the livestock.

A couple of cuties who'd been skating together came out
after a while, chewing gum and swinging their little tails

like crazy, and Gunner watched them closely, his eyes sort
of squinting like an appraiser, and after they passed, giggling and pretending like they didn't even notice the guys,
Gunner gave Sonny a little jab with his elbow, and still
keeping his eyes on the girls as steadily as he kept his eye
on the ball playing golf, he took off sauntering after them.

Sonny didn't know whether he was more afraid Gunner
wouldn't get the girls or more afraid he would. Even if he
did, probably both of them would want Gunner, and the
one he didn't take would probably be pissed off at Sonny
for being stuck with him. He tried to look at things from
their point of view, too. Some guys didn't even think they
were human, it didn't even occur to them that the girls
have feelings too, but he tried to remember that. You
always hear guys, when they spot a couple girls, talk about
who's getting the dog and who's getting the cute one,
sometimes they even flip for it, but they never figure that
the girls might be thinking the same thing about *them*.

Gunner was talking to them, making a lot of gestures,
and Sonny could tell he was pouring it on, but he didn't
seem to be making much headway. They just kept staring
at him and chomping on the gum, and finally he threw up
his hands like he gave up, and they turned away real huffy
and went off waving their tails even harder. The goddam
prick-teasing bitches—boy, would Sonny like to fuck them
till their ears fell off. As if he could. Maybe after his cure,
though. . . .

"Screw 'em," Gunner said when he came back. "Let's
haul ass outa here," and Sonny didn't ask him anything
more about it.

They kept going north until it got dark, and stopped at
a little diner, one with oilcloth on the tables that had
coffee stains and a couple dead flies mashed into it, and one
of those big old stand-up electric fans that made a lot of
noise and just blew the hot air around. Gunner had the
pork-chop special dinner, with peas and mashed potatoes,

and three Cokes and two pieces of gluey blueberry pie with vanilla ice cream. Sonny had a grilled AC and a glass of iced tea.

"I know a guy in Chicago," Gunner said, "where we can probably sack out for a while. If he's still there. He was a young guy at the agency."

"Great."

"If he's not married."

Gunner rolled his napkin into a ball and said, "Shit, he wouldn't get married. He was getting laid all over Chi."

Gunner lit up a cigarette, and Sonny had one too.

" 'Course we don't have to get to Chi tonight," he said. "We don't have to get anywhere. We'll just take off and see what happens."

"Terrific."

What happened was they ended up in Cal City around ten o'clock at night.

3

Sonny had heard about Calumet City ever since high
school, but he'd never been there. He always wanted to go,
but he'd have been afraid to do it on his own. You had to
be careful or you'd get beat up and rolled. A lot of guys
from the region who worked in the steel mills would come
into Cal City and get horny and loaded out of their skulls
and what they didn't blow in the bars and the strip joints
they might get rolled for by the thugs who were just
waiting for a guy who'd cashed a big paycheck. Or a
serviceman. Or a couple of veterans. But Gunner knew the
ropes.

"It's really a crappy place when you get right down to
it," Gunner said, "but if you've never been there you
ought to go at least once." He laughed and said, "See Cal
City and die."

There was this main street all lit up like a carnival with
flashing neon signs and barkers trying to get you in the
strip joints, all of them saying the main attraction was just

coming on no matter what was actually happening. It was just a little country-town street except that it was nothing but bars and strip joints, and all that mothering neon glaring and blinking in the night, and behind it, in the sky, the reddish-orange glow from the steel mills, like the skyline of hell.

They went in a joint called the Port O' Call, pushing their way past sailors and servicemen and brawny guys from the mills, and they got a table pretty near the stage. You had to drink a minimum then, but at least you could sit down and not get crunched by the other horny bastards. Gunner advised they only drink beer, since usually all the other drinks were watered. They ordered two beers and had barely started to drink when these two really sexy-looking fairly young babes slid off their stools at the bar and kind of slinked over and asked if the guys wouldn't like to buy them a drink. Sonny could feel himself start trembling and getting hot and if he could've gotten a word out he'd have told them sure, but Gunner said, "No, thanks, ladies, not in the market, sorry, *no chance—*" and made a swift, short gesture with his hand, like he was cutting off any further talk about it, that was all she wrote, the end, curtains. They took the hint, but before slinking back to the bar, one of them, a really young-looking pretty girl with big eyes and thick brown hair with bangs, blew a contemptuous puff of smoke at Gunner and said, "Screw, punk."

Gunner just laughed. "They're B-girls," he said. "Just B-girls. They let you rub your hand up around their pussy if you buy 'em enough fake champagne, but that's all you get, for something like twenty bucks, maybe."

"Yeh, I know," Sonny said.

He knew because he had been one of the suckers who did that once when he was stationed in Kansas City. He knew it was a B-girl place but he was loaded and all sexed up and this girl was being real nice and chummy and gave

him the usual bullshit about how she'd meet him later at
an all-night drugstore down the street and he actually went
and hung around the damn place about forty-five minutes
before he got the idea. Guys are really stupid when it
comes to stuff like that. Mainly because they *believe* the
damn girl, even though they know what the setup is.
Sonny even told the girl that he really liked her, "as a
person." Oh, his aching ass.

And still he'd been ready to buy that one a drink, who
had just come over, telling himself that, well, he'd find *out*
if she was just a B-girl, maybe she was the real thing. He'd
be tough about it and find out just what the price was and
where they'd go, and if she was just giving him the come-
on, he'd kick her ass out and not buy her any more drinks.
Probably that's what most of the guys told themselves.
Every time they went back and every time they spent
twenty bucks or so for some watered drinks and a little
feel. The thing that really shook Sonny was that these
weren't just kids, or innocent servicemen away from home
for the first time, or boozed-up businessmen getting taken
for a ride, these were goddam *steelworkers*, the brawniest,
biggest, toughest, hardest he-men in the goddam country.
Which didn't speak too damn well of the country.

"It's sick," Gunner said. "It really is sick."

"Fuckin'-A," Sonny agreed.

A stripper came on, one of the old ones with sagging tits
and blotchy legs. Those kind are usually the worst doing
their act, too, because they know they're not much to get
sexed up about, so they try to act real bored and like they
don't give a shit. Sonny could understand how they felt, in
a way, maybe he'd do the same thing if he were them. If
they really gave it all they had and tried hard and nobody
clapped or got worked up or anything, it would really
make them feel bad. But this way, by not even trying, they
could figure that if no one paid much attention to them it

was because they weren't really trying. Gunner looked over the stripper and went back to talking again.

"They say prostitution is evil," he said. "But at least with a whore you actually get something, you at least get your rocks off. What's really sick, if you ask me, is the B-girl shit where you pay all that money for just looking and thinking about it, but not really doing it."

"Do they have that in other countries, the B-girl thing, where nothing actually happens?"

"Yeh, but not as much as here. The thing about Japan is, there are places like that but there are also places where you can really go and get laid. And damn well, too."

"It must be great," Sonny said. "To know it's there if you want it."

"Sure it is. Hell, if you had a real prostitution system set up here, with clean girls, I bet you wouldn't have all your alcoholics and all your suicides. I mean—well, I'm sorry. I was just talking in general."

Sonny could feel himself blushing, but he knew Gunner hadn't meant to get him thinking about his wrist, and besides, he figured Gunner was right.

"The thing about the way it is here, in America," Sonny said, "is that they get you thinking about it all the time, there's all this stuff to get you sexed up, and then a lot of the time you can't do anything about it. It'd be better if they had women wearing those old Puritan outfits with dresses down to their shoes, and cover everything up, and just try to forget about it unless you're married. But the way it is now you see all these boobs and great-looking legs every day, and there are sexy ads of women in their underwear in all the papers and magazines, and strip shows and B-girls and dirty movies and jack-off magazines, and then after you're all fired up by all this stuff coming at you all the time, if you don't have a regular girl or something, what can you do? Guys like Billy Graham talk about all the sex and how our society is corrupted by so much sex,

but it's mostly to look at, not to touch. It's like putting a
kid in this great toy store and then telling him he can look
at all the terrific toys but he can't really have any of them or
play with any of them."

He never really said all that to anyone before, but he
sure as hell thought about it a lot. Sonny really trusted
Gunner, knew he wouldn't kid him about it like a lot of
guys would. Most guys just try to sound like they're big
cocksmen and get all they want, and you have to pretend
you do too, or they laugh and make cracks like maybe
you're a goddam queer or something. That was what
Sonny liked about Sparky, him telling that story about the
seven hundred bucks and not getting laid. Most guys
would have pretended they had made out like bandits and
had all these great call girls licking honey off their cock.
That was something Sonny wanted to try sometime.
Buddie would probably do it, but he didn't *want* her to
do it.

Gunner was nodding at what Sonny had said. "Too
true," he said. "Too true. Like Sparky spending the seven
hundred bucks and not getting laid. In Japan, he could
have bought him a girl for a couple months for that and
she'd have washed and ironed and cooked for him on the
side, and they would have lived in a nice house."

They ordered more beers, and another stripper came on
who wasn't as bad as the first one. This one was younger
and had a pouty kind of mouth, and kept rubbing her
hands over her body like she really was hot for herself.
There wasn't a real band, just a record, and when it
stopped and somebody backstage had to turn it over, the
first broad had just stood there real bored like, but this one
kept rubbing her hands around herself, cupping them
under her boobs and admiring them, stuff like that. When
she took off the evening-gown thing she started out with—
they always started out with a long outfit like an evening
gown, so you didn't see too much at first and that made it

seem like you were seeing more later—when she got down to the bra and panties, you could see this scar on her stomach. Maybe she had an abortion. Or maybe some wild lover gashed her with a knife. They said most strippers had pimps who beat the shit out of them a lot. When she took off her panties and bra and got down to just the pasties on the tits and the G-string with a little silvery thing covering her cunt, she turned around and wiggled her ass a lot and rubbed her hands over it, and a lot of guys clapped and whistled. Then at the end she slipped her finger under the string of the G-string like she was going to take it off and they yelled like mad, even though everybody knew she couldn't take it off because it was against the law, but she rubbed her hand over the little silvery patch and looked pouty, like she *wished* she could take it off, and everybody liked that.

She was really the best at the Port O' Call. They sat through the others, though, there were about five in all, and had about five beers watching them, and when the bored one with the flabby tits came on again, they paid the check and took off. They walked up the street, sort of window-shopping in the different joints—usually you couldn't see too well inside, which made it easier for the doorman hustler to tell you something terrific was just starting 'cause it was hard to tell. You could look at the photographs, though, they all had photographs of the girls in sexy positions, like a theater marquee that shows you shots from the movie that is playing, except in some cases a great-looking girl in a picture outside might not be in there at all, they just had her picture, and inside were a bunch of old broads with flabby tits. Another thing they did to fool you was make up names for the strippers that were almost like the names of great strippers, but one letter or something was changed, so they couldn't be sued for libel. Sonny almost got taken in, but Gunner set him straight. Sonny got all fired up when he saw that one place

had the great Lilly St. Cyr, who is so sexy it is painful, but
Gunner laughed and said, "Shit, man, you think Lilly St.
Cyr is in Cal City?"

"Well, how can they say she is then, if she's not?" Sonny
asked.

"Look how they spell it," Gunner pointed out.

The big sign spelled the last name "Cir" instead of
"Cyr," but it was close enough to have fooled Sonny and
no doubt lots of other dumbasses, especially because you
wanted it to be the real one, and so you helped fake yourself out. There was a lot of other cheating shit they did
like that too. Like they went into this one place, the
Arabian Nites, because outside was this picture of a delicate blond babe with a chain around her neck being
carried off by a gorilla. They figured that was not to be
missed, but there wasn't any goddam gorilla at all, there
was a blonde but she didn't even have the chain around
her neck. Gunner got pissed and he said to the MC,
"Where's the gorilla?"

"Where's what gorilla, buster?" the MC said real
smartass.

"The one outside in the picture," Gunner insisted.

"Where's the gorilla?" the MC asked in this smartass
way to the audience, mocking Gunner. "Boy, we get a lot
of weirdos in here, I tell ya that. Ya hung up on gorillas, go
to the zoo."

"How come you got him in the picture outside then?"
Gunner asked, and suddenly from out of nowhere there's
this monster of a guy hulking over Gunner, wearing a
shiny blue suit and a big diamond pinky ring and he says
real calm but in a way you knew he wasn't crapping
around, "Let's not have any trouble, boys. We don't like
having trouble here."

"Sure," said Gunner, and they finished their beers and
cut out of there. They didn't want any trouble, either, not
from that guy. Not even Gunner. The bouncers they have

in those places, you never notice them until something happens and then they appear on the spot, looking like they'd just as soon mash a guy's nuts as look at him.

They hit a couple other places that didn't have much worth writing home about, having a beer at the bar so they could see if it was worth taking a table but it wasn't. Then they checked into another place called The Sharp Slipper, and there was a real Amazon blonde who looked worth taking in, so they got a table and caught the last of her act, which wasn't too bad. There was at least a live combo there, the usual bored old zombie-looking gray-faced guys on sax and trumpet, and a colored fella on drums who looked pretty knocked out. He wasn't your grinning happy kind of colored fella, but the kind who looked blank, like he'd seen stuff you wouldn't even want to think about and he wanted you just to leave him alone. Sonny really felt awful when this goddam joking MC came on—those joking MCs in the strip joints, they look like they probably haven't changed their underwear for five years even though they may have some terrible shiny new suit on, there's something truly scummy about them—anyway this one told some shitass joke about the "Soo-preem Court Decision," trying to imitate a colored guy's accent, and Sonny never really got the joke if there was one, but there was a lot of stuff about "us coons" and "nigger heaven" and there were some guys who whooped and laughed. There are some guys who would whoop and laugh if you just said coon or nigger. All the time this colored guy was just sitting at his drums with a blank stare, not moving or changing his expression, just sitting through it like he probably had to do every night, and it got Sonny really feeling like shit, but what could he do?

Then he forgot about the colored fella altogether when the next stripper came out. She was Frenchy La Rome, the feature attraction. She was real young, not any more than twenty at the most and probably less than that, but she

acted like she was queen of the goddam world and took no
shit from nobody and by God you were lucky as hell to be
able to see her in action. She had thick blonde hair that
hung to her shoulders and wasn't curly but sort of wavy
and lush and part of it fell over her face like Veronica
Lake. Instead of one of those evening-gown outfits she had
on a shimmery gold-silk sheath dress that came just to her
knees, and long gold gloves to her elbows and sheer black
stockings and black high heels. That really got Sonny
excited in itself, because most of the strippers don't wear
stockings, but the ones who did went into a big production
of rolling them off and that always sexed him up like mad,
the slow, tantalizing way they took them off. But the thing
about this girl was not just the outfit or even the curvy
body all tight under the sheath, or the sexy, full-mouthed
face with catlike green eyes, hung with that goldish hair.
The thing that really got you about her was that way she
had of seeming like she knew she was such hot stuff.

You could always tell when a really good one came on,
because the place got suddenly hushed and everyone
stopped crapping around. When the bad ones or even just
the so-so ones were on, some guys were just talking to each
other and laughing, or yelling stuff at the stripper like
"Give us a little grind, baby" or "Hey, I got somethin' just
for *you,*" and all kinds of crap, but when the really good
ones were on, nobody felt like horsing around, everybody
was drinking in the scene, trying to store it up in their
head so they could run it back to themself some lonely
night in bed and jack off like crazy thinking about it.
That's the way it was when Frenchy La Rome was on.

There was a little runway that came out into the audience, and she paraded up and down it, swinging it around,
and then went back to the stage and unzipped the sheath
and wiggled out of it. She talked, too, saying stuff like
"Don't you boys wish you had a little a this," and slapping
her ass or petting her boob, and running her tongue

around her mouth. You could almost hear the perspiration coming off all the poor horny bastards. When it came to taking off her stockings, after she got one almost off she wouldn't pull it clear off but hooked it on the toe and then pulled it back like a slingshot or something and flipped it out into the audience, and man, these fucking steelworkers were diving for it like it was worth a million bucks, and two guys got in an argument over one of the stockings and ripped it in half and the bouncer had to get them settled down. With just her high heels and G-string and pasties on she came parading back down the runway and she'd stop and tousle some poor guy's hair or crouch down with her legs apart and wiggle her cunt at him, and the place started whooping and whistling then. She stopped right on the runway at a place near Sonny and Gunner's table and crouched down and gave them the old cunt wiggle, right in their faces, and she could see their tongues were hanging out and she said, "You fuckin babies, you oughta be home suckin' on Mama's tit," and then she turned around and waved her ass at them and when she finally finished, after laying on her back and humping up and down, with a big crescendo from the combo. Sonny was pressing his legs together against the hard-on he had, dizzy and almost sick with lust. Even Gunner looked like he'd been through a wringer.

"Too much," he said. "Too much."

"God, what I wouldn't give for that."

"You'd give plenty, and you probably wouldn't get much, either."

"Yeh, I know. God, though. God almighty."

"What the hell are we doing here?" Gunner asked.

"I dunno."

"Torturing ourselves, that's what."

"Yeh, I guess."

"Come on, let's go to a regular bar and just have a beer. If we can find one."

He meant one that didn't have a strip show, and they finally found one, a real mucky joint that didn't have a name but just had one of those neon signs that said, "Bar," like if you wanted any frills you could take your business elsewhere, this was just a goddam Bar, period. Gunner said he figured they didn't water the drinks in a regular bar like that, so he had a Cuba Libre and Sonny had a seven-and-seven. They had already had God knows how many beers and Sonny suddenly knew he was getting soused, if he hadn't already gotten there. He didn't want to admit it, though, even to himself. He was all sexed up and felt desperate, like he had to do something, something to get relief from a woman, or at least have a plan for doing it, a course of action, a goal to aim at and look forward to, some hope, whatever, anything.

"Listen," he said, "have you thought of anything? About what I can do? About a woman. About women. I have to do something."

Gunner grasped at his head, grimly, and said, "Yeh, we gotta do something. We gotta figure something out."

"We really do."

He took a slug of his drink and shook the glass around, rattling the ice cube. "I been thinking," he said. "Have you ever spent any time with a woman, alone? I mean, where you had a lot of time in the sack and didn't have to worry about doing anything else for a couple days?"

"Not really. Buddie stayed in my room down at Bloomington a few nights. But you know, that's another story. Mostly, though, it's been on some fucking couch with people in the next room or upstairs or a golf course or shit like that. You know."

"Yeh. Well, what I was thinking was, if you got some gal who you were hot for and you had a lot of time to relax and play around with her, off in the sack someplace, that might do it. It might work out real good and you wouldn't have to worry so much."

"Yeh, it might," Sonny said, but he was drunk enough to admit the real fear that flared in his head when he thought about it. "What if it didn't, though? What if it didn't work?"

"I dunno, man."

Sonny hated to hear him say it, but he was being straight. "Anyway," he said, "who would I get to do it with me? You can't just go up to some girl and ask her to do that."

Gunner finished off his drink and ordered another. So did Sonny.

"I was thinking," he said. "How do you feel about DeeDee Armbrewster?"

"How do I feel about her?"

"Yeh. I mean, does she sex you up?"

"Well, yeh. But why?"

"Well, she's really good. Sexually. I mean, aside from all that crap about marriage. But with sex, she really likes it, she likes to do anything, and she knows how."

Christ, back at Shortley Sonny had even jacked off about DeeDee sometimes, sort of like he would about the stripper, knowing she was out of his reach, he could never do anything but just think about it with her, pretend he was doing it with her. He still didn't see what it had to do with his cure, though, the fact that one of Gunner's old girls was sexy and good at doing it.

"But what's DeeDee got to do with it?" he asked.

Gunner rubbed at his brow, hard. "Well, I was thinking. Maybe she'd do it. Maybe if I sort of explained, not everything, but maybe if I sort of told her you'd had a bad time with somebody and you really needed some action, it was important, maybe she'd just do it."

"Jesus."

Sonny could hardly believe it. That Gunner would even try to get her to do it for him, much less that she'd do it.

But he could tell Gunner was serious; he really wanted to help. Even with one of his own old girls.

"The trouble is," Gunner said, "her getting this marriage bug. That might screw things up. If she's thinking that way."

"Yeh, I would think so."

"Man, if we were only in Japan. What a fuckin shame. That you didn't get over there."

"I know."

"Well, shit. Here we are in Indiana, surrounded by Ohio, Kentucky, Illinois—" He stopped, hit his forehead with the palm of his hand, and said, *"Illinois!"*

"What about it?"

He took out a cigarette and offered Sonny one but he didn't want any distraction; it looked like Gunner was on the trail of some plan, but he couldn't imagine what the hell Illinois had to do with any plan about getting laid.

"Tell me something," Gunner said. "Have you ever been to a whorehouse? I mean, does the idea of a good whore turn you off? Lots of guys just don't like the idea."

"Oh, I like the *idea* O.K.," Sonny said, "if it was really a good one. But the time I went to one was pretty crappy."

Once in service he had taken a ten-day leave with a buddy in his office and they went to California and on a Sunday shot down to Tijuana for the bullfights. Afterward they started boozing it up in the bars and strip joints and got very horny. They went to a whorehouse that was crowded as hell, mostly with Mexican guys, yelling and arguing. You sat on a little bench, like waiting for a doctor, and when a whore was finished, she'd come down this hall and try to get you to go to her room. The whores were mostly pretty moldy-looking, and Sonny got dragged off by one about forty-five who was pretty fat but didn't look too syphilitic or anything, as far as he could tell. She got him in the room and asked if he wanted to suck or fuck and he said first he'd like to suck and then fuck and she said that'd be three dollars. She opened his pants and examined his prick, then put some Kleenex over it and started sucking away, and before long he shot his wad real good. He started to take off his pants then to fuck, but she said he had already got his money's worth. He tried to argue, but she said she would make trouble, and with all those wild Mexican guys out there, Sonny didn't want any. So he'd paid three bucks for a Kleenex-wrapped blow job.

Gunner said he asked because he just remembered that once in college some lodge brother from Chi had taken him and two other guys to a really great whorehouse. It wasn't in Chi, it was in this little jerkwater Illinois town, about forty miles south of Chi. The weird thing was it seemed just like a little farm town, but for some damn reason there was this great little whorehouse there, ever since anyone could remember. The girls were young and really nice and they played around with you and let you talk to them just like it was a real date and you were a real person. The little town was called Gladiola. Gladiola, Illinois. Sonny said it sounded to him like the ideal place to spend the night.

It took them a couple of hours to find Gladiola; it wasn't even on the map and they kept getting lost. They bought a fifth of bourbon before leaving Cal City, and that kept their inspiration going, even though it was pretty damn discouraging, finding Gladiola. When they got there, the only light on was a night-light in the general store. Gunner knocked and knocked and finally an old toothless guy came down and peeked out. Gunner asked him how to get to the Gladiola House—that's what the place was called.

"Been gone," the man said. "Shut down a couple years ago. All gone."

He shuffled away and Gunner said, "Fuck me in the teeth. What a fuckin piece of luck."

"It's *my* luck," Sonny said. "They probably heard I was coming."

It was almost four in the morning, and there they were in Gladiola, Illinois, and there wasn't any Gladiola House anymore.

"I guess we're up shit crick without a paddle," Gunner said.

Sonny couldn't say anything at all. He wished he was dead.

"Fuck it, we might as well go on to Chi now," Gunner said.

Sonny just nodded. He didn't care.

They came roaring into Chi through a night torched by the steel-mill fires, eerie and hellish. Gunner kept swigging on the fifth and he got too loaded to drive anymore. Sonny said he'd take over. He was past the point of knowing or caring whether he was loaded or not. Somehow he guided them into the stone gray outer web of the smoking city, and he felt that was something, anyway, he was getting them there. His eyes kept closing on him, though, and he'd wake with a jerk, just in time to keep on the road. He tried hard to keep concentrating. They came to a curve and Sonny took it all right, but then, too late, he saw it curve again—it was an S—and he knew it was too late, too late even to put on the brake, and as they headed straight into a cement abutment, he just said, "Jesus Christ," and then they smashed.

There were flares and sirens and Gunner was bleeding, saying, "Oh, shit," wiping blood from his face. Sonny wasn't bleeding but he felt like his whole body had been wrenched out of place. He couldn't believe it was happening. It was a scene like you pass on the highway and think Oh, shit, the poor bastards, and never thought it could happen to you. Sonny grabbed Gunner's arm and started crying.

"Shit man, I'm sorry, I'm so fuckin sorry."

"We're O.K., it'll be O.K.," Gunner kept saying.

In the hospital they found that Gunner had a broken

jaw and needed some stitches. The doctor on duty said
Sonny was just shaken up a bit, he could probably go home
the next day, but Sonny kept insisting something was
wrong, his back was on fire. Finally they took some X rays
and than came running in with sandbags and pulleys and
told him not to move. It seemed he had broken a vertebra
in his neck and if he'd jerked his head around hard he
might have been killed or paralyzed. As awful as he felt, he
was glad he hadn't knocked himself off. They said he
would have to lie in traction with his head in this thing
that pulled it back to straighten out his neck and back, and
then he'd be put in a cast, and then he'd get a neck brace,
and then maybe he'd be O.K.

He knew he ought to be thankful, thankful to God for
saving his ass and not killing anyone else either, but all he
could think of was that if God had really given a shit there
wouldn't have been an accident in the first place. If God
had been a really good guy, he wouldn't have spirited the
Gladiola House away so Sonny couldn't fuck.

Sonny didn't even much mind the idea of being for a
couple months in the hospital. He hadn't known what to
do with himself outside, anyway. Maybe lying there all
tractioned up he'd be able to figure things out better. His
parents got him out of the ward into a two-person room
with an old guy who had suffered a heart attack and was
trying to recover. He was Mr. Weyl and he turned out to
be damned interesting. He told good stories to Sonny
about how he had educated himself, working in the stock-
yards and going to night school and getting a law degree;
he had even invented things that were patented, and he
patented a new soft drink once called "Cherokee Cola"
and lost his fortune in it, but he didn't even seem to mind,
he seemed to think it was an interesting experience, losing
your fortune, especially on something called Cherokee
Cola.

After a couple of days Sonny's parents had to go home to

get back to work, which was really a relief to him, not having his mother looking at him like he was a poor invalid, and his father making those long, despairing sighs. They kept saying how happy they were he would be all right, but it wasn't exactly glee he saw on their faces. His mother kept crying, saying they were tears of thankfulness to the Lord for saving him, but they seemed to Sonny like ordinary miserable tears. Sometimes he could see her sitting with her head down and her lips moving silently, and he knew she was praying. It made him feel like jumping out of his skin.

Gunner got out of the hospital in just a couple days, after they took some stitches under his lower lip and put some clamp kind of thing on his broken jaw. He went and stayed with the old friend of his who lived in Chi, and decided as long as he was there to settle the thing about the ad agency—whether he would go with it or not. He came every day and visited Sonny in the hospital, telling what all was going on and making great stories out of it all.

Rumsley, Klinger, and Faxworth, the three sharp young guys who had started this agency of their own, sounded like comic-opera characters as Gunner told about them. They were wining and dining him, and offering the princely sum of seven-five as a yearly starting salary, but Gunner found that instead of being impressed with them like he'd been when he worked there before going into service, they seemed now like a cartoon strip that might be called The Young Execs, what with their three-martini lunches and Madison Avenue phrases and talking of how they would help him "get a leg up on things" even though he had been in service and wasn't aware of all the latest advances in the Ad Game. When he began to sound like he didn't think it was his meat, they urged him anyway to take a personality test which would help him decide on what career he was best fitted for, and if the ad game wasn't his line, they'd shake on it, no hard feelings, and wish him well in his chosen career, whatever it might be. The personality test, which was administered and interpreted by a special psychological counseling service, revealed that Gunner would do well in the fields of forestry, aeronautics, and charity work.

"I guess what I ought to do," he told Sonny, "is fly around national parks dropping food packages for the bears. That would make use of all my talents."

The psychological people also revealed some dark aspects of Gunner's personality. On one part of the test you were supposed to draw a picture of yourself, and Gunner said he just drew a picture of a guy casually standing with a drink in his hand and the other hand in his pocket. They told him this showed tendencies toward alcoholism and masturbation.

Gunner thought the whole thing was full of shit but pretty funny, and he almost keeled over when he found out it cost Rumsley, Klinger, and Faxworth five hundred smackers to have him take the test and have it analyzed for him. Rumsley, Klinger, and Faxworth were pissed off at the results, and they even were suspicious that Gunner had cheated on the test, though he tried to explain he would never have been able to figure out how to cheat in a way that would make him turn out as a flying charity forest-ranger, with tendencies toward masturbation and alcoholism. They agreed, grumbling, that maybe the Ad Game wasn't his cup of tea.

Gunner went right to the V.A. office after all that and came one day to tell Sonny he had decided to take off right away for New York. He could probably get into Columbia for the second semester and get the GI Bill started then. In the meantime, he didn't want to hang around Indianapolis any longer and he was going to go there and pick up some gear, take Nina out for a farewell dinner, and hit the road for New York. He figured he could get himself a room and land a job at the post office there. He knew some guys in service who said you could always get work sorting mail at night in the New York Post Office, and he would get a chance to really learn the city and psyche things out.

"By the time you get on your feet," he said, "I'll have the place down cold. You can probably get into Columbia for the spring semester—I brought you the catalog, and the GI Bill forms and shit. We'll have two-twenty a month between us just from the bill. We can chip in on an apartment, live on spaghetti and wine. Do the whole thing. *New York*."

He made it sound as exciting as when Sonny met him on the train and he spoke in that same tone of awe and adventure when he talked of "Ja-*pan*."

"O.K., buddy," Sonny said, smiling. "You're on."

Gunner was catching a train back to Naptown that night; when he made up his mind, he didn't let any grass grow under his ass. He stood up quickly, seeming all business and rush, and said, "Look, let's not have any good-bye shit, I'll write from New York, and you'll be out there in no time."

"Right," Sonny said.

Gunner reached down and squeezed him on the arm, his hand warm and strong, and said, "Take it slow, buddy. Don't let 'em get to you. It won't be long."

"Thanks," Sonny said. "I mean it. Thanks a lot."

Gunner waved his hand away, brushing off any thought that thanks were needed for being a great friend and helping a guy figure out what the hell to do next, helping him be able to do it. It reminded Sonny of the way Gunner would brush off credit for his touchdowns or his Purple Heart, his exploits as a cocksman or his loyalty to friends.

He was gone, and Sonny first felt a scary kind of loneliness, and then began to calm down, thinking of the great days ahead in the great City of New York, a place of teeming life and triumph and glory. Surely in a place like that his real life might begin.

Sonny's parents came up every weekend and sat around the room. His mother brought him magazines and slipped copies of the inspirational booklet "The Upper Room" in between the *Lifes* and *Newsweeks* and other stuff he asked for. Sonny never mentioned it, not wanting to start anything. His father got him a portable radio, and some kind of reading glasses fixed so that you could hold a book in your lap and be lying flat on your back and be able to read it by wearing the glasses.

Sonny told them once he had filled out forms for the GI Bill and applied to go to Columbia Graduate School in the second semester. He had spent hours pouring over the catalog Gunner had given him of the School of General Studies at Columbia, which was sort of their night-school branch and was easier to get into. Gunner was going to take some philosophy—he couldn't get the bill unless you took stuff leading to a degree, so painting was out, but he could do that on the side—and Sonny figured he might try philosophy, too. If you had a guy you could talk to about it, maybe you could make some sense out of it, maybe learn some of the real secrets of life discovered by the great thinkers. When he mentioned this plan to his parents, his mother started to cry and his father said, "Well, there's plenty of time to think about it."

"I've thought about it," Sonny said.

He left it at that, knowing there would be scenes and terrible arguments later when he got back home, but there was no use going through them in advance. Sonny tried to keep the talk to just gossip, which passed the time and didn't make scenes and kept his mother from getting sad while she was telling the latest—how the lady Sonny had met when he first got home had gone back to the little Wop grocery-store man, after all he had put her through; how Uncle Buck didn't pay any rent to Grandma Lee-no, even though he had enough money to go out carousing every night, and had only last week been discovered in Lee-no's rollaway bed in the dining room with a woman Lee-no swore was a gypsy!

"How could Lee-no tell she was a gypsy?" Sonny asked.

"Well, she was very dark-complected, and she had on those big hoop earrings they wear, big as bracelets!"

"I bet Lee-no called out the Army, the Navy, and the Marines that time." Sonny smiled.

Mr. Burns snorted, smiling himself. "And the Air Force and the Coast Guard," he said.

"Let's change the subject," Mrs. Burns said. She didn't like anyone to make fun of Lee-no or Buck, and Sonny and his father were always doing it. Just in a little way. It was one of the few things between them, a private kind of joke that they had to be careful about going too far with in Mrs. Burns' presence.

The trouble was, when the news and gossip was over, the three of them were stuck again with nothing to say. And Sonny couldn't get up and walk out, either.

His favorite amusement got to be listening to the late-night radio programs. He could pick up Randy's Record shop from Gallatin, Tennessee, with hillbilly music and all kinds of advertisements of weird stuff like "the flowering blue rose bush" that was guaranteed to make an entire fence of blue roses tall enough to hide your house. They also advertised all the Jesus stuff, the emblems and statues that glowed in the dark, Jesus stickers for your car, Jesus trinkets for your charm bracelet. "Just send a postcard to Jesus—that's J-E-S-U-S, care of this station." There must have been thousands and thousands of people out there, saving up to buy statues of Jesus and flowering blue rose bushes.

Sonny got postcards from Gunner of Columbia University, Grant's Tomb, the Brooklyn Bridge, saying stuff like "Great!" and "Wait'll you see it!" He wrote a letter saying he had got himself a room up near Columbia where there were a lot of students living and you shared a moldy kitchen, but it was cheap. He had actually landed the job in the post office, sorting mail, and met a lot of interesting people, people from all over the country who really wanted to do something, wanted to figure things out, and Gunner was really getting to know the city, had been to a party in Greenwich Village already and learned how to get around on the fucking subways. He said for Sonny to get on his feet and get his ass out there, he'd have everything set up.

The mail was mostly those postcards from Gunner and get-well cards from Buddie Porter. Once Sonny's parents brought her up as a special surprise when they came on one of their weekend visits and she sat around the room with them uneasily, and Mrs. Burns made a big point of dragging Mr. Burns off and saying they ought to give Buddie some time alone with Sonny, giggling a lot and making Sonny embarrassed as hell.

"How are you?" Buddie asked him.

"O.K. Just fine."

"I'm glad. When you get back home, I can drive you around—I mean, if you want to go someplace."

"O.K."

"I love you."

"O.K."

Finally his mother and father came back and they were all uncomfortable together, which was better than just him and Buddie being uncomfortable alone. The nurses later kidded him about having a girl friend, and that made him a little glad Buddie had come, anyway; it raised his stock with the nurses, being a guy who had a girl that came to visit.

It got to be autumn, the clean time. The old hot sticky life of summer cooled down, the wet lush bursting leaves curled into rich golds and reds and browns, falling, lazily, gathering for pyres that would turn to fire and drifting smoke, signals of summer-end, of possible crisp beginnings. Sonny asked Mrs. Garraty to keep the windows open. He wanted to breathe it, the healthy invigorating chill that cleared the hot lungs and the stuffed-up mind. Mrs. Garraty, Jean, his daytime nurse. With her long straight chestnut hair and madonna smile. Married to a potter, an artist, no doubt a sensitive guy, a guy who had a hard time of it. Maybe he would die of some artistic disease and Sonny would get to marry Mrs. Garraty and adopt her two little kids and they would all live happily ever after, in some perpetual autumn of peace and drifting smoke. If the Bomb came, they wouldn't even try to hide. They would sit in a circle on the front lawn, holding hands and smiling and letting it come. That way you wouldn't run all the time till it happened by worrying about it, wondering when it would be and what you would do. That's what the papers meant by "living under the shadow of the Bomb." Fuck that shadow. There were too many shadows you lived under anyway.

Finally they took Sonny out of the traction contraption and put him in a body cast that came down to his waist and came up over his head, just leaving his face out and cutting away a part so his ears were free. At first it was hot and tight and Sonny was scared shitless he'd never be able to live in it, even for the two months they said he had to before he got a regular neck brace instead of the plaster, but then after a couple days he began to get used to it. Maybe you could get used to anything if you had to, sleeping on nails or any damn thing.

Sonny got to practice starting to walk. His legs were weak from not being used and he had to work them back into practice. First he just walked around his room and then he got to go up and down the halls. He was something of a special attraction in his weird cast, and he found he was able to be more friendly to people than he ever had been in his life. He stopped and visited with people confined to their bed, told stories, entertained the nurses, played with little kids who were visiting sick relatives. He was such a popular guy in the cast he wondered if maybe he shouldn't keep it on for good. Maybe he could wear it to New York and get a job in a nightclub or something—stories and songs by The Man in the Cast! Everyone would love him.

On one of the clear autumn days that smelled of a special crisp poignance, Sonny secretly got dressed. He usually made his rounds up the halls wearing his terrycloth bathrobe, but this time he got out some clothes from the suitcase his parents had brought for when he was ready to use them. He put on a shirt, even though the cast was so big he could only button it up about halfway, and some old corduroy pants, and his shoes and socks, and a raincoat that he bundled up around him, pulling the collar up, hiding as much of the cast as he could, and he snuck downstairs and went across the street to a little diner. It was a nice old-fashioned sort of place with frying smells and a counter with stools, and pieces of pie underneath a glass case. Pumpkin pie, his favorite, was in season now, and Sonny had a piece of that and a cup of coffee. The pie was soft and soothing, and the hot coffee invigorating. He couldn't remember when he ever enjoyed eating anything so much. Maybe because it occurred to him that he might have never again been able to eat a piece of pumpkin pie if he'd snapped his neck a little further.

Outside he stood for a while on the sidewalk, just breathing deeply and feeling the pleasure of being alive in the fall. A sharp breeze tingled his flesh and made his eyes get a little watery, and when he blinked and opened them, it seemed for a moment as if everything was bathed in a soft gold light, like a blessing. It was just for a moment but it gave Sonny a sudden sense of joy that seemed to spread through his whole being. He had known those moments before, in different times and places, and they had seemed so intense and so real that everything else was like sleep. Such moments made you feel completely alive, reminded you of being alive, and Sonny wondered if perhaps that's what "real life" was after all—those moments. He didn't find it depressing, but felt perhaps it meant that his real life had been going on all the time, that the moments were to remind him of it and let him feel it. He figured the truth was maybe you lived hundreds of lives within your time, that you never started and continued on a straight path that kept going higher but that you got lost, crashed into things, were crashed into, and began again. There wasn't any last beginning until death did away with you or took you away to some other place. He didn't know about what happened then or even care much at the moment, but he did have a sense of what he was doing now, doing again, as he planned for New York, as he broke from home; whether it was smart or dumb, good or bad, to do those things, he knew at least in one way what he now was doing and was going to continue to do in different ways and in different places and with different people, as long as his heart beat and his blood ran, until he came to this life's end:

Begin.